AT THE DAR[K] [OF]
DAWN, HE CA[ME] [A]
SECOND TIM[E] [IT WAS]
MORE EASIL[Y] [BUT IT]
WAS MORE D[...]

He moved with a long stride across the room to where she slept, curled on her side facing him. He saw for the first time how beautiful she was – even with that strange cropped head. Reaching out a thin finger, he stroked the curve of her sleeping face down to her moist and parted mouth. Desire rose in him as he felt her warm flesh; she smelled of woman and sleep. His fingers traced her full lips, and Rose stirred restlessly, flinging herself over on to her back . . .

ABOUT THE AUTHOR

Sheila Holligon was born and educated on Teeside, and now lives on a farm on the North Yorkshire moors near Lealholm. She has had four collections of poetry published, and several short stories, and writes regularly for American and Canadian papers about breeding rare poultry. She is currently working on a new novel to be published by Signet Creed later in the year.

SHEILA HOLLIGON

NIGHTRIDER

creed

A SIGNET BOOK

SIGNET

Published by the Penguin Group
Penguin Books Ltd, 27 Wrights Lane, London W8 5TZ, England
Penguin Books USA Inc., 375 Hudson Street, New York, New York 10014, USA
Penguin Books Australia Ltd, Ringwood, Victoria, Australia
Penguin Books Canada Ltd, 10 Alcorn Avenue, Toronto, Ontario, Canada M4V 3B2
Penguin Books (NZ) Ltd, 182–190 Wairau Road, Auckland 10, New Zealand

Penguin Books Ltd, Registered Offices: Harmondsworth, Middlesex, England

First published 1995

1 3 5 7 9 10 8 6 4 2

Filmset in 10/12pt Monophoto Baskerville
Typeset by Datix International Limited, Bungay, Suffolk
Printed in England by Clays Ltd, St Ives plc

For Emanuel Z.

And for Philippa Gregory,
who gave me so much help and encouragement

If I wake he rides me like a nightmare
I feel my hair stand up, my body creep:
Without light I see a blasting sight there,
    See a secret I must keep.

  – 'A Nightmare' by Christina Rossetti

Chapter One

TOWARDS morning, the scarred man came to her for the first time. He stumbled out of the shadows, confused and unsteady, for it had been a long time since he had been able to take form here. The dark came together and grew thicker until he had made himself a body. It was as ill-fitting as an old coat, but recognizable as a man.

He stood and listened. He could hear her breathing.

Stretching out his arms, he moved towards her, knowing little except that only a woman could give him shape in this place. He shuffled towards the bed and looked down at her where she lay sleeping. He reached out a hand to touch her pale face, but there was no strength yet in him; he needed to feed on her.

It was too soon.

The old flesh barely brushed against her warm skin before he began to fade back. Only the smell of him, dank and musty, lay on the cold air.

Even his desire for her could not keep him here. Not yet.

Some time later Rose woke suddenly, hearing a sound below her in the kitchen. She lay for a moment not knowing where she was, wondering why she felt so tired. Then memory came slowly in a series of blurred images of herself driving up to Yorkshire from London, crossing the great divide between South and North, coming to the ancestral home to claim her inheritance: one small, damp cottage, with troublesome drains if you judged by the strange smell in this bedroom. This desirable property was set in a large patch of what appeared to be genuine Yorkshire mud, from the little she had seen of the garden last night. Stop bitching, she told herself firmly. Lots of people would love to own a cottage on the moors like this one.

If she could only find one of those idiots, they could have the place, for all she cared.

Christ, it was cold in this bedroom. She pulled up the faded patchwork quilt round her ears and shivered. She watched the shadowed branches flicker across the uncurtained window and listened to the silence. Nothing. No traffic, no nice friendly honking taxis. But there had been a sound: she had heard it. It came again, high and wailing, startling her until she realized what it was. Only the cat – she had forgotten the cat. She added it sourly to her list: one cottage, one garden, one scruffy cat. It wasn't that Rose didn't like cats, just that she'd never stayed in the same place long enough to own one. Have camera, will travel had always been her motto. And the further she went the better. They didn't call her Rambling Rose for nothing. When the letter from the solicitor came, all she had wanted to do was to set off running and keep on going. What did she want a cottage in Yorkshire for – especially from him? Even now that he was dead, she still didn't want anything from him.

The cat wailed again, raucous, insistent. She would have to go down and let the thing out. He. She. It. Whatever it was. All she'd seen of it when she arrived so late last night was a black streak rushing in past her when she opened the cottage door. Where it had hidden itself after that she had no idea.

The cold damp wrapped itself round her bare legs as she pulled on a sweater over her pants and T-shirt. She tugged her socks over her cold feet and went carefully down the narrow stairs into the kitchen. She switched on the light. There was a feeble glow from the unshaded bulb hanging over the big table that filled the centre of the room, and it showed the cat crouching by the door. 'Puss, puss,' she crooned softly to it as she unlatched the heavy door. It swung inward slowly, scraping across the flagstones, swollen fat with damp. The cat slipped between her legs, prickling her cold skin with the brushing of its tail, and then was gone.

There was a hard crescent moon pinned among the trees at the edge of the garden and she could hear water splashing. She thought that there must be a stream beyond the trees – it had been too dark and she had been too tired to start beating nature trails about the place last night.

There was one small light shining in the long, narrow valley below her. That must be the Bransdales' farm, where she had stopped to pick up the key. Someone there kept late hours. Rose shivered and scraped shut the heavy door.

The fire in the black range, which she had lit with such difficulty the night before, was out. She poked at it crossly, but it lay grey and dead. She stood and examined the range, wondering how it had escaped from the local museum. There was an open grate in the middle of it, high up off the floor, with dead ashes heaped below it. On either side of the fire were big side ovens. She supposed that she should be grateful she didn't have to try to cook on this monstrosity – at least the cottage had electricity.

Rose filled the kettle from the tap at the shallow stone sink and put it on the cooker; she was grateful to have that working, though it was thick with grease. She rinsed out the mug she had used earlier and dropped a tea-bag in it, then sugar. Sitting down at the table to wait for the kettle to boil, she thought with nostalgia of the bright, warm kitchen which she had left behind in Islington.

Isabel would have been asleep under her electric blanket for hours, all snug and cosy. They were cousins – daughters of two sisters – and so a little alike, but Isabel was a smaller, daintier version of Rose. Not so full blown. There had been a room in Isabel's house for Rose since her mother had died six years ago. Not that she used it much, but it was there, waiting.

Isabel was a medical secretary, working in Harley Street, living alone since her divorce. Rose could never have done Isabel's job, coping with patients for the surgeon whom she so much admired. Typing all those letters, making all those appointments getting the London Clinic, the patient, the surgeon and the anaesthetist together at the same time. Isabel came home some nights looking white and exhausted. Rose had said to her more than once that it was silly giving so much of herself to her work. Isabel smiled and said, 'What about your camera? It's the same thing.' Which it was, Rose supposed, and Isabel needed to be needed. Some days Rose thought that what Isabel did was a lot more important than what she did. For all that Rose did was to chase down images, to reduce the world to black and white in sets of frozen moments.

It was all Isabel's idea for her to come up here, thought Rose resentfully. She would have been half-way across Europe now, given the choice, and travelling fast. But Isabel had said no. 'You have to go, Rose. He was your father and you can't keep running for ever.'

'Like to bet?' asked Rose.

Isabel had insisted that Rose come up here to sort out the cottage. To lay the ghosts and then decide whether she wanted to sell the place.

Rose looked round the kitchen and groaned. She could

4

not imagine how the old man could have lived like this. Pigs must be better housed. And who would have thought that he would die so very suddenly: dead at seventy on the stone slabs of this floor. She shuddered, got to her feet and filled the mug with boiling water. She added dried milk from the congealed mass at the bottom of the tin and angrily crushed the clotted lumps which formed with an old spoon.

Leaning against the cooker, she looked round the room. It was thirty years since she had last stood in this place – not that she could remember herself here then, for she had been two. All she knew was that one day in spring, just after Rose's second birthday, her mother had packed a bag and left, hurrying down that steep track, hauling little Rose behind her.

Rose wondered now where they had gone, for she hadn't realized that this cottage was so remote, so far from any railway station, from any main road. Wherever her mother had gone for help, she had ended up in London with her sister. She would never talk to Rose about why she left; she would tighten her mouth and say nothing. They lived in the basement of Auntie Kitty's and Uncle Bill's house, and there had been Isabel to play with. And Uncle Bill was big and gentle and never got into rages – somehow Rose knew that her father had not been like that. Rose had been happy there. She had become a city child, street-wise and independent.

For years her father had been nothing to Rose.

She had thought herself free of him, but in the end he had got his revenge. Rose had been in France, doing a feature on street markets around Paris, when Isabel phoned to say that the old man was dead, and that the funeral was to be three days later, up here in the village church. Rose had refused to come back for it – she had let Isabel drive up on her own. She had wanted nothing

5

to do with her father when he was alive: why should she go to him when he was dead?

And then she thought that it was finished, that at last she was rid of him, until that bloody letter came from the solicitor telling her that her father had left her the cottage in his will. Why pick on her? Why couldn't he have left it to a cats' home? Thirty years of him ignoring her and then this. He hadn't even gone to his wife's funeral. Rose cupped her mug in her cold hands and sipped the hot tea.

'Which is why I wouldn't go to yours, damn you,' she said bitterly.

Then there was the money. Thirty thousand pounds. Where had he scraped so much together? He certainly hadn't wasted any on wallpaper and paint, judging by the state of this room. Rose and her mother could have done with some of that money in the hard years when she was at school and then college. Ironic that it should come now, when she was beginning to earn enough from her photographs. Now it was far too much and far too late.

And what had he been? What had he done? He'd worked as a Farm Manager at some place or other, and all his life been bounded by this valley, all his years spent living in this dirty little cottage.

It was even colder in this kitchen. The flags of the stone floor were freezing off her toes, one by one. It felt sticky with dirt as she crossed to the stairs, holding the precious mug of hot tea carefully to avoid spilling any. She crawled back into bed, keeping on the sweater and the socks as well this time, and drank the tea greedily. There was something carved into the old bedhead which was digging into her spine. She turned to see what it was, but could make nothing of it in the moonlight, only that there was a carved panel with an angel and some letters under it. She yawned wearily and then grinned as she thought of Edward's face if he could see her now – guarded by an angel, sweatered and socked and not at all seductive.

Edward. He rose up before her in his smart suit and waistcoat, neat, civilized and immaculate. And although she blamed Isabel for sending her up up here, she knew that the reason she had come was Edward.

He'd asked her to marry him two days ago. She knew that he'd been waiting a long time to do it, but she had headed him off whenever the subject came up. She liked Edward, she probably even loved him, but she didn't want to marry him.

'Me a housewife? Come off it, Edward.'

'You wouldn't be a housewife. You'd be my wife. There is a difference.'

'Mrs Martin, wife of an eminent psychiatrist – that's who I'd be. And where would Rose Thorpe, photographer, be?'

'Still there.'

'Not when I got itchy feet I wouldn't.'

'Even Roses have roots.'

'Yes. On the bleeding compost heap.'

Edward had not appreciated being compared to a compost heap. Rose had ended the row which had followed by throwing a book at his head and storming out of his flat.

He phoned her briefly to wish her a safe journey before she left for the North and told her to take care. Then he asked her to think again about marrying him, told her that he loved her and rang off – presumably to call in his next patient and sit and listen calmly to the problems in her life. Sometimes when Edward sat and looked at her so consideringly, Rose felt that she could easily be his next appointment.

7

Edward and London seemed a long way off. She supposed that they both existed, somewhere. Leaning out of bed, she put the empty mug down on the floor. Through one of the small panes of glass in the window she could see the faint star of light which was still shining at the farm below. Reassured by the evidence that some-one else existed in the night, Rose pulled the quilt over her head to blot out the hard moonlight, curled herself up and fell at once into a heavy, dreamless sleep.

* * *

The Chinese have a saying that the future is only the shadow of the past. In this narrow valley of Moordale, high on the North Yorkshire moors, the shadows lie deep where time fractures and splits, and loops back on itself, as if caught there. It reels and unreels, playing back the lives of the families in the three homes in the valley – Throstle Hall, Ghyll Farm and Haggabacks Cottage. The passing of the years changes very little here.

Of the three, Throstle Hall is the most imposing. It stands high and grey on the hillside, dominating the entrance to the valley. Stone arches lead from the road to a paved yard, where the buildings stand empty since the Farm Manager died so suddenly. There is only an old couple living there now, but in times past this was the squire's house and a place for the gentry.

Further up the valley, on the opposite side to the Hall, stands Ghyll Farm, never a prosperous place, for the land there is wet and poor. The black-faced sheep grazing in the scrubby fields are small, though hardy enough – they would not survive otherwise, for winters up here are long and harsh. The Bransdale family, who live on the farm now, have owned it for generations; their family Bible shows how it passed from father to son, father to

8

son. The farmhouse is rougher than the Hall, for any spare money goes out on four legs on the land.

Above the farm, below the lip of steep moor, is the poorest of the buildings. Haggabacks is built of rough stone, bodged and patched over the years. Yet, for all its air of poverty, this place is the power-house for the valley. It is the point where time ebbs and flows like a strong spring tide. The other two places have always been handed on through the men's line, but this one was a woman's house. Nan lived here, not entirely alone. She had her companions. Sometimes it was a cat sitting with her beside the fire; sometimes there was a long-eared hare crouching by her as she weeded the herbs. The hare knew this place well, for she was running through the valley before the first stone walls grew out of the bitter land, and still her dark ears came bobbing across the sparse fields.

Seasons come and go and little changes.

There was a point where one man entering the valley did have a terrible effect on the lives of all the people there for generations to come. His name was Nicholas Brett, and it was a winter afternoon late in the 1700s when he rode across the moor for the first time.

He crests the ridge behind Haggabacks in the fading light and pulls his mare to a halt. She stands breathing heavily, for he has ridden her hard these past few days, and the wind is strong on this high ridge. It stings at the fresh scar on the rider's face and he winces, turning up the collar of his dark coat and hunching his face down into it. He runs his cold fingers lightly over the wound and curses the woman who gave it to him. It is her fault that he is sitting out here in the middle of a deserted heath miles from anywhere, without even a bed for the night.

Elizabeth James.

He spits her name out into the cold wind, and as soon as he has said it, the room comes flashing up into his head again. The room where she died.

He had been wary of involving her in the first place – it was risky, using the young daughter of Harry's groom. But there was no telling Harry. He insisted he had paid the man enough, whatever happened, that there was no danger in them using her at the next meeting of the Club.

The girl had been afraid as soon as they took her into the reeking room, even half drunk as she was. That cellar room below Harry's house in Chelsea stank of damp and worse: it was sour with the things which had happened there in the year the Club used it for their meetings. There were stains on the floor by the altar stone which needed no explanation. It had begun as a game, a wager, this dabbling in the occult that the five of them practised there – a wager to find the secret of Eternal Life. Then it had deepened and blackened for Nicholas, until it became a driving obsession.

Let the other men mix their vile concoctions with cockerel's blood and black cat's piss. They were mistaken. It was the blood of a virgin that would do it.

But how she had fought, Elizabeth James.

They stripped her lean body of clothes and spread her, half unconscious, on the altar. Nicholas had not intended to kill her. Not that. Only to take a little of her lifeblood. But she saw the knife in his hand and reared up at him, full of a terrible, unnatural strength, reaching for it before anyone was quick enough to stop her wrenching it from his hand. She sliced the point down his face, which tore as easily as a piece of old cloth.

The pain blinded him: he forced the knife from her and slashed down, stabbing until the others pulled him off. And then it was too late for her.

He left a sick and white-faced Harry to rid them of the body. The Thames flowed near the house: one more rotting corpse in there would make no difference. Then Nicholas saddled his red mare and rode out of London. It seemed to his weary bones that he had hardly stopped since then. It had all been for nothing. Elizabeth James was no virgin.

For a moment longer rider and horse stand outlined against the grey sky, then Nicholas Brett tightens his reins, the mare lifts her head and steps forward, picking her way carefully among the loose stones of the track. They disappear down into the valley and the skyline is empty. Only the dead bracken stirs in the wind. But from now on, things begin to change.

Chapter Two

IT was late in the morning when Rose woke with a shock for the second time to a sound, but this time there was no doubt as to what it was.

'Now then,' came the deep voice again from the kitchen below.

'Anyone about?'

Rose sat up and blinked at the strong sunshine flooding the room. She crawled in a panic out of bed before the voice could advance any further, pulled on her jeans and hurried down the stairs. Whoever the voice belonged to, he had no right to be in her kitchen – she must have forgotten to lock the door in the night when she put out the cat.

'Yes?' she said crisply, crossly.

The man leaning against the table had one of the most beautiful heads she had ever seen. It looked incongruous against the dirty, patched jeans and the sweater with a great hole in one elbow. It should have been on some old Greek statue. It was the face of a faun, with slanting dark eyes and thick, dark hair curling almost to his shoulders. The curve of the skull and the line of the long mouth had Rose lusting for her camera. She felt vulnerable, empty-handed without it. And who the hell was he, anyway, looking so very much at home?

She shoved her hands in the pockets of her jeans defensively and waited. Very southern, very civilized. The man looked startled.

'Now then,' he said again, nodding his head and staring at her.

He in his turn was surprised at the sight of her. His sister Maggie had run out with the cottage key in the dusk last night when they heard the car stop at the gate. She'd come back into the farmhouse full of the big car and the woman driving it, all dolled up with a sort of black cowboy hat on.

'By, she is posh!' Maggie had gone over to the mantelpiece to pick up the postcard again. She must have looked at it a dozen times since the thing had come, and all it said in black, spiky writing was 'Arriving Thursday, will collect key from you late afternoon, Rose Thorpe.'

Rose Thorpe.

It suited her, did Rose, he thought. She was like one of those big, old-fashioned creamy roses. All pink and white, and that fair hair. Cropped as short as a hay field after it's cut, but soft and fluffy. She was a grand, big lass. Looked as if she could work outside in the fields all day and never weary. She looked tougher than Maggie, for all her years in London. What's bred in the bone, he thought. By, she was like the old man. He eyed her up and down with interest, her crumpled jeans and a sweater that looked as if she'd slept in it. He saw with surprise the hardening of her nipples through the soft sweater as he stared, and wondered if they were on his account.

Rose saw where he was looking and moved quickly over to the sink. It was his face she wanted to have, not the rest of him – and then only from behind a camera. She filled the kettle, speaking back at him over her shoulder. 'Sorry to keep you waiting. Can I help you?'

He grinned lazily at her. 'Other way round. I'm here to help *you*. I'm Jack Bransdale, from Ghyll Farm down below. And I could do with a mug of tea if you're making one.'

She put the kettle on the cooker and switched it on.

13

'Then you know who I am,' she said, opening a cupboard and rooting about in it for a couple of mugs.

'Aye. You're the old man's daughter. You're like him an' all. Same blue eyes. Same colour hair.'

She didn't want to know. Didn't want to look like the dead man.

She peered into the mugs, ignoring him, and made a great show of shuddering at what she found inside and going to rinse them.

'Did you mean what you said, about helping me?'

'Oh, aye. I've been coming up here every day since the old man died.'

'Stopped short, never to go again,' went the old song skittering through her head.

'Well, I was coming up here before like, after he took badly. Chopping wood and that for him when he couldn't manage. Just keeping an eye on him. I'd not have walked in on you like I did but there was no smoke from your chimney. And no answer when I banged on the door – I thought summat was up.'

'No smoke without fire,' she said, putting a mug of tea in front of him and pushing the bag of sugar and tin of dried milk across the table. He looked blankly at her. 'If you really mean it about helping me, please could you get that horror going again?' She nodded crossly at the dead fire.

'You cold?' He looked surprised. 'It's a grand bright day, warm for December up here.'

He hadn't even got a jacket on, she realized, just a shirt and that raggy sweater. And his sock had a great hole in it too. Why was he here in his socks anyway? Surely he wasn't wandering about the countryside like that? She looked round, puzzled, and saw a pair of wellingtons standing neatly side by side on the door mat.

14

He gulped down his tea and stood and stretched.

The man was enormous. Six feet two, three even. He towered over Rose, and at five feet ten she was used to being eye to eye with most men. He was like a great black bear. He shook himself and strode over to the door, where he pulled on his wellingtons. But where was he going, she wondered? All this putting on and off of wellingtons must be a local custom.

'I'll not be a minute,' he said. 'I'll just fetch in some firewood.' The door closed behind him. She watched him pass the window, probably on his way to pull up the nearest tree. While he was gone, she nipped upstairs to the loo and washed her face and hands, wincing at the cold water. She ran her fingers through her short hair and pulled a face at her reflection in the spotted mirror over the cracked sink. She looked very lived-in this morning. Hearing footsteps below her, she went down to find Jack lighting the fire.

Rose curled up in the chair next to him and watched carefully, thinking that she'd have to do it herself from now on. He knelt in front of the range, broke up some stick wood and found a yellowed newspaper. He coaxed at the damp wood until it flowered into flame. Still he knelt patiently, feeding it until it settled into a sulky blaze; then, balancing a log and some small pieces of wood on it, he opened the side door of the oven and neatly stacked the remaining wood inside it.

'That's for tomorrow,' he explained carefully. 'That way it'll be dry, then the fire should light straight off. It's the bread oven really, is this, but I doubt you'll be making your own bread?'

He grinned at the expression on her face. 'Aye, I thought not. I'll fetch you in some logs before I go.'

He stood and looked round the kitchen. 'Is the cat about? Have you fed her? Tins are at the bottom of that cupboard there. I must feed Lady now, she'll be wondering where I've got to.'

Rose watched him go over to the door and pull on his wellingtons again. She wondered who or what Lady could be. She wasn't sure that she really wanted to know. The scraggy cat was enough for her. Reluctantly she prised herself away from the growing heat and found a tin of cat food. The pink coloured meat smelled horrible. She wrinkled up her nose at the fishy taint of it, and poked out a lump of it with a fork on to a saucer she found in the pantry. The one from which the cat had been eating was encrusted with old, dried food, and she picked it up between finger and thumb to thrust it down into the carrier bag which she was using for rubbish. She put down the saucer full of food beside the sink and went to the partly open door to call for the cat.

'Puss, puss!' At the sound of her voice the cat came slipping in from the garden and, as she edged past Rose, a long, wailing cry came from the outbuildings next to the cottage. Rose slammed the door shut on it and went nervously over to the fire, wondering what it could have been. She watched the cat gulping the food from her saucer as if it were liquid. She licked the saucer bone-clean, then went over to the range and leaped up on top of the side oven, where she curled her tail neatly about herself and began to wash her face.

She was a very non-cat really, thought Rose, all black except for a grubby white bib under her chin. She stretched out a hand to stroke her, but the cat growled softly at her and glared resentfully from pale green eyes. Rose apologized hastily and stepped back.

'There y'are then, Tibby, back in your old spot,' said Jack, coming in with an armful of logs. He leaned back against the door and kicked off his boots yet again. It must help to pass the long winter days, thought Rose, all this business with wellingtons.

Jack stacked the logs in the hearth and, sitting down in the chair next to her, stretched out his long legs comfortably. This annoyed Rose, seeing him so sprawled out and relaxed, practically licking his paws along with the cat. He was more at home than she would ever be in this place. And he wasn't going to mention that strange noise she'd heard either.

'Who's this Lady, then?' she said sharply. 'Was it her making that noise I heard?'

He sat up and looked round at the door, startled. 'What?' he said.

'You said you were going to feed Lady. And there was a noise – like a child shouting almost.'

'A bairn?' He laughed and leaned back in his chair again. 'No, Lady's your nannygoat. The old man had a flock of them at one time. This one is the last of them. She's in the building yonder. D'you want to come and have a look at her while I'm here? Best put your coat on. We don't want you catching cold.'

'But I don't know anything about goats . . .' began Rose in dismay.

'She'll soon teach you,' said Jack cheerfully. Rose picked up her coat and followed his broad back.

The cottage was built of grey stone, with a red pantiled roof. The outbuildings were joined on to the cottage in the old way, huddled against it as if for shelter. It lay at the head of the valley with a track running off up behind it to the high moor. The valley itself was a patchwork of poor, scrubby fields, dotted with sheep. Apart from the Bransdales' farm below, Rose could see only one other house, a big sprawling place far off on the skyline where the valley widened out.

The Bransdales' farm lay at the bottom of a steep

stretch of track down from the cottage, on either side of which was a long, narrow field. Jack took her down the path and leant on the garden gate. He pointed to the distant farmhouse.

'That's Throstle Hall. Right old place. Your dad worked there, he was Farm Manager for years. They thought a lot of him. They say that was where the Lord of the Manor lived, times past. And that's our spot, Ghyll Farm. Then yours, Haggabacks.'

She looked blankly at him. Nobody had told her that she would need an interpreter.

'Throstle?' she repeated.

'Thrush. See these two fields by the track, they're yours an' all.'

'Mine?' she said in surprise, looking at them more carefully. Standard green, bounded by ragged stone walls, and in each of them a small group of sheep. They had black faces and querulous voices. They moved stiffly on elegantly thin legs, cropping the sparse grass.

'The sheep,' she said. 'Are they yours?'

'Most of 'em. There's half a dozen that are yours, we run them with our lot and lamb them in return for the grazing. You'll have nowt to do for them.'

Rose was relieved to hear it. She had no desire to set herself up as a modern-day version of Bo-Peep. She looked more closely at the nearest ones. 'Why have they all got that red patch on their backs – it's not blood, is it?'

This obviously amused Jack. City girl shows appalling ignorance. 'Nay, that's not blood. That's the tup's mark. Ram, you would call him likely; we call them tups up here. He's been running with the ewes late this year. It's to show which ewes he's covered, see, we strap the marker on his chest and when he covers them he leaves his red mark on them. They should be a good lot of lambs come April, we put the young tup in with them.'

She stood and listened to the plaintive bleating of the sheep and watched them graze. This was all getting much more complicated than she had imagined; she had assumed that the cottage was all that she had inherited. Suddenly it was goats and sheep and goodness knows what else. It was not going to be as easy to get rid of the place as she had thought.

Jack turned and led her off through the orchard to the left of the path, telling her that the trees were of little use now; old and left unpruned for too many years, they produced few apples. He stopped at the edge of the stream running beside the trees and peered up and down it.

'You've some mallard ducks here on the beck, your dad used to feed them. You'll get ducklings later on.'

'Is it curable?' she said, then added quickly as she saw his bewildered face, 'I don't suppose I shall still be here by then.'

She felt as if she were submerging under an avalanche of fluffy animals. She wandered back through the trees and stood looking at the cottage. It was growing fingers, clutching at her.

'You'll sell it, then?' he said, coming up behind her. 'You'll not hang on to the place?'

'I'm a photo-journalist. I can't imagine that I'm going to find much work up here.'

'Photos,' he said derisively. 'Plenty of photos if that's all you want. Look up there.'

She turned and looked up the valley. A flock of gulls was wheeling silver over the dale, and sunlight lying on the tawny bracken, thick as fur, was giving it an almost purple bloom. To the right the linen-folded hills opened out into a small flat plain in the distance, and in the middle of this plain was a curiously smooth, round hill, like a great green molehill rising up.

'Fairy Hill,' said Jack, seeing where she was looking. 'The old back road to the village goes round that way, over Fairy Cross Plain and past the church. Don't you use it, though, it's a bad road – it'll knock hell out of your nice car.'

'Thanks. Fairy Hill? Fairies?'

'Little green men with red hats on,' he said gravely. 'And not so long since neither. Never been ploughed, hasn't that hill. Never will be either. Come on, you've not seen Lady yet.'

They walked across the garden to the corner of the cottage, where a once-white gate led through into the yard. The first outbuilding held kindling wood and a great pile of split logs. From the smell of the place the cat had spent a lot of her time in here. The middle building held bins of foodstuff for the goat, and a stack of baled hay filled the far end. There was a tap in this room, which Jack pointed out with great pride.

The end building was Lady's. She put up her feet on the half-door and leant on her elbows, watching them and bleating loudly. Jack tickled her ears and she nibbled at the frayed cuffs of his shirt. She was a big goat, fawn with pricked-up ears and a satanic little beard.

'Keep her hay rack full all the time so she can pick at it,' said Jack. 'Clean water in that bucket, concentrates in the other one – just a handful twice a day . . .'

Morning tea and toast, the daily paper, a milky drink and a hot-water bottle at night, added Rose in her head.

'Just while she's inside, like. I've not had her out while there's been no one to keep an eye on her. You've no need to milk her, that's one job less for you. She's not been to the billy yet. You let me know when she's ready and I'll see to her for you.'

Does he mean personally? wondered Rose.

'And how do I know when she's ready for the billy? When I find her writing out wedding invitations?'

He grinned and looked sideways at her. 'Oh, you'll know soon enough, the row she'll kick up. She's like all females, she'll create until she gets what she wants. She'll let you know right enough when it's time.'

She shoved her hands in her pockets and moved off towards the cottage. She felt as if she'd been round an entire safari park. If he wanted to stand here in the cold and discuss the sex life of a nannygoat, she certainly didn't.

'Thanks for showing me everything,' she called back to him as he slowly followed her. Not that he'd shown her quite everything. If she stood here for another ten minutes with him he could well start showing her How Tups and Billies Do It. With illustrations.

'Jack, I need to stock up on food. How do I get to this village you were talking about? Is there a shop there?'

'Oh, aye. Ainsby. Go back down the road you came in on to the end of the valley and turn left at Throstle Hall. Takes you straight to the village. There's a Co-op there and a post office. Maggie would have got you some more stuff in, but we didn't know how long you'd be stopping.'

'Neither did I. Is there a bank there? I need to cash a cheque.'

'Aye, there is, but it's Friday. It'll not be there today.'

She looked at him blankly. 'What d'you mean, it won't be there today? Where does it go on a Friday, for God's sake, down the nearest rabbit hole?'

He laughed at her cross face. 'Now don't take on so, lass. It's a mobile bank, see, it only comes to Ainsby on Monday mornings. They'll take a cheque in the Co-op, though, don't fret. Your dad's name's good enough round here.'

The miracle of plastic cards hadn't reached Ghyll Farm yet, obviously. Rose thought ruefully of how much her name meant at the bottom of a picture spread in London, and of how much it meant here. Bugger all. The irony was that her father's name meant more.

'Right.' She turned to go inside, aware of how many hours it was since she'd had a proper meal. She'd had enough of the lecture tour for now. He was pulling creatures out of the woodwork. Send the man home before he brought on the dancing bears.

'I'll see you later, then, and thanks again for all your help.'

'Aye. I'll be about if you need me. Mother says she's got plenty of eggs to spare, so don't go buying any. I'll get our Maggie to pop up with some later on.'

He went leisurely down the path, turning to look up at the roof of the cottage from the gate.

'You've a few tiles loose up there. I'll go up and fettle them before the weather turns.'

And he was gone, striding off down the path.

'Rose, my girl,' she said very sadly to herself, 'I think you've got more than a few tiles loose.'

*   *   *

The sound of the red mare's hooves rings loudly in the frosty air as the stranger clatters under the stone arch and into the yard. He pulls the stiffly moving horse to a halt and looks about him with relief. He has ridden the length of this valley and passed only a hovel fit for pigs to live in at the head of it and a rough-looking farm below it. This building is the only one which looks as if it may have civilized people living in it.

The valley is a wretched place to be out and abroad in

22

at dusk, especially on a late afternoon as cold as this, with now a scattering of snow stinging the cold air. He is grateful to have found this house. It will serve him very well to spend a night here – it cannot be any worse than the flea-bitten inn where he had stayed the night before. He still itches from that bed. The mare is weary. He will take her no further.

He slides stiffly from her back and leads the mud-spattered creature across the yard. Everywhere is dark and silent. Surely the house is not shut up and empty for the winter?

Nicholas Brett swears and calls out urgently, angrily. After a long moment a bent old man appears from the nearest outbuilding. He shuffles to the mare's head and stands peering at the stranger.

'Aye?' he says laconically.

'Aye?' repeats Nicholas in disbelief, staring in horror at the ancient leather breeches and waistcoat the old man is wearing. 'What kind of greeting is that for a stranger on a winter's night?'

The old man sniffs and wipes his nose on the back of a dirty hand. 'We don't get ovver many strangers in winter hereabouts,' he says sourly. 'Not many folks that we know either, come to that.'

'Do you not?' says Nicholas thoughtfully. A place where there are few visitors is what he needs, and surely he cannot get much further from London, and the hue and cry he left behind him there, than this lost place.

He pulls a coin from his pocket with cold fingers and hands it to the old man. 'See to the mare for me. She is hot: be careful not to let her drink too much. Only a mouthful to freshen her at first. And rub her down well. Is your master at home?'

'Maister? Where else would he be?'

'Good. I'm ready for a meal. Will he be at dinner?'

The old man snorted. 'Dinner? At fower o'clock? Nay, we had our dinner at proper time, lad. Twelve mid-day.'

'God's teeth, where have I landed?' groaned Nicholas. 'Where am I that they still eat dinner at noon?'

'Throstle Hall in Moordale's where thoo art. And thoo'll not get much forrader neither, there's a deal of snow on t' way.'

The old man clicks his tongue at the mare and, turning his back, leads her off across the yard.

'But where do I go? How do I get into this benighted place?'

'Throo t' door's usual fashion. Reet in front of thi face.'

Muttering about daft furriners, the old man disappears with the mare and slams the stable door behind him.

Nicholas Brett stands for an instant longer, looking about him. This Throstle Hall is a lonely place, a long way from any village. He could lose a few days, a few weeks, as easily here as anywhere. Chance having brought him here, he will make use of it. Brushing a clod of earth from his spattered breeches, he straightens his coat, crosses to the heavy door in front of him, and pushes it open.

He steps into a kitchen, and the smell of rank fat and greasy food after the pure moor air halts him in the doorway. There is a little servant girl on her knees at the fireplace; she yelps and drops the peat she is holding. A woman standing at the table snaps crossly at her: 'Whativver is it, Tully?' She is busy serving out food with her back to the door; all she is vaguely aware of is a bitter draught of air around her swollen ankles. Tully kneels, all squeaks and wide eyes, and somehow cannot get a word out.

'I fancy that I startled her, madam,' says the stranger smoothly, shutting the door gently behind him and stepping forward into the candlelight. And the woman whirls and gasps to see an unknown man in her kitchen, and she and Tully stare in a frozen silence at the angry red scar stitching his eye corner to his long, narrow mouth. It seems to both the frightened women that something dangerous has come into the house.

He stands patiently and waits for speech to return to them, eyeing the shelves lined with pewter dishes, the thick beams hung with strings of black puddings, hams, fat sausages and great flitches of bacon. If it were to snow from now to Easter, he thinks, there will be no shortage of food in this house. He smiles at the women, especially at the little one kneeling by the hearth. Tully, he thinks. Chance has done more than bring him to the right place: it has brought him to the right person. For this one is all blue eyes and innocence. This one is an unused little virgin. He holds her fast in his gaze for a moment, then looks away to the heavy woman at the table. She is watching him as intently as Tully. He will need her on his side to get to the girl. He smiles wider than ever, and his voice is as smooth as cream.

'I am Nicholas Brett, from London. I have lost my road in the poor light, and wondered if I might speak to your master, to prevail upon his hospitality for the night?'

This is the first time that Martha has seen anyone from as far away as London, and she is flustered, anxious as to what she should do.

'Aye, surely sir,' she begins. 'He's having a bite of supper, through t' door there . . .' She nods at the half-open door at the far side of the kitchen, but her eyes slide back to his scar.

'Martha!' comes a bull-like roar from beyond the door. 'Am I to have no meat tonight? I'm fair clemmed here waiting for summat to eat . . .'

'Master?' says Nicholas very gently, lifting a narrow eyebrow.

Tully giggles, then whimpers at the sound, clapping a hand to her mouth as Martha whirls on her with a glare.

'Tek t' London gentleman in to Master Latimer, Tully. And give ovver being so silly . . .'

But the London gentleman has gone, and the door into the far room is closing soundlessly behind him.

Chapter Three

THE light in the valley had changed by the time Rose climbed out of her estate car and lifted out the heavy box of groceries. The late afternoon sun lay pale and soft above the black ridge of hills, and all about it clouds were forming, silver edged. The air felt much colder.

This time, Rose left the car at the bottom of the track to Haggabacks. Driving up it the night before in the poor light, she had not realized what a rocky road it was. Carrying everything up the track was going to be a nuisance, but the alternative would be to change the car for a Land Rover. And that would mean she was stopping – which she definitely was not, thought Rose gloomily as she toiled up what felt like the bed of a river.

She was pleased to see the thin scribble of smoke drifting from the cottage chimney. At least the fire was still burning. She put the groceries on the wall as she opened the gate. There was nothing very exciting in the box, but enough to keep her going. She was not much interested in food – especially if she had to cook it herself. It was only fuel to keep her moving. Isabel would spend two entire days getting food ready for a dinner party, and think the time well spent. Rose would rather open a bottle of wine and a packet of cheese biscuits.

The village had been prettier than she had imagined, with stone cottages round a village green. There was even a smithy, with a man shoeing a small, grey pony. And the old pub, the Running Hare, which looked out over the green, had been warm with a log fire, shining horse brasses and low, dark beams. The chicken and chips in a basket had been modern enough – hot and well cooked. Rose felt better now that she was full. She closed the gate behind her and heaved up the box again.

A long, wailing cry on the cold air startled her, until she realized that it was only Lady, singing for her supper. After dumping the box on the kitchen table, Rose threw a couple of logs on the fire and went straight out again to feed the goat before the light began to fade.

She wasn't looking forward to this. What if she got the amount of feed wrong? She would fill up the hay rack first. That was the easy bit – even she could get that right. With an armful of hay prickling under one arm, Rose opened the goat-house door. Lady stood back politely to let her in, took a hard look to see what Rose was carrying and, seeing only hay, shoved past her with a loud cry of derision. Dashing across the yard, she leapt up on to the wall of the garden and, with a brisk twitch of her fat, stubby tail, disappeared over it. Rose stood stupidly clutching the hay, then pushed it into the empty rack and set out after her. The goat had found a straggly row of Brussels sprouts, and was delicately picking them off like some exotic fruit. Her sharp little hooves were churning the lower leaves into the mud. Rose opened the gate and called to her.

Nothing happened. Exactly what Rose had expected.

'Come out of there, you!' she bawled. Lady pointedly ignored her, and went on picking sprouts. Rose set off along the path towards her, threatening death and destruction. Lady swung her elegant head, gazed at her with wicked bright eyes, then, skipping happily up the path to Rose's feet, stood up on her hind legs and butted her.

Taken by surprise, Rose sat down abruptly in the muddy earth at the side of the path. She sat in the thick, wet ooze and watched the goat trot back to her sprouts. Picking up a handful of the chocolate-dark clay, Rose hurled it at her, screaming, 'Bloody goat, call yourself a fucking Lady . . .'

There was someone standing at the garden gate, watching her.

Rose crawled stickily to her feet and went down the path, ignoring Lady, uneasily aware of the wet mud sticking to her bottom.

'Sorry about that,' she said to the girl at the gate. 'It's Maggie, isn't it?'

The girl looked like Jack. She had the same dark hair, but hers was lank and straggling down her back. Brown eyes like his too. She was nearly as tall as Rose, but what shape she was it was difficult to make out, for she was wearing a sagging tweed skirt and a baggy anorak. Her sturdy legs in mudstained stockings ended in the inevitable wellingtons.

She pushed the basket she was holding into Rose's hands. 'Here. Hold the eggs. I'll get her in for you.'

Walking straight past Lady, who was now playing leap-frog round and round the garden, Maggie disappeared into the buildings. She came out holding a feed bucket.

'Lady, Lady, come up, then!' She clattered the bucket as she called, and the goat halted in mid-hop with her ears pricked, then hurried across the garden and through the little gate. She followed Maggie meekly into her house as if it had not been her idea at all to leave it in the first place. Maggie closed the door firmly behind her.

'I'll feed her up for you. She needs a drink,' she called to Rose.

'Make it a double whisky. And the same for me,' said Rose to herself, carrying the basket of eggs into the kitchen.

She peeled off her jacket and kicked off her mud-caked shoes, unzipped her muddy jeans and dropped them on top of the jacket. Hearing footsteps behind her, she turned to thank Maggie and found instead a young, red-haired man staring at her legs.

Maggie came bustling in to find her brother Paddy standing admiring Rose with what Maggie called 'his daft look' on his face.

'Our Paddy, what are you doing here?' she snapped, annoyed at him for turning up when she was enjoying the importance of having Rose all to herself.

'You'd forget your head if it was loose. You were supposed to bring the chicken that mother had ready.'

He turned back to Rose, eyeing her knickers as he spoke. 'It's gutted ready for you. Mam thought it might be a bit beyond you, dressing it out. She'd have brought it up herself, but she was a bit busy.'

Oh, why not have mother as well? thought Rose. Are there no stray cousins anywhere about? No aunts or uncles, no aged grandparents? Let them all come. See the new neighbour's muddy knickers. Walk up! Walk up!

'I'll just go and get cleaned up,' she managed in a brittle voice. 'Maggie, would you be very kind and put the kettle on for me so we can have a cup of tea? I'll be down in a minute. Do excuse me.' She turned her mud-stained rear to them and went up the stairs, stiff-backed and stately.

'Oh, *do* excuse me!' Paddy minced round the table with one hand on his hip.

'Ah, don't,' said Maggie filling the kettle. 'She's nice. She talks lovely. And did you see those knickers she was wearing? Red, and all that lace. I wish I had some as pretty as that.'

'You have enough trouble keeping the passion-killers you wear on.' Paddy began to root through the box of groceries. 'What's she been buying, then? Three tins of salmon. Oh, very nice.' he slipped one of the tins into his pocket. 'She'll never miss one.'

'Stop it, our Paddy, it's not right . . .' began Maggie anxiously.

'It's not right she can afford three fucking tins of salmon when all I can manage is a tin of sardines. She's not the one on Income Support, is she? She's got loads of money, living in London, owning this place and that car. Then there was all that money her dad left her.'

'Well, she was his daughter, wasn't she?'

'Aye, well, she should have bloody well behaved like one then, and come up here now and again to see the poor old sod. What else has she been splashing out on?' He began to poke about in the box again, picking out a packet of Instant Soups. 'She's not going to waste much time cooking, is she? Mind you, with her looks she must spend most of her time flat on her back.'

'Shut up, Paddy!' Maggie snatched the packet from him and put it back into the box, leaning across it protectively to keep his hands out.

'Our Jack never said what a sexy bit of stuff she is, did he? I don't suppose he even noticed those great long legs of hers. He wouldn't notice anything that wasn't covered in white wool and going baaaaaa.'

'Not like you,' said Maggie under her breath.

'Not a bit like me.' He grinned and moved behind her, holding her arms and pinning her against the edge of the table. 'I bet she knows her stuff, that one. I can just imagine her, strutting about in black stockings and suspenders.' He began to rub himself gently against her, and she felt him harden. 'You've got long legs. You could wear them an' all. Give me summat nice to look at for a change.'

Maggie was getting hot and flustered. 'Leave off, will you? And don't talk so daft. Whatever would I want to wear them for – to feed round in? Get off me, will you, she'll be coming down again in a minute . . .'

She swung a sharp elbow into his ribs and snatched up the box. He kissed the bent nape of her neck with a loud smacking sound and grabbed an apple as she hurried past him into the pantry. He leant against the table chewing it, listening to her clattering and banging about. Poor cow. Jealous as hell. Things were definitely going to get more interesting with this Rose around. He grinned as he tossed the apple core into the fire, imagining Maggie tottering out in high heels, stockings and suspenders to feed the sheep.

When Rose came downstairs there was a bright fire burning, and one end of the table was spread with a grubby white cloth. Set out on some old blue plates were a rich, dark fruit cake and a block of creamy-white cheese. A big brown teapot stood steaming in the hearth, and Maggie jumped up from where she was sitting on the hearth rug and began to bustle about, pouring out the tea.

'I hope it's all right me getting everything out like this. I've put your groceries away in the pantry. Cake's one of my own. I've put your jeans to soak in the sink.'

Paddy looked up as Rose thanked Maggie and sat down in the chair opposite him at the table.

'She's well known for her fruit cake, is our lass. Wins every year at the village show with one. About the only time she ever gets anything right, isn't it, Mags?'

Rose looked at him more carefully. Maggie was beaming and nodding as if she hadn't really taken in what he'd just said, but there had been something very sharp, very nasty, about the way he spoke. Something not at all teasing. He was like a fox, this one.

Jack was a bear, big and powerful, but this one was nothing like him. He was all narrow angles. Sharp-faced, with high cheekbones and a shock of red hair. His queer, empty eyes were staring far too hard at her.

He lifted up his long nose and sniffed. 'By, you smell nice,' he said.

'Eh, Paddy, where's your manners?' Maggie frowned at Paddy and handed Rose a mug of tea. She cut a thick slice of cake and put it on Rose's plate with a wedge of cheese.

Paddy scowled at her. 'All you and Mam smell of is sheep. It makes a nice change. Rose doesn't mind me saying that she smells nice, do you? Roses are meant for smelling. You just have to watch out for pricks, that's all.'

Rose did not like the tone of his voice, let alone what he was saying. She was sure that he didn't like her; it was there, underneath in his voice. But why? Maybe it was women that he didn't like – he didn't seem at all fond of his sister. Rose wondered if he were gay, if that was why he was so antagonistic? No, it wasn't that, those pale blue eyes were undressing her where she sat. She was not going to play games with this one; he was best just ignored.

She took a bite out of the cake. 'Oh Maggie,' she said. 'This is lovely.' And it was too, rich and dark and crumbling in her mouth.

'Very nice!' Rose said again through a second bite. Maggie looked pleased and cut her another slice.

'While you're here, Maggie, how do I get any hot water in this place? I'd love a bath.'

Maggie exclaimed and jumped to her feet. 'It's this

33

switch here, by the cooker. Jack should have told you, I bet he didn't tell you half the stuff he was supposed to. Did he get you told that the postman doesn't come up the track to your place, he leaves your post in the box on the wall at the bottom there? And if you have any letters to go, you leave them in the box and he'll take them for you.' She came and sat down again. 'There. That should be hot enough for a bath in half an hour. It's a nice little bathroom, isn't it?'

'It would be if it were clean,' said Rose without thinking.

Maggie sniffed and bridled and cut herself another piece of cake. 'We did what we could,' she said flatly.

'Oh, I didn't mean that . . . you must all have done a lot for my father. I do appreciate it, it's just that I'd like to do some decorating, do the place up a bit.'

'Why d'you want to bother to do that, then?' Paddy's voice was sharp. 'Are you planning on selling the cottage?'

'Maybe. I don't know yet. I haven't really had time to think about it, I only got here yesterday . . .'

Yesterday? Impossible. It felt like weeks ago, months ago since she had arrived here. It couldn't be only two days since she had last used her camera. It felt like a lifetime. Tomorrow she would get up early, ignore the cottage, go out and start recording this valley. There must be somewhere, one of the rooms, that she could fix up as a darkroom. Until she sorted it out she would send off the film to be developed, instead of doing it herself as usual. Back in far-off Islington, the long-suffering Isabel had let her convert the basement into a darkroom. She was spoilt. She would just have to do the best she could here.

The work itself would be different as well. She was used to catching action, things happening, people's reactions – all of which looked like being a bit thin on the ground here. Rose hadn't done much landscape work – how did she start to capture the sky, the emptiness of the moors? The light, she thought, would be very difficult . . .

She became aware that Paddy was saying something to her. 'If you want some help with your decorating, Maggie can come up to give you a hand. She's done a fair bit at the farm, wallpapering and such. There's not much doing on the farm at this time of year. She'll be better off up here helping you.'

Very nice, thought Rose. Don't ask the poor girl, just volunteer her. He hadn't offered to help out himself, she noticed. Which was a relief – she would much rather have Maggie.

Maggie looked apprehensive as she turned from Paddy to Rose. 'Well, I don't know. I'm not that good at it.'

'Oh, please, Maggie, would you help me? I'll pay you of course, I don't expect you to do anything for me for nothing. Where would I get the paint and paper?'

'If you think I could help you . . .' Maggie hesitated and looked at Paddy's cross face. 'But I'd like to give you a hand,' she went on hastily. 'We'd need to go to Stokesley to get the stuff. There's a nice shop there sells real cheap paint. I could come with you, it takes about half an hour.' She was excited at the idea now. 'It's a lovely drive, you go right across the moors. You'll like that.'

She looked like a child invited to a party. What must her life be like, wondered Rose, if going over the moors to a place called Stokesley to buy some tins of paint was such a big event?

'Fine,' she said. 'I'd like to make a start right away if we can. Could we go there tomorrow, d'you think, about one o'clock if that's okay with you?'

35

'I'll be waiting at the farm gate,' promised Maggie happily.

Rose imagined her standing there waiting with her party frock on and clutching a red balloon on a string.

Maggie sighed contentedly and, standing up, began to collect the dirty pots and take them to the sink.

'Now then,' she said, pulling on her anorak. 'Have we told you everything? Postman. Oh, and the dustmen don't come up the track either, you have to push your wheelie-bin down on dustbin day. Make sure the lid is tight on else the foxes come down from the wood opposite and make a terrible mess of them. And if you want the milkman to leave you some milk, put your crate down by the post-box with a note in it for him.'

Rose wondered if anyone ever did actually venture up the track to the cottage? What about the doctor? If you were ill, no doubt you had to stagger feebly down to the post-box and lean against it, clutching your fevered brow. What kind of place had she come to? Living up here seemed to be the rural equivalent of having leprosy. She watched with interest as the pair padded across to the door and tugged on their wellingtons. She was going to have to buy herself a pair of these essentials and start practising. A gust of cold air came in as they went out of the door and banged it behind them. The sound of their voices died away down the path.

Dusk seemed to fill the room as they left. Rose sat in the firelight, watching the flames. The fire was blazing well now, and the kitchen was losing the edge of its damp smell. The cat had come in when Paddy and Maggie left, and was sitting by her empty dish, her front paws tucked under her, waiting.

It was feeding time. Then there was a list to be made out for tomorrow, and Rose should really write to Isabel. It felt strange and cut-off not having a phone here, not being able to pick it up and talk to Isabel. There were a lot of things missing in this place when she started to look round, things everybody else took for granted. There was no fridge. No washer. No TV or radio. The cat wailed unhappily, and Rose got up from her chair and picked up the empty dish. The half-empty tin of cat food in the pantry smelt even worse now. She wrinkled her nose at it and went on with her list of missing objects. A microwave oven, a split-level grill ... and the ICA Gallery, the British Museum and Islington, she added crossly. An electric kettle was going to be the first thing on her list tomorrow. That should make life a bit easier. Why her father had to live like this with thirty thousand pounds in the bank, she could not imagine.

She stood watching the cat eat her supper, more slowly this time and less as if she were starving. If Rose decided to sell this place, there were two ways of doing it. Get the builders in and all mod cons or keep the rural charm and paper over the cracks herself. Whatever she did, the new owners would probably rip it all out anyway. Take the walls back to wattle and daub with a toothbrush and a pair of tweezers. Dine out for years on what they found behind the ancient peasants' range. There could be anything behind that monstrosity. Probably a couple of ancient peasants.

Why did she keep thinking 'if she sold it'? Of course she was going to sell it. What else could she do with it? Funny how the Bransdales were so interested in her plans for the cottage, as if it affected them. Jack had pricked up his ears when she'd mentioned selling, and now Paddy had done the same. And very foxy ears brother Paddy had too, not as nice as Jack's by a long way. Paddy walked oddly, as if he had something wrong with his leg. Why was he lame, she wondered? She yawned and stretched. It had been a busy day. Helpful as they had all been, Rose felt as if she had taken an overdose of Bransdales.

She walked across and picked up the cat, put her outside and turned the old key. She wanted no more stray Bransdales wandering in, especially not when she was in the bath. They'd seen far too much of her already.

*   *   *

It is midday when Nan sees the three horsemen riding up the valley towards her cottage. The day is mild, with snow melting under a watery sun. She has been gathering up the dead twigs from under her apple trees, and she steps back into the shadow of their gnarled trunks.

She knows the first two riders. They are the Latimer lads, Nathan and Joshua. Long ago she had known their grandfather, Thomas Latimer, known him very well. But these two are nothing like the fine man that he had been. They are empty-headed, and all the more dangerous because of it.

The last time that they came this way on their fine horses they rode them round and round her garden, and her herbs were trodden flat into the soil, and all was to plant again. The lads are afraid of her, and rightly so, for all she is an old woman now, but they had not harmed her that day. Spoiling her garden was enough sport for them.

Time was, they would have had more respect for her; now no one stops them at their pranks. She is nothing to them. Even the young women of the village do not often come to her cottage, when once they turned to her for help. They are afraid of her too, and have turned away from the old ways. Her time has gone, but the power is still there if she needs it.

She peers through the lacing twigs at the third rider,

38

and catches her breath sharply as she sees the scar on his face, sees the Devil's Mark drawn so clearly on him. She knew he was there at the Hall, for news of a stranger travels fast in this valley, but she has not seen him before.

She is puzzled that he is so far north in winter-time. The two leading horses come level with her, splashing through the mud and past her. The stranger pulls on his mare's reins and slows her to look curiously at the cottage. He turns his head to the trees and sees Nan, and for a moment the two look silently at one another; then the red mare tosses her head and springs forward to follow her companions. They crest the ridge of the moor and are gone.

Nan holds on to the trunk of the tree, for her legs do not belong to her, they will let her fall flat on her back in the muddy garden. She can feel flames licking at her skin and smell smoke, and the world is wheeling in a black crackle of pain round her.

The stranger is a death-bringer, and she fears whose deaths he brings. He wears that scar through a death; there is blood on his hands and more to come. She claws at the trunk in a terrible choking fear, then there is something brushing her legs, and there is a sound like a murmur of bees. She looks down shakily and sees her cat, her great yellow cat with his tail swollen with rage and his green eyes glittering. His purr roars in his furry body, and he weaves himself between her legs, rubbing his great round head against her.

'My pretty, my pretty,' she says unsteadily, and the flames dwindle and fade, the bitter smell of smoke clears from her head and she bends to touch his warm fur. She turns to look at the cottage, and it is safe. All is well. No smoke plumes the still, grey air from the thatch of her roof, only the thin thread from her peat fire.

Nan sighs and looks after the horsemen, but they are long gone, and the track is empty. She moves slowly up the path with the cat; the cat's soft feet padding beside her, her wooden clogs with their iron tips and heels clopping over the damp, mossy flagstones.

Chapter Four

Rose lay back in the hot water and groaned with pleasure. She had poured in half a bottle of bubble bath, feeling that she needed cosseting. She lay and looked at the island of her body, gleaming pink through the bubbles. It seemed a very long time since she had actually seen all of herself at once.

Certainly it was the first time that she had been warm since leaving London. She stretched out her toes and wriggled them happily. All the bits and pieces seemed to be in working order. Nice-shaped feet with high arches. Long legs. Big hips and bum – bigger than fashionable really, but Edward liked her that way. Neat waist. Nice round tits. A good, useful body, she told herself firmly.

And the fact that it was bloody useless in bed was not apparent.

And not important, she said wearily again, as she had done so many times over the years. She slid her hand down between her legs and touched the wet mouse of herself gently. Anything it needed she could give to it, and still wake up next morning with nobody beside her. The very idea of sleeping all night in the same bed with someone horrified her. To let anyone see her sleeping, to trust anyone as much as that, was beyond her.

She had never let Edward stay the night at the Islington house – she went to his place in Devonshire Mews; that way she could leave when she wanted to.

Rose thought back to the first time that she had met Edward, when she fell for him at the ICA. Literally fell for him, and knocked him off his feet at the same time.

Which exhibition had it been? It must have been Robert Mapplethorpe's. Rose liked the ICA – it had a nice, relaxed sort of atmosphere. People talked, you didn't feel reduced to a whisper, and the work they showed was exciting. One of these days Rose hoped to have her photos up on those walls.

She'd wandered round the vestibule before she'd gone into the room where the photos were hung, collecting up a handful of leaflets of forthcoming events. There had been the usual crowd round the bookshop and the post-cards, glossy and colourful as a cloud of chattering birds. She'd been so busy looking at the leaflets that she hadn't been watching where she was going on the shallow flight of steps into the exhibition room. She tripped over her feet and went flying into Edward, who was standing reading a poster at the bottom of the steps.

God, how stupid she felt. She knocked him to his knees, and she was flat on her back with every single person in the place staring at them. But he was so nice about it; he picked up her shoulder bag and helped her to her feet. Then he walked round the photos with her. Even then, before Rose had known what he was, she had been intrigued by the way the faces of the people looking seemed to interest him as much as the photos. The watchers watched, the viewers viewed.

Edward stood for a long time in front of a photo of a male nude, watching the women's faces as they looked, and there were a lot of women looking. It was a beautiful photo of a man with skin like shining ebony, and a great carved penis like a piece of sculpture.

'Come and have a coffee with me?' he said afterwards. And since the coffee bar was just along the corridor, it was easy to say yes. When he sat down and put her coffee in front of her, he looked at her and said easily, 'I'm Edward Martin, thirty-five, divorced. I live behind

Devonshire Place in one of the mews cottages. I'm a psychiatrist. Your turn.'

When she asked him what a psychiatrist was doing at the Mapplethorpe Exhibition, he grinned and said he liked photos. They were secrets, he said, and he liked secrets.

He asked her for her phone number and she hesitated, then shrugged and gave it to him. He brought out a leather wallet from his camelhair coat and carefully wrote it down on the back of one of his cards. He pushed another card across the table to her. She shoved it into her pocket without looking at it. She didn't expect to hear from him again, and she didn't think that she would ever ring him.

Isabel liked the sound of Edward from the first time that Rose mentioned him, that night when she made a funny story out of knocking him off his feet.

'A psychiatrist? Oh, he might know my boss, then, I'll ask on Monday and see what I can find out . . .' Isabel was all interest.

'No, you won't,' said Rose curtly. 'I don't know what he specializes in and I don't want to. I shan't hear from him again, so it's a waste of time. It's not worth fussing over.'

Isabel shrugged. 'If you say so. But if he's as nice as he sounds, I think he'll ring you.'

Isabel was right. Edward did ring. And he was nice. He was kind; he listened. He was trained to listen of course – sometimes Rose wondered if one of the reasons that she didn't want him to get too close to her was the way she could never say anything casually to him. He had a way of looking at her when she was talking that made her wonder exactly what she had told him. Living with Edward would be a bit like living with a light-house, illuminated by the bright flashes of his attention.

Sometimes Rose wished he wasn't quite so understanding, so gentle. Sometimes he offered her too many choices when she just wanted . . . what?

Heathcliff, probably, since she was in the right place for him.

The bath water was almost cold, losing its heat rapidly in the damp air of the room. Rose yawned and sat up. All this fresh air was getting to her. She had to unpack her camera bag if she did nothing else before she climbed into bed. She must see what film she needed – better take her camera with her tomorrow to this Stokesley place.

She must remember to send off a postcard to Edward to let him know she'd arrived safely. He'd been worried about her driving so far on her own, which should not annoy her, but it did. She pulled out the bath plug with a jerk, and, standing up in the soapy water, shuddered and reached for a towel.

She had found a one-bar electric fire, tucked away in the bottom of the wardrobe for some reason, and had left it switched on while she was in the bath. The bedroom was slightly less than frigid when she went back into it now, wearing the vast pair of men's pyjamas she'd bought in the Co-op. The only alternative had been pink nylon, dotted with flowers.

Rose knelt in front of the fire and towelled her hair dry, then pulled her camera bag towards her and began to check its contents, the way a child checks its toys, as if to reassure herself that she was still a photographer and that Rose Thorpe still existed up here in the frozen north.

She lifted out the camera first, very carefully. A well-used 35mm SLR which she wore round her neck like a piece of much loved jewellery. Her Nikon lenses. She stood the unused film like a row of soldiers on the chest of drawers and counted them. Twenty-five. She could see that getting fresh supplies was going to be difficult. A packet of padded envelopes to send off the film. Spare batteries for the flash. A couple of small screwdrivers for emergency repairs. She left the camera on the chest of drawers with a fresh film in it.

Tomorrow, she promised it. Tomorrow I will begin.

Rose shivered her way down to the kitchen, made herself a mug of cocoa, and put it on the bedside table with a packet of biscuits. The bed was warmer tonight – she pushed her feet down to the two hot-water bottles she had bought in Ainsby and groaned with pleasure. She had even treated herself to a photography magazine at the post office. She picked it up and, leaning against the headboard, dunked one of the biscuits in her mug. A disgusting habit – one of the many which she would have to give up if she married Edward. Tough luck, Edward.

She sucked happily at the soggy biscuit and studied the magazine cover. Inevitably, a naked woman, near enough, but a good photo all the same. Very well lit. Rose wriggled uncomfortably. This bloody hard headboard – why she had to have an angel digging into her spine she couldn't imagine. It made her feel anything but holy. She turned round and thumped it crossly.

Under her hand, the panel with the carved angel moved slightly.

She thought she'd cracked it; then, as she looked more closely, saw that there was a thin slit down the edge of the panel. She put the tips of her fingers into the crack and pushed.

The sliding door of the small recess had not been opened for years. It was swollen thick with damp. She pushed as hard as she could, but it would only open far enough for her to slide in her fingers. An old, musty smell seeped out of the opening as she scrabbled inside it.

She thought it was empty, and then her fingers touched paper. She caught hold of the edge of it, easing it out through the crack. She reached inside again, but she couldn't feel anything else. There was only the damp stained envelope in her hand. She left the little panel as it was, and pushed her pillows up against it. She turned over the old envelope, and saw that it was fastened with a red blob of cracked sealing wax. She ran her fingers over the seal, and absent-mindedly gulped her cooling cocoa.

Why had her father hidden this so very carefully? For she supposed that it was her father who had hidden it there. Oh, my God, she whispered under her breath. Suppose that it was another will so carefully sealed and hidden? Suppose that she was sitting here in someone else's bed . . . in someone else's cottage . . . Slamming down the mug, she pushed her fingers under the brittle seal and ripped open the envelope. She peered inside.

It wasn't a will. It was photographs. It was a handful of old, faded black and white photos.

She lifted them out gently and spread them across her knees. They were all of a woman. She registered that much before she took in the actual contents. Then she gasped, picked up the nearest with shaking hands and stared at it, not believing what she was seeing.

These could have nothing to do with her father, he could never have taken them – they must have been French studies which he'd picked up somewhere.

But the woman was lying on a bed – and it was this bed, for there behind her was the carved angel with the outstretched wings.

The woman was wearing only a pair of dark stockings. She lay on her side, one arm propped under her head, smiling at the camera. The thick bush of pubic hair stood out against her pale, round stomach. Rose could tell by her face that this was no modern pin-up. Nowadays nudes wore their nakedness more easily, so that even their bodies looked bored. When this photo had been taken, there was still a naughtiness in having bare breasts, a delicious guilt which no longer existed. It showed in the glint in the woman's eyes, in the curves of her heavy bottom and thighs. This was someone's private peep-show; someone's private erotica.

And again: the next photos showed the woman kneeling against the side of the bed, showing off the heavy, round whiteness of her haunches. And here she was holding up her creamy breasts with their dark, plum nipples towards the camera, here lying with open legs and one hand trailing down to the mossy cave of herself. There was a close-up of her face, orgasmic and joyful. Then there was one last one.

In this photo the woman was lying face downwards on the bed, her long, dark hair spread like a fan around her head. She was lying passive, submissive, as if she were waiting for something. Or someone.

But superimposed across her was the shadow of a man.

Shadow. Image. Rose looked more closely but she couldn't make it out. There was something wrong about the man's shape, as if it were some kind of double exposure. It reminded her of the photos people produce of ghosts. It had the same fuzzy quality to the edges of it. The man was reaching out a hand to touch the woman's back but his head was turned towards the camera. Only the dark shape of a face showed, but the flash had somehow caught his eyes so they gaped like black hollows of bone.

This last photo terrified Rose. Finding them had been bad enough because her father must have hidden them there, but this one . . . this one felt very bad to her. She shivered and pushed all the photos back into the envelope, letting it fall to the floor beside the bed. She reached out a hand to switch off the light and hesitated, then left it on. Somehow she didn't want the room to fill with dark just now. She pulled the bedclothes up round herself and lay clutching her hot-water bottle as if she had been taken ill suddenly. She felt cold and sick.

Rose was a London woman, and would have described herself as tough, unshockable. She had seen things on the walls of the ICA which were in themselves more shocking than these photos of a woman. It was not that. She didn't want to think that her father had taken them, her father had done that, here on this bed with that woman.

And who was she? It was the same woman in all the photos, Rose knew that, but they had not all been taken at the same time. Time passed in them. The light changed; in some of the photos you could see that the branches of the tree outside the window were in leaf, while in others they were bare. And in that last one, in the one with the shadow of a man, there was snow on the window.

The woman wasn't Rose's mother – she had been slight and fair, nothing like this dark woman's lushness.

When had he taken them? After his wife left him? If it had been before, then maybe that was why her mother had run from this place so suddenly, if she had found out about the dark woman . . . Rose had thought that taking photos was something private of her own. She knew she was good at it, that it was a special gift she had been given. But there was an eye for line in her father's photos and a certain appreciation of form and image which echoed her own work. She didn't want to think that it was from him she got her talent, that she owed him that much.

Images of her father came up to Rose, erotic, lustful, goatish. She saw him rutting on this bed with the heavy-breasted woman, and heard her cries of pleasure. But the image which disturbed her uneasy sleep all night long was the black shadow which lay across that last photo. Once she woke herself screaming out, terrified that the dark hand had reached out and touched her, but there was nothing.

*　　*　　*

The room is all in shadow except for the small, round table pulled close to the smoking peat fire, and there the candle flickers in the draught from the door. Nicholas Brett shivers and rubs his cold hands together. Opposite him at the table, Joshua tips up his mug of ale and drops the empty mug to the floor between his sprawling legs. Nathan is sitting with his head on his folded arms, gazing into the pale, smoky light of the fire.

'If thoo were in London now,' begins Joshua, and trails off into a hopeful waiting.

'If I were in London now,' says Nicholas and shrugs, pulling out his snuff box from his coat pocket. Joshua leans forward to watch him take snuff on his little silver spoon, breathing it up his nostrils with a practised air. Nicholas closes the ornate silver box and holds it for a moment so that Joshua can see it. 'Made by the very best. Fribourg & Treyer,' he informs the pair, and pockets the box.

'But what would thoo be doing?'

'I'd not be sitting in a cold room, waiting until it was time for my bed.' Nicholas glances round at the window, where a sudden wind scatters a shower of hailstones against the small panes.

'Do you know that in London the men wear colouring on their faces?'

49

'What? Like lasses?' Joshua grins, and Nathan lifts a sleepy head from his arms.

'Pink and white. Very pretty, I assure you. Imagine a room. A drawing room. Around the walls are great gilt mirrors, reflecting and dazzling. The room is very crowded and noisy with people, so that you cannot hear yourself speak. The women are magnificent. Their hair is dressed high, and threaded with ribbons and jewels, with as many feathers fluttering as a cock's tail. There are so many candles burning that the women glitter with light, and the air is full of their sweet perfume. There isn't a pox mark to be seen, only complexions as pink and white as any milkmaid's.'

'What, men an' all?' grins Joshua.

Nicholas nods and for a moment the drawing room is more real to him than this cold place. He sighs, wishing that he were there in that crowded, sweet-smelling room, instead of here in this fusty damp place smelling of mice.

Silence falls on them again.

Nicholas yawns and covers his mouth with a white hand. Joshua drums his feet on the floor, and Nathan scratches his greasy head.

Nicholas looks at them both and says slowly, 'Shall I show you a thing my close companions and I learned this past year?'

Their eyes glint in the candlelight as they turn to him and wait.

'Your father is well a-bed? There is no chance of him interrupting?'

'Nay, if thoo oppen that door thoo'll hear him snoring. It's past eight. He'll be hard on by now.'

'Past eight,' sighs Nicholas. 'So late already.'

'Show us,' says Nathan.

'I need a wine glass from the kitchen. Have you such a thing? With as broad a base as possible.'

Joshua's chair scrapes across the flagstones and the door bangs behind him.

'Have you some scraps of paper to mark letters on?'

Nathan scowls around the room.

'We have an auld book somewhere. Aye, that's it on t' window-seat. We use it to prop window open in summer time. It'll mebbe have some blank pages at t' back.'

Nathan brings the crumpled, damp endpapers over to Nicholas.

'But what am I to write with?' says Nicholas patiently.

Joshua comes back into the room with a gust of cold air, and the peat fire puffs out a cloud of smoke as he slams shut the door. He puts down a glass on the table.

'Martha says she wants it back in one piece or else there'll be trouble.'

Nicholas nods, fingering the goblet.

'Something to write with?' he asks again, and, getting to his feet, kneels beside the hearth to pick up a half-burnt twig lying there. He tears the brown-spotted paper into small squares, and on each one he marks a letter. On the last two pieces he writes the words 'Yes' and 'No'. The boys watch him as he puts the upturned goblet in the centre of the table and spreads his scraps of paper in a ring round it. He moves the candlestick nearer to the glass, and shadows flicker across the black letters.

'Now,' he says softly. 'You must pull up your chairs, and each one put a finger of both hands on the edge of the goblet.'

They slide a glance at each other, but they do as he asks. He puts his fingers next to theirs and waits. Joshua sniggers and falls silent as Nicholas looks coldly at him.

'This is not for sport,' he whispers. 'Listen to me. Watch the goblet.'

'Is there someone there?'

The glass slides across the table to the word 'Yes' and

returns to centre. The boys look at each other and back to Nicholas's white face; the three faces are like masks now, hanging in the dark air.

'Tell us your name,' coaxes Nicholas, and the glass begins to move. Nicholas says the letters carefully as the glass moves, and it is sliding freely, smoothly, and it is not the boys' fingers pushing it.

They cannot work out how Nicholas is doing it, but the glass is moving.

'E', says Nicholas. Then 'L' and then in a horrified whisper, 'I'.

There is a terrible tension growing in him now as the glass slides and spins about the table in the candlelight, a terrible stiffening in him as he watches.

'Z' he whispers hoarsely, and then there is a pause. The glass moves jerkily.

'A' says Nicholas in a rising yelp.

The glass hesitates, then spins to the next letter. It pauses briefly at the letter 'B' and Nicholas says, 'Ah, no, not you, not you . . .'

He grips the edge of the table and over it goes with a clatter as the candlestick falls and the light dies. The candle is out, and the glass shatters on the flagstones. Only the sound of the boys' terrified breathing fills the room as the door slams behind Nicholas.

Chapter Five

R OSE sat and stared at the blank sheet of paper in front of her. She really should write to Edward; he would be worrying how she was managing up here on her own.

'Dear Edward,' she wrote, then sat and stared at it. She couldn't get any further.

'Dear Edward,' she said brightly into the silent room, 'I still don't want to marry you. Love, Rose.'

It was not possible for her to write to him without saying that; she couldn't bring herself to hurt him by writing him an entire letter without so much as mentioning his proposal. She wished he hadn't asked her to marry him. She resented him doing that to her. It made her feel uncomfortable every time she thought about it. She screwed up the paper crossly and threw it at the sleeping cat.

She would write a postcard to him. That was safer, nobody puts personal things on a card. It was Isabel she wanted to write to, Isabel she was missing. Pulling another piece of paper towards her, she began again.

Haggabacks Cottage
Very late. Wednesday

My dear Isabel,
Here I am at last with the letter I promised you – did you get the postcard I sent you from Stokesley? I can't get used to having no phone, I feel as if I'm gagged.

I don't know where to begin!
The journey up was no problem. But the cottage – oh, Isabel,

what a state it's in! It's dirty, it's damp and it's forgotten what paint looks like. I couldn't hope to sell it in this state. I'll have to do it up first. Yes, I know what my experience is with a paint brush. Nil. But I'll have to try. I think the best thing I can do is stop on here for a few weeks, at least until after Christmas, cover up the cracks as far as I can and put the place on the market after that, in the New Year.

The only person I can see wanting it is a masochistic hermit. I'm only just getting the damp dried out. I really wanted to be back with you in London for Christmas, but it's just not possible. How did my poor mother ever live up here? It's beautiful in a wild sort of way, but my God it's bleak. I never knew that Heights could actually Wuther before, the wind round the cottage is eerie. The Ancient Britons needn't have bothered with woad up here. They'd have been naturally blue with the cold. The only place I ever get warm is in the bath, and then I lie and dread getting out again.

I yearn for your lovely central heating and being able to wander about half-dressed instead of having on as many layers as an onion, and that's just to go to bed. The cold makes me lazy in a queer sort of way, I don't seem to want to do anything. The Bransdales (people at the next farm, more later) never seem to feel the cold. They think I'm a southern hot-house flower. Not fit for bedding out.

I wanted to show you what the cottage looked like and the moors, I did try to take some photos but the place defeated me. How can you photograph emptiness? There's nothing but these wild skies and hills that go stretching away into the distance for ever. I took a few shots of the cottage and gave up.

Oh, yes, I was going to tell you about the Bransdales, wasn't I.

I'm not totally cut off, the Bransdales live at the next farm. I've only met the children so far. Grown-up ones. Jack is about my age, he has a face like Pan and I lust to take his photo. Not married. Then there's the younger brother Paddy, about twenty-five, fox-red and wicked faced. He limps badly, but no one mentions this. Then there's poor old Maggie the daughter, aged twenty-three going on fifty. She's not married either. She dresses in tweed skirts and layers of sweaters and lisle stockings by the look of them. The boys treat her very badly – Women's Rights don't seem to apply to Maggie.

I haven't met Mrs Bransdale yet. She sent me up a chicken, dead, thankfully. I don't think there is a Mr Bransdale, there's no sign of him anywhere about. They all live in a kind of cocoon on the farm, nothing seems to happen to them and they never do anything.

Apart from Maggie, who must have done something at least once, she has a Dark and Wicked Past which I found out by accident. She took me to a place called Stokesley to buy paint and wallpaper. It was a lovely drive over the moors, through lots of little villages. Maggie chattered all the way.

So there we are, going through a little wood, and a magpie crosses in front of the car. She peers round, all serious, looking for something. Turns out to be another magpie, but there isn't one in sight. So she says, all polite, 'Good afternoon, Mr Magpie.'

'Sorry?' says I. I mean, talking to the birds for goodness' sake. She looks at me as if I'm beyond hope, and says very patiently, 'There's only the one magpie, on its own, that's right unlucky, that is. You have to say summat like good morning to it, then that makes it all right.'

News to me.

'Just magpies, is it?' I hoped it was – I thought that she was going to be having meaningful conversations with every sparrow between there and Stokesley. Luckily it's only lonely magpies that you have to acknowledge.

She really believed it, Isabel, she really thought we'd have a terrible afternoon and all sorts of evil would descend on us if we weren't respectful to Mr Magpie. I ask you!

We had a very nice afternoon, it was fun. Stokesley is a lovely old place with a very wide main street, full of Georgian houses.

And a shop that sells the best fish and chips that I've ever tasted. I'm obviously returning to my Yorkshire roots — we sat in the car and ate them out of the paper. Delicious.

Then we went to a paint shop and bought enough paint and paper to decorate Buckingham Palace. I found a shop selling off clothes cheap and bought a couple of tracksuits to work in for myself, and two for Maggie — only fair if she's helping me. She was pink with excitement — she's never had one before.

We went into a newsagent to buy some mags for me (I've no TV, Isabel!) and she bought a comic. She took ages to choose one, I don't think she can read very well. Then she chose a little red car and a box of Jelly Babies. She saw me watching and went scarlet. 'They're for the bairn,' she said.

'Whose bairn?' I said, as ever in with both feet.

'My little lad, Thomas,' she said.

And it turns out that she has this boy of five that nobody had mentioned. And who his father is I have no idea. They don't seem to go a great deal on fathers in this valley. Seem to manage quite nicely with just mothers.

Maggie and Jack treat me like the fairy at the top of the garden. And there are fairies, real ones with red hats, just round the corner on Fairy Hill. Maggie exasperates me watching everything I do, but she means to be helpful. Paddy has only been up to the cottage once to look me over. He saw more of me than is usual because I was running about in my knickers at the time. Maggie and Jack seem to be convinced that I am simple-minded as well as a Londoner. Or maybe because of it. Everything I suggest doing they shake their heads at and say, 'Nay, that'll never work . . .' When they've gone home I do it anyway.

Maggie turned up at half past eight on Monday morning to work, so work we did. She had one of the tracksuits on and I gave her a quilted waistcoat of mine to go over it. She has a nice figure under all those layers. She looked a bit more modern than usual — then she carefully put a big flowered apron on top in case she got it all dirty.

I'm sitting in the kitchen writing this to you, and the room is nothing like the one I walked into last week. Maggie has blackleaded the range, and I have learnt how to keep it alight. The black cat Tibby sits on the side oven warming her four paws. Maggie and I scrubbed for two whole days and then painted the walls in Summer Blue. I'm not sure what you would have called the colour that they were before. Greasy Grey possibly. The floor is flagstones under the dirty rugs that were down. Clippie mats, Maggie calls them. You prod cut-up lengths of old clothes through sacks in the long winter evenings to make them.

I burnt them in the garden when she'd gone on Monday. Very cross she was too. I got a big square of rush matting in Stokesley. Much as I love the colour of the old flags, they're too cold to leave bare. The dresser is polished and turns out to have nice brass handles under all the black. I found some blue pottery in the pantry and set that out. Polished the chairs and scrubbed the table. See how domesticated I'm becoming? Only because I couldn't bear to live in the room as it was. At least I have one room now as I want it. I did want blinds for the window, but Maggie said not, she thought heavy lined curtains would be better. She was right as well; even as I'm sitting here the curtains are lifting slightly in the draught.

Tomorrow Maggie and I attack the little parlour – Maggie's name for it. Jack has been up on the roof and fixed some loose tiles so that should keep out the rain. I didn't realize that there were so many problems with having a house – I'm not convinced I'll ever enjoy owning one, they have too many needs for my liking.

I can't work out what they all do on the farm; Jack finds the time to be up here most days helping. The few sheep that they have can't support five of them. They do have something else called suckler cows, whatever they are.

Tibby is asking to be let out. It's after midnight, and I must end this vast scrawl. I still haven't told you about my goat, Lady, or the ducks on the beck – see how I'm picking up the language? Next time I see you I'll be wearing my green wellies and will greet you with a loud, 'By heck, lass, it's grand to see thee.' It will be too. I do miss you and Islington. I sleep alone and chaste in winceyette pyjamas. I expect now you're on your own you've filled the house with beautiful young men. I prefer my hot-water bottles. I must go to bed or else I'll never cope with the parlour tomorrow. Maggie puts Thomas on the school bus and rushes straight up here, panting with eagerness.

Write to me, Isabel, enormous letters full of lovely details about pavements and shops and warm feet. Much love,

Rose

Rose sat and looked at the letter. It was a long one, but she had not mentioned either Edward and his proposal, or the one thing which she needed to tell Isabel about. She picked up the pen again and scrawled blackly, heavily, at the bottom of the page.

Isabel — I found something very strange hidden away behind a panel on my bedhead. A set of photos. And my father must have taken them but they're weird. Nasty. They really upset me — I thought I was broadminded and I'm not at all. They're of a woman — not my mother — and the only woman within miles of this place is Mrs Bransdale. Surely they can't be of her?

(Rose thought again of that last photo, the one with the dark shadow across it, but how could she explain that to Isabel?)

So he took photos. And I take photos. Do you suppose that's where I get it from? How much of the old bastard is there in me, then? More than I thought, perhaps.

R.

Rose stretched and yawned. She picked up a postcard of a sheep and scribbled on the back of it without pausing for thought.

Edward — any tips on photographing sheep? I'll not be back in

London for Christmas, there's too much to do at the cottage.
Getting quite domesticated. May yet learn to cook Yorkshire puds
– by heck aye lad.

Love, Rose

Lad, thought Rose, sitting looking vaguely at the card.
The last thing that you would call Edward was a lad.
There was a very wise old man lurking in there somewhere behind those black-rimmed glasses. Rose could
imagine him lying as a baby at his mother's breast and
looking up at her, nodding gently and listening to everything she was saying, noting every incautious 'Whose
Mummy's ickle darling, then?' He was probably born
with those specs on. It took him all his time to take them
off when he was in bed with her. Then he complained
that he couldn't see her face.

She yawned again. She was so tired with not sleeping
properly, with all the physical effort of decorating. She
pushed her letter to Isabel into an envelope and stuck
down the flap. She held the letter and card in her hand
and wondered what time the postman came to the box.
She wanted to get these two off as soon as possible.
Better take them down to the box now and make sure
they went in the morning.

Pulling on her wellies and coat, she found the torch
she'd bought in Stokesley. The light pricked its way
down the path in front of her, making the intense dark
on either side seem blacker. A white shape glimmered at
her beside the track and cried 'ma-ma' to her in a low
throaty growl. By the time she realized it was only a
sheep, she'd flown into the dark and was leaning against
the post-box with shaking legs. She took a deep, unsteady
breath, told herself not to be silly, and pushed the card
and letter into the box. She slammed the door and
fastened the catch.

The silence of the dark valley pressed in on her. There was a light at Bransdales' farm again. Maggie had said that it was Paddy's light when Rose asked her about it. Paddy couldn't sleep much at nights. He got up late, slept most of the morning.

It must be Jack who does all the outside work, thought Rose. Jack and Mrs Bransdale. Maggie talked as if she did most of the cooking and cleaning, as if her mother were busy elsewhere.

Far off at Throstle Hall a light pricked on and went quickly off again. Mr and Mrs Latimer on the prowl. An old name – Edward would know the history of this area. He would look it up in one of his hundreds of dusty old books. He knew more about most things than Rose did. He had more books than furniture in his mews cottage, but he said that his books *were* his furniture. Edward. She wondered what he was doing now, while she stood here wool-gathering in the middle of the night. He would be sleeping, no doubt, with his book fallen to the floor beside him, bedside light on as usual.

Rose turned and set off back up the track.

At the darkest hour before dawn, he came to her for the second time. He took on a body more easily now; his tall shape was more defined. He moved with a long stride across the room to where she slept, curled on her side facing him. He saw for the first time how beautiful she was – even with that strange, cropped head. Reaching out a thin finger, he stroked the curve of her sleeping face down to her moist and parted mouth. Desire rose in him as he felt her warm flesh; she smelled of woman and sleep. His fingers traced her full lips, and Rose stirred restlessly, flinging herself over on to her back.

She was dreaming of Edward, dreaming of being in a small, dark room with him. But something bothered her:

his hair. The colour of his hair was wrong. It was long and dark, and his eyes were dark. Something had hurt him. There was an ugly scar puckering his wax-white face from eye to mouth corner.

'Edward,' she moaned. 'What have you done to your face, your poor face?'

The scarred man narrowed his eyes at the sound of another man's name on her lips. She belonged to him: she had no need of any other man. Not any more. He would use all of her. He frowned and caught her roughly round her full throat, his fingers biting deep into her skin, holding her fast.

He bent his head towards her with an effort.

His force was leaving him. He was fading into dark, into nothing, and he was gone.

Rose muttered something incoherent, rubbed crossly at her throat, then turned on to her side again to sleep more deeply.

*　　*　　*

A week after Christmas, Tully is trudging back along the lane to Throstle Hall, singing happily to herself and swinging her empty basket. It was right good of Martha to let her go home for a whole afternoon, and such a basket of stuff she'd given her to take. Cheese and gingerbread, oatcakes and fat ham and t' pickings off a goose. And a bottle of her elderberry wine.

Her dad had been sitting in front of t' fire, hunched up like an auld man. There was a sheep badly and it always worried him, losing stock. He was muttering to himself about all t' mouths he had to feed, going on about her dead brothers and sisters.

Tully thought it was mebbe a good thing that t' poor little souls had died. How ivver could her mother have fed another six bairns? There were still plenty of 'em left without any more. She'd poured her dad a taste of t' wine and given him some gingerbread, and that had brought a smile to his face. Young Emily had unpacked t' basket with eyes like plates at so much food. Then t' questions had begun. Most of 'em about Master Brett.

Master Brett.

Just that, just saying his name to 'em all had made her feel that good. Even her mam had sat down for a minute and listened while Tully told them about London, about t' crowds there and t' way rich folk lived. She'd caught her dad watching her with a frown, and straight out she'd said to him that he wasn't to fret. She wasn't getting above hersen, waiting on someone as fine as Master Brett. She knew her place. And he'd nodded, satisfied.

But Tully knows that she has changed since Nicholas Brett walked into their kitchen that day. It is as if he has put a sort of magic on her, so that all she wants to do is to listen to his voice and follow him about like a little dog. There is something about his eyes and the way he looks at her, as if she matters to him, somehow. His poor face doesn't bother her, not now, for his scar is not as raw looking as it was at first. She wonders what it would be like to touch it, to put her mouth against his poor skin . . .

There is a puffing and a snorting in her ears and such a flurry of movement beside her that she cries out, startled, slipping in the mud to sit down heavily. There is a wild whinnying and there are four great legs stamping around her, and Tully is sure that she is killed.

'Steady now, steady,' says Master Brett, and the mare stands at his voice. He sits and looks down at her in amusement. 'Mistress Tully, my apologies. The mare meant you no harm.' He leans from the saddle with an outstretched arm. 'Up you come, sweetheart. Put your foot on my boot.'

And all in a scramble, Tully finds herself sitting sideways in front of Master Brett on the red mare. She has mud on her skirt, and her heart is beating fit to burst so that she doesn't know where to look.

'Am I forgiven?' he says, and turns her face to his and kisses her startled mouth.

Her cheeks are ablaze and she feels very strange. His arm is round her waist, holding her tightly to him, he called her sweetheart and he kissed her. And as the mare picks her way through the mud, all Tully can think of is how can she mek him kiss her again?

Chapter Six

BEFORE nine o'clock next morning, Maggie was banging on the door. Still in her pyjamas, Rose came sleepily down the stairs to let her in.

'I'll put the kettle on before we get started,' said Maggie, taking one look at Rose's face. 'I'll go and feed Lady for you while it's boiling. You go and get some clothes on. I can hear your teeth chattering from here.'

She pulled off her anorak and hung it behind the door, then put on her big flowered apron from the basket on the table. A gust of cold air rushed in as she banged the door behind her, and Rose went back upstairs, looking longingly at her bed and wishing she could crawl back into it. She really couldn't cope with this cold, it sapped all her energy, made her aware all the time of her grumbling body. But she wanted to get on with the cottage – the sooner it was finished, the sooner she could get rid of it.

She hated every inch of it today. She could put a match to it quite happily. Though the place was so damp that the match would probably go out.

She pulled on two sweaters and her jeans, and paused a moment in front of the mirror. There was a dark shadow on her throat – was it a bruise? She touched it gently and winced. It hurt – how could she have done that to herself and not noticed? Faintly into her mind there came the echo of a dream. Something about Edward. Something about . . . his face?

Rose shrugged and pulled up the collar of her sweater to cover the mark. Maybe it was rising grime. A high

tide mark. Edward had a *scar*, that was it, she remembered now. Leaning forward closer to the mirror, she
drew a line down her face from her eye corner to her
mouth. Then she shivered and ran quickly down the
stairs for her mug of tea.

The little parlour smelt strongly of damp. It felt unused
and musty. Rose walked into the middle of it and looked
round her.

One small iron fireplace, possibly Victorian, in the
wall opposite her. One small paned window looking out
on to the garden and the path, with a good, broad
window-seat. Nice, that. An oval table, once polished,
with four balloon-backed chairs. An old blanket chest. A
carpet which might be worth saving. And the inevitable
clippie mat in front of the fire. That could go, for a start.

There was another door in the far corner of the room.
She'd looked in there before, when she first arrived. The
tiny room wasn't much more than a cupboard, full of
boxes and piles of old newspapers. They could wait.

'Right, then,' said a beaming Maggie, appearing
behind her with a mug of tea. 'Let's get started. That's
Lady fettled for a bit. By, I am enjoying coming up here
to help you. Beats helping mother any day.'

'Why?' said Rose curiously.

Maggie hesitated and looked away. 'Well, I get things
right for you like. I get everything wrong at home . . .'
She trailed off unhappily.

'Maggie,' said Rose truthfully, 'I could never have
managed all this on my own. I really don't know what I
would have done without you.'

Maggie straightened her apron and perked up. 'Aye.
Now our Jack's coming up later on, when he's fed round.
He says to tell you he wants to clean out this chimney
before you try to light it. He says it'll be full of muck and
birds' nests and such, it's that long since it was lit. Your

dad never came in here much, he lived in the kitchen. Right – where shall we start, then? D'you want the furniture moving out?'

'Don't move anything just for a minute. I want to take some photos before we start, like I did in the kitchen.'

'Oh, you and your old photos,' said Maggie indulgently. She was just beginning to get used to Rose and her camera; just beginning to ignore the lens pointed at her, instead of freezing stiffly every time it swung in her direction and shuffling hastily out of view-point with her head down. She leant against the wall and sipped her tea, watching Rose as she began to pin down the room.

By mid-morning the furniture was piled in the kitchen, and the carpet was over the line in the garden, being given what Maggie called 'A good going over'. She had found an old-fashioned carpet-beater in the pantry and was happily raising clouds of dust with it. Rose watched her through the window for a moment and thought that it looked more like some form of therapy to work out your frustrations. She looked at the wallpaper. It ought to come off next. Not that it was going to take much energy to move it; most of it was peeling off the walls like dead skin.

She began on the corner by the fireplace. Here the paper was clinging to the walls a little harder, perhaps because the heat from the fire would have kept this wall drier. Rose caught hold of a loose corner of the faded paper and pulled. There was not just one layer of the stuff, but four or five, and they ripped off in one lump, covering her with a foul-smelling dust. She threw the paper behind her and sneezed and swore, then looked at the wall in front of her with surprise.

There was something under the paper – it looked like the corner of a small wooden door. She pulled off another strip of paper. It was a cupboard, set flush into the wall,

66

and so thickly papered over that nothing had shown through.

Rose stepped back and stared at it. Another secret. There were too many secrets in this house. She thought of the photos she'd found, of that strange double image on one of them, and wondered if she really wanted to know what was inside this cupboard. She went slowly into the kitchen and picked up the camera from the table where she'd left it safely out of all the dust. She clicked off some shots of the cupboard as it was, then very carefully began to peel off more layers of paper, each time recording it, until the little door was uncovered.

'Very Alice in Wonderland,' said Rose, standing staring at it.

She reached out a hand doubtfully, telling herself that it would be empty behind that little door, but there was no knob, no handle of any kind. It was wedged tightly shut.

Coming in rosy and wind-blown from the garden, Maggie exclaimed in surprise. She knew nothing about the cupboard being there, but she knew what it was for. 'It's next to the fireplace, see, it'll be the old spice-box. We have a couple next to our fire, to keep stuff dry.'

The cupboard sat in the wall looking blind-eyed at them. Rose was cross with herself for being so cautious about it and went for the bread knife. Even that didn't open it. Maggie stood and watched her and seemed less eager than Rose to get it open.

'Leave it. Leave it for Jack to open, Rose.'

It was late in the afternoon when Jack came up, just as they finished stripping the walls. He laughed at Rose's discovery.

'I keep telling her, there'll be nowt in it,' said Maggie quickly.

'Aye, it'll be empty, bound to be. I'll have a go at it when I've done this chimney. Maggie, get yourself out into the garden and watch out for the brush for me.'

Maggie went out into the windy garden and stood looking up at the chimney, holding down her flapping apron.

Jack pulled off his sweater and rolled up his shirtsleeves. Rose saw the tuft of dark hair at his open collar, and wondered how far down it grew like that.

He knelt beside the fireplace and spread an old sheet on the floor, then screwed in the first rod on to the brush-head. He worked with an easy, unhurried movement, adding on rod after rod, undisturbed by the pieces of clotted soot and old plaster which fell on to his wrists.

'You're a Jack-of-all-trades,' said Rose admiringly.

He grinned over his shoulder at her. 'Aye. Well, you have to be out here, time you get a man to come in from town to do it, there's ten more jobs need doing.'

'I'm very grateful for your help . . .'

'No bother. It wasn't safe, lighting this till I'd done it.'

Rose put a fresh roll of film into the camera, and began to photograph the bent, arching back and the muscles on the strong bare arms. He sat back on his heels and wiped a soot-stained arm across his face.

'I reckon you see with that thing,' he said.

'Yes. Yes, that's clever of you, actually I do.'

'Fancy taking pictures of me when I'm all in my muck. I look much better when I'm clean.'

'You'll have to come back another time, then, and I'll do some more of you.'

He looked carefully at her to see if she meant it, and nodded.

'Aye, I might just do that.'

A sudden banging on the window startled them.

Maggie's face was pressed against the glass. 'Get a move on, will you, our Jack! I'm freezing out here.'

'Wait your hurry, woman, I'm nearly done – just you keep an eye on that chimney.'

He screwed in the last section and thrust the long, stiff rod up the narrow chimney, turning to look at Rose as he did so and grinning broadly before giving one last thrust of his wide shoulders.

A wild yell from the garden let them know that the brush was in sight.

Jack grunted with satisfaction and began to pull down the rods. While he carried brush and rods to stand outside the kitchen door, Maggie hurried in and bustled about, gathering up the sooty sheet, complaining that her hands were that cold she couldn't feel them.

'All right for you two, nattering in here,' she said crossly, glaring up through her tangled hair at Rose.

'Sorry, Maggie. We'll have a cup of tea as soon as Jack opens this cupboard for me.'

Maggie sighed. 'Do you have to? I've been thinking about it while I was all that time out there in the cold. I've got a funny bad feeling about that cupboard. I think maybe you should just leave it shut. I mean, it didn't get papered over by mistake, did it? Someone knew what they were doing. Mebbe they had a good reason for covering it up. Let's just paper over it again. I would, Rose, honest I would.'

Maggie was voicing all Rose's earlier doubts, and she didn't want her to.

'Oh, come on, Maggie, you said yourself there would be nothing in it, so what difference does it make if we open it? It looks a nice old cupboard, I could use it to put china in or something . . .'

'But once it's opened then it's too late, isn't it?'

'Too late for what?'

Maggie hesitated, pressed her lips together and shook her head.

There *was* something in the cupboard.

When Jack forced it open with his knife, there at the bottom of it, covered in a fine brown dust, was a bundle. It was wrapped in what once must have been a white cloth. It was yellowed now, rotten with age. There was an old, musty smell clinging to it.

'There you are,' said Jack cheerfully. 'It's all yours.'

'Don't touch it!' screeched Maggie. 'Don't you touch it, Rose, it's something bad is that . . .' She backed away from the cupboard, wrapping her arms up in her apron for comfort.

Rose looked at her and hesitated, then lifted her camera and began to photograph the bundle.

'Why should it be something bad?' she said, concentrating on using the side of the cupboard as a frame.

'Why is it all fastened up in there if it's not?' wailed Maggie.

Rose hesitated with her hand stretched out to the cloth, then saw Jack grinning at her. He thought that she was as frightened as Maggie. She caught hold of a torn fold and ripped back the cloth.

It was a dead cat.

Inside the cloth there was a dried-up, mummified cat, with tufts of hair still clinging to its blackened skin, its thin lips drawn back from its yellowed teeth.

If Rose had expected anything, it was more photographs, not this dead travesty of a creature. She turned and clutched hold of Jack as Maggie began to wail behind her.

'I told you! I told you to leave it be! I knew it was something bad and you wouldn't listen to me. You've let something out now, let it out in the cottage. You should have kept it fastened up like I said . . .' Tears of distress were rolling down her face and her voice was getting more and more shrill.

Jack pulled Rose towards him and put his arms round her.

'For God's sake, will you shut up! You're scaring Rose as well as yourself. It's been dead too long, has that thing, to hurt anybody. It's only a dead cat, you daft bitch.'

He looked down at Rose. 'D'you want me to get rid of it for you? You'll not want to keep it, do you? I'll bury it in the orchard . . .'

Maggie's howl cut him off short. 'Keep it? Keep that? It's a bad thing, you musn't keep a bad thing like that in the house . . .'

'Will you give over? Get yourself out into the kitchen and make Rose a cup of tea if you don't like being in here with it.'

Maggie didn't need telling twice. The door closed behind her with a bang. Rose moved back from Jack, annoyed at herself for clinging on to him like that.

'Sorry,' she said. 'Yes, please get rid of it for me.' He reached out for it and she caught hold of his arm.

'Hang on a minute.' She lifted the camera and made her unsteady hands hold it properly. She focused in on the bundle of bones and fur, and this time, because she was behind the camera, it was easier.

'Why would anyone want to put a dead cat in there in the first place?'

'I have heard of them being put in foundations when they've been building round here, years back. Something to do with keeping the witches off. Bringing good luck.'

'Not for the poor cat,' said Rose unsteadily, and followed Maggie into the kitchen.

She found her standing by the kitchen window, staring out into the garden.

'Are you all right now?' said Rose, but Maggie didn't answer. She stood watching as Jack came out with his spade and began to dig in the dark winter earth.

Rose filled the kettle and put it on the ring. 'I think I'd better scrub out the cupboard.' She filled the washing-up bowl with hot water and disinfectant. Still Maggie said nothing.

'Make the tea when the kettle boils, will you? There are some chocolate biscuits in the red tin.'

Rose went back into the other room and put down the bowl on the floor. She picked up the scrubbing brush and, as she reached inside the cupboard with it, she saw that there was a piece of paper wedged in the crack at the back of it. She eased it out carefully and brushed off the dirt.

It was a half-sheet of letter paper, intricately folded. It had been sealed with three black seals, and, sticking out from between two of them, was what looked like a piece of dried, brittle skin. The damp paper unfolded easily. Inside it was drawn a pentacle, with a circle, and round this circle some words were written. Rose went over to the window-seat and sat down.

'What have you found now? Something else out of that place?' Maggie came in nervously, carrying a tray with three mugs of tea and a plate of biscuits.

'And what's that nasty thing on the floor?'

Rose moved over absent-mindedly so that Maggie could put down the tray next to her.

'What nasty thing?'

'That, next to your foot.'

'It must have fallen out of this paper.' Rose peered at the faded writing. Maggie bent down to look more closely and gave a horrified moan.

'It's skin,' she whispered. 'It's horrible dead skin. Oh, Rose, what have you found now . . .'

Coming in from the kitchen, Jack groaned.

'You're not off again are you, Rose will think you're as daft as a brush. What are you on about now? You mean this on the floor here?'

He bent and picked up the scrap and looked at it curiously.

'It is skin. Looks like it could be off a cockerel – part of its comb.'

He tossed the frail thing into the fireplace and came over to Rose. 'What's the paper, then?'

'It was in the back of the cupboard. That piece of skin was inside it. Listen.' She began to read the old words. '"In Him shall be the strength of thy hand. He shall keep thee in six troubles, yea, even in seven shall no harm come to thee." And look, round the pentacle it says something else. I don't understand a word of it. Is it Latin, d'you suppose? *"Agla el oh nalgah Adonai sadai."*'

'There's something else at the bottom,' said Jack peering over her shoulder. '"Ye are everlasting power of God. Theos Hoc in Vince."'

His deep voice echoed and died in the damp, musty room and Rose felt the hair on the back of her neck prickle. She shivered and stared at Jack.

'But what is it?'

'Witch charm, I should think. To keep them away. Same as the dead cat.'

'But why was whoever put them there so afraid of witches?'

Maggie sniffed and pushed a mug of tea into Rose's hands. Words on a piece of paper frightened her less than that old bag of bones had done.

'Don't you know, then?'

'Don't I know what?'

Maggie shook her head and looked away.

Jack leant against the wall next to Rose and folded his arms. 'Well, it's this place, see. Haggabacks. It's always been known as the witch's cottage. It's in the right place for a start, on the edge of the moor and right away from the village. Lonely like. They say her name was Nan – didn't your mam ever tell you about her? Your dad was real keen to call you after her, but your mother stuck out against it. She said it would ill-wish you.' He hesitated, looked at Maggie and away again. 'It's probably just tales like, but they do say that Auld Nan died a bad death here. But like I said, it's nowt but old tales.'

Rose let the paper fall to the floor.

Jack's face seemed to loom large and white above her in the failing light.

She died a bad death here, old Nan the witch.

*　　*　　*

The crowd is cheek by jowl in the crypt, pushing Nicholas back against the damp stone wall. He winces and brushes down his coat, and the man standing pressed against him in the crush eyes the thick gold ring on Nicholas's finger with an astonished greed.

Nicholas breathes in the foul air, stinking of sweat and chicken shit and thinks this place is too like the Chelsea cellar of Harry's house for his liking. There is something about a cock-fight which excites him the same way: the blood and the ceremonial dying. He remembers how he slashed down the knife into Elizabeth James and the way it had felt. His anger at the bitch and the pain she caused him is still there, buried deep.

But now he has young Tully instead.

He thinks with pleasure of how she trembled when he took her on the mare in front of him. And such a sweet kiss he had given her! He could have turned her end

74

over end in front of him on the saddle and had her then, with one thrust, she was so pliant under his mouth. But it was not the right time. He wanted to build up the tension in her, make her beg for him. Then at the year's high peak in Midsummer, when the power was strong, then he would have her. He would break the seal in her, unlock that tight secret. He would let his own cock strut the walk. And taste her blood. This time, it would all work as he planned it. The elixir of life would be his, and he would have life everlasting. Tully's blood would give him what he burned for.

Nicholas shifts uncomfortably, aware of the stiffening between his legs. There is a great roaring noise around him now as the crowd begins to shout the odds on the cocks to come in, so that he blinks, confused, and comes back into himself with a jolt.

'Five to four on the Black.'

'Two to one against the Brown Red.'

'Three to one against the Brown Red.'

'It's a grand cock, is the Brown Red.'

Gideon is pressed closely against the other side of Nicholas. Nothing but a good cock-fight would have brought him as far as Lastingham on a winter afternoon. His sons are standing uneasily in front of him, anxious that the birds will not be up to the standards of their London companion.

Nicholas thinks that the cocks will have to be remarkable to make that cold ride across the moor worth while. He thinks with regret of the cockpit he frequents in London. Nothing could be more different from this cold crypt under the church than the Royal Pit in Birdcage Walk, St James's Park, where a main of cocks was a delight to the eye. He looks round at the rough crowd of farmers and landowners and wonders what the birds can be like.

'The Black's nowt but an auld shake-bag!' bawls Gideon red-faced and sweating, and his neighbour turns on him happily.

Then in come the first two cocks and the noise dies as they are carried in and dropped to face one another. Nicholas raises his eyebrows in surprise as he peers over the heads of the crowd. The birds are big for their weight; their thighs are muscular and firm. The quality delights him. He nods at Joshua, who is watching him anxiously. Nicholas has put fifty guineas on the Brown Red, and that seems a fearful lot of money to Joshua. He fears that Nicholas will lose it.

The birds stand motionless and reaching, then raise their hackles, skirmish briefly, stand back from one another and attack with both legs. At the first stroke of Brown Red's spur, Black is touched in the throat, and stands back.

His breathing looks laboured, and a drop of blood falls from his beak. Brown Red attacks again, and they fall in a bundle of feathers which sways and rises. Brown Red is loose: he springs on the flank of Black. His spur paralyses his opponent.

Brown Red has won, the Black is dead and for an instant Nicholas sees the room through the red eyes of Brown Red, feels how the blood runs hotly through the bird, feels the lust to kill in him. He recognizes the same lust inside himself. It was a good death, a ritual killing, and Nicholas is considerably the richer for it.

The victor and the dead bird are taken out and the cries go up again. There is a good Grey to come in. Yorkshire Greys take some beating – or so Nicholas has heard, but they are a strain he knows little about. He pats Joshua on the back and smiles at him. This is more like it, he thinks. Yorkshire does have something to offer him after all. He touches the heavy bag of guineas on the inside of his coat, and knows that he will do well out of the afternoon.

'How many birds did you say, Gideon?'

Gideon is puffed up with pride. He knew all along that the Brown Red was a good 'un. 'Plenty more yet,' he says happily. 'There's a main of twenty.'

And the new birds are in, and the Grey is a beauty, with pearl eyes, a yellow beak and legs and a black saddle, with hackles the colour of straw. It is the bird which he faces that causes Nicholas's eyes to widen for it is a Muff, a Black-breasted Red. Nicholas has seen this breed only three or four times at the Royal, where it is still a novelty.

'How will it fight?' he whispers eagerly to Joshua, and settles to watch as the Grey and the Muff stand motion-less with hackles raised, eyeing each other with a red stare. It will end in a death, and Nicholas stares intently, not wanting to miss a blow.

The crowd are equally intent. Only the man standing at the far side of Nicholas takes his eyes off the birds to glance quickly at the bulge in Nicholas's coat where the guineas lie. Then he turns his head back to the birds, and a roar goes up as the Grey strikes, and blood spurts and stains the feathers of the crouching Muff.

Chapter Seven

'**W**HAT...'

Rose ran through the apple trees, her bare feet scrunching on the cold snow. She could hear him breathing close behind her, the padding of his soft paws. He lifted up his long grey muzzle and howled, his frozen breath smoking the falling snow.

'What time...'

In and out of the trees she ran, ducking under their clutching twigs, round and around, and his breathing was closer and closer. The snow was falling heavily, covering her blanched skin. It was filling her mouth so that she could not breathe. She clawed at her crusted eyes, the clotting snow sliding like tears across her wet face, and then she felt the first touch of him. His sleek, dark head brushed against her leg; his long red tongue snaked out and licked at her white thighs. The rasping of his tongue sent shivers of desire as sharp as needles pricking through her. Her legs trembled, folded under her. She sank to her knees in the soft, white cushion of snow.

'What time is it...'

His dark fur brushed her back and his claws scraped her bent, submissive neck. His teeth crunched down into the soft fruit of her throat. White skin tore, peeled to red flesh, peeled to white bone. Blood beaded her and ran between her breasts. He sucked the sweet marrow of cracked bone and in the red kiss of that bite she came to the final orgasm of death. Rose-red in the white snow.

'What time is it, Mr Wolf?'

'Time to let me in, my dear!'

Rose screeched and woke, shuddering and sweating, wailing her terror into the dark, not knowing who or where she was. Her hands clutched at her throat, pattered around her in the dark.

She was safe.

There was no wolf-dog. It had only been a bad dream. She was Rose Thorpe; it was the night before Christmas Eve and she had had another bad dream. She wiped the sweat from her face and breasts with the sheet and made herself breathe evenly steadily. What was it about this place which gave her such fearful dreams? She never had them in London. She didn't want them here. Rubbing her hands across her face, she lay back on her pillows and turned on her side. She yawned and closed her eyes, still wondering why she had dreamed up something as nasty as a wolf-dog. But it was all right now: she was safe. She could sleep.

He came out of the dark fully formed, and he was on her: he was gripping her shoulders and his mouth was clamping down on hers and his legs were wrapped round hers. Then he had her by the throat with one hand, and the other defined her body, cupping the roundness of her breasts, measuring the soft curve of her stomach.

It was a dream again . . .

It was the next part of the dream . . .

She whimpered and flailed out uselessly at him, desperate to wake up. His hand caught her under her chin, forced back her head. His nails delicately scratched at the soft skin there and then cut down, at first marking her with a pink thread, then scraping deeper until he was drawing a bloody furrow to the round full-stop of her navel. Then down again until his fingertips slid into her and held her still.

Dreaming, she was dreaming and it was not true . . .

She forced open her eyes until the room swam in red. Then his mouth was kissing the burning seam with which he had marked her, and he was licking, sucking at the red seep. All along the length of her body he kissed with a sticky mouth, and as he reached her cunt she bucked and arched in a frenzy, flailing at him and clawing at his back.

'Nothing but a dream,' she croaked at him, and she heard a laugh, rusty and unused, growling in her ear.

Then she was on her own in the dark, curled up in a ball, holding the bedclothes tightly round herself, not knowing what was real any more.

But in the morning, half-asleep, she stumbled out of bed and pulled off the T-shirt she had slept in and looked down in horror at the mark which bisected her.

It was impossible then for her to stay alone in the cottage. She needed people round her, normality. She pulled on her clothes quickly, hiding the laceration – if she couldn't see it, it wasn't there. Nightmares and fantasies. Any marks on her, she had made herself. Dreaming.

It was Christmas Eve. She would take the presents which she had bought for the Bransdales down to the farm.

In the early afternoon Rose walked down the track carrying the box of brightly wrapped gifts. Christmas here had crept up on her as a surprise, if not a nasty shock. She picked her way carefully down the muddy track, and wondered at how different time was up here. In this place the days seem to be sufficient in themselves; they didn't link up with one another the way they did in London. There were no hooks to hang the coming days on. It was like going back to childhood diaries: 'Got up.

Did nothing. Went to bed.' Only the weather made any change in the pattern of the days, and all it seemed to do was to get colder.

The Bransdales lived like this, so that any break from the routine, anything unexpected, became too important. Too big somehow.

Rose had realized a couple of days ago how few shopping days to Christmas she had left if she wanted to send off a present for Isabel. And Edward. So when Maggie arrived at the cottage all set to work for the day, Rose casually announced a change of plan. They would go to Whitby that afternoon. She hadn't been there yet, all she knew about it was that it had an abbey. And the sea, of course.

She thought Maggie would have been glad of a change, pleased to go into a town and see some life.

'We can't do that,' said Maggie very quickly, looking as shocked as if Rose had just suggested a quick trip to Siberia.

'Why not? It's not that far, is it? It must be only about ten miles from here. Out on the coast road. It would be lovely to see the sea.'

'Aye, but you never said anything about it yesterday, and there's the bairn's tea and everything . . .'

'Maggie, I couldn't have said anything yesterday because I only just thought of the idea half an hour ago. And you know you're never in when the bairn comes home from school because you're here, helping me. Your mother always gives him his tea.'

'But I'm not ready . . .' wailed Maggie.

Rose got cross. 'I am going to Whitby after lunch. I would have liked to take you with me, but it's entirely up to you whether you come or not. Of course you're ready, all you have to do is to take off your apron and put your coat on. You look nice in that tracksuit. We're only going shopping – oh, come on, Maggie. We deserve a break. It'll be fun.'

Maggie eyed her, unconvinced.

'Have you got everything for Thomas's stocking?'

'He never has one,' said Maggie in surprise. 'I never bother. I've got him a present, though,' she added hastily as she saw the look on Rose's face. 'Knitted him a new jumper for school.'

'Well, this year he's having one,' said Rose. 'We'll go straight after lunch.'

This turned out to be an understatement.

Rose sat and waited in the car at the farm gate for forty minutes while Maggie went in to see if her mother wanted anything from the shops.

'She had to make out her list in a rush, see, with her not knowing we were going,' said Maggie, all flustered, climbing back into the car bristling with baskets and purses.

Rule one, thought Rose. Wear your wellies at all times. Rule two. Always give twenty-four hours' notice before venturing into civilization.

But when they finally got there, the little town was well worth the trouble, for the tide was high, and the smell of the sea was everywhere, and there were carol singers in Victorian dress standing round a Christmas tree down by the harbour. And in Woolworth's the girls were dressed as fairies and Santas, and Maggie sparkled with excitement, and young Thomas was going to have a stocking bulging with delights this year.

When they'd piled all their heavy bags in the car, Maggie took Rose across the swing bridge over the River Esk, along the cobbled street which led to the flight of a hundred and ninety-nine steps up to the church and the abbey. They had arrived at the top breathless, and stood watching the sea crashing white and wintry far below them against the cliff face, with the abbey black and gaunt behind them. Rose had taken a roll of film, but it was difficult to avoid a cliché in such a beautiful place.

While Maggie was shopping for her mother in the butcher's in Church Street, Rose had quickly bought presents for the Bransdales. She stood now with her hand on the farm gate, hesitating and looking down into the box. She'd thought the gifts were right at the time, but now she wondered how they would accept them. Maybe they would think them over the top, excessive. Thomas's present was fine; he would like the big yellow tractor and trailer done up in shining gold paper.

It was Maggie's present she was doubtful about. Three pairs of French knickers had seemed like a good idea in the shop – she'd seen Maggie admiring a pair of her own hanging up in the bathroom to dry. The poor girl could do with a little luxury in her life. The tin of biscuits for Mrs Bransdale was safe if lacking in imagination, and there was a bottle of whisky for Paddy, since Maggie had once said that Paddy liked a drink.

And Jack. Rose had wanted to get something special for him. She had offered to pay him at first for all the help he was to her around the place, but he'd refused so curtly that she hadn't liked to offer again. He was too nice to be used for nothing in return. She'd bought him a sweater – a thick, dark blue one, the largest size in the shop, with a pattern of white sheep knitted into it.

Then she'd bought a silver ring with a stone of Whitby jet for Edward, and an antique cameo brooch for Isabel.

Rose crossed the yard and stood listening at the kitchen door. It was half open but there was no sound from inside it. She had never been as far as this; Maggie always met her at the farm gate when they went out in the car. She peered round the door.

A sheep-dog got up stiffly from the hearth rug and

growled at her. She took a quick look round and backed out hastily. It was bitter cold in the room, the fire half dying, and the place had a comfortless feel. There was a queer carved post at the end of a long wooden settle piled high with boxes and clothes. No wonder Maggie had been so surprised when Rose grumbled about the kitchen at Haggabacks. This one was just as bad.

She went across the yard to the outbuildings and, hearing a voice from the nearest one, leaned in the doorway and looked round. The place was full of feathers. It was like some ancient ritual she had walked into. There was an old boiler steaming away in one corner and standing next to it was a tall woman in a filthy coat, tied round the waist with a piece of hairy string. She was lifting a goose, a great white one, from the dripping, steaming water. It had a plastic bag where its head should have been, stained red with the blood dripping from the neck stump.

Mrs Bransdale at last.

And, looking at her, Rose knew exactly what she was going to think of the presents for her children. Corrupting one with naughty knickers and one with strong drink. And Rose could just imagine Mrs Bransdale's face when she saw the cute, fluffy white sheep gambolling happily round Jack's sweater.

Mrs Bransdale strode across to an upturned wooden box and hung the bird by one leg from a hook at the level of her head. She sat down heavily and began to pluck the bird, tugging out the feathers with strong red fingers. All this time she had not once looked at Rose, except for a very brief glance when she appeared in the doorway. Next to her, on another box, Maggie was plucking furiously, white down clinging like fine snow to her hair and coat. She looked up at Rose now and nodded quickly.

'You two look very busy,' said Rose brightly.

The words dropped away for ever into a heavy silence. Neither of them appeared to have heard her – they weren't going to answer something as obvious as that if they had.

'Mrs Bransdale?' she began again. 'Sorry I picked a bad time. I brought Thomas his present down. And something for the rest of you, just to thank you all for being so helpful . . .'

There was nothing but the sound of feathers ripping from the soft flesh for a minute, then Maggie said reluctantly, 'What you got the bairn, then?'

'A yellow tractor. One of the ones with a trailer that fastens on behind.'

'Oh grand. He'll like that, won't he, Mother?'

The mother lifted her head, on which she appeared to be wearing a green teapot-cover pulled well down over her ears, and looked coldly at Rose. 'Oh, aye,' she said. 'He'll like that.'

As soon as Rose heard Mrs Bransdale speak, heard her cold, sneering voice, she knew her feelings about the presents had been right. Mrs Bransdale wanted nothing from Rose. Rose felt over-dressed, like Lady Bountiful from London, all done up like a dog's dinner. It was there on Mrs Bransdale's face as she sat and watched her. Christmas and shiny wrapping paper meant nothing to the woman.

Rose saw now why Maggie was like she was – her mother had eaten her alive years ago.

All the same, Maggie could have stopped pulling out feathers long enough to come and take the box of presents. She wasn't even looking at Rose; only her fingers moved, pulling and tugging at the dead goose.

There was an old table just inside the doorway. Rose dumped her box on top of it and felt a hard anger rising in her. Bloody peasants. They could at least have said thank you. She caught hold of the camera on its strap round her neck.

'You don't mind if I take a few photos?' she said. She didn't bother waiting for an answer; she framed up Maggie's hands among the feathers.

Mrs Bransdale began to laugh, a harsh, unused cackle of sound.

'I told you what she was like for taking photos . . .' began Maggie, looking at her mother in astonishment, her hands stilled on the bird. Seeing her mother laugh like that was as rare a sight as snow in August.

'Nay, it's not that. Summat she reminded me of,' said Mrs Bransdale, and, bending her head forward, began again to rip savagely at the soft breast feathers.

Rose was not really listening to her. She was trying to catch something of what she had seen when she came to the doorway – a sense of time past, of a dim line of women all down the years sitting like this, preparing the Christmas feast. She shot off a film quickly, as if it were her eye closing and not the shutter. She was not there any more for the women; they had closed her off now completely, intent on getting off all the feathers before the geese cooled.

Rose took one last shot from the doorway, framing the women in its old wooden square. She called out a deliberately formal goodbye, and turned away with relief, glad to be out of the sour smell. She brushed the clinging flecks of feathers from her jacket as she crossed the yard.

As she reached the gate on to the road, she heard a man's voice raised in anger, echoing round the outbuildings in the still air. There was the sound of a blow, then Thomas appeared weeping, running across the yard to find his mother. Rose closed the gate behind her, wondering what all that was about – it must have been Paddy,

86

she thought, for she couldn't imagine Jack hitting the little boy like that. Much more likely to be foxy Paddy snapping and snarling. He'd never been back to Haggabacks, not after that first time. Summed her up and found her wanting, obviously.

She couldn't work out what Paddy did with himself all day. When she asked Maggie about it, asked if he helped with the stock, Maggie shrugged and was off-hand about it. 'Sometimes he helps Jack. If he feels like it. His leg plays him up.' Then she'd been very busy with her scrubbing brush and said no more.

It had been Paddy's light which Rose had seen that first night. Doing what? He didn't read, according to Maggie. He watched TV but that was hardly a full-time career. Rose wondered about his sex life. He never went out; nobody ever came to the farm. Jack went out now and again in his old Land Rover, but Rose didn't imagine he went off chasing women in it. He seemed to go to Ruswarp Mart and back, once a week. And Maggie . . . now Maggie must have had a sex life at some point. She'd done it once, obviously. All three of them, thought Rose, leading such chaste lives. They must take a lot of cold baths. Or else Mrs Bransdale was shoving handfuls of bromide in their tea. And having seen the woman now, Rose could well believe she was doing just that.

Rose considered her own sex life. All nicely sublimated into her work. Nearly all, anyway. And, wondering how the photos would turn out of the goose-plucking, Rose closed her garden gate behind her.

'That's her, then, is it?' said Mrs Bransdale.

Maggie looked at her in surprise. Her mother's hands were in her lap, doing nothing, and she was looking out of the door to where Rose was crossing the yard.

'She's a bonny-looking lass.'

Maggie scowled and ripped out a few feathers. Her mam had never said that about her.

'She's like her dad,' went on Mrs Bransdale. 'Charm the birds off the tree. But she's trouble here.'

'No, Mam, she's nice, I keep telling you how nice to me she is.'

'There's not just you here,' said her mother tersely. 'There's the lads as well, think on. I don't like her being here. She should have stayed in London. There's things that will start up again now she's here.'

Maggie's mouth fell open and she thought of the dead cat. 'Things?' she said fearfully. 'What sort of things?'

'It's been quiet up there for years,' said her mother, ignoring her. 'She could be the one to bring him back.'

'Him?' Maggie's eyes were bulging. 'Who?' she screeched.

Her mother hesitated, then opened her mouth to answer.

The sound of Thomas wailing in the distance interrupted her. He hurled his stocky little body across to Maggie and clutched her knees.

'He hit me, Uncle Paddy belted me one!' he roared. Then he saw the box of parcels on the table and his roar stopped in mid-stream. 'Mam?' he said. 'Has he been?'

'Who?' said Maggie in a fading whisper.

'Santa,' said Thomas, peering up at his mother's white face as if she'd gone daft.

'Has Santa been, Mam?'

Rose fed Lady and scattered a handful of corn for the ducks on the river. She brought a sack of logs into the kitchen and stood it by the door. That was enough of country life for the day. She hung up her coat and kicked off her muddy wellingtons. Then she went into the little parlour and closed the door behind her, leaning against it for a moment to admire the room. Dusky pink walls and white woodwork, the oval table shining now, with a deep glass bowl full of scarlet-berried holly standing on it. The room smelt clean, of fresh paint and beeswax polish. The faded reds and blues of the carpet fitted in well. Yes, she was pleased with this room. Strange how she had never bothered to decorate her room in Isabel's house, she'd left it all to Isabel. It was just a place to come back to between trips, a jumping-off point. Yet this room satisfied something in her now; it was as much her creation as the ordering of images in her photos.

Rose bent and put a match to the fire. When it was well alight, she went upstairs for a bath. She sprayed herself with her favourite musky scent and put on the long green velvet housecoat she'd bought in Whitby when she got Jack's sweater. Underneath it she was wearing a long white lawn nightie from the same shop – it had long sleeves and a tiny lace frill round the high neck. It wasn't the usual kind of thing she wore, but it was a distinct improvement on the winceyette pyjamas.

Christmas Eve.

She would celebrate it in her own way, this first Christmas in a place of her own. She went back into the parlour, where the fire was burning brightly now, throwing flickering shadows on the beamed ceiling. She knelt in front of it, rubbing dry the soft pale feathers of her hair, and thought suddenly of Edward.

It was a Christmas Eve the first time she went to bed with him. She'd been out with him several times and knew that he wanted her, but he left the timing of it up to her. She liked that. They went for a drink in Marylebone High Street, and she thought how tired he looked. When she asked him why, he said it was because so many of his patients were depressed, suicidal even, at Christmas.

That surprised her. 'I'd have thought this time of year would have cheered them up.'

'No. They see everyone else joining in and having fun, as they see it, and they're cut off from it all. Lonely people suffer badly at Christmas. Now and summer holidays are my worst time.' He yawned. 'Sorry, Rose, I'm out on my feet. Like to come round and have a coffee with me? I might wake up if I'm full of a strong black brew.'

Rose liked Edward's mews cottage. The ground floor was the garage now, but it had formerly been the stables, and the green-tiled wall at the far end still had the racks for hay, and the horses' names above them. She followed him up the narrow flight of stairs and into his living room, which was knee-deep in books. But he had a big jar of tawny chrysanthemums standing in the unused fireplace, and a tank full of brightly coloured guppies. She walked over and knelt beside the tank.

'My personal relaxation therapy,' he said. 'I'll make the coffee.'

She followed him into the kitchen. Real ground coffee, none of your instant for Edward. He carried her mug over to her and stood beside her, looking so weary and vulnerable that she melted inside towards him.

'Ho ho ho, little boy,' she said in a deep gruff voice. 'And what would you like for Christmas?'

He looked startled, then grinned. 'You,' he said simply.

Rose took him by the hand and led him into the bedroom.

It had been so good, that first reaching out for him. He spent a long time on her breasts and she loved that, for they were very sensitive. He was a generous lover, watching her carefully to see if she was happy, talking to her as he touched her. She thought when his mouth first touched her nipples that this time she was going to manage it, this time it was going to be different. But then he stroked her cunt, and a terrible despair shook her as she realized that it was going to be no easier for her with him.

She felt herself grow wooden, numb.

She tried to pretend for him, for she saw that he wouldn't come in her until he had satisfied her. But he had known.

Afterwards, when he had come quickly in her, he looked at her face and kissed her. 'My fault,' he said. 'I wanted you very much, and it's been a long time.'

'It doesn't matter,' she said dully. As she always said. 'I don't come. Ever. I've never . . .'

She stopped and swallowed, the stupid tears at her feeling of failing sliding wetly down her face.

'You will next time,' he said. 'I love you, Rose, whether you come or not. And it's not a test for you – nobody's giving you marks out of ten.'

Then he yawned and put his arms round her. 'Stay with me till morning,' he said.

But she wouldn't. She waited until he slept, and was out of bed and off down the narrow stairs. It was still early enough to pick up a taxi in Baker Street. And when she opened her bag to pay the driver, there inside it was a small box, neatly wrapped in glittery paper with a card: 'To Rose, with love from Edward.'

She opened it as soon as she was inside the house, opened it as anxiously as if it were bad news, not a present. It was a heavy silver chain bracelet, an antique one. She held it in her hand for a moment, thinking of him lying asleep as she had left him. Then she pushed the chain into a drawer.

No chains, even for Edward. She'd never worn it, and he'd not mentioned it, but she thought he must have noticed. And he probably knew why.

Rose ran her fingers through her hair and sat up. She was half asleep thinking of Edward. The fire was dying down. She began to pile wood on it, and as she did so she heard a voice calling to her from the kitchen.

* * *

Ben puts down the pails of water next to the table and scowls at Martha.

'There y'are, then. What thoo wenches do with all this watter . . . Ah spend half my day at that pump, ah do.' He sits himself on a stool and rubs his aching back.

'Do with it? We wash our hands now and again. Aye, and our clothes. Not like some.'

Martha sniffs and fills a mug of ale for the old man, thinking that those leather breeches of his have a life of their own by the end of winter. He picks up the mug and drinks noisily, wiping his mouth with the back of his dirty hand. The door behind him opens, and Tully comes through it carrying a pile of soiled linen.

'He's gone, then,' says Ben maliciously to her, watching her face. Tully stands and looks at him. 'Who has?'

'Yon fine London gentleman. He's away to t' South on his red mare. Went off first thing this morn.'

Martha looks sharply at Tully. She is standing in the middle of the floor clutching dirty bed-linen with a face to match it.

'Get that lot out through t' back,' she snaps, and Tully jerks herself into a scurry over the muddy floor.

Ben watches her go, and turns to look at Martha.

'Happen it would be best if he nivver came back,' he says.

Martha allows herself the luxury of propping her

bottom on a stool next to him. She thinks of all the times she has caught Tully standing gawping at Master Brett with more than candlelight in those big eyes, and sighs.

'If there'd been a mistress here in t' house then mebbe he'd not have got to stop so long in t' first place.'

'She was a bonny lass, was Sarah Latimer,' says Ben, thinking back to a summer's day when Gideon brought his young wife over t' threshold that first time. Ten pairs of oxen to draw t' bride-wain from t' church, and all t' beasts' heads fluttering with bright ribbons. And her dead of a fever so young, when t' lads were nobbut bairns.

Ben puts down his empty mug and thinks that women are frail things at the best of times.

'A bonny lass,' he says again. 'Those lads could have done with a mother. Master Brett was a bit of company for 'em. Maister has no time for 'em. Never has had. It'll be quiet again for 'em now he's gone. Happen ah'll get a bit of help outside again now. If t' pair on 'em haven't learnt ovver many airs and graces from t' furriner.'

'Hardly that, Ben. He's a Londoner.'

'Same thing,' says Ben crossly. 'We're well rid of him sniffing around young Tully. Him and his fancy ways. And what was he holing up here for? Cooling his heels for summat. Give us a sup more ale, Martha.'

In the cold back place Tully stands, still clutching the pile of linen to herself. Master Nicholas on his red mare is riding over that black moor all t' way to London. What if he nivver comes back again?

But he must come back to her.

He had kissed her so sweetly that day weeks ago, he called her sweetheart and she thought that was all he wanted, as it was all she wanted. Only kisses. But he took more than kisses. Tully feels sick now, thinking of how much she let him do to her. These last mornings when she went into his room with his hot water, he lay there on his bed with the covers back and all of him bare. And she touched him. And he lifted up her skirt and stroked between her legs until she cried out, and he clapped a hand across her mouth.

What if she has a bairn? Tully doesn't think she will, not from just touching him there. She'd seen the tup with the ewes often enough. She doesn't care if she does. If she has his bairn, then he'll have to come back to her.

She wipes her tear-stained face on the soiled sheet, sniffing wetly thinking that now all the days will be t' same for her, going on for ever full of nowt but work and doing what Martha says. And listening to auld Ben grumbling on. Tully will have nowt left to hope for if he doesn't come back.

And why didn't he take her with him?

She was frightened of crossing t' moor, frightened of t' very idea of London, but she would follow Master Nicholas anywhere he wanted her to . . .

Then Martha shouts to know if Tully is going to be out there all day, and she throws the linen down on top of the great heap already piled up. A mouse runs squeaking from it across her feet. Tully squeaks louder than the mouse, and scurries back to the kitchen.

Chapter Eight

Rose was startled, hearing the voice, then she recognized it.

'I'm in here, Jack,' she called, standing and stretching.

He came padding to the doorway in his stocking feet and hesitated. His eyes widened as he took in the velvet dressing-gown, the bare feet below the long nightie.

'I'm sorry,' he began. 'You off to bed?'

'No, it's all right, Jack, I've just had a bath. Come in.'

He was holding a little Christmas tree in a plastic bucket. 'Where d'you want this, then?' he said gruffly.

The spicy smell of the dark little tree filled the room, bringing back the Christmases of Rose's childhood. 'For me? It's lovely – I do like real Christmas trees. Will it stand on the window-seat?'

He smiled at the pleasure in her voice and, crossing the room, put the tree carefully on the centre of the seat. 'There,' he said, standing back to look at it. 'How's that?'

'Lovely,' she said again, going over to stand next to him and touching the dark spines of the branches. 'What a nice thought, Jack, thank you very much.'

He nodded, and began to look in his pocket for something.

'Here,' he said. 'Our Maggie sent you this.'

'But what is it?' she said laughing. 'Leaves?'

'It's an ash sprig. Because it's Christmas Eve see, you put that under your pillow tonight and you'll see the man of your choice. You'll see your coming lover.' The word sounded awkward from him, as if it were one he hadn't used much.

'Does Maggie do it? Does she put a piece under her pillow?' Rose took the ash sprig gently from him.

'Oh, aye, she does it,' he said seriously. 'So she says, any road. But she'll never let on who it is that she sees.'

Rose wondered if Maggie saw the mythical father of the bairn.

Jack hesitated, then went on quickly, 'She does see a lot of queer things, does our lass. That's why finding that old dead cat in here the other day upset her so much. She shouldn't have made such a daft fuss about it all the same . . .'

'It was a horrible thing to find. It upset me as well. I don't usually clutch the nearest man for protection.'

He grinned down at her. 'I didn't mind.' He glanced across at the cupboard which had its door firmly closed. Rose felt better somehow with the door shut.

'I must be off. I've another tree to do up now for the bairn. We've never bothered with one before, but Maggie's got him a stocking full of stuff and nowt will satisfy her but a tree as well for him. I got them both out of the wood yonder – I've left you the roots on, so you can put it out in the garden when you've done with it in here. You like it, then?'

'I don't like imitation trees at all. We always had a real one when I was small. You must have had one when you were little, didn't you? And stockings?' She put the brittle spray of leaves down on the table.

'Nay,' he said, looking surprised. 'Mother never had time for stuff like that.'

She looked at his face and something of how it must have been for him as a child in that bleak farmhouse at Christmas-time came over her in a wave of sadness. Nobody ever seemed to have had much time for Jack –

he did most of the work on the farm with little thanks, and Rose used him when she needed something doing but gave him little in return. She'd never so much as asked him up for a meal or suggested going out for a drink. He had gone to so much trouble with the little tree, just to give her pleasure.

She moved towards him and put her arms round him, saying, 'Happy Christmas!' and kissing the long curve of his warm mouth. He stiffened and stood rigid for a moment, then his arms came round her and she felt his body hard against hers. She leaned into the strength of him and felt safe there, felt she could give herself to him in the firelight with the scent of the little fir tree heavy on the warm air. She reached up to touch his cheek and took his hand to bring him to the rug in front of the fire. He pulled his mouth away from hers and stood looking down at her, then shook his head.

'Happy Christmas, Rose,' he said hurriedly and strode off across the room. The door closed behind him.

Rose stood and listened. The far door of the cottage banged shut and she heard the Land Rover start up. She had upset him, and she hadn't wanted that. She had wanted . . . what? To give herself to him like a Christmas present? Most days here, dressed in grubby jeans and several layers of sweaters, she didn't feel in the least erotic, she simply felt cold. But because she'd just had a bath, smelled nice and felt clean – she felt different. Female. Fragile. She wanted to be loved, she wanted Jack's hands on her, wanted to lie bare in the firelight beside him. She wanted him inside her. But she'd gone too fast for him; he wasn't expecting her to be any different from what she usually was. Ah, but it would have been so good, she thought, kneeling in front of the flickering fire, cuddling her arms across her breasts where her nipples were ready for his mouth.

She had felt him hard against her through the soft velvet; she knew he had begun to respond to her. She would have made up to him for all those sad Christmas Eves when Santa never came.

He had said her name – for the first time he had called her Rose. The Bransdales never called each other anything; 'him' and 'her' were as near as they ever got. Certainly they never touched one another.

And he had brought her the tree. The scent of it was strong now with the heat of the little room, dark and evocative. She turned to look at it. It was a perfect shape as it stood; it needed nothing to decorate it. She would leave it bare. There had been a parcel from Edward in the mail, and one from Isabel with a bundle of cards she had forwarded on. Rose would put them on the window-seat next to her tree, and that would be Christmas.

She would go and get something to eat now, and then she was going to bed. She was tired, sad at what had happened with Jack. And at what hadn't happened. Perhaps after Christmas she would try again to get him to let her take some photos of him. She felt again the strength which had flowed from him as he had held her, and she wanted his hardness in her.

Not once had she thought of Edward.

Marry me, Rose, marry me . . .

Edward was in another place, and she was someone else.

Rose was in bed long before midnight. She lay drifting on the edge of sleep thinking of Jack and Maggie as children, of Thomas and the nativity play which Maggie had taken her to at the village school earlier in the week. Such a tiny little school – two classrooms and a kitchen. Maggie had enjoyed showing Rose off, her friend from London who was a photographer.

It had been a very matriarchal afternoon. Both of the

teachers were women, and the audience consisted only of proud mothers. Not a father in sight. The only man there had been the Vicar, and everyone treated him as something different from a man. More of a spiritual eunuch. The bairn had been one of the Shepherds, trailing a vast dressing-gown down to his feet with a tea-towel tied round his head. He was clutching a toy lamb with three legs. The voices of the children singing 'Away in a Manger' had sounded sweet and pure, and it didn't matter that the chubby little King who gravely presented his gift to the baby had announced that he brought Frankenstein.

Thomas's face had been beautiful when he saw his mother. Rose wondered sleepily what colour hair he had. She'd never actually seen it, for he was wrapped in a thick balaclava round the farm. It was probably dark, like Maggie's.

Maggie.

Rose jerked back from sleep as she remembered the sprig of ash leaves. She'd brought it upstairs and left it on the bedside table, not really sure whether she intended doing anything with it. Reaching out now, she picked it up and laid it carefully under her pillow, and wondered if Maggie had done the same.

Out of the night he came to her again.

He came striding easily from the shadows, for his strength was growing by her very presence in this place. This time, as he stood beside her bed, he knew that he could take her.

She was as fair as an angel, and he wanted her.

Rose came up slowly from a dream of being out alone on the moor in the dark, feeling that her legs were cold. She stirred restlessly and opened her eyes. There was a thick silence pouring through the room, where even the small window showed no paling of the night. She reached down and touched her bare legs. The bedclothes were gone from her, and her nightie was bunched above her breasts. The cold air lay wetly on her stomach. She thought that she had done it to herself, kicking off the clothes in her dream, then as she lay she felt the first faint pressure of him on her skin.

Cold against her and growing heavier, skin against skin, she could feel his chest and legs fastening her down, and hard between her open legs she felt his erection. And now she heard the sound of his harsh breathing.

Dreaming. She must be dreaming, it was another of those bad dreams like the one she'd had before, when she had scratched herself so badly. She must be able to tell the difference between a bad dream and reality. She'd been lost out on the moor. *That* was the dream. But she was here in her bed now, so what did that make this?

There was something terribly familiar about it all. It was the same man, the one who'd clawed her like a cat . . . and the scream bubbled out of her, rasping her throat and emptying her. She hadn't known true fear before, not this pure terror. No one could hear her; no one could help. He would rape her and then he would kill her. Her useless scream went sliding down the walls as his fingers scratched at her nipples.

But she'd locked the door. She knew that she had locked it, so then how?

Jack.

It must be Jack with his own key, come to her now in the night. She groaned with relief and forced herself to reach out and touch him, to know him by his long hair. But her shaking fingers met old skin, cold and hard, in a thick seam of scar which ran from eye to mouth.

Her mouth stretched wide, gasping for air, sucking in a scream as a mouth came down on hers, covering it so that she couldn't breathe. His narrow tongue came sliding into her dry mouth, soul-kissing her down into dark. Then, as she fell away from him into a spinning blackness, he lifted his mouth and fastened his lips on her nipple, licking until she burned and prickled and the whole of her body was a hard, dull ache. And it was not pain she was feeling now but a desperate desire for something out of reach. The air was cold on her breasts as he left them, sliding down between her legs to lick at the hidden folds of her. Not that, not that, not even Edward had ever . . . and her hands clawed down at his unseen face, and his tongue was lapping like a cat at the cream.

She had locked the door, and it was not Jack, this scarred man wasn't Jack. Far off inside her at the flicking of his tongue something was gathering, fading and swelling in waves breaking white against the cliffs of her body, and she had never felt this, never, never.

She took her hands from his face and covered her own and began to wail, a long orgasmic cry that tore her as she tensed and stiffened and came. He lifted himself and eased his long prick into her, snaking it into her singing, throbbing cunt.

She died back into silence and stillness. Back into fear. He had taken what he wanted. Now he would kill her. She couldn't stop him; he was too strong. She lay beyond all hope, and as she lay he knelt above her and kissed her gently on the mouth and began to leave her. Once he had come in her, he was spent. Only an insubstantial shadow of a man lay for an instant longer on her, then he was gone.

Rose was fastened to the bed by terror. She lay and listened, not daring to breathe, but there was nothing to hear. How could he have gone? He must be there, standing beside the bed, waiting until she moved to catch her again. She couldn't bear it; she had to know if he was there and scrambled from the bed, clawing at the wall for the light switch, sobbing now with hoarse, rasping cries. She caught the switch in her clawing hands and the pale, orange light showed her that the room was empty.

There was nothing there.

She slid down the wall on to her haunches as her legs gave way under her, her nightie rucking up at her back, and hunched herself as small as she could. She rocked backwards and forwards in a terrible numb anguish and saw with horror a faint, wet smear on the inside of her leg. And, as she looked, it faded into nothing.

*　　*　　*

On a mild, starlit night, some days after Nicholas Brett has ridden out of the valley, three men on foot come over the moor top behind Haggabacks. They are nervous, flinching at shadows, staying close to one another as they come near to the cottage. They whisper thinly as they see the thread of smoke curling up from the chimney, and stand hesitating at the threshold. Then the door opens slowly, and Nan asks them sharply if they are going to stand there all night, gawping about for anyone to see?

They get themselves inside the door and there they come to a halt, huddling together and peering round as if expecting to see a half-eaten baby somewhere about. But the light of the peat fire shows only a hunched figure on a stool by the hearth, a sleeping cat at her feet, and a table. And on the table there is something wrapped in a white cloth.

'Is that it, then, mistress?' asks the boldest of the three, nodding towards the table, wanting to be well out of this place and on with the night's dark business.

'Aye. There's your hand.' Nan sits very still on her stool with her back to them, and the sandy-coloured cat at her feet stirs and settles herself again.

'Two silver pieces. We agreed on that, mistress?'

Nan answers not a word.

He steps forward and puts the money down on the table with a soft clink.

'Best look at it afore you go. I took a deal of trouble with it,' she says coldly over her shoulder.

He swallows nervously and glances round at his friends, who are edging back to the door now; then, stepping forward, he peels back a corner of the cloth.

Nan's voice cuts into the silence. 'Lame Jem's hand. Taken from him where he swung in his chains. I made it as I would make bacon, masters, by rubbing in saltpetre and then drying. And there is a candle with it, made of his fat, mixed with pure beeswax, and a lock of his own dark hair. You must take t' candle and thrust it into his fingers and light t' wick. Lame Jem won't mind. Not any more he won't.'

Nan sniggers and rocks on her stool and her long hair writhes in the firelight.

'Then they'll sleep fast. Oh, how they'll sleep. Not a waking soul in the house. And you must keep them sleeping. You must say out loud:

> "Let those who rest more deeply sleep
> Let those who wake their vigil keep
> O Hand of Glory shed thy light
> Direct us to our spoil tonight."

There'll be little spoil for you tonight but that'll keep you safe enough.'

She nods towards the table, where the Hand of Glory lies stiff, the nails on the dead fingers glimmering like pearls against the wax-grey skin.

'And then you'll bring it back to me when you're done. And you'll not be caught – though you'll bring little away with you from Throstle Hall. Why there?'

The men's glances slide fearfully now from one to another, for how can she already know enough to hang them all?

'Why there?' she says again sharply.

'T' stranger was at Lastingham, at t' cocking. Ah stood next to him there. He wore a gold ring on his finger and he had a purse full of guineas. He was wagering high. Where does he get that money? What's he running up there at t' Hall?'

'He's no smuggler. He runs nowt. And he's not there now; he's back in London where he belongs. All you'll get at Throstle is a few pewter plates and silver spoons – unless Martha sleeps with them under her mattress. There's more pickings at t' big house in Farndale.'

The men shuffle their feet and say nothing. She is trying to make them give up the idea, with her tales of Martha and her spoons, but the talk for miles around is how the stranger can wager so high. They think of the gold and watch Nan. She shrugs, enjoying their discomfort.

'Think on,' she says. 'One that lights t' candle must be t' one to put it out, else it will take blood to quench it.'

And the cat moves by the hearth, and suddenly the men see that she has no tail, and her ears are very long, and she is sitting up in the firelight and she is too big, too big for any cat.

'See these gentlemen out, my Moll,' says Nan gently, and the hare comes leaping towards the men, who are fumbling and sweating at the door, half blind with terror. It's true, then, it's true that she has a great hare that does her bidding . . .

The door bangs behind them, and the Hand of Glory lies safely wrapped in its white cloth inside the coat of the leader. Its fingers lie stiff and cold against his beating heart.

Chapter Nine

Very early on the morning of Christmas Day, Rose was walking in the orchard. The day was mild and sweet, with a pale sunlight slotting through the trees. And trees, now that Rose looked so carefully at them, were not brown, as she had always supposed them to be. The alders along the bank that she was busy photographing were wrinkled lizard-green, and the tips of their twigs were tinged with purple. She stood and watched where the water leaped and bubbled over a big rock in the middle of the river.

Beck, Jack called it. A nice, homely sort of a word. Round the bend of the river came the mallards, the drake leading his two ducks, resplendent in his shining green head feathers and white clerical collar. To own this stretch of water seemed to Rose to be a very precious thing. She concentrated very hard on ducks, on trees, on water.

For if she did not, if she let go of the tight hold on her mind for one minute, then the film of last night would start to replay again. She had been over and over it so many times, lying curled up in the dark shivering, waiting for the night to end and the window to begin to pale off into dawn. As soon as it was light, she crawled out of bed with a violent, sick headache and went down the stairs as feebly as an old woman. The door was locked; she knew she had locked it last night. No one came through it in the night.

There was a sound behind her in the apple trees and she jumped, whirling round and backing away, but it was only the cat. She had followed Rose into the orchard and was climbing one of the trees, her whiskered face peering down through the gnarled fingers of twigs.

'You look like the Cheshire Cat,' said Rose unsteadily.

The Cheshire Cat had faded away as well and left nothing but a grin. And she felt him again fading from her body, dissolving out of her, back into shadow.

It had only been a dream. A dream of desire, because she dreamed of Edward in the firelight, because she wore a green velvet gown. Because she kissed Jack.

But how could it have been a dream, for she had been dreaming before that; dreaming of being lost up on the moor. She had woken from that dream.

So it had not been a dream, and he was real. Then to be real, he must have been hidden in the cottage when she locked the door; he had been behind the door of the unused bedroom. A real man of flesh and bone.

But then how had he gone? Not out of the door. He had melted from her; he had thinned away into nothing. He kissed her mouth and then he was not there any more. She had switched on the light and he was not there. She remembered how at first she thought it was Jack, and she desperately wished now that it had been.

She stood looking at the cat's face, framed in the twigs.

'So what was he, then, Tibby? A ghost. The spirit of Christmas past. Nothing but a haunting, and more of gravy than the grave. I don't believe in ghosts.' And a horrible memory of Isabel telling her to come back and lay the ghosts made her feel sicker than ever.

She took a quick shot of the cat's face and walked slowly down the dark avenue of trees. It wasn't only the way that he disappeared, or even what he had done to her. What frightened her most was the terrible way that she had responded to him. She didn't respond like that to Edward, who loved her. She had never felt with any man what she had felt last night. She saw now that what she felt with Edward was only a faint foretaste of the pleasure which her body could give her. And the label of frigidity which she had pinned on herself so many years ago was perhaps not true.

The last time Edward had slept with her, he said that maybe he should make love to her with her longest camera lens, since that was what she responded to most. He had been laughing when he said it, but at some level he meant it. And at some level it was true. It was sad, because Rose really liked men, the way they thought, their hard bodies and their ridiculous, endearing pricks.

But she couldn't give all of herself to a man; there was always something at the back of her head which flashed up a warning sign saying, 'No, be careful now, that's far enough.'

It wasn't that she was afraid of getting pregnant, for she'd been on the pill since Edward. She was afraid of letting go, of coming down in a different place and being out of control.

She leaned against a tree and watched the sunlight flicker through the leaves. She sighed and shifted uncomfortably. Even now she wasn't right; she wasn't back to her comfortable state of more or less ignoring her body and just letting it get on with things. She had had a bath, scrubbing the memory of him fiercely from herself, but she still felt wrong. Today she was nothing but a body. She felt like the pictures she had seen of the old figures of the Sheelah-na-gig, as if she were nothing but a grinning face and a great, swollen slit leering like a welcome.

She felt again his mouth on her and the snake of his tongue between her legs.

Dream. Ghost. Incubus.

Incubus. Dear God, now there was a word to play with.

Leave it, leave it, she thought, feeling the sour sickness rising in her again. It was Christmas Day in the morning, and she had dreamed a horror. Call it a foretelling perhaps, and the presence of a lover still to come.

And then for the first time, she remembered the ash sprig that she had put under her pillow. But no, it couldn't have anything to do with that; she didn't believe in the old ways as Maggie did. Perhaps putting the sprig there had sent her to sleep dreaming of a lover. But then it should have been Edward's body that came to her. She thought of the thick seam of scar on the man's face. Somewhere recently she had seen a scar like that . . . her head was too fuzzy to think straight. It hadn't been Edward who came to her and it wasn't Jack either. She wasn't going to think about it any more. She was just going round in circles. The one thing which was left to her today, her one constant, was the eye of her camera. That was unchanged; it would give her no false images; it would show her nothing but the cold reality of this place. No dreams; no visions.

Lifting the camera, Rose began to photograph down the corridors of trees.

It was still only mid-morning when she made herself go back into the kitchen. The rest of the day stretched in front of her, endless and flat. She had cleaned Lady out and fed her, glad of her warm, hungry presence. For the first time since she came to the cottage she wanted noise – a television, a radio, a cassette-player. Why hadn't she thought of it in Stokesley or Whitby? Maggie's chatter had covered up how silent this place was. Even the wind had dropped now, and the whole valley lay in a great silence.

There was no hope of seeing Maggie for days, not till

after Christmas, not with Thomas being on holiday from school. There must be something Rose could get on with on her own today, something that would stop her thinking. She put down her camera on the table and, looking at it, wondered about the camera her father must have used. She hadn't looked at the photos from behind the carved angel since the night she'd found them. She'd brought them down here and wondered whether to burn them, but had instead pushed them in the deep drawer of the kitchen table. Her father must have taken them with a plate camera, must have developed the plates himself. For he could hardly have taken them into Boots to be developed, especially all those years ago. So where was it?

She'd asked Maggie if she'd seen a camera anywhere, and Maggie said vaguely that there was a lot of stuff packed away in the store-room off the little parlour.

There was nowhere else that it could be. Rose had a sudden desire to hold her father's camera, for although the photos had upset her so much, it intrigued her that her father had taken photos at all. The image she had of him was of a rough and solitary man, not of someone who saw the world through the camera's eye as she did. She needed to follow up this link with him; she wanted to take her own photos of this place with his camera. She could give him that much of herself. A quick mug of coffee and she'd make a start on the store-room.

It was cold and damp in the little room. She ran upstairs for the electric fire, going reluctantly back into her bedroom, slamming the door shut on it behind her. She plugged the fire into the one wall socket, then switched on the light. The small window overlooking the moor was so dirty and thick with cobwebs that very little light was coming through. Crouching in front of the fire's amber glow, she sipped at her scalding coffee and looked round her.

What rubbish is left from a lifetime, she thought in dismay, seeing the heaps piled round her like wrack at low tide. He couldn't have thrown out a newspaper for years – stupid that they were still here and he wasn't. Nothing remained of her father – except herself, of course. It wasn't much to mark a lifetime. An unloving daughter and a broken-down old cottage. But then, what would Rose have to leave? A room full of black and white images. Frozen time. Nothing more than that.

There was a little bow-fronted chest of drawers filling one wall which was too good to leave in here. She'd have that out when she'd emptied it. There were four tea-chests of assorted junk, a few old books among the papers. An old trunk, a battered little suitcase carefully tied with a length of hairy string and that was it. She would begin with the chest of drawers. There were some empty feed sacks piled in one of the outbuildings she could use for the rubbish. She brought the two top drawers over to the heat of the fire.

Hours later, she found something wrapped in a red paisley shawl at the bottom of the trunk, and knew by the tripod next to it that she'd found the camera. She picked the bundle up and cradled it on her knees, thinking of the dead man who had held it last, of the photos he had taken with it.

She pulled off the shawl.

It was as she had thought: a plate camera. Big and solid, it sat on her knees like a promise. She smoothed the shiny wooden sides and ran her fingers round the brass rim of the lens. It was beautiful in itself as a piece of art. She wanted to go out now and start taking photos with it, but there was so much she needed before she could begin.

She got to her feet clumsily, for she was stiff, and rubbed her aching back. Later, when she was all finished, she would have another bath, but the light was fading and there was Lady to feed again. She carried the heavy camera slowly from the store-room. Holding it steady between her hands, she pointed it towards the window and looked down into it. There was the tree on the window-seat, outlined darkly against the fading sky, and on the seat next to it her unopened presents, which she had forgotten about. And all was upside-down, all inverted by the shining lens. She carried the camera over and put it down beside the gifts, patting it gently as if it were a living thing.

She shivered and, turning, saw how the fire had died to a red eye. The room was cold. She would build up the fire, feed Lady and give Tibby a festive tin of sardines. There were four bulging sacks of rubbish to drag out and store in a building until the dustmen came again. She had done well – all that was left to sort through now was the battered little suitcase. And she had kept her head busy as well as her hands, and the horror of last night was less now; she was beginning to put it away behind her. She knelt and began to stack dry logs on the fire, and a contented satisfaction filled her at the thought of the camera sitting on the window-seat. It was hers. All hers.

Lady bleated companionably when she saw her, thrusting her nose into the pocket of Rose's coat, where she knew that there would be a biscuit. She had pulled out all of the hay from her rack and made herself a sweet-smelling nest in it. Rose filled up the rack again, and watched as Lady stood on her hind legs and lipped delicately at the long, dry seed-heads. She turned her head and bleated briefly as Rose went out and bolted the door behind her.

Rose stood for a moment listening to the silence. There was a queer, waiting feel to the air, a brooding quality to the late day. A light shone at the farm below. Rose wondered if Thomas liked his tractor. And whether Maggie was skipping about in a pair of new knickers. She grinned at the thought of Mrs Bransdale's face watching Maggie unwrap them. Going into the wood store, she filled a paper sack with split logs and half dragged, half carried it into the house.

'Tart,' said Mrs Bransdale softly. 'Getting you stuff like that.'

Maggie went red and clutched the opened present more closely.

'She's not, then. She wears stuff like this herself and she's not a tart . . .'

'Aye, and' you'd wear them an' all, you mucky little bitch!' Mrs Bransdale reached across the table. 'You give them here.'

'I'll not. It's my present from her. It's nowt to do with anyone else what I wear.'

Leaning against the mantelpiece, Paddy sniggered. 'It's not what you wear that's your problem, it's keeping the things on . . .'

Mrs Bransdale's chair scraped back across the cracked lino as she stood. 'Shut your mouth, Paddy,' she snarled at him. She wrenched the parcel from Maggie's hands, pushed him out of the way and flung it into the heart of the low fire. The silvery paper caught at once, bursting into blue flame, then the lace trimming licked into red tongues of fire. Maggie gave a loud wail and buried her head in her arms. 'It's not fair,' she moaned. 'I never get owt pretty . . .'

'And you. Out!' said Mrs Bransdale, catching Paddy by the shoulder. 'Get yourself outside and get some bloody work done for once.' She hit out at his head, but he was lurching heavily to the door, white-faced and furious.

The smell of the burning material filled the room.

Under the table, safe beneath the hanging tent of the chenille cloth, Thomas clutched his tractor to his hurting chest and very carefully did not listen to the sound of his mother weeping and weeping above him. 'Brumm brumm,' he whispered softly to himself. 'Oh, brumm brumm brumm.'

This time after her bath Rose pulled on a clean pair of jeans and a thick sweater. No more green gowns. No more night visitors.

She opened a tin of beans and made some toast, then carried it into the parlour with a fat, brown pot of tea. It was a strange Christmas dinner; she wondered what Isabel would be eating far away in London. And Edward. She couldn't imagine either of them sitting down to beans on toast.

She ate the food quickly, as another job to be done, sitting on the rug in front of the fire, then pushed the dirty plate aside and brought over her two parcels from the window-seat. Isabel's first. Under the brown paper was a gold-wrapped box, tied with a red ribbon. Rose opened it carefully, smoothing out the paper and stroking the silky ribbon. She lifted the lid of the box. Isabel had sent her a set of thermal underwear. Rose stood and held the dark blue long johns against herself and let out a snort of laughter. Dear Isabel! What a very useful present, much more sensible than French knickers. Rose folded up the underwear and put it on the chair behind her.

Edward's parcel now. She wondered what he was doing today and if he were missing her. She unfastened the paddibag reluctantly, pulling out the staples as carefully as if she intended reusing them as well as the bag. There was a book inside. Patricia Bosworth's book on Diane Arbus. How like him to find such a perfect gift for her – this was the photographer whose work Rose loved most, wanting to get into her own photos the raw truth she saw in Diane Arbus's slices of life, which seemed to freeze the moment and hold it for ever. Arbus had once said something to the effect that a photo was a secret about a secret, and the more it told you, the less you knew.

Rose sat and looked at the book, and wondered if she would ever take a photo that would become as well known as an Arbus. She opened it to see what Edward had written inside. Neat and precise in his black writing his message said, 'Happy Christmas, Rambling Rose. Don't stay away too long. I miss you. Love, Edward.'

There was a letter from him tucked inside the front cover. Rose turned the fat white envelope between her fingers. She didn't want to open it. She knew what it would say, and it was nothing that she wanted to see. She propped the envelope on the mantelpiece. She would open it later.

Now she wanted to find out what was in her father's suitcase, then she was finished with him. She dragged it on to the rug, untied the piece of string round it and lifted the lid. There was a fat sealed packet inside. Nothing else. It tore as she lifted it out on to her knees, showering her with what looked like old Christmas cards. A strange thing for him to have kept. She picked up the top one and looked at it, puzzled. Why had he wanted this? It looked hand-made, childish. There was a lopsided, cut-out Christmas tree glued on the white card, with silver peeling stars on the branches, and a lot of dirty fingerprints round the edge.

Rose frowned at the tree in its red pot. Why was it so horribly familiar, that red pot?

She opened the card and saw inside the sprawling crayoned letters: 'To Daddy, from Rose.' She dropped it as if it had burnt her fingers, and snatched at half a dozen more. They were all there, every single card which she had determinedly sent him over all those years. All those years when she had watched for the postman coming along the pavement, waiting for him to bring her a card from Daddy. And every year there was nothing. The old bastard hadn't even cared enough to send her a Christmas card.

She was five again and hurting, understanding none of it, waiting for a card which never came. She crumpled a handful of cards between her fists, crushed them as she swore at him, thrusting them into the red mouth of the fire. She held them down with the poker until they charred into flakes of black ash – Santas, glitter, robins, snowmen and angels with dirty wings all gone to nothing.

She was six, she was seven, she was eight, and the years when he had shut himself off from her were pressing down on her head. A terrible rage gathered itself from a needle of hurt a long time buried inside her and came roaring through, through the child which she had been.

Love from Rose, love from Rose, but there was never anything back from him. It had all been for nothing, all run to waste. Great wrenching sobs shook her as she knelt with her face scorching from the blazing fire.

'I hate you,' she began, her voice rising to a scream. 'Hate, hate, hate you. Damn you, Daddy, for what you did to me!'

She lifted the poker and brought it down hard into the middle of the burning paper. Flakes and clots of ash spewed silently across the hearth. Rose sat back on her heels and wiped her face, leaving a black trail across her pale skin. She picked up a log and dropped it like a full stop on the remains of the cards.

There was still one big unopened envelope lying on the rug. Rose picked it up to throw it on the fire, then hesitated. She ripped open the brittle paper.

She sat with the contents on her knees, snuffling wetly to herself, and saw with renewed horror how her entire life was there, all spread in front of her. There were cuttings from the *Fulham Gazette*, from the time when she and her mother had lived there for so many years. There were her O-level results, her one A-level in Art; there she was smiling out of a bunch of school girls; there was the report of the big photo competition she had won at sixteen. And there was a thin bundle of her own photo spreads, cut from magazines and papers over the years.

There she was, then. This was what she had given back to him. No husband, no grandchildren. A handful of photos instead. These were her only reality. And he had kept them, had cared enough to follow what she was doing from a safe distance.

But how had he got them? He could hardly have bought the *Fulham Gazette* for fifteen years on the off chance that Rose would pop up in it. Her mother must have done it; she must have sent him the cuttings. Another betrayal – another secret about which Rose knew nothing.

But he had still not got in touch when her mother died. He hadn't gone to her funeral. Isabel had done everything, all the arrangements. That dreadful service at the crematorium where Isabel had held Rose's hand all the way through. She had helped Rose to pack up the Fulham flat, then taken her home to Islington. There were months then when Rose couldn't read the word cancer without feeling sick.

She felt sick again now, thinking about her mother. Rose had failed her; she hadn't gone to the hospital to see her that last week. Rose knew that her mother was dying; she knew that she wouldn't see her again, but she could not force herself through those swing doors at the entrance. Twice she got as far as the steps outside the hospital; she put out her hand and pushed open the doors and caught a whiff of the smell inside – antiseptic despair. Twice she turned her back and ran away down the steps. She had not been given a third chance. Her mother died in the night, peacefully enough in the end, but she died alone.

Rose had been blind and dumb with grief and guilt for a long time, until slowly images once more began to form for her in front of the camera, and work became her reality again. But it had been a very bad time.

She got shakily to her feet now and tossed the packet of cuttings on to the table. Kneeling beside the window-seat, she took the plate camera into her arms and cradled it. Work was the only answer, the only truth, the one thing that didn't let you down. She would use this camera, would find her own vision of this place. She felt washed clean, burned out by the rage she had let out of herself. Her father couldn't harm her any more, not now. He was as dead as the blackened ashes on the hearth. It seemed to Rose that it was the living who haunted you, not the dead. Living, her father had chased her down the years; her hate for him had spurred her on to achieve, to become somebody, to survive. And, since nothing comes by chance, she would take his camera and make it work for her.

*   *   *

It is spring in London, and Nicholas stands by the window and gazes out with a sigh of satisfaction. He can see a sunlit street, a road, people and carriages. There is no mud anywhere, and pale pink blossom is fluttering from the tree outside the house. The very air is different – balmy, soft.

'So you holed up in Yorkshire, did you? You were very lucky.'

The voice is soft and drawling and falls as sweet as honey to Nicholas's ears, after the harsh accent he has heard for so long.

'Lucky?' he says, half turning to where his companion leans against the marble fireplace. 'Lucky to be in York-shire in mid-winter? My dear George!'

'You know very well what I mean and how you were lucky. The woman's family were bought off far too easily. A death is a death, even if Elizabeth James was of little value.'

'It was an accident. She was not meant to die.'

'No? There have been some strange tales about you in your absence. About exactly how she died, and what you and your companions get up to in that Club of yours. You will do yourself no good by what you are dabbling in. You must be more careful, Nicholas.'

Nicholas turns his head to look out of the window again, and says nothing. His companion watches him in silence; then, seeing that he is going to get no response no matter how much he tries to warn Nicholas, he strolls across to the window to join him. He rests a hand on his shoulder and asks lightly, 'So will you stay here in London with us now that it seems safe for you again?'

Nicholas grins at him. 'They have some good Grey cocks up in Yorkshire, but little else.'

And he pauses.

He thinks of Tully, waiting at Throstle Hall, rosy-faced and eager. She will be all the more eager for him by the time he crosses that moor again. A month or so without him and she will be ready to do anything he asks of her.

'. . . Brown Reds?' asks his companion.

Nicholas considers him vaguely.

'I said, do they fight Brown Reds up there in the wilds?'

'Yes, good ones. And would you believe, a strain of the most excellent Muffs,' says Nicholas, and the thought of Tully sinks to the bottom of his mind and lodges there.

Talking of spurs and weight, the two men leave the room to stroll the sunlit streets, and Yorkshire is very far away.

Chapter Ten

ROSE made sure that she would sleep as soon as she went to bed that night, staying by the fire and reading her Diane Arbus book until she was almost asleep where she sat. She did consider remaining where she was, well away from that bedroom, but she was sure that what had happened last night had been only a bad dream. Still, she was edgy, scratchy, at going back there to sleep. But it had been a dream, a terrible dream, and he would not come again.

And that night he did not come.

As she slept, the weather turned. It grew colder. A bitter small wind began to blow, changing direction now and not coming from the moor, as it had done for every day since Rose had arrived at the cottage. Now it came straight up the valley and full on to the front of the house. The cold grew piercing, and towards dawn the first snow began to fall.

The cold woke Rose early. The room was full of a strange, white light; shivering, she drew back the curtains and looked out on to a world transformed. The trees in the orchard were all a white-lace filigree, a delicate tracery of iced twigs against the grey sky, where a cold sun gleamed. And in all the valley there was a great white silence.

She dressed quickly, thankful for the peaceful night, and went out to stand on the bank of the frozen river. There was a narrow channel of open water moving sluggishly in the centre of it, and here the mallards were swimming crossly up and down with a great deal of complaining. She smiled at their struggles to scramble over the ice, and scattered their corn on the knife edge of it, where they scooped it up hungrily. She used up a whole roll of film on them, and another where a stretch of river round an outcrop of rocks had iced over, and the water came booming over the shining boulders with a cold, dull sound.

Everywhere there were tracks in the snow. Rose hadn't realized how much traffic was passing through her garden. Here were rabbit tracks leaping along beside the river, there the neat marks of Tibby. And everywhere the spreading fans of birds' wings, and the feather-stitching of the birds' small feet. She captured them all in quick, sharp images, wishing that she had some sheet film for her father's camera. There were blue shadows on the far bank of the river, and points of light glinting scarlet and silver as the sun caught the sugary surface of the snow.

Rose discovered that her hands and feet were going numb with cold, and that Lady was shouting loudly for her breakfast. Wood, thought Rose. She must drag in as much as she could carry, in case there was more snow on the way. She found the snow strangely exciting – at least it was something different happening. It was like a declaration, a kind of challenge.

In mid-afternoon Jack drove slowly up the track in his Land Rover with a load of split wood in the back. He found her trying to fix up a bird table with an old tray outside the kitchen window.

'Here, I'll do that for you,' he said, crunching up the path. 'There's some stakes in the buildings, you need good strong legs on that, else the wind will have it straight in the beck.'

She helped him to carry the wood into the building, offering as usual to pay for it, but he would have none of it. 'It's old, dead stuff, is this. I was clearing out a place in the fold yard where the ewes will have to come in if it worsens. I needed the space.'

Rose left it at that. There was an edge to him today that wasn't usually there. He was watching her more closely, and showing his pleasure at being able to help her. He knocked up the bird table quickly and efficiently, braying the stakes into the hard soil. Rose exclaimed at the hold the frost had on the earth, but he shrugged it off. 'It'll do the garden good. You need a bit of frost to break up the ground. Things grow all the better for a bit of frost.'

By the time he finished, the sky along the ridge of hills was a bright pink, as if it were on fire. Light reflected on the snow-covered trunks of the trees, so that one side of them looked as if they were thick with pink icing. Clots of snow fell heavily from the branches as the small birds made their last feed.

'Have you got plenty of candles?' asked Jack, carrying a heavy sack of logs into the kitchen.

'Candles? I don't know. I've never looked.'

'You'd best start looking, then. There's more snow on the way. Sky's full of it. And we can be without electricity three or four days at a time round here if the wires come down. And another thing: water. That tap'll be frozen outside, is it?'

'Yes,' she said. 'Yes, there's no water coming out, I meant to tell you . . .'

'It freezes up first out there. The water comes from the moor top, see, and the force isn't that strong, it soon freezes. Keep your water heater on but don't empty your hot-water tank right out, and leave a cold tap running all the time, just to keep it flowing. You'll have to carry water out to Lady till that tap out there thaws. And take the chill off it for her with a drop of hot water in her bucket. We were carrying water out to the stock for six weeks last winter till the thaw came.'

Suddenly the snow seemed a lot less exciting.

'You'll be warm enough,' said Jack cheerfully. 'And you can always cook on the range if the electric goes off.'

'It's warm enough downstairs, it's the bedroom I can't cope with. That one-bar electric fire is useless – I'd have to take it into bed with me to feel any heat.'

He looked amused. 'We don't bother with heating bedrooms up here. Not unless you're poorly. Crawl into bed and pull up the blankets and you're soon warm enough. But if you want a fire up there you've got one. Didn't you know? It's behind the head of the bed. It's got a sheet of hardboard nailed over it, but it's there all right.'

She was half-way up the stairs before he'd finished. He pulled off his boots and padded across the floor after her. She was pushing crossly at the heavy bed with little effect. He grinned at her efforts, and thrust the bed along the wall towards the window. He knelt and examined the hardboard.

'I'll just go and get summat to jemmy this off with. I'll not be a minute.'

Rose sat on the edge of the bed and looked at the square of thick fluff where the bed had been. She would decorate this room as soon as Maggie turned up again. What colour, she wondered . . . something warm. Peach? Apricot? It sounded more as if she were making a fruit salad. A nice bright cherry possibly.

The last of the pink light was fading into a soft deep blue by the time Jack had lit the fire in the little Victorian basket fireplace. He sat back on his heels and watched it critically, anxious in case it smoked after being so long unused. As the growing heat reached him, he unzipped the old anorak he was wearing and pulled it off. Rose saw for the first time what he was wearing under it. She knelt down beside him and touched his arm.

'Thank you, Jack. You've got the sweater on – it's nice. It's a good fit.'

'Aye,' he said, concentrating on the fire, carefully not looking at her. It was just as well that she had not been expecting effusive thanks. She looked more closely at him. He was wearing a clean pair of jeans, he'd washed his thick hair, and he'd shaved. For her? He saw her looking.

'I'm all clean today,' he said smiling at her, then lowered his head away from her gaze.

'You said that I could take some photos of you when you were clean.'

He busied himself putting wood on the fire, saying nothing.

'Jack, can I take some? Please?'

He shrugged and still said nothing, still held his face away from her, but she saw the tension in his long back and thought that he had come here this afternoon for just this. She went for her camera.

He was standing leaning with his back against the mantelpiece, hands thrust defensively in his pockets, when she came back. She smiled and began to take photos of him as he stood, talking to him as she did so, telling him how good they were. And his head was as beautiful in the eye of the camera as she had thought it would be.

'Will you take off your sweater and shirt now?'

He hesitated, but she was businesslike, occupied with the flash, her head bent.

'Aye,' he said slowly.

He was, as she had thought, a very hairy man. It lay thick on his chest like a pelt. He stood with his hands by his side. She would have liked him to strip off entirely, but that was too much for him this first time. She would not push him. He stood patient as an animal as she began to focus on him. She caught the line of the long neck and shoulders, where his long hair curled down almost to the white skin. In the firelight he was beautiful, white where the weather had not coloured him, hard and muscular. She did not try to pose him; she took him as he offered himself.

She finished with some close-ups of his profile and the thick column of neck. Putting down the camera reluctantly, she came back to his living presence as if she had been on a journey, came back into herself with a sigh. She saw that he was not, after all, unmoved by this close attention from her. He glanced down at himself and grinned shyly, and she moved and put her arms round him. This time he pulled her close and held her tightly; this time his mouth was warm on hers.

Rose slid a hand down to touch the heavy bulge, and he groaned softly, pulling back from her to ease off the rest of his clothes. He stood and waited, the firelight flickering on the hard white curve of his buttocks. He did not touch her; still he stood and waited.

She wanted him.

He stood so heavily, so still, filling the room with a soft calm. Because he was demanding nothing from her, she wanted him more. She pulled off her clothes unhurriedly, then reached up and kissed him, feeling him rise against her, swollen and thick from the dark thatch of hair. She led him to the bed.

He lay with his arms round her, and he smelt of the outdoors, of hay. He stroked her back with his large warm hands and folded her into him and she was safe. He was gentling her as if she were a wild thing that would fright, and she liked it. Liked the silence of his holding her, the slowness of his hands on her. He came to her breasts and touched them softly, stroked them with his thumbs. And his mouth on her nipples was just as gentle, his long mouth demanding nothing from her except that she should let herself fall away into him. She opened her legs as his hand touched her cunt, and he covered her with his great dark body.

He was mixed now with her dream, her ghostly lover, and surely this was what the dream had been foretelling. She began to move to that high peak which she had reached with her night rider, feeling herself unfold.

Jack lifted himself and looked at her for a moment, then whispered softly, 'You're my bonny wild Rose,' and thrust himself urgently into her.

As if he'd turned a switch, pulled out a plug, so the wanting drained out of her. She was back in her head watching herself again, feeling him now as something hard and foreign banging away at her. She hated this, his banging at the soft walls of her. She lay wooden as a puppet doll as he moved on top of her, coming with a long groan. He slid out of her, and lay alongside her with one outflung arm heavy across her breasts.

She lay and listened to his deep, slow breathing and knew that she had been wrong. He was nothing to do with her night rider, this stranger beside her.

His arm was heavy, pinning her down. She was filled with a terrible sadness; a grey waste land came over her as she lay. He said something muffled by the pillow and sat up.

'What?' she said vaguely, not caring, for it was all wasted for her.

'I'm sorry, love. I was too fast for you. I came too quick. It was the first time for years and you're that beautiful . . .'

He stopped and bent to kiss her face gently stroking his hand over her short hair. She ran her hand down his back and he groaned, moving his head down to her breast again.

The sound of the wind grew louder, and there was a hard flurry of snow against the window. Jack lifted his head and listened. 'I'll have to go. I'll have to leave you, lass. I've got my sheep out in this.'

'Are they still out in the fields, still out in this snow?' she said in surprise. She thought how it must be for them, patient and uncomplaining all night out in the falling snow.

'It's not that lot I'm worried about; they're all right for now. I've got some ewes up on the moor. If it starts to blow I'll lose them.'

He was off the bed and tugging on his jeans, pulling his shirt over his head.

'I wish I could stop here with you.' He came and knelt on the bed, stroking Rose's hair. 'The other day when you kissed me. I didn't mean to ... You took me by surprise.'

She smiled at him and shook her head. 'It didn't matter.'

'Aye.' He stared out of the window as a gust of wind rattled a white cloud of flakes against the glass. 'I must go. The sheep get behind a wall up there and get buried. There's a couple of old ewes will mebbe lead them down to the stack yard, but the young ones know no better than to stop up there.'

'You go. Hurry before the light goes altogether.'

He kissed her quickly and strode across the room, pausing in the doorway.

'It'll be better for you next time, lass, I promise.'

The door closed behind him.

Rose curled herself under the clothes and pulled them

up about her ears and listened to the wind blowing the snow against the front of the cottage.

She'd never been left in mid-fuck for a sheep before.

She thought of Jack making his way up the track to the moor in the wild white snow and shivered for him. He had been very confident that there would be a next time, something she hadn't thought about. She wished that it had gone right with him, hadn't been such an anti-climax. It had seemed the natural thing to do, somehow, to go to bed with him, for she had identified so closely with him when she was taking the photos. It had been an extension of learning his body through the camera.

She hadn't thought how much it would mean to Jack. Maybe he would expect her to marry him now that he had slept with her. Make an honest man of him. She groaned and had a vision of herself forced into a shotgun wedding at the village church, with Mrs Bransdale holding the shotgun in one hand and the blue sweater which Rose had given Jack in the other; evidence of corruption.

Marry me, Rose, marry me . . .

Damn it, she had come up here to get away from Edward pushing her to marry him. The last thing she should have done was to let herself get as close as this to another man. And what was Edward going to say when he found out she'd slept with Jack? If he found out. What did she think she was trying to prove to herself? Rose, you are an idiot! she wailed crossly to herself.

A log settled on the fire with a crackle, and tall leaping shadows moved across the ceiling. The light was fading fast now; Rose could just make out the snow whirling past the darkening window. She lay on her side with her knees pulled up, watching it dreamily, remembering the feel of Jack's body against hers, his mouth on her breasts.

She must have slept: the room was suddenly full of the sound of a dog barking, of sheep bleating as they passed the cottage, startling her fully awake again. The noise of their crying died away as Jack's Land Rover started up with a roar. The headlights swept round the room as he drove off down the track after the sheep, then the dark lay thicker than before in the warm room. He had found his sheep, then.

She felt guilty, keeping him here in her bed until the light had almost gone. The snow was rattling heavier than ever against the window, but the fire crackled hotly as it settled.

And he came again to her.

She felt a cold chill along her back, and there was a strange smell in the room, like the one she had smelt here that first night. Like the smell that came out of the old chest in the parlour when she opened it for the first time. A very old and earthy smell.

Along her back as she lay shell-curved there came the first touch. She tightened in on herself, folding her arms protectively across her breasts. Fear trapped her there like a mouse, and he was the cat rasping at the back of her neck with a red tongue. But this cat had a prick: she could feel it pressing against the curve of her where she haunched away from him.

The narrow tongue was moving now down between her shoulder blades, and a terrible numbness came over her as the old confusion filled her again – she thought that she had been asleep, but surely she was awake now?

She lay staring blind at the falling snow, and, drawing down her spine, the wet tongue lipped and lapped, down between the curving haunches where all of her was wet and ready for him, as she had not been for Jack. His hands parted her legs and the very tip of him pecked at her and began to move slowly in and out of her, but so sly, so small were the movements that the friction of him against her became unbearable, and she cried out to him to let her come, to finish it. He slid into her and, as he did so, stroked a hand down and scratched with long nails at the very core of her. She came triumphantly, and he held the nape of her neck as she convulsed and shook, kissing the white fullness of her throat. Then, as she slowly became still again, he bit hard at the soft skin so that she cried out in pain.

For he was angry with her.

She was *his*. She had no right to take another man into her bed, to be so free with her favours. She must learn.

He was leaving her, his warmth turning cold against her back. For a moment longer the strange smell lingered in the room, then there was only the smell of woodsmoke on the dark air.

* * *

Nan stands by the table and crumbles the bitter herbs into the old pewter mug, crushing them to a fine powder with her long, thin fingers. Going across to the fire, she lifts off a pot of bubbling, steaming spring water and pours it carefully over the herbs. They give off a pungent, acrid smell, and she sniffs at it, satisfied. It smells powerful and strong, and that is all it needs to do, this time. She leaves the drink on the table to cool and sits herself again on the stool before the fire.

It is early in May, and there is a pale, green sunlight coming through the half-open door, but the wind is cold.

The lass will be here soon.

Nan has had no word, no message brought to her, but half an hour since, busy in her garden, she had known clear as if a voice had told her that t' lass would come, and why. She is not coming for t' usual reason – the unwanted bairn on t' way. Sometimes Nan thinks there are far too many bairns altogether. Look at Margaret at Ghyll Farm. An auld woman afore her time with so many, and there was no need, no need. Better to live without a man than to live like an animal.

Nan sighs, pushing back her straggling grey hair and looks at her hands, held out to the flames. They are well-shaped still, but the skin is wrinkled, blotched with brown stains. Old. Time was, time was.

She didn't feel any lack of a man now, but there had been years when she had burned for one between her legs. Days when she had let the young Squire take her, young Thomas Latimer. How old had she been then – fourteen? Fifteen? As young as this one coming to see her now.

Thomas Latimer had taken her on the high moor under a blue sky with the heather prickling her bare back. She hugs her shrivelled breasts and remembers how he suckled at their young ripeness, like a great, fair baby. He had given her a green gown, and he had sung to her.

'Greensleeves was all my joy . . .' she hums softly to herself, rocking backwards and forwards in the hot sun of a long gone summer. And Thomas Latimer married the Squire's daughter from the next valley when the leaves began to fall. By then Nan had been round with her own daughter.

Nan stirs uneasily and looks towards the open door. Not long now. She feels that she is deceiving the lass, giving her this to drink when it is not what she is coming for. All this will do is cool her blood, when what t' lass wants is a charm, a love potion to drink that will bring back that scarred devil all the way from London to her.

But Nan will do nothing to bring *him* back.

She thinks of flames, sees smoke, sees thatch crackle into fire. And it is not just that; there is a darkness round Tully when Nan thinks of her with Master Brett. Something about Master Brett frightens Nan. Tully needs a strong protection from him, a warding off of evil, but Nan feels that there is nothing she can do to keep off t' bad that she knows is coming. It will take more nor a drink of herbs in an old pewter mug to keep Tully safe.

She glances across at the mug. There is only a thin scribble of steam drifting now from the dark mirrored surface. It is ready. She begins to whisper to herself, watching the steam.

> 'By t' power of land and sea
> By t' might of moon and sun
> As I do will, so mote it be
> Chant t' spell and be it done.'

Her voice dies away into silence, and as she sits she hears Tully's foosteps coming hesitantly, fearfully, up the mossy path.

Chapter Eleven

'WHAT'S up with our Jack?' said Paddy. He was watching Maggie as she ironed.

'Nowt is there?'

'He's like a cat that got at the cream. He was lucky with them sheep yesterday. They were half-way down the track to Haggabacks when he managed to get himself up there after them. Mam would have killed him if owt had happened to them in that snow. Where was he all afternoon anyhow?'

Maggie shrugged, then pulled another crumpled shirt out of the overflowing basket at her feet. 'I dunno.'

'Maybe he was tucked up in Rose's bed. Where there's a Rose there's a prick.'

Maggie banged down the iron angrily. 'Shut up will you, she's not like that. She's nice, is Rose.'

He watched her cross face for a moment without saying anything.

'Has she paid you yet, Mags?'

''Course she has. Pays me every day I go up there. You know she does, you should do – you've had half of it off me.'

'Lend me a fiver.'

'What for?' She put aside the shirt and bent down for another.

'I want to send off for summat in the post. You'll like it.'

'Oh, aye? Like the Christmas present you didn't give me, I suppose.'

His face tightened. 'I've no money for presents,' he

said softly. 'You bloody well know that. No money, no job, no woman. No nowt.'

She glanced up at him and saw how angry he was getting. 'Only me,' she said bleakly, pulling a five-pound note out of her apron pocket. 'Here.'

It disappeared into his pocket like a conjuring trick.

'You're a good lass,' he said, touching her bent head. She looked up at him and was about to say something when Thomas burst into the kitchen, covered in snow and weeping.

'My hands have fell off, Mam!' he wailed.

Maggie put down the iron with a sigh. 'Don't be daft, they've not fell off, they're just cold.'

Her voice was rough, but the way she pulled off the little boy's gloves and coat and brought him to the fire was not. She knelt and began to rub his cold fingers between her warm ones, as Paddy stood and watched them.

Rose walked down the track from the cottage to the postbox, thinking only of the weather. She wouldn't let herself think about what had happened yesterday, for this time she couldn't explain it away as a bad dream. The weather was taking on a terrible reality – she was used to city streets where there *is* no weather. Today there was nothing else. The snow was driving hard and small in her face, stinging and hurting her. The Christmas-card flakes of yesterday had turned to ice. The wind had found itself a voice in the night, wailing and howling up the valley.

She reached the box and leaned against it to get back her breath. It was covered with congealed snow. She wiped it off and forced open the little door. It was empty inside, but surely the postman should come today – she tried to work out the date. It must be the twenty-seventh. Normal delivery then – possibly by dog sledge.

She had put all her post inside a polythene bag. There was a fat letter to Isabel which was a lie from beginning to end by what it didn't say, for she had mentioned neither Jack nor her night stranger. She had finally got round to telling Isabel about Edward asking her to marry him, and what her answer had been. Isabel wouldn't be too surprised at it, thought Rose, for she knew her very well. The rest of the letter had been thanks for the thermal underwear; somewhere under layers of clothes she was wearing Isabel's gift and appreciating the warmth. Even if she did feel she ought to be wearing a cloth cap to go with the long johns.

There was a brief note of thanks to Edward for the book, scrawled on the back of a postcard of Whitby Abbey.

There was a pack of film to be developed; not that she expected much from the results, but there should be some she could send to Isabel.

And lastly there was an order for darkroom stuff, this time for plate film for the big camera, for chemicals and trays. Once they came, she could begin.

Rose pushed the polythene bag to the bottom of the box and closed the door tightly. Below her down the lane the farm was blotting out in a grey flurry. There was no colour in the grey landscape. A wind was taking the loose snow from the fields and blowing it across the road like smoke.

Below the wall the sheep huddled, their fleeces clotted with snow, their black faces masked by it. She grieved to see them standing so patiently in the trodden wisps of hay. Surely Jack would come to take them down to the fold yard? She looked up at the high shrouded moor and shuddered at the thought of Jack going up there yesterday as the light went. The film she had taken of him was in the box now, off to be developed. She hoped the photos came out well, for her sake as well as Jack's, to show him that she was good at her work. She pulled up the hood of her coat round her face and began to make her way back through the deepening snow to the cottage.

She started to sneeze as the door closed behind her.

By the evening of that first lost day she was ill.

Her throat was sore, her chest hurt when she breathed, and her nose had sprung a leak. She could not get warm. There were only a few soluble painkillers left in the box she'd brought with her. It was a long way to the nearest chemist's.

She put two cushions on the hearth and sat with her back against the warm door of the old range. The falling snowflakes seemed to hold her fast there in the early dusk. They swarmed like fat white bees against the window until her head stung with the clustering of them. The cat leapt from her place on the side oven and came to sit on Rose's knee, purring in a rusty, unused thread, kneading her aching flesh with needle claws. Rose stroked the soft fur and felt the cottage shrinking round her to a black dot in a waste of white.

Getting out of bed on the second day, she felt her legs shake; she was as frail as an old lady creeping down the stairs. But still there was Lady to be fed, and wood to be dragged in from the buildings. The goat's water in the bucket was frozen; Rose had to break it with her fingers to refill it. She crept along the wall back to the cottage, dragging as much wood as she could manage in a plastic sack behind her – she was very much afraid of losing her fire. Only the snow and the wind had any substance; she herself had little reality. There was nothing but the warmth of the fire and the soft breathing of the cat on her lap. Time passed only as an alteration of light on the snow-clotted window.

She took the last of the painkillers on the morning of the third day, and by mid-morning her head felt as if it had an iron band round it. She tied a woollen scarf tightly over her unwashed, greasy hair. She washed now as the cat did – a quick cat lick. Each morning she pulled on the few clothes she took off at night. She could smell herself where she sat, musky and feverish. The cottage had shrunk to two places for her: her place on the hearth and her bed upstairs.

Some time on the third day she got it into her head that there was someone in the cottage with her. She knew at the same time that there was not, but the rooms felt different. If he came to her now, when she felt so ill, she thought that it would be the end of her.

Creeping down the stairs from the bathroom, she found herself listening to sounds which were not there. She stood shaking and dazed, but there was nothing. Only the rooms did not seem as empty as before.

Still the wind howled against the cottage, wailing along the electricity cable as if it were singing to her – wanting her to come out to play. She huddled against the range and fed the fire anxiously, coughing and sick as the wind poked a bony finger down the chimney and sent a gust of wood smoke over her and the cat. Late on that third day her fever reached its height. She had been three days without speaking to anyone, apart from the goat and the cat. Her throat felt as if it had sealed up.

In the early dusk she slipped into an uneasy doze and woke sweating and terrified.

She could hear her name.

Rose, Rose, Rose, it came hissing.

Rose, Rose, Rose, it came whimpering down from the upper rooms, wailing down the stairs and into the kitchen with her, ballooning out until it pressed against her skin, pinning her back against the range door.

The cat's fur rose on end and she spat, yowled and ran.

Rose put her hands over her ears and screamed, and the sound rasped at her throat with red pain.

He had her name now, he had that much of her. She was beginning to belong to him.

Then it was only the wind in the wires; only the snow blowing against the windows.

She dragged herself up the stairs some hours later and stood hesitating in the doorway of her room. She pushed open the door slowly, peering round with held breath. The room was empty, but there was something different. Nothing she could see, nothing she could hear. It was something she could smell. Faintly into her blocked-up head there came an old, evocative scent.

She knew what it was now. He had left her a gift. Heavy on the cold air the scent of roses filled the winter room. At first it was delicate, only the warm softness of half-open rosebuds, then it began to change. It thickened, became full blown, and the first faint smell of decay reached her. The rotting graveyard smell strengthened, filling her nose and mouth with a rank taste so that she gagged and swallowed, and, clutching at the doorpost, she heaved and retched at the stench. She slid to her knees and vomited, the bitter sickness spewing up from her, and the sour smell of it mingled with the smell of rotting, decaying roses.

'Rose,' he whispered gently. 'Rose.'

And he was laughing at her where she crouched in the empty room, over and over wiping her sour, wet mouth with her shaking hands.

'Uncle Jack!' shouted Thomas. 'There's a great big car come up the lane after the snow plough and it's at our gate, come and see!'

'In this lot?' Jack cut through the string on the bale of hay he was opening for the sheep. 'Who the hell would be daft enough to come out on the roads in this snow?'

He followed Thomas across the piled-up drifts in the yard to the half-buried gate.

Getting out of his car into snow above his ankles, Edward looked in dismay at the enormous man looming out of the falling snow at him. He had a tattered sack over his head and shoulders and was holding an extremely long, sharp knife.

'Excuse me,' he said carefully. 'I'm sorry to disturb you – I'm looking for a place called Haggabacks Cottage.'

'Oh, aye? Who were you wanting, then?'

'I'm trying to find a friend of mine, Rose Thorpe.'

'Are you now? And is she expecting you?'

Edward stared at the bulky figure. 'Could you just direct me please?' His annoyance showed in his voice.

Jack grunted and pointed up the lane. 'Straight on. Last one in the valley, you can't miss it. But you'll have to walk.'

'Fine. Is it okay if I leave my car in your gateway? Not in your way, is it?'

Jack shook his head. 'I'm not daft enough to be going anywhere.'

Thomas's small head peered out from behind Jack's knees as the stranger slammed and locked his door. Pulling a great armful of parcels from the boot, Edward set off up the track. Thomas's eyes widened at the sight of all the things the man was carrying.

'Uncle Jack,' he said. 'Is that Father Christmas come back again?'

'No, it bloody well isn't,' said Jack tersely. He shoved Thomas aside and stomped back to his sheep.

*

Edward dined out for weeks on the story of how he got to Rose's cottage after being cross-questioned by the keeper of the cottage wearing a sack. He struggled up the track, dropping parcels in drifts above his knees and losing all the feeling in his hands and feet. Afterwards it was funny, but not then.

He came out of the smoking, wind-blown snow in a place where there were no footprints but his own and leant, breathless, on Rose's gate. He was thankful to see that although the snow on the path was untrodden, a thin line of smoke was curling from the chimney.

There was too much snow piled against the gate to open it. He scrambled over, landing in an undignified heap on the other side.

He went down the path and banged on the door. There was no answer. He banged again impatiently and shouted her name, but the wind swallowed his voice.

Rose had heard the knocking. She sat by the fire and looked at the door.

Here I sit by my own hearth with my black cat on my knee. The cat is my companion. She licks my milk-white skin. Why, she is getting quite familiar. Knock at my door as hard as you like. I don't believe in you, whoever you are. I will not let you come in. By the hair on my chinny chin chin I will not let you in . . .

Edward stretched out a cold hand and tried the latch of the door. It lifted and the door creaked slowly inwards.

. . . then he'll huff and he'll puff and he'll blow my house down. I do not want you here. My black cat is my companion. I will not spell it out again for you . . .

He slammed the door behind him with his foot and leant against it, peering round short-sightedly for Rose, then pulled out his glasses from an inside pocket and slipped them on.

'Rose?' he said in dismay, and again more loudly, 'Rose?'

She sat there glaring at him so oddly, making no attempt to greet him, only tightening her arms round her bent knees. Her eyes glittered at him in the firelight from a wax-pale face. The cat on her lap sprang to the floor with a hiss and ran off into the shadows.

'Are you real?' she said at last, harshly, rustily, as if from a very long way off.

'Real enough. And very cold,' he said, making his voice cheerful and reassuring as he saw how disturbed by him she was. 'It's me, Rose, it's Edward.'

He crossed to the table and dropped his parcels on to it, then took off his sheepskin coat and shook the snow from it. He knelt in front of her, taking her hands in his, and was alarmed to feel how they were shaking.

'Edward. I thought you were . . . I thought you were him . . .' she began. She reached out and touched his cheek, brushed the snow from his thick fair hair, not even aware of the tears streaming down her face.

He had never seen her cry before. It shattered him. He took her in his arms and cuddled her, feeling the fever in her burning her up.

'You're ill,' he said, relieved that that was what was the matter with her.

'Yes,' she agreed. 'I was ill, I had a bad cold.'

Feeling began to seep back slowly into her. Edward was here, and there was something she should tell him about. But if she didn't tell him, it wouldn't be true, it wouldn't have happened to her. She was aware now of how dirty she was, her hair greasy under the crumpled scarf.

'I didn't know you were coming,' she said vaguely.

'Yes, you did. Of course you did. I told you in my letter, in with the book I sent you. I said that I would be in Newcastle taking a day course, and I would call in on my way back down south. Rose, you never read the letter, did you?'

She looked at him blankly. It was on the mantelpiece in the parlour. She remembered now putting it there out of the way, not wanting to read what it said. She gazed sadly at him.

'Poor Cinderella. You've been having a hard time all on your own. You're not with me yet, are you? Maybe I should go out and come in again dressed as Buttons. It's New Year's Eve, my love, and I've come to first-prick you or whatever the quaint customs are up here.'

The snow flurried hard against the window, and she thought of the journey which he had made to get to her. She saw the black dot of his car creeping through the snow-filled lanes to her.

'Where's your car?'

'It's down at the farm at the bottom of your track. The snow plough had been as far as their gate. A jolly green giant of a man with a sack round his head asked me a lot of questions about my intentions before he allowed me to leave the car and come up to see you. There seemed to be a very small dwarf hiding behind his knees. Neighbours of yours, are they?'

Jack and Thomas. Edward and Jack being polite to one another. Edward so fair and southern, Jack so dark and rough. Beauty and the Beast. She saw for the first time that Edward was wearing a ring on his little finger; the one she had sent him at Christmas time.

'Dear Edward,' she said, and kissed him.

'That's better,' he said, hugging her to him tightly. 'Hello, Rose, where've you been?'

Oh, Edward, where I've been is off inside my head somewhere.

Where I've been is in bed with an incubus.

Opening my legs for a ghost, Edward, that's where I've been.

'Come on, Little Ash-Pussy, get yourself out of the cinders and show me round, then I'm going to unpack some of the stuff I've brought and treat you to a little luxury. You certainly look as if you could do with some.'

She showed him the cottage. The parlour smelt musty again – he laughed to hear her call it that. He picked up his letter from the mantelpiece and looked at her for a moment, then shrugged and tore it in half, dropping the pieces on the black ash of the cards she had burnt there on Christmas Day. So long ago. There was a smell of soot in the room, and already a faint brown line showed above the skirting board, where the damp was creeping back and nibbling its way up the walls. She saw with dismay how pine needles from the dying Christmas tree sprinkled the window-seat. She had forgotten all about Jack's little tree.

Rose took him up to the bathroom, showed him her bedroom, aware of the grubby sheets on the bed and the smell of herself in the room.

'"Thou God Seest Me",' he read in delight from the carved headboard of the bed. 'What's that, Victorian contraception? It's enough to quell any incipient erection. What's behind the angel?'

'Nothing now,' said Rose. 'I found some photos behind it. Weird ones.'

He looked carefully at her and nodded. 'That kind of photo. Curiouser and curiouser. And you've a fire in your bedroom. Delightfully decadent. I'm going to light it, and you run a bath for us.'

While Edward was downstairs finding sticks and wood, Rose dragged off the sheets and pillow cases and thrust them to the bottom of the wardrobe. She found some clean lace-trimmed ones in the airing cupboard, pulled them on and sprayed them with a quick burst of scent. She straightened the patchwork quilt and drew the curtains against the falling snow. Switching on the bedside light, she checked the room quickly. Much better. For of course he would stay all night with her – where else would she sleep?

'Get undressed and into the bath,' said Edward. 'I'll be with you as soon as I've lit this.'

He knelt beside the fire and piled on small pieces of wood, watching the little flames tongue redly at them.

Rose lowered herself stiffly into the hot, scented water. She lay back and stretched out her legs, slipping down into the heat until only her face was uncovered. She was almost asleep when he came in to her; she was only vaguely aware of him pulling off his clothes and coming to stand beside the bath.

He stood looking down at her. 'You've lost a lot of weight. I expect you've not been eating properly on your own, have you?'

She thought about it. She couldn't actually remember eating very much for several days; not since the snow began. It had been soup in a mug mainly.

'Sit up,' he said, and climbed in behind her.

He began with her hair, tipping back her head gently so that the apple-scented shampoo didn't go in her eyes. He rinsed it carefully, then began to wash her arms, her back, her breasts, as efficiently and quickly as a well-trained nanny.

'Stand up now,' he said briskly, rinsing the soap from her long back. Like a good girl she turned to face him, while he knelt and washed her legs. He came to the pale bush of her cunt, which he touched gently.

'The Chinese had a word for this.' He coated his hands with the thick, creamy lather. 'Several, in fact.

144

They called it "The Open Peony Blossom", and "The Golden Lotus", or sometimes "The Cinnabar Gate".' He rubbed softly at her, easing the tips of his fingers into the wet folds, then cupped his hands and let the warm water trickle over her until she was pink and clean, the curling tendrils of hair flattened like feathers to the high curve of her pubic mound.

'And what did they call this?' she asked, crouching in front of him. She lifted his penis and held it in her two cupped hands like an offering. He grinned with pleasure as it began to stiffen at her touch.

'That, my Rosebud, is my Red Bird, my Heavenly Dragon, my Coral Stem. My Jade Stalk.'

'You made that last one up. Jade's green.'

'Ah, yes, the ordinary vulgar jade is. But there is a very precious creamy white variety. Very rare. Hence Jade Stalk. You may kiss it very humbly, if you like.'

She cradled him in her hands, looking down at him. He had a small, neat prick, curving slightly to one side. A highly individual prick, she thought now. Just like its owner. She bent and took the soft wet end of it into her mouth and, wanting to give him more, slid her mouth forward along him, taking him in until her lips almost touched his fair wet thatch of hair.

He shuddered and caught hold of her hair, lifted her head and looked down at her in surprise. 'I said a kiss, not rape and pillage. You must have missed me more than I thought. Come on, you musn't get more cold.' Stretching past her, he pulled out the plug.

'Out you get. Where are the towels?'

The warm, soapy water drained away with a loud gurgle. He dried her quickly, roughly, so that she was warm and pink.

'Right. You go and dry your hair by the fire and find something nice and long and Victorian to wear. I'm going down to get us something to eat. Have you got a dressing-gown I can borrow?'

He went off down the stairs in a swirl of green velvet. Rose thought how Jack would laugh at him if he could see him like that. She went to find her white nightie, wondering what Edward had brought for them to eat – she was hungry now.

'You don't have a lot of food in your cupboard, Mother Hubbard.'

Edward came in carrying a heavy tray. 'Luckily I brought plenty of stuff with me.' He put down the tray in front of the fire and sat cross-legged with his back to the heat.

'Ah, this is nice,' he said. 'Come here and sit next to me and let me feed you.'

He gave her morsels of food as if she were a small bird, sliding them into her eager mouth with his fingers, fragments of thin, smoked salmon, tiny white slivers of chicken in a rich sauce. Isolated into splinters of taste, the food became a succession of rich textures. Towards the end of the meal, she no longer had any idea of what she was eating; she was aware only of his slippery fingers easing into her mouth. She sucked at them greedily.

Finally, he wiped his fingers and opened a small jar of peaches in brandy. He took one out and gave it to her, watching as the thick brandy juice trickled down her chin, caught in the hollow of her throat and fingered down into the cleft of her breasts. He knelt behind her and pulled her back on to his chest, sliding his hand to rub a nipple with his thumb, lapping the juice from her long throat as delicate as a cat. He slid his tongue into her peach-wet mouth, and the taste of him was the climax to the feast. The half-eaten peach rolled slowly across the floor as he lifted the long folds of her nightie, stroked her narrow ankles and behind her knees, kneaded

146

her flesh until she was all sugar and spice for him, pooling to liquid at his fingers on her. And he entered her delicately, carefully, easing himself over the rim of her as if she would spill.

He held the curve of her throat and came into her almost absent-mindedly, for he was watching her face. Something in her was changing. Something which had been land-locked for all the time he had known her was being stirred by a far-off current. What was it, he wondered, that had begun to break the ice? Living so much alone, perhaps, or coming back here where the memories of her father had to be dealt with. There was something else, though. She was not as open as she usually was; she was not meeting his eyes so easily. It intrigued him, this feeling that he was shuttered off from her. There were dark shadows under her eyes and she looked weary. He put his arms round her and rocked her to him, then pulled her to her feet.

'Come on. Time you were tucked up in bed. I'm knackered after that long drive. We'll have a couple of hours' sleep, then we'll celebrate New Year.'

He piled some logs on the fire, then, climbing in beside her, kissed her briefly, turned his back on her and seemed to fall instantly asleep. She lay listening to him breathe, disturbed by having him in her bed next to her. It was strange having him here. She should have read his letter, she felt bad about that. She sighed and shifted uncomfortably. Her head was tired, but her body had only just woken up. Edward had penetrated her so carefully she'd hardly felt him.

. . . and the breath was slammed out of her as his body covered hers, and the anger in him was coming off him in a raging heat. Because of Edward, because of Edward she realized, and felt how hard for her he was already.

For the first time she wanted him, and her need was greater than her fear. She reached down and caught hold of his prick, groaning with pleasure at the size of it. He took hold of her short hair and wound his fingers in it, pulling back her head and biting her swollen bottom lip until it bled. She arched up towards him, tugging at his hips now, desperate to have him in her. He thrust into her as if he were wounding her, spearing at her again and again until she felt as if she were hollowed out entirely by him. She moaned her pleasure at him, and it seemed as if the whole of her body were coming endlessly. He fell forward across her, his long hair brushing her face, and as suddenly as he had come, he left her . . .

She wiped her mouth on the sheet, dropping back from a great height into herself, waiting until her breath steadied itself again.

She turned her head. Edward was still sleeping beside her.

She had let her night rider take her with Edward sleeping as sweetly as a baby next to her. Rose didn't even care if he had been a dream or not She had wanted him. Now she must forget him: concentrate on Edward. She moved across and cuddled him, curling herself into him. He muttered something happily and settled into the warmth of her. Within minutes, she was sleeping as deeply as Edward.

*   *   *

It is summer now in the valley. Very late one moonlit evening Martha is sitting by the table in the kitchen at Throstle Hall, waiting. She is waiting for Tully, who should have been in her bed long since. Martha has a feeling that wherever Tully has got herself to, Master Nicholas Brett will be there with her.

Summat about him frightens her. For a start, she

doesn't know why he keeps coming back here. There is nowt as far as she can mek out that would bring such a man all the way from London. Ben says he's hiding from summat, but this is a very long way to come to hide. Ben calls him a forriner, and it is true that he is so different that he might as well be one. He is always right smooth and courteous with Martha, but she had seen how Tully had faded that first time he left, early in t' spring. Her skin had turned like whey, and her eyes had blue shadows under 'em. She'd gone pattering off down the lane to see Auld Nan one afternoon soon after he left and came back full of a secret, but Martha trusted Nan. She'd not encourage t' lass in owt that would harm her. Not with a man like that.

A man like what? Martha isn't sure. She has noone to measure him against. T' Latimer lads have made him their leader, somehow. They never need Gideon at t' best of times, but then not many folk do. As long as he has his ale and his sheep he cares nowt for owt else. The lads have allus been a bit wild, being motherless, but since Master Brett came calling they've been wilder than afore.

What frightens Martha, what she sits turning ovver and ovver in her head, is a little bit of talk she heard.

She knows it all by rote, she's told it over to herself so many times. There'd been some heat in t' days, a bit of warmth in t' sun. Martha had got up good and early, just on fower o'clock, for she'd got it into her head to do a wash. First since Christmas and t' linen in t' back place was piled high, with mice raising families in it. Martha had crept downstairs, opened up t' peat fire to start t' pans of water heating, and it was when she knelt there blowing away at it that she heard voices.

It gave her a start, for she'd been nervous ever since those men had come thieving round t' place months back. She'd fettled t' first one who came through t' back door with a warming pan over his head, and they'd all turned tail and run. Ben had been no help; he knew nowt about it until next day when she told him. He was getting as deaf as a post these days; sleeping out there above t' hosses he was less use than a dog. He didn't even bark.

But that morning, kneeling there by t' fire, Martha knew it wasn't thieves again when she heard them voices. She went pattering to t' inner door and opened it, and she heard Master Brett laughing in a queer, fuddled way. She crept down t' passageway to t' parlour door, and put her eye to t' thin crack of light down t' edge of it. There were candles guttering on her good polished table, and Joshua and Nathan were sitting there with their eyes fair bulging like goosegogs.

'If it had worked, then . . .' Nathan was a bad colour in the candlelight. Master Brett shrugged. 'If it had worked, then . . .' His voice trailed off and he swore. 'Then I would not be sitting in this benighted hole with a pair of drunken owls.'

The younger Latimer blinked at him. 'But how did thoo get that scar?' he whispered.

'She had a knife.' Master Brett ran his long, white fingers over the livid scar.

'And t' woman – what happened to her?'

Both the boys had their eyes fixed on his scarred face.

There was a long silence in the little room, then his soft London voice came thinly to Martha where she listened at the door.

'The woman died,' he said.

Then Martha's feet pattered back into the kitchen and she slipped on her pattens and made a noisy clattering and banging, singing like a bird to herself, and all t' time, all t' time, she could see his face as he answered.

'The woman died.'

And thick as a swarm of bees t' questions came into her head – what woman was it who died, and why? All Martha knows is that it was Master Brett who killed her.

The sound of a soft giggling in the yard rouses her. The door opens a crack and closes gently, and Tully stands in a patch of moonlight on the stone floor. She stays with her hands pressed on the door behind her, startled at seeing Martha sitting so heavily, so solid, at the table.

'And where have thoo been, Tully?' asks Martha softly.

'It was that hot, I was all of a sweat,' begins Tully glibly. 'I went out in the yard, just for a breath of air, like.'

'And he just happened to be out there in t' yard as well, did he?' Martha's voice is even softer.

'Who d'you mean?'

'Don't act so daft!' bawls Martha crossly. 'I mean our fine visitor, Master Scar-face. Him who's been haunting our doors for months back. And for why, is what I want to know. What does he want to keep coming back here for?'

Tully shrugs and says nothing, but she knows why, because Master Brett has just told her why. He comes back to see her. And the bitter drink Auld Nan gave her has done it; it has drawn him back to Tully away from all those fine London ladies. He has brought her a red ribbon. It is tucked away out of sight between her small breasts, and Master Brett put it there himself.

'Get yourself ovver here and sit down next to me, Mistress Big-eyes, and tell Martha what was happening out there with that gentleman in t' moonlight.'

Chapter Twelve

THE alarm on Edward's watch bleeped them awake just before midnight. Edward yawned and stretched and hurried off downstairs, complaining loudly of the cold. As Rose came back from the bathroom, he re-appeared waving a bottle of champagne and two glasses. Rose curled up sleepily in the bed again and watched him open it. He climbed in beside her, shivering, and filled her glass.

'Ten minutes to midnight. Here's to next year, my darling. Here's to you and me, to a lot of good photographs, a lot of rich patients.'

She hesitated, then echoed him. 'To us,' and thirstily emptied her glass. She slid a hand down him and felt his prick small and defenceless against her palm.

'Sorry, Rose,' he said. 'Beautiful as you are, I can't at the moment rise to the occasion.'

She leaned over him and put her empty glass on the floor. Picking up the bottle of champagne, she filled her mouth, then, kneeling astride him, she took his prick into the cold, wet bubbles.

He stiffened and groaned and began to harden.

She sucked on him gently, then began to flick her tongue up the length of him, sticky with champagne. And, as she had done in the bath, she took his prick deep into her mouth, feeling the soft, round head of him smooth against the high cave walls. Holding him tightly there, she began to suck more strongly.

Edward caught hold of her head and said jerkily, 'I'm going to come . . .'

She hesitated, wondering whether he wanted to come in her mouth. Wondering if she wanted him to, for it was something she had never let any man do to her.

'Rose . . . .' he said again, more urgently and, lifting herself, she knelt above him and lowered herself on to his prick, feeling the warm gush of him as she did so. He thrust up at her and held her astride him, looking at his watch.

'Midnight. Happy New Year, my love. Nice timing. I can't think of a better way to start a new year.' He hesitated, then pulled her down on to his chest. 'I'm not asking you again now, just reminding you that I do love you and want to marry you.'

She looked sadly at him and began to say something.

'No. Not now. This is perfect. Let's not spoil it now, Rose.' And he pulled her mouth down on to his and sealed off her reply.

They finished the bottle of champagne between them and slept again, waking late in the morning to find that the snow had stopped falling, and a thin sun glittered through the clouds.

Rose busied herself with the jobs that had to be done, feeding Lady and introducing her to Edward, who gravely wished the goat a very happy New Year. He helped her to bring in more wood and cleared the garden path of snow. The cold air and the exercise made him hungry. They sat at the kitchen table eating bacon and eggs, and she laughed at his rosy face.

He pushed his empty plate away and sighed. 'Right. Come on, then. Time you started packing.'

She looked at him blankly. 'Why should I pack?'

'Rose, don't be silly. You're coming back to London, now, with me. I'm not leaving you here on your own like this.'

'I'm not going anywhere with you, I'm staying . . .'

'You were in a dreadful state yesterday when I arrived. I can't leave you here.'

'I had a bad cold, that was all. I'm fine again now. I'm not ready to leave here yet. Don't bully me, Edward, I'm not one of your patients . . .'

He looked crossly at her. 'You can be so obstinate. Of course you're ready to leave, this place is a dump. You've seen what it's like; you've faced up to coming back and I know that was difficult because of the way you feel about your father. There's nothing to keep you here. Unless . . .'

'Unless what?' she rasped.

'Unless there's someone to keep you.'

She stared wide-eyed at him, then looked away.

'When I came in yesterday, you said something about thinking I was *him*. Who did you think I was, Rose?'

She sat in a frozen silence and would not look at him.

'You thought I was Heathcliff from the farm, didn't you? Answer me please, Rose. Did you think that was who I was?'

She turned her head slowly to face him. He could not know, he must not know about her night rider.

'Yes, of course,' she said. 'There was no one else it could have been.'

He watched her carefully. 'Have you slept with him, Rose?'

'Yes. Once.'

He sighed, pushed back his chair and walked over to the window, where he stood with his back to her.

'I wish I hadn't asked. Or that you'd lied.'

'To you? You don't lie to a psychiatrist . . .'

'Christ!' he shouted, swinging round and striding over to her chair. 'You never miss a chance to have a go at me. It's what I am, just like you're supposed to be a photographer.'

'Supposed to be? What the hell do you mean by that?'

'You say you won't marry me because of your career, you say you have to be free to run around the world taking your photos, that they come before a husband and children. So where's your darkroom here? Where's the work you've done since you came? I don't see photos anywhere – you've been here long enough to have something to show me but there's nothing. You must have spent your time running round after Heathcliff. I didn't realize that you liked them rough, Rose.'

'He's not my bit of rough – and stop calling him Heathcliff. His name's Jack. And I'm sorry, I shouldn't have slept with him. I should have realized it would hurt you.'

'Yes. Yes, it does. I wanted to marry you, of course it hurts me.'

The past tense of the word fell like a stone between them.

He sat down slowly. 'This Jack, then. Where has he been these past few days when you've been so ill? Christ, Rose, you could have died up here on your own for all the care he took of you.'

'There was the snow, he would be busy with the sheep . . .'

'Too busy to see if you were all right? How long d'you think you'll be happy coming second to a flock of sheep?' He reached across and caught hold of Rose's hands. 'Look. Never mind this Jack. Come back with me anyway. You don't belong here. You belong with me . . .'

She pulled away her hands and scraped back her chair. 'I'm staying here. I'm not finished yet, and I'm not running away just because you say so.'

He stared at her cold, cross face. 'And you won't marry me,' he said flatly, accepting.

'No. I won't marry you.'

She stared at his bent head and knew that it was over. She should feel sorry for him, but all she wanted was for him to be gone.

She stood by the fire and waited as he gathered his things together then walked with him to the door. He pulled her to him and kissed her, holding her close to him.

'I hate leaving you here; I think you're staying for all the wrong reasons. I'm still your friend, Rose, I still care. Take care of yourself.'

Then he was gone, and she closed the door behind him. She leant back against it and listened to the silence in the cottage. Edward was wrong: she *did* belong here. And he was wrong when he said she wasn't a photographer. She hadn't understood that he saw her work like that, as an excuse not to take on any responsibilities. She would prove him wrong: she would make the store-room off the parlour into her darkroom, and take some photos with the plate camera which would make him eat his words. And choke on them.

'Goodbye, Edward. And good riddance,' she said harshly out of a hard, cold anger, and the words hissed and settled in the silent, approving rooms.

There was no more snow in the night. The morning was mild and bright, as if the weather had paused for breath and relaxed its iron grip. The red post-van crawled cautiously along the lane from the village and reached Ghyll Farm at eleven o'clock. Crossing the yard, the postman looked at his watch, and thought that he was in the wrong place for any elevenses. A smile from this lot would make his day, never mind a mug of tea. He clattered loudly on the door of the farm and shouted, 'Post!'

Maggie came hurrying out and nodded at him, looking in surprise at the big bundle of mail he was holding.

'I can't get any further up the lane than here – can I leave Haggabacks' post with you?'

Maggie nodded again and held out her hand. 'Aye. Jack'll take it up for her when he sees to the sheep.'

'Thanks.' The postman handed over the bundle and set off back through the snow, thinking that was about the longest conversation he'd ever had with a Bransdale.

Maggie stood by the kitchen table and sorted through the post. Most of it was for Rose, and she put that carefully to one side. There was a big, brown envelope for Paddy. She turned it over curiously. Paddy never got any post except his giro for the Income Support once a fortnight.

'What have you got there?' said Mrs Bransdale, crossing the room on her way out to the stock.

'It's for our Paddy.'

'Oh, aye? Give it here.'

Maggie handed over the envelope obediently.

Mrs Bransdale glanced at the name and address, sniffed and ripped it open. She looked at the brightly coloured magazine it held and her face tightened.

'The mucky little toad,' she said roughly. She flicked over the pages. 'I never saw such stuff . . .' she began, her eyes widening. She got to the centrefold and froze, then rushed across to the fire and pushed the magazine to the back of the flames.

'What was it, Mam?' Maggie stood with her mouth open, wondering who was going to tell Paddy.

'Your dirty-minded little brother bringing filth in here. Wasting his money on stuff only fit for burning. Best place for it is the fire back. I'll not have stuff like that in my house!'

She nodded at the fire, where the flames were curling

round the edges of the pages. 'Where did he get money from to waste on muck like that? Did you give him it?'

Maggie went red and shook her head.

'I hope you've more sense than that. You know what he's like. Needs a bucket of cold water over him at the best of times.'

Maggie gazed at the fire, where a pair of breasts bigger than she had ever supposed possible popped into flame like two pink bubbles. Her mother followed her gaze and sniffed, rattling at the half-burnt pages with a poker.

'Get summat done, then,' she said. 'Don't stand there gawping all day. I'm off to see to the beasts. You can get Sleeping Beauty his breakfast when he manages to crawl out of his bed, and you can tell him what I've done with his mucky magazine.'

She marched out of the kitchen, slamming the door behind her. Maggie knelt by the fire, wondering if she could rescue any of the pages for Paddy, but all that was left was a high-heeled shoe, a black stocking and a garter with a red rose.

Rose was spreading scraps on the bird table, enjoying the sunshine, when Jack came crunching up the path with her mail. She beamed happily at him, pleased to see him.

'Happy New Year!' she called as he came towards her, then stopped in surprise as she saw his face. He strode past her without saying a word, went into the kitchen and threw a packet and some letters down on the table. Rose scattered the rest of the food hurriedly and went in after him, wondering what could have happened.

He swung round on her aggressively and said, 'Who was that daft bugger, then?'

She was so taken aback she could hardly believe he

had said it. To give herself time to take in his words, she crossed to the sink and filled the kettle. 'Sorry?' she said.

'I said who was that daft bugger, out in his car in this weather? He must have been a townie, whoever he was. Nobody else is soft enough to be wandering about in this lot. Nancying about in a pair of shoes.'

Rose spooned coffee into two mugs, thinking that Jack should have seen him in the green velvet gown.

'He was a close friend of mine actually – Edward Martin. He's a psychiatrist.'

'Oh, aye? He wants his own head looking at, coming out here in this weather. He was lucky to get out of the place yesterday when he did. He could have been stuck here for days, making a right nuisance of himself with his daft car stuck in our gateway. Mebbe you'd not have minded him being fast in here with you, though – kept your bed warm for you, did he?'

She leant back against the sink and considered hurling the jar of coffee at his thick head. She had been so ill and he had not been near her for days; now suddenly he was telling her what to do.

'He slept with me, yes,' she said, pouring boiling water into the mugs.

He went on as if he hadn't heard her, but she could tell by his face that he had. 'Bloody daft townies. They should stop where they belong, in towns.'

She looked at him. He hadn't shaved for days. His hair was greasy, his hands were dirty and he smelled of sheep. That he should stand here in her kitchen being so rude, so ignorant, so Northern, she thought in a fury. She had been going to tell him that she was finished with Edward, that he wouldn't be coming again, but not now. She wasn't telling him anything when he was in this mood.

'Edward is my friend. I'd been ill and he took care of

me. I don't have to have your permission to have visitors. Or to go to bed with them if I want to.' She marched across and slammed his mug of coffee down in front of him. 'So shut up about him and drink that, or else go away and leave me in peace.'

He hesitated for a moment. 'I didn't know you'd been ill. I meant to get up to see if you were okay but I was that busy with the sheep. If you were sleeping with this London bloke you should never have let me go to bed with you – fancied a bit of a change, did you? You know what you are? You're nowt but a mucky little bitch!'

He picked up the mug of coffee and hurled it against the wall. The door slammed behind him.

Rose stood and watched the coffee crawl like blood down the fresh, pale paint of the wall. There was something wrong with the way it was trickling down; it was moving as if . . . as if someone were smearing it. There was a great round circle appearing before her and a curling snake . . . Rose backed across the room in horror. There was the letter R now and an E, and there was her name scrawled huge and dark across the wall, and the kitchen was full of the scent of her night rider, old and musty. And just once, he said her name.

ROSE . . .

Rose's legs gave way under her and she sank to the floor with her hands over her ears. Edward had gone, Jack had gone, but he was here in the cottage with her. This was the one she was left with.

Long after the smell had faded from the room and the coffee stains were dried on the wall, Rose still sat shaking. She made herself fetch a cloth to get rid of her name staring at her. She picked up the broken pieces of mug and threw them away. The mail which Jack had brought was still lying on the table. She gathered it up and sat down on the hearth again, holding on to the reality of it.

The big packet held some hope for her – it was her darkroom supplies, and film for the big camera. She could begin again.

Pushing it aside, she looked at the two envelopes. There was a fat letter from Isabel, full of details about work which Rose read greedily, and at the end of the letter Isabel came to the subject of Edward's proposal. 'Do what you feel is right for you, Rose,' she finished. 'I like Edward very much, but I'm not convinced you would make each other happy. Marry Edward if you can't live without him, but only then. I wish I could talk to you on the phone, but my thoughts are with you.'

Rose thought how good it would be to talk to Isabel, but then there was so much that she couldn't possibly tell her, that she couldn't tell anyone. Edward already seemed nothing more than somebody out of her past. She pushed the letter back into the envelope: she would read it again later. The last envelope was a set of photos back from being developed. She had lost Edward, she had lost Jack, but she still had herself – Rose Thorpe, photographer. She ripped open the packet and pulled out the folder of black and white prints. She concentrated on them, the whole of herself fixed on them. They had been taken mostly as snapshots for Isabel, but even so they had to be right. Rose never threw any of her work away, for it was still hers, however bad it was, but she never showed anyone anything which didn't come up to her high standards.

The ones of the interiors of the rooms were just records, surprising her by how different they looked now. There were three very good ones of Maggie and her mother plucking the geese; she put these aside as possible sellers. The last ones in the pile were the ones which she had taken in the orchard on Christmas Day. She went through them slowly, then stopped, frozen into a shocked stillness, looking down in dismay at the last one she had taken.

She had shot the photo down the row of trees, wanting to catch the pattern of branches against the sky. But there was a figure in it; there was a man disappearing among the trees at the far end of the row. He had his back to her, and was dressed in something dark, something old-fashioned. She stared at the oddly blurred figure walking through the crisply defined trees. He was stepping out of the picture – into what?

She could find no reason for it, this strange, hunched figure hurrying through her apple trees. It must be a double exposure. She scrabbled wildly at the thought, wanting it to be that, wanting it to be a fault at the labs.

But she knew that it wasn't.

How could she have taken a photo of a man who wasn't there? And if she hadn't seen him except here, did that mean he was haunting her orchard whenever he chose to? She didn't want to keep this proof of him. She ripped the image into shreds and threw the white petals on to the fire. For an instant the man's head flared into prominence, glowing redly, then disappeared into blackness.

Maggie pulled up her mud-splashed skirt and lay back in the hay. 'It tickles,' she giggled, shuffling her bottom uneasily on the sweet-scented hay.

'You should be used to it by now,' he said. 'And you are supposed to take your wellies off as well as your knickers.'

'Sorry.' She kicked them off and lay waving her legs happily in the air. 'Are you sure there's nobody about?'

'I told you. There's nobody about.'

'Are you still mad at our Mam?'

'I wish Jack would bury her in a bloody snowdrift. Of course I'm still mad at her. She's got no right to open my post, no right at all. It was my magazine, that. Nowt to do with her. I wanted to show it to you; you'd have liked to look at it, wouldn't you, Mags?'

'Would I?' she said doubtfully. She began to giggle, remembering. 'There were some really big tits in it, Paddy, I saw them before they got burned up.'

Anger whitened his face again.

'Rose has got lovely tits,' she offered him quickly, pulling up her three sweaters and peering down at her own. 'Have I got nice ones or are they too skinny? You never say owt nice about them to me. I could be built like a bleeding cart horse for all you say.'

'I don't fuck cart horses.'

He unzipped his jeans and knelt above her. She groaned at the sight of his prick springing up and reached for it.

'You don't ever talk to Rose about you and me, do you?'

'No, no, of course I don't, I've never told anyone, you know that. Even Mam and Jack think I got Thomas that night I was drunk after the show.'

He looked at her carefully. 'I'd kill you if you told anyone . . .'

'I'll not, I'll not.' She was almost in tears now, desperate to turn away his anger.

'And it's me you care about, me that you belong to?'

'You know it is!' she wailed unhappily. She reached towards him again, but he pulled away from her.

'Greedy. Earn it.'

'I don't know how. I can never think of owt, you know that. It's no good . . .'

'Yes, you can. Here.' He pulled out a candle from his pocket.

She looked in amazement from it to his face. 'Put that up me you mean?'

He nodded and watched her coldly, avidly, as she took it nervously from him, patted at herself as if for reassurance, then touched it to the thick bush of dark hair. She began to rub the candle gently backwards and forwards, liking the feel of it.

He leaned forward and touched her, stroking the soft inside of her thighs; then he moved her hand from the candle, took it and slid it slowly into her. She came at once, yapping like a vixen, and he covered her mouth with his hand, wishing that she took longer to come, that she was not so easy. He waited until the jerking of her body died away and she lay still in the hay; he eased himself into her, coming quickly and silently, withdrawing at once. He knelt beside her and watched her for a moment.

'Why did you come out with that about her tits?'

'What?' she yawned lazily.

He nipped at her bare stomach.

'Ow, that hurts. Rose's tits? I saw them once when she was still in her nightie. They're not that big, but they've got real big nipples. I bet she knows a lot of stuff.'

'What sort of stuff?'

'Oh, you know. Stuff like you're always getting me to think of. Why don't you find out?'

'What, and have our Jack break my neck? No, thank you.'

'Don't be daft. There's no chance of him doing that now. He had a bad row with her this morning when he took her post up. About that man that stopped the night with her. I was in the kitchen when he came back, and he was calling her all the names under the sun. Says she's a dirty little bitch. He's not going up there again. She must have gone to bed with that man, whoever he was. So she'll be on her own up there now. Why don't you go up and keep her company?'

'Clever lass,' he said. 'Why don't I do just that? Pay a visit to Haggabacks. I've as much right to be up there as she has anyway . . .'

'What? what are you on about now?'

'Never mind. I'll pay her a visit. Then I can tell you all about it, can't I?'

She nodded uncertainly. 'If you like. But you be nice to her, she's lovely, is Rose. She's so kind to me . . .'

'Let's hope she's kind to me as well, then.' He was surprised to find himself hardening again at the thought of Rose.

Maggie was delighted to have pleased him so much.

'Do it again, our Paddy,' she whispered eagerly. 'Do it to me again.'

*　　*　　*

Tully slides on to the stool next to Martha and says nothing.

'Well?' says Martha. 'What was happening with Master Brett out in t' yard?'

Tully sighs. 'Nowt. We were just talking, Martha.'

'Aye? Talking about what?' Martha takes a deep breath. Her fear for Tully is hurting her, making her chest so tight it is hard for her to breathe. 'Telling him t' best way to clean pots? Because that's where thoo belong, lass, all among t' grease. Not talking to London gentry.'

Tully sits and wonders just what they had been talking about. She couldn't mek head nor tail of what he said anyway, if t' truth be told.

'Magic,' she says suddenly. 'He talks a lot about magic. He wanted to know about Nan. If she does charms and that . . .' Her voice trails off into silence as she thinks of how she drank that bitter stuff from Nan's pewter mug, and of how Nicholas Brett rode into their yard seven days later.

'Nan's but a poor auld woman now who knows a lot about herbs and such,' says Martha impatiently. 'There's nowt magic about her these days, if there ever was. I hope thou told him that?'

'Oh, aye, I did,' agrees Tully promptly, not believing a word of what Martha was saying. She certainly hadn't told Master Brett that it was one of Auld Nan's charms that had brought him back across the moor.

'Well, then? Thoo can't have spent all that long time out there talking about an auld woman. What else?'

'Fairies. He's seen Fairy Hill. He knows its name. He wanted to know why it's called that. Wanted to know if anyone's seen anything up there.'

'What Sally Ford over there at t' crossroads says she's seen many and many a time? Little green men is what she's seen, with red caps on their heads, coming out of that culvert at the roadside there. She reckons they live underground inside the hill, like mowdiwarps do. She's seen 'em right enough. Thoo'd not get me crossing that plain after dark.'

'Nor me,' agrees Tully quickly. She leans her bare arms on the table and yawns. This hot kitchen is making her sleepy. Crossing by Fairy Hill after dark would be a fearsome thing, but surely at dawn it would be safe enough? Master Brett has said that he is taking her to t' top of Fairy Hill at sunrise on Midsummer Day next week. He will not say what it is for, only that it is a secret.

Tully thinks that she knows why he is taking her up there on such a magical day. She thinks he is going to ask her to become his wife. She is still a maid, but he has kissed her and touched her. And he told her he came back from London just to see her, to take her up Fairy Hill on Midsummer Eve.

They will climb the hill and at sunrise he will give her a gold ring for her finger, and he will ask her to become Mistress Brett. And Tully looks down all t' years to come and sees herself bustling about her own kitchen, with her own shining plates, and a baby swinging in a cradle.

'Is that all, then?' says Martha sharply, peering closely at her.

'All what?'

'Your wits are fuddled! Is that all he did, just talk about fairies?'

'Oh, aye,' says Tully most convincingly. 'He just talked.'

But when he had done talking, he had kissed her until her legs had gone as tottery as a new-born lamb's, and his hand slid down inside her bodice with a knot of red ribbon he'd brought her all t' way from London. And his fingers curled round her breast and stroked it, and how strange it still felt to her, his fingers on her there.

'Think on!' snapped Martha, still not satisfied. 'Talking won't leave thee with a bairn in thy belly. Talking's safe enough. Though why he should want to tek thoo out in t' moonlight to talk about fairies I can't think. But talking leads on to other things, most times. Best if thoo doesn't spend so much time alone with him, Tully. From now on keep out of his room upstairs. I'll see to his bed-linen and his hot water and such, think on?'

Tully imagines Master Nicholas's face when he wakes up to the sight of a red-faced Martha, puffing and panting, beside his bed with his hot water, and she giggles.

'Yes, Martha,' she says meekly. Promising to keep out of his room is one thing, going up Fairy Hill with him to see the sun rise is a different thing altogether. She feels his fingers brush the soft skin of her bare breast again, and shivers.

Martha eyes her in amazement. How can the lass be shivering when t' place is so hot her shift is sticking to her?

'Here, get off to bed,' she says. 'Best place for thee.'

Tully slides from her stool and says goodnight to Martha, and goes slowly up the stairs to the very top of the house, to her narrow bed under the eaves, there to sleep with the knot of ribbon in one hand, dreaming of Midsummer Day.

Martha sits at the table and worries. Maybe there is summat she can do, someone she can tell? But no one will listen to her in this house, only Ben, and he's not much use. All she can do is to watch Tully very, very closely. Mebbe after all she's only being a daft auld woman, seeing danger where there is none, but Martha knows what she heard through t' crack in t' door that morning, she knows what Master Nicholas said.

'The woman died,' is what he said, and Martha shudders now, remembering his face as he said it.

Chapter Thirteen

THE wind had dropped in the valley, but the cold intensified. There were some small, hard snow flurries, but it seemed too cold even to snow. It got into Rose's very bones. Winter in London was never like this. Sometimes there would be a thin covering of snow on the morning streets, but it would be gone by midday. People dressed a little differently, wore fun furs and big boots, but it was all a game, really. Inside the houses there was no season of winter. Here there was nothing but the weather.

In the first days after Edward left, Rose tried to make herself keep going. She began taking some photos but the cold defeated her. Her hands were too cold to work the camera; her imagination was too cold to work, or so she sourly told herself. On the third morning after he had gone, she woke into a cold such as she had never imagined. The air in the bedroom seemed wet against her head; her cheek-bones ached with it. When she drew back the curtains, there were thick frost ferns covering the inside of the window. She didn't know windows could do that, not inside. She blew on the glass and watched the frost melt in a ring, giving her a squint-eyed view of the trees before it began to rime over greyly as she stood.

The water in the kettle downstairs had frozen over. The loo flushed sluggishly; the water in the taps seemed less somehow. She thought of what Jack had told her about keeping it moving, and left the cold tap downstairs turned on.

She had to force herself to go out to Lady and to drag in more wood. It seemed to her that she had been living here for ever, doing nothing more than this – looking after Lady and feeding the hungry fire.

She was back in her old place by the fire again, with the cat licking and slurping at her cold paws behind her. There was nothing for her to do. She yearned for a TV, a radio, a cassette-player. Anything to blot out the sound of her own thoughts. She sat and made out long lists in her head of the things that she would buy the next time she escaped from this place. Always supposing that she could get her car to start, of course. The poor thing must be in a worse state than Rose.

She filled the hot-water bottle to sit and cuddle, made herself a mug of soup and wrote a letter to Isabel. She sorted out some photos of the cottage, of Stokesley, of Maggie busy painting; and put them all in the envelope. That filled in an hour successfully. She peered at her watch. It was four o'clock, and the light was already dimming in the kitchen. The birds were coming down to the table for their last feed of the day. She sat and watched them. Blue-tits, great-tits, chaffinch, blackbird, and a pair of big thrushes such as she had never seen in London, with creamy white breasts and waistcoats of dark freckles. As she watched, they all scattered soundlessly, flying low across the snow into the trees. She looked round for Tibby, thinking that it must have been the cat which had frightened them, but Tibby was sleeping behind her with her paws tucked in.

When Rose looked back at the bird table, there was a kestrel perched on the far side of it, gazing in at her. His carved, heraldic head alarmed her. Kestrels don't come to bird tables. What did it want from her, with its sheening feathers and hard, shining eyes?

She hunched down into herself and looked away from

it. When she looked back, the table was empty. Only then did she think of photographing it. And this did worry her, for Edward's words had gone very deep with her. If she was not a photographer then she was nothing. It was her only definition of herself. She should have been reaching instinctively for her camera. It was all ready with a film in – not the big one, that would have taken too long to set up, but her own little camera.

She had intended taking the big camera out today and starting some still-life compositions of the snow-furred branches. So why hadn't she? If she sat here on her bottom much longer waiting until it got warmer, the snow would all have melted and defeated her object.

Something inside her was clenched too tightly to let her work. There was fear, yes. She had not imagined the scrawling of her name on the wall; there had been a ghost man walking in her orchard. But there was something threaded in with the fear – something so sick and strange that she did not want to admit it.

Her night rider had not been for too many nights, and she burned for the release which he brought her. Edward and Jack had dropped away from her now as if they had never shared her bed. It was not them she was waiting for through the dark night hours, not their hands she wanted on her. Like a fatal illness she would not acknowledge, her desire for him lay beneath every waking thought.

She got to her feet impatiently, weary of herself. Dusk was heaping itself in the corners of the room. She crossed the floor and switched on the light. Nothing happened. She went into the pantry to get a new bulb, and switched on the light in there. Again there was nothing. Rose stood with her hand on the switch and felt the cottage cold and silent about her. Two bulbs gone? Oh, let it be just that . . . She hurried to the foot of the stairs to try the switch there. But she knew there would be nothing. Rose sat on the bottom step and cradled her head in her arms. She felt as if she were falling away into a deep black hole.

Dark, dark. She had to keep out the dark. Jumping to her feet, she ran back into the pantry, bumping herself on the corner of a shelf, scattering tins and packets as she felt for the box of candles she'd looked out earlier, when Jack warned her that this could happen. Three or four days, he'd said. She couldn't manage, couldn't survive all that time without light.

Her fear of him surfaced to blot out everything else. What if he came to her now, in this dark, when she could not switch on the light and send him back into the shadows? She must have some light. She knelt with the candles in the pool of firelight and lit them with shaking hands, placing them on saucers, in egg cups. She lit them one by one until she was sitting crouched in a circle of candlelight, pale crocus buds of flame flickering in the draught from the door. Then she picked one up in each hand and began to walk through the rooms of the cottage, placing the candles on the window-seats where they bloomed against the black, wet glass. And every room had these small points of light in the window, flickering in the dark.

As he limped from the cow-warm buildings back towards the farm-house, Paddy looked up towards the cottage and saw all the windows pricked with light, and saw them as the message he needed.

Hurrying inside, he went lurching up the stairs to find the unopened bottle of whisky which Rose had given him for Christmas. Maggie was in the kitchen as he came back with it, lighting an oil-lamp at the table. His shadow swelled and fell across her, and she looked up, startled.

'Where are you off with that?' she began, but the door closed behind him in a gust of cold air, and he was gone.

Mrs Bransdale saw him padding fox-black through the white snow with the bottle in his hand. She turned and looked up at the cottage, and saw the candle flames. She stood and cursed the bitch for taking the second of her sons from her. The woman had already upset Jack with her fancy London ways, flummoxed him so that he didn't know whether he was coming or going. She'd taken his mind off the ewes, and just when it should have been on them. Putting ideas into his head. And in Maggie's, come to that. Her and her French knickers. As if Maggie didn't have enough daft ideas in that direction on her own already. Now there was Paddy away wagging his tail after the woman. Mrs Bransdale stood and watched him cross the yard and go out of the gate.

'Moths to a candle flame!' she bawled after him in a rage, and repeated it as she went into the kitchen, startling Maggie considerably.

'That's all they are, daft buggers, moths to a candle flame.'

Through the blue, crackling ice-shadows Paddy lurched, his breath smoking thinly in the frosting air, his lame foot trailing behind him. He leant for a moment on the cottage gate, getting back his breath, watching the guttering candle flames.

Rose heard the gate click; she heard the dragging footsteps coming slowly up the path; she heard the tap on the door.

Tap, tap, tap.

She thought in horror of the story of the little goat kids, and of how their mother warned them and warned them not to open the door while she was gone, not to anyone at all.

Again the tapping came, but she sat without moving. Was it him, coming to her out of the night? Had her candles drawn him in to her? There was a long pause, then once more the tapping came, knocking at the very centre of her fear and desire. She got to her feet like a sleep-walker and went step by step and foot by foot across the floor. She pulled open the door.

Paddy stood and looked at her. He held out the bottle.

'I saw the candles that you lit for me,' he said. 'I got your message.'

Rose hardly made sense of what he was saying. She was confused, not knowing if she felt relief or disappointment. She caught him by the arm and pulled him in out of the night, shutting the door tightly behind him.

They sat one at each side of the table, the bottle between them, a candle at each side of it. The light made Paddy's face look strange and ghostly. He had a thin face with high cheek-bones, and the shadows lay blue beneath them. And his pale eyes glinting in the flame never left Rose.

The whisky lay warm inside her; it was the first time that she had been warm for days. She said so to him very carefully, very confidingly, and jerkily. He filled their glasses again.

'Paddy,' she said. 'It's very kind of you to come up here to see me. I was frightened on my own when the lights went off. When you knocked on the door I thought it was . . . I thought it was someone else.'

'Our Jack?'

She shook her head. 'Who's he?'

He grinned with a snarl of white teeth. 'Aye, who *is* he? I don't mind coming up to Haggabacks. If we had our rights, maybe it would be me sitting behind that table anyway, and you would come tapping at my door to come in.'

She thought about this slowly while she emptied her glass again.

'Why would I be doing that?'

'Because of your dad and our Mam, that's why,' he said. 'Because your dad should have been red-rudded, then we'd all have known for sure.'

'Rudd-redded?' she said, thinking that it didn't sound quite right somehow.

'Marked. Like the tup, show who he'd covered.'

'Like the tup,' she agreed, and giggled a lot. 'I found some photos that he'd taken . . .'

'Your dad? What sort of photos?'

'Rude sort.'

'Show me them.'

'Too rude.'

'Show me how rude. Show me just one.'

'Just one.' She slid open the table drawer and pulled out one of the photos from the packet, pushing it across the table to him. The dark woman lay in a pool of candlelight, lifting her heavy breasts to Paddy and smiling at him. Paddy sat dumb and frozen looking at her, and his face was whiter than ever.

Rose stretched across and pulled back the photo, shoving it back into the drawer and closing it.

'I told you they were rude,' she said. 'Isn't she a rude lady?'

'Isn't she just,' he said with an effort, and poured himself another glass of whisky.

Rose was swimming now in a golden haze of whisky on an empty stomach. There was a glow round Paddy when she looked at him, and he was wearing a skull for a head. She took another gulp from her glass and leant across to him.

'Paddy,' she said earnestly. 'What do you do?'

'I don't do owt,' he said bitterly. 'I just am.'

She considered this in a muddled sort of way, and thought it made sense.

Paddy reached across and took hold of her hand. 'I want to fuck you,' he said very politely.

'No, I'm so sorry, I can't let you do that,' she said, equally politely.

'You let our Jack,' he said in a hurt voice. 'And that London bloke. Why can't I?'

He pushed back his chair and walked round the table to her, holding on to it unsteadily. He weaved and shimmered in front of her. She emptied her glass, looking wide-eyed round it at the bulge in his jeans.

'Paddy,' she said. 'You're very lame. Why are you so lame?'

Ice formed in the room; there was a wind roaring round her and his pale eyes were burning her up.

'It's the Devil's Mark,' he whispered.

'Silly. Silly. No, it's not,' she began to say, and suddenly felt very tired. She yawned, put her head down very carefully on to the table, and was asleep, falling away into a whirling blackness.

He took her by the shoulders and shook her angrily, but she was gone. Reaching into the drawer, he pulled out the photo she had shown him and pushed it into his pocket.

He stood and hated her. Hated her because she had laughed at him and said no when he wanted to fuck her. So how come she'd let Jack do it to her? Jack with his two long legs. He was always going to be limping along after Jack. Why should Paddy have nowt and this bitch have everything?

He wanted to hurt her. He reached out and punched her angrily, but she only muttered and settled again. He ran a hand over her breast, but he was too much in awe of her to do more. He wanted to spoil her. Picking up one of the candles, he held it unsteadily to the back of her head. Her hair flared briefly, frizzling with a horrid smell of burning. He put down the candle, picked up the bottle and emptied the dregs of whisky on to her blackening hair. He cursed her briefly and left, leaving the door wide open behind him.

The cold woke Rose some hours later.

She woke into a sick terror. Dark as thick as velvet muffled her, so that she couldn't think where she was or what had happened. A blurred memory of Paddy came seeping back to her, of him being angry with her, coming round the table and wanting . . . She couldn't remember. The candles had long since guttered out, and the fire was dead. She could feel a stream of cold air coming through the door at her, and there was a nasty smell of something burnt in the room.

She ran her fingers over her face and through her hair, stopping in horror as her fingers found the burnt, wet stickiness at the back of her head.

Oh, God, she thought. It's blood. He must have hit me with something. I'm bleeding to death . . . then she caught the smell on her hands. Whisky.

She sat huddled in the chair, too much afraid to get out of it, too sick and weary.

Then faint and thin and full of a terrible wanting sadness came his voice whispering her name, gentling her to him, drawing her into him.

Rose, Rose, Rose . . .

She got unsteadily to her feet, clutching at the table and stood listening. She went towards the stairs, and heard the desire in his voice deepen as she moved across to the bottom step. She lifted one foot to go up to him, fumbling for the wall to support her, and doubled denly with pain. She was going to be sick . . . she ran for the door, knocking over a chair, and as soon as the cold air hit her she vomited her terror into the piled snow by the doorway. She was sick until she thought that there was nothing else left inside her to part with.

She leaned against the wall and heard Lady bleating. Lady was warm, she was safe. The pale, reflected light from the snow was enough for her to scrabble along to Lady's door. She unlatched it and the goat came running to lip at her hands for a biscuit. Rose knelt in the straw and cuddled her, hanging on to her as a last link with normality. Lady mouthed at her hair, tugged at her sleeve, intrigued at having Rose sitting in the straw with her. She had pulled most of her hay out of her rack again as usual. Rose gathered it up into a heap and curled herself up in it, sick and shivering. The goat came and settled at her back, and the warmth of her came slowly to Rose. Still half knocked out by all the whisky she'd drunk, she escaped into a black sleep, her head full of candles and Paddy, of the sound of her name in the dark.

Rose woke at first light, cramped and stiff, covered with hay seeds and smelling of goat. Lady was still sitting next to her with her feet neatly tucked under her, mouthing her cud like a wad of chewing-gum.

Rose clambered awkwardly to her feet. She opened the half-door and fed Lady, giving her a handful of small apples as a treat. Every light in the cottage was blazing – the bright kitchen hurt her eyes, but she was very grateful to have electricity again. The place stank of whisky, of candle grease. She switched off the lights and made herself a cup of tea – it was all she could face, sick as she felt. Sick of herself as well. She had been so stupid to drink all that whisky when she never usually touched the stuff. Paddy must have given her a lot of that bottle.

She remembered him coming round the table towards her. And she had said . . . what? It had stopped him, whatever it was. She dropped the empty bottle into the rubbish bin. She would light the fire again, make sure that it was burning properly, then she was filling her hot-water bottle and going to bed for the day. And she was locking the cottage door first.

What she had done with Paddy was something she could cope with, but that other memory of herself going towards the stairs, going towards her night rider, was one she was not prepared to accept.

In the late afternoon she surfaced again, pale and reluctant to do anything. She should have a bath but it was too much effort. Her head hurt, her stomach hurt. The towel felt like sandpaper on her frail skin. Her face in the bathroom mirror reproved her. She peered in closely at it. She looked now as she would look in ten years' time. Emptied out and faded.

'Your petals are fading, Rosie dear,' she told her reflection sadly. She stood and looked at herself for a while, then went for her camera. She set it up with the extension cable and stood by the window where the light was best. She pulled off her nightie and dropped it at her feet, then leant back against the damp stained wall, staring straight at the camera in a flat statement of herself.

Here she was, then. Rose Thorpe at thirty-two. She was sick, she had a headache. She had been bloody stupid the night before, and somewhere she knew that she was lucky to have come out of it so lightly. She pressed the rubber bulb between her fingers: this was Rose as she would be.

This photo would turn out to be the first of a series of self-portraits, the first because Rose had never been very interested in her own body or the way she looked. She had just accepted that it would do what she told it to, but she had never connected it with what she thought of as Rose. Since she had come to this place, her body had betrayed her so many times by its actions and responses, surprised her by how little she knew about it. She pulled on her jeans and sweaters and began to think of earlier photos. Were there any? When her mother died, Rose had gathered up all her papers and things and shoved them in a box. Up in the attic in Islington, in that box. That's where they must be.

She remembered a few of them vaguely. One of herself at three, smiling and holding on to her mother's dress with one hand. Her first school photo at five, looking miserable. She had hated school, every day hoping that it was Saturday or Sunday when she didn't have to go. The other kids had laughed at her because she didn't have a dad and what was worse, didn't even know she was supposed to have one. She could remember coming out of school that first afternoon, seeing her mother standing waiting in a blue flowered dress. Rose had rushed over and started kicking her, hitting out at the soft flesh. And the other mothers made such disapproving noises, drawing back their own kids in case it was catching. She had been so angry with her mother for not telling her, for not warning her that not having a father mattered so much.

Herself at ten, tall and sturdy with long legs. Clever. Her body that last summer at junior school had been totally hers as it would never be again, when it was every day the same. Reliable. Then sex came up in her like yeast the next year and she wanted to know it all, try it all. Mickey from next door had given her a ring with a green stone, and she had promised to marry him when she was sixteen. Mickey and his family moved soon after that, but she kept the little ring for years. Somewhere there was a photo of them with their arms round each other. Pieces of Rose.

She would look for the photos when she got back to Islington. They were the beginnings of herself, the first letters of her alphabet. Now where was she up to? P for Photographer. And that, she told herself firmly, was what she should be doing. Out there with the plate camera. She might feel better in the fresh air. She couldn't feel much worse.

*   *   *

John Bransdale is out very early checking his ewes, and is startled to see something coming bobbing towards him through the grazing flock. Then he sees it is a hare leaping through the grass, her long ears with their dark tips flat against her sleek back.

'Puss, Puss,' he calls to her respectfully as she goes, but the fine boned head does not turn to him. He will not harm her, although they could do with the meat. He licks his lips at the thought of hare stew, but the hare is bounding away up the track to Haggabacks.

John stands and watches her. They say that witches take the form of hares and all night run wild through the dark, coming home now as the sun rises. And it takes a silver bullet to kill one. John doesn't think it's Auld Nan herself who's just run past him, but there again they say she has a hare who keeps her company like a cat does, and maybe this is the one.

A strange big creature it is, thinks John as she disappears out of sight. She is safer up this end of the valley than the other.

Nothing with fur or feathers is safe for miles around Throstle Hall. Nathan and Joshua Latimer will kill anything that so much as twitches, tossing the poor bloody bundles on to Martha's clean scrubbed table however much she grumbles at them. It doesn't occur to them that animals can feel pain, for what can't talk can't feel is the way that they see it, when they take the trouble to think about it at all.

Once as a jest they tossed a fine red dog fox they had shot on to Martha's table, but she had slammed out of the house and not come back for two days. Two days of being served bread and cheese by a surly Ben, accompanied by the swearing and ranting of Gideon, had made sure that little jest was not repeated. But Martha never says no to a hare, for Gideon is very fond of one. Jugged.

To end up jugged is a poor sort of finish for an animal with so much magic in her. She has been running in this valley before any of these people came, and she has had many names. Owd Sall, Moll, Grimalkin, Bawtie Bandy and Katie. Old women's names. No coincidence, that. Time has turned round on her since she was sacred, and the White Mother protected her, but still she runs through the grass, a moon creature, a trickster, the bringer of renewal. She runs through the grass, and the years turn at her passing.

Nan opens her cottage door and looks out for her now, and the long ears come bobbing past her as the hare brushes her long skirt with dew-wet fur and comes to sit beside the fire.

Nan nods and smiles at her, says, 'Good morning, Moll', and stands for a moment longer at the door. She peers up towards Fairy Hill. Just for an instant she thinks that she sees something move up there, right at the very top of the hill, small and black against the rising Midsummer sun. Then it is gone. She rubs her old eyes and mutters to herself, closing the door and crossing to join Moll by the fire. She sits down on her stool, and the hare turns her head to look at her. Nan reaches out and strokes the silky head, and sighs. Something has moved on: she can feel it. There is something wrong, and something big and bad is coming. She knows now who it is that she has seen up there on Fairy Hill, and though she cannot see it all, not yet, she knows that there is blood in it.

Chapter Fourteen

WHEN Rose went through the kitchen on her way out, she noticed that the table drawer was half open. She stood looking down at the photos inside. Why had she opened the drawer? She had a sudden horrible image of showing them to Paddy, of pushing something across the table to him. Surely she had not? Not to him of all people. She snatched the packet and looked inside, but the photos were still there. She put the envelope carefully back, shut the drawer, and stood thinking. She could remember nothing. All of last night was a whisky-coloured, shadowed blur, and a recollection of a great fear. Best forgotten. She shrugged, wincing as her head crackled, and went out into the garden.

Rose set up the big camera on its tripod at the end of the garden. She would start with the cottage. It wasn't going anywhere, it would just sit there patiently for her, however long it took to get it into focus. It was strange to her, taking so long over everything. She was used to snatching images. This frozen, static landscape was empty, yet she felt that she should be able to make photos out of it. Perhaps taking so long was the right way to coax out the pictures, easing them out of their locked silence.

She was used to working quickly; this camera needed a lot of preparation. It had no separate view-finder. She had to open the shutter, set the lens aperture to its widest diameter and then study the upside-down image on the focusing screen.

The cottage was standing on its head.

Rose stood and gazed in, and thought that it was like looking into one of those old-fashioned glass paper-weights. If she shook the camera gently, snow would begin to fall about the little cottage.

She focused in sharply, bringing it in from the edges in hard, clear lines, giving herself up to a fierce concentration on what she was doing, and began to photograph.

'Whatever is she doing now, piddling about in the snow?' said Maggie, stopping half-way across the yard and screwing up her eyes at the cottage, where she could see Rose small and black against the snow.

'How should I know? Putting spells on the lot of us. Hexing the cattle. Making Jack's prick fall off.'

Maggie giggled. 'He never uses it anyway. Not for that.'

Paddy grinned and patted the curve of her bottom, then began to stroke it.

'Give over. Someone'll see you.'

'No chance. They've all gone down the village in the Land Rover.'

She pushed away his exploring hand. 'Give up, will you. I'm not in the mood.'

He nipped her hard and she squealed. 'Don't you bloody well start. You women are all alike. Nowt but cock-teasers.'

'I am not, then.' Maggie wasn't too sure what he was calling her, but it didn't sound nice. 'I don't know what's up with you today, our Paddy. You're like a bear with a sore head. What did Rose do to you when you went up there to see her? She got Jack in a right state that last time he was there, and you're not much better. She must have done summat to upset you last night an' all, you're all back to front today.'

He said nothing, looking away from her.

She folded her arms and scowled at him. 'You're right mean, you are. You promised to tell me what happened when you went up to Haggabacks.'

'It's not what happened, it's what didn't happen,' he spat at her. Hunching his shoulders, he moved away from her crossly. It hurt him to think about last night. Rose shouldn't have been like that with him, treating him as if he were nowt. He was as good as Jack any day and she'd opened her legs for him. And she shouldn't have got at him for being lame.

'Why are you so lame?' in her prissy London voice. No bloody business of hers why he was lame.

And then showing him that photo when she must have known who the woman in it was. Who else could it be? She must have guessed. Still. He'd got the photo off her, and it proved a lot of things, the way he saw it.

'Here, come on, I want to show you something,' he said. 'Then I'll tell you what happened.'

Maggie followed him up the steep steps and sat down on the bales of hay, watching him. The one small window was netted thick with cobwebs. He could smell the cattle moving restless below them. He stood and looked at Maggie in the dim light and wished that she were Rose instead.

'Go on, then, what have you got to show me?'

He pulled the photo from his pocket and smoothed it out carefully.

Maggie was disappointed. 'Just a photo? Is that it?'

'You take a good look at it. Just you look.'

She took it from him. 'Oh heck,' she said. 'Look at her ...' Then she stopped. 'It's our Mam,' she said in horror. 'Our Mam, showing everything she's got. It *is* her, isn't it?'

'Aye, it is. And you know who took it? The old man

did. Lady Muck's dad did. I told you before there must have been summat going on between those two.'

He stopped and looked at her. She thrust the photo at him.

'It's horrible. Put the nasty thing away. It wants burning, that does. I don't want to listen any more . . .' She pulled down her skirt to cover her knees and turned her back on him.

'Shall I tell you what happened up there, then?'

She shrugged and wouldn't answer.

'Your mother showing her tits like that,' he said softly. 'Letting herself be photographed like that. And she wouldn't even let you keep those nice knickers Rose gave you. She burned them up. And she burned up my magazine as well – because it had pictures of bare women in it, didn't it? Doing things she'd done herself, old bitch.'

'She's not fair,' said Maggie shakily. 'And that photo is horrid, I don't want to talk about it. I wish you'd never shown me the nasty thing.'

'But don't you see what it means,' he began, exasperated at her digging in her feet so. 'If our Mam let Rose's dad take mucky photos of her, there's a fair chance that she let him do a lot more as well . . . so who was your dad, Maggie Bransdale, and who was mine?'

She put her hands over her face and began to rock backwards and forwards.

'I don't want to know!' she wailed. 'Shut your mouth, will you?'

He pushed the photo back in his pocket and looked at the sullen hump of her back.

Crouching in the hay at her feet, he began to bring her back to him. 'Rose was scared when the electric went off. She'd lit candles in all the windows. Place looked like a birthday cake with them all. But they were really a message to me to go up there to her. I knocked on the door, all polite and gentle like, and she was real quick to let me in. She was pleased to see me, she pulled me inside and sat me down at the table. Then she started to talk to me.' He could tell by her half-turned head that she was listening. 'Rose has a lovely voice, hasn't she? And when she leans into you, and looks at you, those big blue eyes and that lovely soft hair, somehow she makes you feel that you matter to her.'

He had her now.

She turned to him and nodded eagerly. 'Aye, she listens as if she really wants to know what you're saying, doesn't she? Go on, then, what happened then?'

'I took the whisky up like you saw. We had a drink out of some thin glasses with stems on them – all she had, she said. By heck, she likes her whisky does that one, it went down like water. We talked a bit about London, then she came straight out with it. Said did I want her because she fancied me. And she stood up and pulled off her sweater and then her shirt, and she had nowt on under it . . . and she does have nipples just like you said, lovely big pink ones.'

Paddy knelt and began to stroke the back of Maggie's neck, where he knew that she liked to be touched. She leant into him, and he remembered again how Rose had refused him, and faltered to a stop.

'Go on,' said Maggie. 'What happened next?'

He took a deep breath. 'Rose came round the table to me with her tits all bare. She knelt down at my feet and unzipped my jeans and she took my prick out, then she put it in her mouth and sucked it . . .'

Maggie gasped and stared at him. 'Rose did that?' she cried. 'Fancy her doing that to you!'

'Then she began to lick me like a little dog. She kept saying how big I was. Couldn't get enough of me.' He watched her and waited.

'You could do it to me just as good as she did. Come on, you do it to me, that's my good girl.'

She looked at him and pulled a face, and he kissed her mouth – a thing he rarely did.

She slid down his zip reluctantly and, gingerly grasping him as if he would explode in her fingers on touch, she bent and put the very tip of him into her mouth. Then just as warily, she spat him out again, snapped her legs together like a pair of scissors and said anxiously, 'Here, you won't do it in my mouth, will you? I don't want that nasty stuff in my mouth.'

'Rose did,' he said viciously. 'Lapped it up as if it was ice-cream.'

'Ice-cream? Funny sort of ice-cream.'

He saw the obstinate look on her face. 'No. No, of course I won't do it if you don't want me to,' he said, gentling her back to him with his hands on her neck.

'I don't,' she said. 'You promise?'

He kissed her mouth again, and pushed down her head gently. 'I promise,' he nodded.

Taking a deep breath, she fastened herself grimly on to him and, closing her eyes tightly, began to suck.

Much as he would have preferred it to be Rose's mouth on him, he loved it. A picture of Rose's fair head fastened on him came into his head and waves of pleasure beat through him. He began to rock gently against her. He looked down at her blind white face and a surge of affection went through him for her.

'Maggie,' he said. 'Oh, our Mags!' And he came sweetly into her warm red mouth.

Two days later, when Maggie came up the track to see

Rose, there was a difference in her. Something in the way that she spoke to Rose, the way she looked at her, had changed. Rose couldn't make out why she was so different, but it was there. Maggie didn't tap at the door as she usually did for a start, she marched in, took one look at Rose and burst out laughing.

'By heck,' she said happily. 'Your hair's a right mess. Whatever did you do to it?'

Rose clapped her hands to the burnt patch at the back of her head. She'd forgotten about that.

'Hello, Maggie,' she said. 'Did you have a nice Christmas? I burnt my hair on a candle.'

'Daft thing to do.' Maggie walked across to the fire and plonked herself down in a chair. 'Christmas? Aye, it was okay.'

Rose had been looking forward to seeing Maggie again. Now she wondered why.

'Bairn's back at school,' said Maggie with satisfaction.

'Don't you miss him?' asked Rose, going to fill the kettle. From the way that Maggie was thrusting out her long legs to the heat of the fire, she was settling in for some time.

'Heck no. He gets fed up at home. Whinges on all the time. No one for him to play with at the farm, he's better off at school.'

Rose poked about in the tin to find a biscuit which wasn't broken. She put what she could find on a plate and looked at it thoughtfully. There was a lot more plate than biscuit.

'I'll have to go into the village and get stocked up again if the road's clear,' she said, and was surprised to find that the idea of actually going out and leaving the cottage seemed too much trouble.

Obviously Maggie didn't feel that way.

'Plough's been right through, the road's okay. I'll

come with you. I've not been over the doorstep for weeks. You get sick of being shouted at.'

'Who shouts at you?'

'They all do,' said Maggie flatly.

Rose thought of the life that Maggie must lead, at the beck and call of her mother and brothers all day long, and her irritation at the thought of taking her to the village in this mood faded.

'Mam's always on at me, I can never get owt right for her. And Paddy can be a devil when he wants. Even our Jack can get nasty. He's been in a right old temper for days, banging about the place and shouting. That's because of you.' She grinned at Rose and crunched her biscuit noisily.

'Why blame me?' said Rose.

'You sent him home with a flea in his ear, didn't you? Gave him his marching orders. You weren't nice to him at all. Not like you were to Paddy the other night.'

She watched Rose slyly from under the curtain of her dark hair.

Rose sighed. It was like living in a goldfish bowl, going round and round, soundlessly opening her mouth, surrounded by watching eyes. They missed nothing, yet at the same time there was no proper communication between any of them, no talking things through, not using actual words. They did it all by bush signals and a queer kind of blind intuition.

Maggie sat watching her over the edge of her mug.

'What d'you mean, like I was nice to Paddy?' said Rose suddenly. Maggie shrugged. 'You know.'

'No, I don't know, that's why I'm asking you,' said Rose, angry at the sly way Maggie was looking at her. 'I had a drink with Paddy, that's all, if it's any of your business.'

Maggie looked startled. 'That's not what he . . .' she began, then stopped and looked away.

'Not what he what? Not what he told you? You're a lovely family, aren't you, Maggie? If he told you we did anything else, then he's lying. And as for your other precious brother, he was very rude to me about Edward coming here, and I didn't like it. You can tell Jack that he can come and see me any time he wants to, just so long as he doesn't try to tell me who I can see and who I can't. It's my cottage, not his.'

Maggie banged down her mug on the table and stood up. 'Aye. And it was Jack cared for the old man, not you. You've never once asked, so I've said nowt, but it was Jack found your dad dead of a stroke on the floor here. It was Jack who had to tell the doctor and the vicar and everyone, seeing as we couldn't get hold of you anywhere. Jack had all the arranging to do, this end. And then every day he had to come up here and see to Lady and the cat, and keep an eye on the place.

'But he knows whose cottage it is all right. Even Paddy knows. It's all yours, Rose Thorpe. Any road, I'm off. I just came to say I'll not be up for a while. There's no point in decorating in this weather. Frost will spoil the paint . . .' She paused for breath.

'Maggie, I'm grateful for what you all did for my father, especially Jack. And I'm sorry that I've upset him so much. I didn't mean to. Will you tell him what I said – that he is welcome to come up here any time, just so long as he doesn't try to start running my life for me.'

'Aye, I will.' Maggie looked relieved and smiled at her. She hesitated at the door. 'Will you take me with you if you're going into the village, then?'

'Yes. Yes, of course. About two o'clock tomorrow, if that's all right with you?'

Maggie nodded. 'Rose?' she said, turning in the doorway.

'What?'

'Is that all you did with our Paddy, then, really? Just had a drink with him?'

'Bloody hell, Maggie, what d'you think I did with him?' snapped Rose.

Maggie went out quickly, shutting the door quietly behind her.

Rose sat and wondered what all that had been about. And she knew whose feet would come pad pad padding next up the track.

It was late in the evening before Jack arrived, then he stood hesitantly in the doorway.

'Can I come in, then?'

'If you promise not to throw any more mugs at the wall, then, yes, you can come in.'

'I'll not do that.' He nodded briefly, and Rose realized that this was all she was going to get in the way of an apology. The usual Bransdale effusiveness.

He shut the door behind him and pulled off his coat and boots. She took him into the parlour, where she had lit a fire that morning after Maggie had left. The table was scattered with photos – she had been sorting them out and doing up some to send off. She had tried to develop the first sheet film herself. It was like some magic ritual, the tray with the developer, the tray with the water, watching the first image come swimming up. She had been very anxious that there was nothing wrong with these photos, that they showed her nothing she hadn't seen for herself. Images of a black and white landscape, with no grain in them, no grey dullness anywhere, had come out of the tray. And no shadowed figures walking through them. The prints were a perfect clone of the negative, showing her a sculptured valley which her own little camera had been unable to cope with.

Rose was feeling good about all this, hugging the satisfaction of working again to herself like a secret. She had missed the feeling that there was in London of moving on, of each day advancing towards some unspoken, unworded goal. Here each day's tasks were sufficient for the day, and every morning you got up to do them all over again. It was enough for the Bransdales, this living in the middle of the days and letting them all flow over you with only the weather to change the pattern. Rose felt that she would sink without a trace here in a year.

Jack stood by the table, looking down at the pictures curiously. 'You've been busy, then,' he said. 'You found summat to photograph in the end.' He picked up a photo of his mother with the dead goose. 'I like this,' he said. 'This is grand, Mam ploating the goose.' He looked through the sheaf of scattered photos and picked out another one. 'Here, this is me,' he said, and stopped abruptly.

'What?' she said absent-mindedly, watching his face and lusting after it again.

'It's me,' he said, a queer flush coming over his high cheek-bones. He brought the photo over to show her. 'You never sent that to be developed like, with the others?'

It was a shot of his back, white in the firelight.

'Yes, I did. I bet the girls all loved it at the labs.'

He looked down shyly at it again. 'Am I as nice as that?'

'Nicer,' she said, laughing at him, and something of how she had felt when she took the photos came back to her. He took it to the table and put it down with the others.

'Rose?' he said hesitantly, looking at her.

She let him take her in his arms and kiss her. He was

hard against her as soon as he touched her, and she leant into him, thinking how easily men were roused and ready.

He had more assurance this time, pulling up her sweater, his mouth cold on her breasts. This was no ghostly lover, this was all solid Jack, and he needed her.

Rose wanted him. Wanted him to take her quickly, needing to feel his skin on hers. She pulled off the rest of her clothes and lay on the rug. The fire was warm at her back, stroking down her spine as Jack came to her. She was falling away under him, feeling herself split open, wanting him in her, and the old nursery rhyme came bubbling up to her, O Jack be nimble, Jack be quick, as she thought that there had been Edward first and then her night lover and now there was Jack, and all three of them had wanted Rose Thorpe, who had always thought of herself as frigid. Then, as Jack stroked the fair bush of hair between her open legs, she heard the voice growling in her ear.

'Rose, Rose, take him for me, Rose . . .'

It wasn't Jack's voice, Jack couldn't hear it. She knew whose voice it was.

'Ride him for me, Rose.'

Then down from the nape of her neck, down the length of her spine, his finger crawled and his nail scraped at her fire-shadowed skin. She felt herself begin to respond to his touch and his fingers scratched down to the base of her spine and began slowly to rub there, round and round and under his hand a cold flame began to burn in her. She was nothing now but this small patch of skin, and his nails bit deep into her and a great column of lust rose in her, fierce and wild as she had never known it.

She pushed at the startled Jack, straddled him and,

catching hold of his prick, lowered herself on him and rode him, howling, witch-rode him dry.

'My little bitch,' said the voice approvingly in her ear. 'Ride him for me, Rose.'

She jerked and threshed on the hook of Jack's prick, and he arched and groaned and came into her. She felt him begin to soften, to slide from her, and rage burned through her. She was only just beginning. She was a great hungry wet mouth to be filled. She was not yet done with him.

'Fuck me!' she screamed at him. 'Fuck me!'

And her nails raked in a bloody pattern down his chest and she bit at the white throat of him and still the voice whispered in her ear that she should ride him, ride him to the death.

Jack swore at the pain, trying to move her off him, but she would have none of it. She gripped him with her long legs and, bending to his prick, closed her white teeth round him. He yelped at the pain, swore at her and knocked her off him with a back-handed blow which sent her crashing up against the leg of the table. She lay shaking her head, whimpering in the silence. She came back into herself slowly, sick and shaking with horror at what she had done to Jack, and at what she had wanted to do to him.

He looked at the bloody seams down his chest with disbelief, scrambling into his clothes and watching her warily. He rubbed his neck where she had bitten him.

'I had a cat once,' he said unsteadily. 'Pretty little thing it was. Used to sit on my shoulders. It went queer one day, biting and scratching at me like a wild-cat. It never got a second chance to hurt me that bad again . . .'

She listened to him leaving and held her breath, waiting fearful in case she was not alone in the room. But there was nothing. She crawled across to her clothes and pulled them on shakily, hating the flesh she was covering. It had betrayed her again, it had hurt Jack.

She could never let Jack make love to her again. Inside her head there was a small, hard image of herself astride him, and this time in her hand there was a shining knife.

Ride him to the death, the voice had coaxed her.

And she knew that next time she would do it for her night rider.

*   *   *

The two small figures move slowly up the slope of Fairy Hill, and the Latimer boys stand at the foot of it, holding the heads of the three horses, and watch. The first figure crests the edge of the round hill and stands out blackly for a moment, then disappears from their sight, and the smaller one following it toils up and disappears after him.

Nathan sighs and looks around fearfully. Fairy Cross Plain at this hour of the morning, before the sun has chased away the shadows, is a strange place.

Next to him Joshua is still watching the top of the hill. 'What will he do with her?' he whispers.

Nathan dare not imagine. All he wishes is that he was safe back in his bed, and that none of this was real.

Tully stops to get back her breath. She had liked riding in front of Master Brett on the red mare, she liked his arm round her, but Master Nathan kept looking at her so strangely and his brother would not look at her at all. She catches her breath and watches the black figure striding ahead of her to the centre of the hill and thinks that mebbe Martha knew what she was talking about, after all.

The figure turns and beckons to her, and her feet trail slowly towards him over the cropped grass. The drink which Master Brett had given her before they set off, to warm her up he had said, smiling so nicely at her, it seems to have turned her legs all to water. She blinks. There is a faint, pink tinge showing in the sky behind him, and she stares at him fuzzily. It seems to her that the figure of Master Brett is growing and swelling until he is filling up the sky.

He is getting bigger and blacker and he is waiting for her, and Tully squeezes shut her eyes, for this is not her Master Brett she's looking at, not any more it's not. Tully wants this to stop now, she wants to turn and run all the way back down the hill to the Latimer lads and the waiting horses, but her legs will not go where she wants them to.

She is drifting across the grass to him and her eyes fly open, for not to be able to see him is somehow worse than seeing him. He is holding something black and sharp, and it draws her, it pulls her to the very centre of the hilltop. She can feel it pulling her, and it drags her sprawling to her knees before him and it holds her there. And all in a jumble Tully knows that this is where it ends for her: she will not see Martha again, or her family, and she has put on her good frock to come here for this.

The bone-handled knife points high in the still air. It stays there for a moment, then draws a black line down to the girl's meek white throat, where the red ribbon which he has given her is tied. The knife slides beneath the ribbon like a caress, and at the cold kiss of it on her skin Tully gives a high, hare's scream of fear which chokes off into silence. The sound of it carries faintly on the quiet air. Joshua and Nathan eye each other uneasily, and wait.

The knife blade begins to turn. The ribbon tightens round Tully's throat, cuts into the white flesh, bites deeper until she is wearing a necklace of bloody red beads.

She dies where she kneels, her hands clawing at her neck.

Nicholas Brett pulls out the stained blade and turns to face the waiting sun. He points the knife, and power crackles along it. Screaming out his strength, he brings up the Midsummer sun.

It is Midsummer on Fairy Hill and Nicholas Brett kneels and very gently, very softly, puts his mouth to the red seep at Tully's throat.

Chapter Fifteen

Rose woke suddenly from a dream of lust. She slid a hand down between her legs and cradled herself, trying to remember what she had been dreaming. But it had gone, only rags of it were left. She had been with . . . who? It had not been Edward, nor had it been Jack.

'You, then?' she asked the shadowed room. 'Was it you?'

She knew that he was not in the room. Not this time. It had been a true dream and nothing more – he had not come to her as she slept.

She sat up in bed and saw the moonlight moving across the blue-shadowed snow, and far off towards the distant ridge of hills she heard a faint, thin howling. She nodded wisely at the sound, as if it were something she had been expecting, and climbed out of the warm nest of her bed.

Like a sleep-walker she went to the long glimmering mirror of the squatting wardrobe and pulled her nightie over her head. It dropped crumpled to the floor and she stood and looked at herself. A dream-changed self. She was warm. Even in this cold room she was burning with heat. Her flesh had a strange pearly quality, so that it shimmered and gleamed in the moonlight. She ran her hands down her arms and shuddered with delight at the satin smoothness of them.

Her body was rounding out as she stood: her breasts filling and swelling, their tips swollen and dark against the pale skin, stiff as buds in the moonlight. She rubbed them gently and leant towards the mirror, where her eyes looked out at her, huge and glistening in her white face. She leant and kissed the full mouth, cold against the glass, and she wanted herself. Wanted to keep herself as she was now.

She went for her camera.

She fastened the flash on it, all the time listening for the howling to come again. Going across to the window, she stood in front of the black glass and squeezed the bulb, released the shutter. She took herself as a lover would take her, then put down the camera carefully on the window-seat, anxious not to spill herself.

Then the howling came again.

It was nearer now; it was coming from the wood on the valley side near the Bransdales' farm. It came echoing round the valley walls, reflecting from the frozen snow with a dreadful baying sound.

Rose stood at the window and waited.

Across the milky snow she saw her coming, a far-off dot against the white. She watched her leaping dark across the snow, her long ears flat against her back. There was a terrible desperation in the way that she ran, and the baying of the unseen dogs after her was rising and filling up the valley.

The hare came slipping through the garden gate and up the path, crouching on her haunches below the window where Rose stood to stare up at her with black, hollow eyes.

But no hare was this size, thought Rose, as she ran down the stairs, her bare feet padding across the floor, pattering to the door. No hare was as big as a dog, had such great eyes. The sound of the dogs was louder still, yelping and screaming shrilly in the night, but the hare was safe, the hare had come home. Rose swung open the door and the sound stopped, switched off into nothing. She looked for the hare, but that too was gone. There were no tracks breaking the snow on the path. Nothing. Only the winter wind creaking the trees, only the hungry moon. Rose slammed shut the door, shut the moonlight away from her bare skin and went slowly back up the stairs.

This photo which she has taken of herself. She will fasten it up on the wall next to her first self-portrait, the one she took after she had drunk so much whisky with Paddy. There is a great difference between the two photos. The first shows a woman in her early thirties, the flesh of her face already beginning to show a faint pattern of emerging lines which the coming years will deepen. The second shows a woman who has no age. She is luminous. Rose has never looked like this. She seems spellbound, her very flesh edible in its perfection. Her face looks as if it is behind a veil, so radiant yet so hidden does it seem. Only her eyes glisten and blaze in the whiteness of her face above a mouth swollen with desire.

And Rose looks from photo to photo, and glances across to the mirror and sees a third Rose, non-committal, understated. And she will take out a lipstick in a gold case and, walking to the wall, will print her name under these two self-portraits in sprawling scarlet letters. And in doing so she will reaffirm herself, lay claim to both these images.

'Maggie,' said Rose next day as she drove the car carefully over the rutted snow on the road to the village. 'Do hares come out at night?'

Maggie looked at her anxiously. 'Is it a riddle? I'm no good at riddles.'

'No. No, I just wondered if you'd ever seen a hare out in the moonlight. I don't know much about them.'

'They're witches' creatures, are hares. Did you think you saw one, like? Maybe you saw Auld Nan's hare.

They reckon she had one, like you have a cat. Why would a hare be out in the night, though?'

'I thought I heard some dogs after it.'

Maggie swung round to her, all eyes. 'What sort of dogs? Ordinary dogs?'

'What other sort is there?' said Rose, concentrating on the slippery road.

Maggie shrugged. 'They say,' she began, then stopped.

The car lurched and skidded on the clots of snow and Rose swore. Maggie giggled.

'They say what? Come on, Maggie, tell me what the stories are round the fire on winters' nights.'

'Big black dogs, they're not real. They're ghost dogs. Sign of a death.'

Rose thought about that one.

'Anything else I should know? Things that should make me stick my head under the bedclothes if I hear them?'

Maggie shrugged again and watched the drifts of snow piled by the roadside.

'There's the gabble-ratchetts,' she said in an off-hand voice.

'The what?' said Rose.

'The gabble-ratchetts. Flying over the house in the night, screaming and crying.'

'Oh, my God,' said Rose. 'They sound terrifying. But what are they, birds of some kind?'

'Mebbe geese. Mebbe not. But they're bad luck when you hear them.'

Rose drove on over the icy-crusted road and thought about gabble-ratchetts.

'You know,' said Maggie suddenly, 'the bairn won't come up to your cottage.'

'Frightened I'll eat him?'

'No. Don't be daft. This was before you even came here. I took him up to Haggabacks with me once just after your dad died when I went to feed Lady. He came into the goat house all right with me, but I couldn't get him to go into the cottage. He kept on saying that there was a man with a bad face at the bedroom window. Your bedroom window. He scared me as well, we both went home real quick. He'll still not come up to see you, though, he's not forgotten.'

Rose said nothing; she concentrated very hard on her driving.

'I can't help what the bairn sees,' said Maggie defensively. 'He's like me, he picks things up. And when I tried to tell Mam about it, she wouldn't listen. She went all queer and told me to shut up. It's a funny place, your cottage, isn't it?'

Rose thought that it didn't make her laugh.

'You never say much about your dad, do you, Rose?'

'Nothing to say. You don't say much about yours either.'

'Never knew him,' said Maggie cheerfully. 'Tractor turned over on him in the bottom field a couple of months before I was born. Killed him.'

So that left Mrs Bransdale with three small children to bring up on her own, thought Rose, and that couldn't have been easy. She opened her mouth to ask what had happened to Thomas's father, but closed it again. She didn't really want to know – and she didn't want to upset Maggie over what was none of her business.

Maggie took for ever in the Co-op. Rose had finished her shopping and was standing waiting at the check-out and still there was no sign of her. Rose went to see what she was doing, and found her hovering by the shelf with the shampoos on it. She moved off crossly when Rose came in sight and scowled at her, lurking at the end of the shelves and obviously waiting for Rose to go away. Rose couldn't imagine what she was buying that was so private, but she smiled and nodded and carried out her full box to the car.

She looked in through the window past the tins of pears and the packets of washing powder, but still there was no sign of Maggie. Rose gave up and strolled over to the post office. She stocked up on stamps and sent off a big packet of film to be developed, treated herself to a daily paper and a dozen bars of chocolate.

She sat in the car eating a Mars bar and looking at the paper. It could have been written about moon country for all the sense she could make of it. It worried her, that she could so easily drop out of what was happening out there in the real world. There'd been some snow in London; there was a picture of a street where it lay at least an inch thick. Rose snorted. They should see this lot. She flipped quickly through the pages and pushed the paper in her shoulder bag.

Oh, come on, Maggie, she thought. It will be dark before we get back if you don't hurry up. And I don't fancy going back into the cottage in the dark after your cheery little tales of men with bad faces peering out of my bedroom window.

Rose jumped as there was a sudden knocking on the window beside her. It was Maggie, beaming and nodding that she was ready to go. She climbed into the car with a bulging carrier bag, which she clutched tightly to herself. All the way home she chattered non-stop, and Rose must have made the appropriate responses, although she had very little idea afterwards of what she had said. She was uneasy away from the cottage; it was a long time since she had left it and she did not like to think of those empty rooms without her. It did not occur to her how far she had come to accept the situation, or why she knew that she could tell no one about it, not even Maggie.

At the farm gate Maggie scrambled out and hesitated, turned and bent down as if she wanted to ask Rose something, but the light was fading fast and Rose only glanced briefly at her, said goodbye and drove the car on to where she parked it, leaving Maggie standing watching.

Rose stood with her hand on the gate and looked up at the window, but it reflected blank and empty at her. She hurried inside with her box of groceries and went straight out again to feed Lady.

When everything was done and the fire was crackling brightly, Rose made herself a mug of coffee. She picked up the paper she had bought in the village and began to turn the pages again as she leant against the table. She stopped suddenly and turned back a page. She looked at the photo at the top of it. It showed a man standing in a clearing in a wood, holding something in his arms. It was a blurred, broken reproduction, difficult to make out. She peered more closely. What was he holding – a cat? Or maybe it was a hare. There was something horribly familiar about this man. She switched on the light to see better and caught her breath as she saw the thin line of scar down one cheek-bone. Her night rider had a scar, yes, but she had seen another image of him staring out at the camera like this . . . and then for the first time she remembered the set of photos she had found when she first came here, the photos behind the angel. She pulled the packet out of the drawer, riffling through the images to find the one she wanted. It was the same head, staring out at her with those dark eyes. The man standing above the figure of the woman sprawled face downwards on the bed, this was the same man staring up from her newspaper at her.

She began to read the piece in the paper impatiently, but there was no sense in it. It was the wrong piece. It had nothing to do with this dark man and whatever he was holding. It was an account of a girl and the pony she had bought, rescued from going as meat in the market. Nothing to do with a man and a hare. How could the paper have made such a mistake? And she had looked at it once already in the car when she was waiting for Maggie – why hadn't she seen it then?

Rose went over to the dresser and found a pair of scissors, then cut very carefully round the photo of the man in the dark coat and the white shirt, crumpling up the rest of the paper to light tomorrow's fire. She laid the photo on the table, and gathered up the photos of the woman to put back into their envelope. There was one missing: there should be another one of the woman holding up her breasts to the camera.

So she *had* shown foxy Paddy at least one of them that night. And he had taken it.

She shrugged and pushed the packet back into the drawer. It didn't seem that important to her now.

She picked up her cup of cold coffee and absent-mindedly began to drink, wrinkling up her nose at the taste and taking the mug to the sink to pour away the bitter dregs. As she stood there, she heard something – Jack's Land Rover coming up the track.

Rose didn't stop to think, she ran across the kitchen and turned the key in the lock, then crouched against the door. Last time Jack had come to her she had hurt him so badly. But it was not that, it was something else. It was not him she wanted; it was not him she had hurried back home for.

She held her breath and listened as the footsteps came up the path. Beside her head, the latch lifted and fell again.

The door rattled at her back.

'Rose? You in there?'

The snow crunched along the wall and the window darkened as he peered in. She shrank herself to nothing and, putting her whirling head down on to her knees, covered her face as if convinced that if she couldn't see him, he couldn't see her.

'Rose!' Jack shouted more loudly. 'It's me, open the door.'

Still she crouched there as he banged once more on the door, and then she heard his footsteps going away, heard the sound of the Land Rover starting up and rattling off down the track.

She crouched there until there was nothing more to hear, then got stiffly to her feet. She walked heavily over to the light switch and flicked it off and crossed over to the stairs. She put her foot on the bottom one and looked up. There was a faint glimmer of light at the top of the stairs, coming from her bedroom.

The pale bloom of light drew her unsteadily up the stairs, step by step in the silence. The bedroom door was a little way open; she put her hand flat against it and slowly pushed. There was a candle burning on the window-seat.

He was standing by it, his back to her, looking out into the dark. He was wearing the dark breeches and the white shirt of the photo; it glimmered in the shadows. His hair was tied at the nape of his bent neck, and something about the angle of his head, the slump of his broad shoulders, filled her with sadness.

He was her night rider; this time she was going to him.

She went further into the room, moving as slowly now as if she were under water, deep down below everything. He heard her coming and whirled round to her. She saw the scarred face and cried out at the hurt of it, but she was not afraid. Not this time. She walked to him with outstretched arms, putting her hands against his chest and staring up into his face. He caught hold of her fingers and pulled her to him.

'Rose,' he whispered. 'Rose, my love.'

This time his skin was warm on hers as he bent to kiss her; this time he smelt faintly of old dried herbs, of lavender and rosemary.

He reached out and extinguished the candle with his white fingers, and led her to the bed.

Long afterwards Rose saw how clever he had been that night.

He let her send Jack away on her own; he let her come to him of her own free will and showed her himself as a reward. And then he played her like a fish, so that she never felt the hook deep inside her mouth.

He came to her as a perfect, courtly gentleman. He treated her as a sweetmeat, nibbling and kissing at her skin as if she were marzipan, tasting her nipples like sweet cherries. That night there were no claws to him, and all he worked towards was her pleasure. He came into her as gently and as slowly as if she were a young virgin, and she came differently to him, easy in a long, cresting curve.

He lay with his arms round her, stroking her back, and he had her fast now. He had caught her with lust, but it was from this night that she began to love him. She fell asleep in his arms, waking alone next morning filled with the thought of him, amused to realize that she still did not know his name.

*   *   *

Martha hurries from fire to table, from dropping plates to letting flies get in at the ham, and all the time she worries as she flusters and bustles. Where can Tully have

209

got herself to? She should have been down here in t' kitchen hours ago, and when Martha has a minute to spare, just as soon as Master Gideon through there stops bawling for his meat, why then she will go up those stairs and heave the lazy hussy out of bed, so she will. Leaving Martha with all to do, and her legs today aching something wicked, and her back like knives in it. But she's allus been such a grand little worker has Tully, such a good lass and biddable. If that Master Brett has turned her head and given her ideas above herself, if she's going to start this sort of daft going-on, why then she can get herself back up t' lane to Ghyll Farm and stop there.

It is Midsummer Day, and the heat in the kitchen from the fire where the fat bacon sizzles is making Martha feel quite faint. The flies are buzzing in a black cloud over the bread on the table; the butter is running away with itself and the milk has clotted sour. Martha trips over a stool and kicks out at it with a wail.

Today it is going to be even hotter.

When Martha finally toils up the stairs to the top of the house, she is about past herself. It is hotter than ever up there. Mebbe, she thinks, when she stops half-way up to get back her breath, holding on to her sides and wheezing, mebbe t' lass is sick?

But when she climbs the last flight of stairs to the poky cupboard of a room which Tully is so proud to have all to herself, Martha sinks thankfully down on to the bed – then sees that Tully is not there at all.

Martha sits and listens to the flies buzzing and the sweat runs down her back, and she sees that Tully's good frock is gone from behind the door, and the one the lass works in is tossed all of a heap on the floor.

So where can she be at this hour, in her good frock?

Martha sits a while and wonders, then she heaves her heavy body back on to her reluctant legs and sets off back down the stairs. She stops outside Master Brett's room and listens, just on the off chance, but there is no sound from in there. She stretches out a hand to try the door, but pulls it back and shuffles on along the passage. She daren't go in there, not without an excuse she daren't.

Ben is sitting at the kitchen table with a face like a rain storm. She can smell his trousers from the doorway.

'Where's my ale and cheese, woman?' he grumbles. 'Ah've been up since all hours, and there's not so much as a crust of bread put ready for me.'

'I can't find Tully, Ben.' Martha sinks on to the nearest stool and wipes the sweat from her red face with her apron. Her aching legs are all of a tremble. 'Tully's gone off somewhere.'

'So has Master Brett,' says Ben sourly. 'Ah found t' red mare all saddled up at first light, and he came striding across t' yard shouting for her. Funny that, though, for she were all of a lather – as if she'd been out somewhere already. And come back home fast, from t' look on her. He went riding out of t' yard as if t' Devil himself were after him. But he nivver had our Tully with him.'

And Martha looks at Ben, and Ben looks at Martha, and a fat, striped bumble-bee comes buzzing and humming about the kitchen, filling up the uneasy silence.

It is Midsummer Day, and the blood-red sun now high on Fairy Hill shows up the patch of bruised grass on the very top of it. And where the grass lies flattened and broken, there is a dark, red stain seeping thickly into the turf, and, at the very edge of it, a scrap of scarlet ribbon.

Chapter Sixteen

MAGGIE came bursting in as Rose was eating a slice of toast.

'Our Jack came up here last night,' she announced belligerently, before she was even through the door. As if Rose didn't know.

'And you wouldn't let him come in.'

'I must have been in the bath then,' said Rose lightly. 'Was it important?'

'How do I know?' said Maggie. 'All I know is that he came home mad as anything again. Shouting and bawling.'

'Sit down and have a cup of tea,' said Rose, refusing to apologize for not opening her own door. She poured out the tea and leant across to where Maggie was standing by the table, and as she did so became aware of a strange smell hanging round her. A strong, chemical sort of smell.

Maggie sat down, pulling her coat tightly round herself and glowering. Rose made her a slice of toast, and she sat and watched her do it without a word. This heavy silence was most unlike her, and when Rose looked at her more closely she saw that Maggie looked very upset, and that she had been crying.

'Maggie? What's wrong? Was Jack very angry that I didn't hear him last night? Did he get nasty with you?'

Maggie snuffled and gulped her tea. She shook her head and tightened the thick headscarf she was wearing.

'What is it, then – is there something wrong with Thomas?'

Maggie sniffed and shook her head again.

Rose looked at her in exasperation. She was going to be here all morning playing guessing games at this rate.

'Maggie,' she said very briskly, 'tell me what's wrong, please.'

Maggie put down her mug obediently and wiped her nose with the back of her hand, then untied the scarf and dragged it off.

'There!' she wailed. 'Look at me. Just look at what's happened to me!'

'Oh, my God, Maggie, what did you do?' said Rose, trying desperately not to laugh.

'It's all our Pad's fault. I was cross with him over summat, and he started to have a go at me about you. About how nice you always look, how smart you are and how scruffy I am. Well, I know I don't have any nice clothes like you do, except of course those nice suit things you bought me. I've not had no money for clothes with the bairn's things costing so much. But now you've been paying me for helping you decorate and that, I've been able to put a bit of money away for myself. And our Pad kept going on about your hair being all styled and looking posh, and I looked at all the women in Stokesley and Whitby when you took me out, and none of them had long, lanky hair like mine. It was all cut real short like yours, or else all crinkly and pretty. So I thought if I could curl it like, it would look better . . .' She paused for breath.

'Home perm?' said Rose.

'Aye. I got it yesterday in the Co-op. I was going to ask you if you would give me a hand with it because I've never done one before, but you were in such a hurry last night. It was the instructions, they were that difficult, I didn't know how long you had to leave the stuff on for, and there was two lots of things you had to do and I thought there was only one packet you had to put on. I got all muddled up with it . . .' She trailed off with a sniff.

I knew that she wanted something but I wouldn't stop to listen, thought Rose sadly. And Jack shouted at her because I wouldn't open my door to him. And that nasty little Paddy wants sorting out. Painfully.

She sat and looked at Maggie's hair. It was a complete disaster area. The smell was even worse without the scarf. Maggie had left the stuff on for too long, and her dark hair was frizzled, sticking out at all angles at the sides. The back had curled in some places; in others, where Maggie had put too much hair in the curlers, it hung lank and sticky.

'Maggie, love,' said Rose gently, 'I don't think that I can do anything with it.'

Maggie wailed and snatched up the headscarf. She tied it roughly on again.

'I can't wear this for the rest of my life . . .'

'No, of course you can't, I haven't finished yet. This is what we'll do. I'll get ready and we'll go to Stokesley. The road should be all right if it's no worse than yesterday. We'll find a hairdresser that can fit us in and get your hair cut short. I'll pay for it, don't worry. I need to go in myself anyway, to get this burnt patch trimmed out.'

'Can I have my hair cut like yours?' Maggie's face lit up. 'It's a lot of bother for you, I thought you could just do summat with it yourself. I've never been to a hairdresser, Rose, you will tell me what to do, won't you?'

When Rose came downstairs again, ready to go, Maggie was leaning against the table looking at the photo which Rose had cut out of the newspaper.

'Right, then, Maggie, let's be off,' said Rose, picking up her car keys from the dresser and pulling on her coat.

'That's a grand little pony that girl rescued, isn't it?' said Maggie. 'What did you cut it out of the paper for – you thinking of getting a pony now?'

Rose glanced at her and walked round the table. She stood looking down at the photo. Maggie was right. There was nothing in the picture except a fair-haired girl and a little pony.

'Rose?' said Maggie anxiously. 'You've gone all white. You all right?'

'Yes. Yes, I'm fine,' said Rose with an effort. 'Nothing wrong with me at all. It must be the cold getting to me.'

She screwed up the cutting and threw it towards the fire, where it fell into the hearth.

'Come on,' she said. 'You don't need anything from the farm, do you? Just come as you are. Tell them where we've been when we get back. It's easier that way, then they can't say anything.'

Maggie looked at her, not convinced. 'I've got my wellies on.'

'So what? It'll give the girls in the hairdresser's something to talk about.'

Maggie grinned.

Which it did.

There Rose and Maggie sat, side by side in the chrome chairs, on the rose-pink carpet with the rose-pink basins in front of them, gazing at their dripping wet reflections. The girl in the cream trouser suit cutting Rose's newly shampooed hair leant forward, pressing her bolstered bosom against the back of Rose's neck.

She spoke to Rose's reflection in the mirror in front of them. 'What did you say you'd done to it again, love?'

'I burnt it on a candle,' said Rose loud and clear.

She saw the smirk in the mirror as the girl glanced sideways at the assistant next to her, who was snipping off long dead snakes of Maggie's hair.

Maggie looked like a skinned rabbit, thought Rose in dismay, and hoped that some of the way she looked was because of the expression of total panic on her face.

'Yours was a home perm that went wrong, was it?' cooed the girl behind Maggie, holding up a particularly frizzled bit and wincing.

'Yes,' quavered Maggie, obviously waiting to have her hands smacked.

'Oh, dear,' said the girl. 'Made a right mess of it, didn't you?'

'Aye,' said Maggie faintly, shuffling her muddy wellies on the pink carpet.

The two assistants looked at one another and raised delicately plucked eyebrows.

Rose had never in her entire life been so glad to be out of anywhere as out of there. She stood in the street and ran her fingers through her hair – what was left of it. It was shorter than usual, boy-cropped and draughty. But it wasn't *her* hair she was worrying about, it was Maggie's.

The girl had cut it very short at the back and sides, longer on the top of her head. It was a very sophisticated sort of cut. Perhaps it looked so odd on Maggie because it was above a tweed skirt and wellies. She had a beautifully shaped head now that you could see it, and the short hair made her look all eyes.

'Maggie? Do you like it? D'you like what they've done to your hair?'

Maggie glanced wide-eyed at her reflection in the shop window. 'Isn't it posh! Does it look all right, though, d'you think our Paddy will like it? He won't go mad at me, will he?'

'Of course Paddy will like it,' said Rose, puzzled. It was an odd thing for Maggie to say – why Paddy? It was

Mother Bransdale Rose would be worrying about. She could just imagine the well-turned phrases which would ring round the farmyard when a shorn-headed Maggie appeared.

'It's lovely,' she said, reassuring herself as well as Maggie.

'By!' said Maggie pulling her headscarf out of her pocket and tying it tightly round her head, completely flattening the entire style. 'Fancy it costing all that money just to have your hair cut, I didn't know it was as much as that.'

And thank you so much for paying, how very kind of you, Rose dear, added on Rose silently. Somebody had to say it, and it was beyond Maggie.

'Let's go and have a cup of tea,' she said, feeling suddenly exhausted. 'And while we're here I want to buy a cassette-player and some tapes. Is it any good me getting one with a radio as well? What's the reception like at Haggabacks?'

'Your dad had a radio. He used to listen to Radio Cleveland on it. Crackled a lot, but you could hear it.'

'Did he? I haven't found one anywhere.'

'Aye, well, he gave it to our Paddy,' said Maggie very quickly.

'Did he?' said Rose again. A likely story.

Maggie looked at her sideways and away.

'What sort of tapes will you buy?' she asked hastily.

'Any sort as long as they're noisy. It's so quiet on my own up there, especially with you not coming up. I miss having you to talk to.'

'Aye? Well, mebbe we could make a start again next week, now the weather's picking up a bit. If that's okay with you?'

'It's more than okay with me, it's the best news I've had for days. I'll get some more paint while we're here.

We'll do my bedroom next, then we can have the fire on to dry it.'

She thought of her night rider's hands on her breasts in the night. She wanted that room perfect for him to come to her again.

Much later, with the car full of tins of paint and fresh brushes, Rose dropped Maggie at the farm gate and watched her go off across the yard, pulling her headscarf tighter as she did so. If only one of the Bransdales would say something nice about her hair . . . but of course they wouldn't. They all found it easier to say something destructive.

Rose parked the car and looked in the post-box at the bottom of the track. There was a postcard in the box. She looked at the neat black writing and recognized it with some surprise as Edward's. She had pushed him so far to the back of her mind; she hadn't expected to hear from him again.

'Thinking of you,' he had written. 'When are you coming back to London?'

She didn't need him thinking of her. And how could he imagine that she would go back to London? The future was something she didn't want to think about, she was thinking only of the night to come.

She turned over the card to look at the picture.

It was the crystal skull in the Museum of Mankind. She had gone there with Edward one wet afternoon to see an exhibition of American Indian Art, but it had been this crystal skull which fascinated her. It was made of rock crystal and labelled as probably Aztec. She had looked at the shining purity of the lines of the skull and taken the image of that away with her at the end of the afternoon.

She stood holding the card and thinking now of time, of the skull beneath the skin, of the long-gone days when her lover had lived.

A door banged in the yard of the farm below her, and there was a long, wailing cry, eerie on the cold air, then silence. Rose listened, but there was nothing more to hear. It had sounded like Maggie. Someone hadn't liked Maggie's new hairstyle. Rose sighed and, pushing the card into her pocket, began to carry the paint up the track. And, as she did so, snow began to fall again unwillingly from the dark sky.

*　　*　　*

The group of mourners come slowly out of the gate at Ghyll Farm, blinking in the strong sun, and gather themselves to move out of the head of the valley. The four young men who bend and slip the white linen towels under the coffin to lift it are Tully's brothers. It lifts very easily, for there is little weight to it. Her father will walk behind the coffin, supporting his weeping wife.

By rights, since it is a girl's coffin, it should be girls who carry it, but the day is hot, and the road winding across Fairy Cross Plain is a long one. So the boys will carry the coffin until the last stretch of turf before the grey stone church, and the girls will take over then.

Tully's sisters, all three dressed in white, walk ahead of the coffin, and the two eldest hold between them a great garland of coloured ribbons, and in the centre of it a white glove. On the palm of this glove is pricked out the letter T and the number 15.

Tully Bransdale, age fifteen, dead of a fall.

And Martha, walking heavily behind Tully's mother and listening to her weep, is thinking about that fall.

That morning, she had missed Tully and searched high and low for her, with old Ben creaking and groaning alongside her, she wondered that there was no sign of Master Nathan or Master Joshua, not for long enough. But when they did get themselves downstairs, it had been those two who had found Tully, and t' pair on 'em that whey-faced and sick at it that it had surprised Martha. She'd thought Tully had been nowt to either of 'em, but mebbe not.

Poor little Tully lay all in a crumpled heap at t' foot of t' cellar steps, and t' story was that she must have slipped in t' bad light, going for a bottle of wine late in t' night for Master Brett and his companions. And there was her candlestick dropped, and t' candle rolled across t' dirty floor. Right enough.

But how come t' fine gentlemen drinking themselves daft had never missed t' bairn? Master Nathan had mumbled summat about t' three of them being ovver drunk to notice that she never came back with their wine.

So why would Tully have put on her good frock to go down to t' cellar? Martha puzzles on that. And her neck, t' little white neck on her. Broken in t' fall was what they told Martha.

And then rats at it, said Master Joshua, and was sick all ovver himself. Martha swallows hard and concentrates on the figures of John and Margaret ahead of her. Somewhere behind her the Latimer lads are following the coffin, but neither hide nor hair of Master Brett has been seen since Ben saw him clattering out of the yard in such a hurry.

Tully's father wonders too about that fall, and grieves.

Maybe he didn't ask enough questions when they came to tell him she was dead, but it had hurt too much. Master Gideon had sent along a fat purse of coins by his sons, a full year's wages for Tully and then a bit more. No need for him to have done that. And word too that in a bit, young Emily can go up to the Hall and take Tully's place. John grieves for Tully, she was his bonny little lass, but he has children in plenty. Feeding them all is his constant worry. With that money from Master Gideon he can buy in a new tup at the backend, and next year's crop of lambs will be a better one.

Little lass is dead, and all the questions – aye, and all t' answers too – will not bring her back to life again.

Martha's legs are aching already, but she will keep company with Tully all the way to the churchyard if it kills her, and it feels as if it will. Martha knows that she failed Tully. She didn't keep her safe enough; she didn't put enough fear into her over Master Brett.

Let the others say what prayers they want. Martha has only one prayer: that Master Nicholas Brett never comes nigh to Throstle Hall again.

For if Tully went arse over tip down t' cellar steps and snapped her neck like a flower stem, then how come there were grass stains on her legs when Martha washed t' body? There were other marks as well, marks which Martha doesn't wish to think about too closely. And bright red blood where there should have been none, not from a fall there shouldn't.

Tully Bransdale, age fifteen, died a maiden pure and spotless.

Did she, though, in the end? Not to Martha's thinking she didn't. And Martha was the one who washed the body. But she says nothing: let Tully's parents think that she was as unused as an unbroken egg. Free of any taint of sin, she goes to her grave a pure-white lamb of God.

The two biggest girls lift high their garland, move off steadily along the path and in high, clear voices begin to chant: 'The Lord is my Shepherd, I shall not want. He maketh me to lie down in green pastures: he leadeth me beside still waters . . .'

The men cast anxious glances back at Haggabacks on the skyline, but the door is closed and all is still up there. The men's deep voices rise to join the girls', and small and black against the sun the group of figures makes its way towards the great breast of Fairy Hill, where a knot of faded ribbon still lies on a patch of rusty grass. The figures crawl like insects between the grey stone walls, and the sound of their voices comes faintly on the sunlit air.

Chapter Seventeen

Rose slept alone that night.

Maggie did not come next morning as she had promised.

Rose stood by the window waiting for her, and wondered where she was. It wasn't like her not to keep her word. There had been that wail last night – that could only have been Maggie. Rose thought that perhaps she should go down to the farm, get some eggs as an excuse, and see what was happening. But since she was the one who had taken Maggie to have her hair cut, she would be no help. She would only add fuel to the fire.

She grew restless, waiting. The day was slipping away, wasting. She wanted to get on and make her bedroom a suitable place for a lover. She lit a fire in it and began to pull off the strips of old, damp wallpaper. It seemed to Rose that she had spent entire weeks of her life since she came North just pulling off old wallpaper. It made her hands feel dry and nasty, and the smell was disgusting.

By midday she had done all but one wall.

When she looked round the room, the walls she had stripped looked even worse than they had with paper on them, for now she could see the holes in the crumbling plaster. They showed the age of the cottage – like a face without make-up. Rose poked a finger crossly in the nearest hole and a shower of plaster fell on her feet. She swore and slammed the bedroom door behind her, then ran downstairs to make herself a sandwich.

Twelve o'clock and still there was no sign of Maggie. The cottage was very silent. Rose took her cassette-player with her when she went back upstairs. A tape of Kate Bush got her through the last wall.

She stuffed the heaps of old paper into sacks and hauled them down the stairs and into the garden. A few flakes of snow were drifting down through the apple trees and a watery sun splintered on the dark river.

Rose tipped out her sacks on to a narrow beach of pebbles on the curve of the water and put a match to the edge of a curling finger of paper. It lit unwillingly, then the flames took hold in a plume of thick, grey smoke, blotting out the cottage from her view so that she saw it wreathed in smoke. Then the smoke rose high like a declaration on the still air, and Rose felt uneasy that she was drawing so much attention to herself.

She tipped the last of the paper sacks on to the flames and wandered over to the water's edge. She scraped with the toe of her boot in the pebbles where the water lapped coldly at her feet. There was something white shining there. She bent and picked it up out of the water. It was a broken piece of pottery, creamy white with small, brown flowers. Rose stroked it with her thumb, wondering what it had been and whose kitchen it had been in before ending here. Now that she looked more closely there were other pieces of pottery, a shard of blue, a piece of bottle-green glass.

And as she bent and looked into the water, there was his face.

On a flat black rock a little way below the surface of the water, his face was looking at her. His dark hair was tied at the nape of his neck and he was wearing a white shirt, open at the neck. He was smiling at her, a twisted, mocking smile, and the scar running from his eye corner to the edge of his curving mouth was a line of thread stitched across the pale skin. The water moved and blurred across the face so that it seemed that the eyes shifted, and, horrified at seeing him there where it was not possible, she threw the fragments of pottery she was clutching, so that the water broke and splintered, covering his smile in a shower of glittering drops.

She straightened and backed stiffly until she was standing on the grass bank. She turned and looked fearfully behind her up the row of apple trees, but they were empty. Only the gently falling snow disturbed the thin twigs. And when she stared back at the rock again, the water flowed smoothly now over its flat, black emptiness.

But in the night, when the rising wind was pattering the snow against the window, the face came swimming up to Rose again. The man on the stone. The man with the hare in his arms. Her night rider.

She switched on the cassette-player next to the bed, and the sound of Kate Bush singing 'Running up that Hill' came flooding into the room. Rose lay and thought of Edward in this bed, and then of Jack, but it was neither of them that she wanted. She wanted her dark lover.

She groaned and touched herself gently between her legs. She reached into the wanting core, feeling the pink wetness close round her fingers like a sea-washed anemone. She began to stroke backwards and forwards across the flesh-fronds, feeling the salt water ebb and flow in her. And the voice of Kate Bush rose above the tide, singing clear and bell-like, and Rose was climbing up the long hill with her, climbing and tensing and wanting.

'Come to me,' she said harshly over the rising beat of sound.

'Come to me, I want you, want you . . .'

The tape now was curiously muted, fading softly back into a hissing noise which cleared and changed itself into her name.

Rose, Rose, it whispered to her, and he was there, forming quickly and urgently. She was ready for him, clutching at him and reaching for his prick. He was growling and nipping at her, thrusting himself in as she arched up to meet him in the thick dark. And he filled her to the flesh brim with his thrusting. This time it was different; it was not the soft dreaming coming that she had before with him, when she had lain down passive below the surface of him. This time she was clawing at his back, bucking under him and coming instantly with a violent frenzy. When he slid out from her, still she was not satisfied, still she wanted him to possess her.

He dragged her over to the edge of the bed and bent her over it, like a bad child waiting to be whipped, a white submissive waiting for him. He reached under and cupped her hanging breasts, pinching the hard nipples, rubbing at her cunt until she was yelping for him. Then he took her from behind like a dog, holding her tightly round the hips so that she could not move from the thrust of him.

And she did not want to move; this was what she had wanted, this losing of herself in him.

This time he made no sound, there were none of the sweet endearments of last time. All was in a terrible silence, it was a ritual taking of her in the dark. This was an ancient ceremony he was performing and he was no longer her courtly lover.

His weight on her grew less. His warmth drained from her and he slid from between her legs, dying back to leave her with a terrible sense of loss.

'Your name,' she moaned into the space he had left. 'Give me your name.'

She lay hollowed out across the bed, grieving for him, and as she lay the voice of Kate Bush rose up again out of the dark, strange and ghostly in the silence.

*

Maggie came up to the cottage late next morning, when Rose was washing down the paintwork in the bedroom, making herself be very busy, making the day be very ordinary – not thinking about what she had done, what she had been, in the night. She finished the door and carried her bucket and cloth over to the window-seat, where she stood looking out for a moment before she began on it. And there was Maggie, standing at the far side of the gate, hunched against the falling snow in a strange, held stillness.

Rose watched her, relieved to see her there, then wondered what she was doing, how long she had been standing like that. She thought that perhaps Maggie was watching something, a bird she'd seen, but there was something wrong with the way she was standing. She looked like a lost dog. Rose banged on the window and shouted, beckoning to her. Maggie looked up briefly and then down at her feet again.

Rose sighed. More trouble, from the look of it. Maggie was obviously not going to come inside on her own; she was going to stand outside in the falling snow until it covered her. Rose ran downstairs and across the kitchen, wrenching open the door.

Maggie was still standing exactly where she had been before, clutching the gate and staring down at her feet.

'Maggie!' called Rose down the path. 'Come on in out of the cold.'

Maggie gave no sign of having heard a word.

Rose called her name again, getting more anxious as Maggie lifted a blind white face and looked at her as if she'd never seen her before. Rose went sliding down the path, feeling the snow edge over her shoes. She tugged open the gate.

'Maggie, love, what's the matter? Why won't you come in?'

Maggie half turned from her, then with a desolate gesture she lifted her hands to her face and pulled off her scarf. She stood with the snow falling white on her bent head, then lifted her pale face and stared at Rose.

'Oh, Jesus Christ!' said Rose, feeling sick. 'Who the hell did that to you?'

Someone had taken a pair of scissors and slashed off Maggie's hair.

It had been cut short before, but now it was shorn. It stood in ravaged tufts, with patches of raw skin almost bare, and the falling snow melted and dripped down Maggie's face with her tears.

Rose put her arms round her and pulled her down the path and into the kitchen, horrified at how stiff Maggie was, rigid with shock. She led her over to the fire and, pushing her down into a chair, knelt beside her. She caught hold of Maggie's cold red hands.

'Who did it to you Maggie?' she said. 'Who did that to you?'

Maggie sighed and groaned, 'It was our Paddy,' and suddenly clung on to Rose as if she were drowning.

Rose sat and stared at the bent, savaged head. She was burning with rage so that she couldn't get a word out. Maggie had been so proud of her new hairstyle; she had so little of anything. Now even the little bit of self-confidence she had was gone from her. How could Paddy have done this to her? Rose was hurting for Maggie. She reached out and touched the back of her bare, defenceless neck – it was as vulnerable as a little boy's.

'I'm so sorry, Maggie,' she whispered, and two great tears rolled down her face.

Maggie sniffed and looked at Rose, startled. Rose in tears was alarming.

'It's not your fault,' she said shakily. 'It was nowt to do with you taking me to have it cut. You were only

228

helping me. I should have left my hair like it was, I should never have even tried to look as bonny as those other women. I might have known I'd never get it right . . .' she trailed off sadly.

Rose sat back on her heels and looked carefully at Maggie's head. Once you got over the violence which the cropped head showed and concentrated only on the shape of it, it was beautiful. The curve of it and the small ears reminded Rose of somebody. It came to her with a memory of a phrase and a strange, flicking action of the hands. Sinead O'Connor. That was who Maggie looked like.

'You're exactly like her!' exclaimed Rose in delight.

'Like who?' said Maggie flatly.

'Sinead O'Connor – "Nothing compares . . ." You know who I mean, you must have seen her on TV. She's beautiful . . .'

'Oh, come off it, Rose! How can I look like her? I'm bloody bald, that's what I am. Ugly and bald . . .' Her tears were streaming again now.

'It's a bit rough today, yes. But when it grows more evenly in a week or two you are going to look fantastic. Will you let me just trim off the tufty bits? Trust me to do that for you?'

Maggie hesitated, then sighed. 'Aye, do whatever you want. You can't make me look any worse than I do now.'

Rose jumped up for the scissors. She began to cut off the wisps of hair standing up at all angles.

'I'm like a plucked chicken!' burst out Maggie again. 'He said if I was going to have my hair cut off and make a fool out of myself then he'd do the job properly. Make a right lad of me. Now I'm worse than when the perm went wrong. I wish I'd left it alone. I should never have had it cut without asking him first. I wish I was dead, I do!' She knocked Rose's hand away and began to rock backwards and forwards in her chair.

'You don't have to ask anybody's permission to have your own hair cut. Paddy had no right to touch your hair, never mind hack it all off like this. Ah, don't, Maggie, don't . . .' She put her arms round Maggie and cuddled her until the sobbing died away.

'Your hair will grow again. Lots of women in London have it cut just as short as yours. Mine's not that much longer. And you've got such lovely thick hair, in a few days it will look quite different when it starts to grow again. You know what you look like now? Like a very expensive London model. Shit, Maggie, I could never afford to take photos of you in London!'

Maggie peered at her through red eyes and saw that she meant it.

'Honest?' she whispered.

'Honest,' said Rose. 'Sit there and get warm while I make us some coffee. I'll put some brandy in, we could both do with it.'

She went to put on the kettle.

When she came out of the pantry with the milk, Maggie was sitting hunched and shivering, staring at something on the mantelpiece. She turned a white face to Rose as she came across with the mugs of coffee. She looked more upset than ever.

'What is it?' began Rose in dismay, then saw where Maggie was looking. The card of the crystal skull which Edward had sent her was propped against the clock on the ledge.

'It's a death,' said Maggie in a hoarse voice. 'Get rid of it.'

Rose took one look at her face and dropped the card into the heart of the fire.

'That better?' she said gently. 'It was only a picture.

Here, drink up your coffee.' She put the mug between Maggie's shaking hands.

Rose stood and watched Maggie.

There had to be some way of giving her back to herself, of putting right the damage that Paddy had done. The more she looked at it, the more she admired the curve of the bent head and the great, dark eyes.

'Maggie,' she said hesitantly. 'Would you let me take some photos of you?'

'Like *this*? All ugly?'

'I keep telling you that you're not – I wouldn't waste film on you if you were. I told you – I couldn't afford to pay for you in London. I will pay you, though, of course . . .'

'You will not, then.' Maggie drained the last of her coffee. 'That was lovely. I'm warm again now. If you think you would like to take some photos of me, then I would be pleased to do it for you.'

She had a queer kind of dignity about her, which moved Rose. She hugged her and looked round the kitchen. 'Not here. It's much warmer up in my bedroom. The fire's been on up there these last few days. Right, then, come along Ms Bransdale, we have work to do.'

Ms Bransdale followed Rose happily up the stairs, still not quite convinced but willing to trust Rose.

Rose sat her on the window-seat. Silhouetted against the small squares of glass in the old window, she would be underlit with the bedside light. Did she need the flash? wondered Rose. She looked at Maggie through the eye of the camera. She was wearing a thick cardigan with a collar, and a crumpled shirt under it.

'Maggie,' said Rose briskly. 'Take off your cardigan and shirt, the collars are in the way.'

Maggie pulled them off in the obedient way of

somebody used to doing what they were told. She hesitated and looked down at her vest and bra.

'These as well?'

Rose nodded.

Maggie sat placidly with her hands in her lap watching Rose.

Rose knew that the photos were good as soon as she began – there was a malleable quality about Maggie, a total lack of self-consciousness, so that she gave herself easily to Rose. There was a strong dichotomy between the boy's head and the full breasts with their dark nipples, between the raw head and the soft, velvet skin.

Rose shot off one film and went for another.

'There's a name here,' said Maggie, as Rose crossed to the chest of drawers.

'What?' said Rose vaguely.

'Here, in the glass on your window. There's a name scratched in it. Nicholas Brett, it says. Who's he, then?'

Rose wasn't listening properly, her head was full of shadows and angles.

'Never heard of him. Turn your head more to look out of the window, Maggie . . .'

She went on taking photos, immersed in what she was doing, until Maggie shivered and said plaintively, 'Are you nearly done? I'm getting frozen sitting here . . .' She crossed her arms and hugged herself. Rose took one last shot of her like that and sighed.

'Lovely,' she said. 'Come over to the fire and get warm. Sorry, I get so carried away once I start working. Oh, Maggie, Maggie, these are going to be so good, I can feel it. You are a lovely model.'

She scooped up Maggie's clothes from the floor and took them over to the fire. Maggie followed her stiffly, stretching and rubbing at her cold arms, and knelt down in front of the flames.

Rose stood looking down at her bent head and the long line of her narrow back above the old tweed skirt. She had identified so closely with Maggie, building up such empathy with her as she sat there so patiently. She had done it with Jack as well, so that she had wanted all of him, not just his frozen image. She reached out a hand and stroked the bent curve of Maggie's neck, and as Maggie looked up, startled, she knelt beside her and kissed her.

It felt strange, a woman's mouth against hers this way. It was warm and giving under Rose's. She stroked down the narrow back and lightly drew a line round each of the round breasts, touching the nipples curiously. This was how *she* felt then, and bending her head Rose took one of them into her mouth. She sucked the stiff little peak as delicately as a ripe grape, and Maggie groaned in surprise and pleasure.

'That's nice,' she breathed softly, stroking Rose's head and leaning towards her. She needed comforting. Her skin was warm now in the firelight, and her arms were round Rose's neck. And still Rose's tongue flicked at the swollen nipple, and this was how women's skin tasted. She wanted more of Maggie, she wanted to explore all of her like a new country, and she reached for the fastener on Maggie's skirt.

And then she heard him laughing.

'Crop-heads!' the voice inside her head said delightedly. 'High-breasted boys pleasuring one another. Oh, my Rose, my Rose!'

He was standing behind her, a dark presence which cast no shadow, which made no sound that Maggie could hear. He was watching her where she knelt, with her mouth on Maggie's breast.

How could she have been so stupid, how could she have risked bringing him to Maggie in the same charged atmosphere that had brought him to Jack?

'Ride him to the death!' he had said, and she thought of her nails tearing at Jack's bare skin.

She jerked back from Maggie as if the pale skin were burning her wet mouth and said urgently, 'Get your clothes on, Maggie!' Maggie looked round at the door, startled.

'Someone coming?' she whispered, snatching up her clothes and beginning to pull them on. At least she hadn't picked up his presence — she had been concentrating too hard on what Rose's mouth was doing to her. She looked at Rose now with big, sad eyes, like a child whose toy has been snatched from her. But she was safe: he was fading back into the shadows.

'Did I do it wrong? I've never done it before with a woman, I don't know what women do to each other . . .'

'No, of course you didn't do anything wrong! I thought I heard someone coming, but it must have been the wind. You're lovely, Maggie, it was nothing to do with you. I've never done it with a woman either, so we're both the same. It's just not . . . not a very good idea. You put your clothes back on, love.'

She bent and kissed Maggie's upturned face and, turning her back on her, began to clear away camera and films, ignoring Maggie as she grieved away to herself behind her. When she was sure Maggie was dressed and only then, Rose took a deep breath, forcing herself back to normality, and turned to face her.

'It's because I'm ugly,' said Maggie.

'It's because you're not. I shouldn't have done that to you, I'm sorry, Maggie. I just got a bit carried away, seeing how good these photos of you are going to be. They are, you know, the contrast between your dark eyes and your skin, and you've such black hair . . .'

Rose was scrabbling about to get them back to where they had been before. She couldn't believe she'd done that now, she was turning into some kind of sex-maniac. First Jack, and then Paddy had tried, and now poor Maggie. There was only Mrs Bransdale left . . .

'Is your mother's hair the same colour as yours? Like Jack's?'

'Aye,' said Maggie listlessly. 'Leastways, it was. It's grey now.'

'What colour is Thomas's hair? I've never seen him without his balaclava on — is he dark like you as well?'

'No, his hair's red like his dad's,' said Maggie. 'Same colour as Paddy, is the bairn's.'

The words went falling and bouncing round the room. What did she mean, that Thomas's hair was red like his dad's, like Paddy's?

Thomas is Paddy's son.

That's why it's always Paddy she worries about, that's why *he* was the one who cut off her hair.

That's why. Oh, Maggie love, Maggie.

Maggie roused herself with a jerk from gazing into the fire and swung heavily round to Rose, white-faced.

'Oh, God,' she croaked. 'Oh, God, I didn't mean to say that, Paddy will kill me if he finds out . . .'

Rose cut in on her loudly. 'Paddy is his uncle. Not surprising if Thomas has the same colour hair as his uncle.'

'Aye. Aye, that's what I meant. Same as his uncle.'

Now it was her turn to search desperately for something to get them both back to normal. She stared frantically round the room and scrambled to her feet.

'You've been getting on in here, haven't you? All the walls stripped. And now you're doing the paintwork. Tell you what, I'll go and mix some Polyfilla and make a start filling in some of these holes in the walls, there's some right bad bits in here, isn't there? Then we can get

235

going with the paint – what colour was it you got for in
here?'

'It's a pink,' said Rose unsteadily. 'I thought it would
warm up the room a bit, a nice warm pink.'

'Rose-pink,' said Maggie with a high-pitched effort at
a giggle, and went scurrying off thankfully downstairs to
mix her Polyfilla.

Rose's hands stilled where she had made herself busy
with her camera bag at the chest of drawers. She leant
her aching head on her arms and groaned. First Maggie's
savaged head, then her own stupid attempt to make love
to her and now this last horror which made everything
else seem like nothing.

Thomas was Paddy's son.

Paddy and Maggie, and the bairn was a fox-cub.

Father and son with that burning red hair.

No wonder that it was always Paddy's name at every
sentence end, and his reaction Maggie was so worried
about all the time. This was the hold he had over her,
then. But what could it be like, thought Rose, sickened at
the idea, what could your life be like if your own brother
was fucking you? Thomas was five now, so it must have
been going on for at least as long as that. And still was,
presumably, since Paddy claimed such dominance over
Maggie.

Maggie liked to be touched, liked being loved. Rose
had found that out for herself. She responded to affection
like somebody starving for it. But to have to go to your
own brother for it . . . better celibate. Better to burn.

Who knew? Did Mrs Bransdale know? Or Jack? Rose
didn't want Jack to know, didn't want him to be smeared
with any of this. Surely he would have stopped it anyway
if he knew about it? Some day Thomas would have to
know – but how could you ever tell a child that?

Incest. It had always been only another word for

Rose, never something that meant anything to her. She saw the years going by empty and bitter for Maggie, and her secret as a knot tying the family closer and closer together in the years to come, binding them all to Ghyll Farm.

Into Rose's head there came unwillingly an image of Maggie as she had just seen her, with her head bent and her breasts bare, and instead of Rose's fair head against that pale skin, there was the blazing red head of Maggie's brother.

*　　*　　*

'But did it work?' whispers Joshua, leaning across the table to his brother.

Nathan shrugs and fills up their mugs again from the flask of ale and gulps thirstily at it. All he wants to do is to get drunk as fast as possible and blot out that burying.

'How should I know if it worked?'

'Aye, but her throat. He'd done what he said. Drunk her blood. Virgin's blood, to give him life everlasting . . .' His voice dies away in the dusk of the room.

Nathan shudders. He'd seen Tully's throat fair enough, where she lay sprawled at the foot of the cellar steps. He was never going to forget seeing it. He gulps again at the ale.

'How did he know what it was supposed to do, anyhow?'

'He read it in an auld book. He tried it afore, with that London lot of his, with that Elizabeth woman. But she wasn't a virgin.'

'And she knifed him,' says Nathan.

'Aye. She knifed him. Right enough.'

They thought of the scar on Nicholas Brett's face.

'It had to be a *lass* whose blood he drank?' says Joshua suddenly.

237

'Tully was a lass, wasn't she? What are thoo on about?'

'If it wasn't just a lass it works with, and if it didn't work for him again this time, then seems to me we'd best keep a close watch on him next time he turns up here again . . . if he turns up.'

Joshua trails off into silence, dreading the very thought of seeing Master Brett sitting opposite him in the candle-light ever again. For little Tully is dead, and somehow her being dead was a very terrible thing which Joshua desperately wishes he'd had no part of.

'Think on,' says Nathan. 'Not just a lass but a virgin. We're no virgins. We're no use to him.'

'Oh, aye,' sighs Joshua thankfully. 'No use at all.'

'Besides,' says Nathan with a hiccup, 'he'll not dare show his face again here. He'll not come back.'

He fills his mug and takes a great mouthful, and there again is the picture of Tully lying at the bottom of those steps, with her red throat smiling up at him, and sour and bitter the sickness spews out of him across the table as he realizes that she is never going to leave him now.

Chapter Eighteen

Rose couldn't sleep that night for thinking of Maggie. She knelt in the window-seat, looking down the valley at the farm where Paddy's light still burned, very late, and she hated him.

As she knelt there Maggie's words came back to her, something about a name in the glass. She would look in the morning, she thought, when it was light.

The pale morning sun showed her his name, bitten deep into the old glass. She had asked him to tell her who he was, and he had etched it here for her. She ran her fingers over the ornate script. 'Nicholas Brett,' she said. 'Nicholas Brett.'

Now she had a name to fit on him. A little more of him to hold inside herself.

It took Rose and Maggie three days to finish the bedroom –three days in which Rose was very careful to keep the atmosphere well away from what it had been the day she took the photos of Maggie. Neither of them so much as mentioned the bairn – or Paddy either. Rose was grateful for the cassette-player, though by the time Maggie had played Kate Bush a dozen times she was beginning to wonder.

But Maggie seemed quite cheerful with her, which was a relief. She seemed to have buried whatever Rose had touched in her along with her secret. And as the days passed and her hair began to grow again as a dark cap on her carved head, she got her self-confidence back. Rose caught her several times standing admiring herself in the mirror.

Jack had not been up to Haggabacks again. Rose knew that it was only a matter of time until he came, and she didn't know how she was going to handle it. She couldn't keep locking the door against him. She liked Jack, but she had nothing to give to him. And Edward was fading out of her thoughts like an old photograph, going brown round the edges.

All that she wanted was the incubus.

She had his name now when he came so easily to her out of the dark. And every time that he came to her she was pushing back the boundaries and the taboos of her own body, so that in the daylight hours her desire was shocking to herself.

During the day, splashing on pink paint and listening to Maggie happily singing along to Kate Bush, Rose couldn't connect the person that she was then with the person of the night. She knew who she was during the day – she was Rose Thorpe, photographer, telling a wide-eyed Maggie about some of the places she'd been to and some of the things she'd photographed. Maggie had little to offer in return, for she had been nowhere and done nothing. But in one way she had travelled further than Rose, for she had gone beyond the boundaries of family taboo. Of that they didn't talk. Maggie was a good listener. She defined Rose to herself during these hours together.

But in the hours of dark, then Rose was somebody quite different, and a stranger to herself. She knew how to bring him to her now, each night she drew him in with the ceremony of her own fingers on herself. She cried his name into the dark as he wrenched orgasms out of her with his nails and his tongue, making her come until she thought that she would dissolve into nothing beneath him. In the mornings she saw how her arms were bruised with the marks of his fingers and her back had a furrowed trail where his nails had brought her into flame. In the daylight hours she knew that she shouldn't want this, and knew that women are not to be used through pain, but in the dark – ah, then there was nothing he could do to her that she did not like, that she did not crave more of. He was edging her closer and closer to something, something which frightened her in the day. Not at night, when he was in her like a drug, and the sweet flowering of pain she felt with him was an obsession.

Incubus: an evil spirit supposed to descend on sleeping persons; a nightmare; a person or thing that oppresses like a nightmare.

He was her nightmare and her dreams, and now she had a terrible disregard for her own safety. And after her nights with him, she woke in the early light filled with a strange, wild energy, prowling the empty rooms of the cottage, knowing that she should not let in a force which was taking her over so completely, yet already longing for the night when he would come again to her.

Her incubus.

Maggie didn't stay long on the third day, for there was nothing more to do in the bedroom. She came in laughing, waving something at Rose.

'I've brought your post up. It's better than the last postcard you got.'

It was from Isabel: a postcard from Provence, where she was having a few days' holiday. She propped the sunlit scene against the clock. Isabel, she thought vaguely. She really must write to her again . . .

Maggie went home to get the bairn's tea ready, and Rose stood in the middle of the bedroom. Pink walls, white woodwork, a freshly scrubbed floor. The fire crackled softly to itself, and Rose wondered why it all depressed her so much.

For what did she do now?

She'd had enough of home-making. She had a room for her lover and that was all she wanted. It was time to get back to her own work. She went downstairs to her little darkroom and closed the door firmly behind her with a sigh of content. This was where she should be, and this was what she should be doing.

Rose began with the photos of Maggie, knowing that they were going to be good. As she watched them come one by one out of the tray, she couldn't believe that she'd taken them. For the first time, she had found a voice of her own and found what she wanted to say.

Maggie was beautiful in all of them – the difficult part was showing them to her, for they were erotic, breathing a heavy, dark sexuality. They showed all the feelings Rose had backed away from afterwards. It was all there in the photos, in the curve of a breast, in the line of the mouth. Rose couldn't hand them over casually to Maggie, yet she must see them, they were so good. It was not just the photos, professional as they were. It was Maggie herself. As Rose had known, she was a natural model, giving herself to the camera as easily as talking.

Rose felt sad, looking at them, knowing how wasted Maggie was. She would most likely never leave the farm and this narrow valley. But the photos of her would hang on a gallery wall in London – Rose was set on that.

She left them to dry and went on to the first group of plates she had taken with her father's camera, some landscapes of the valley and the cottage in snow. Something had smeared across the first one. It looked like blood, but of course it couldn't be, she had made a mistake with the chemicals somewhere. The second one she developed was of her cottage, and that was very good, sharp and crisp, but on the snowy path outside the door there was a hare sitting.

How could she have taken a photo of a hare when there hadn't been one there? It was happening again, this horror of images appearing on her prints. She had thought that the camera couldn't lie to her, that it was a fixed idea of truth, but even that was changing.

She watched the next print come floating up to her in a frozen stillness. This was the last one she was doing. If there was something wrong with this one, she was finished. She stared at the image which lay just below the surface of the liquid in the tray in despair, for it was a place she knew she had never seen before.

It was a hilltop somewhere, and there was a man pointing something black at the sun. And the rays of the sun had been full on the camera, so that there was a glittering sunburst almost obscuring him. Only his arm showed clearly, and the thing he was holding – a knife, was it?

But she knew the man.

She knew him by Braille, by the feel of his skin in the dark, by the mapping of his body with her tongue.

There was something pale on the grass beside him; a bundle of rags. No. No, it could not be just rags, for surely that was a hand at the man's feet.

The fingers twitched as she looked.

Rose swayed and clutched the edge of the table. The photo dropped from her cold fingers. She bent stiffly and picked it up by one corner, turned it face-up and stood staring at its white emptiness. It was blank and empty. She ripped it across and threw it from her, then she was out of the room and the door slammed behind her. She leaned against it, feeling ill and sick.

She could not have seen those fingers move.

It was the strong chemicals making her eyes water.

But she hadn't even taken a photograph of that place. She was taking photos of things which weren't there, out of a dead past . . . and what had her night lover to do with a knife and a bundle of rags?

The loud knocking on the door terrified her, pinning her where she stood. Now she was being threatened by something outside the cottage as well as by something in the darkroom behind her. She couldn't breathe; her heart was racing as if it would shake her apart. She was fastened here against this door and there was nowhere for her to go.

The knocking came again, louder than ever, then a voice.

'You there, Rose? It's me, it's Jack.'

It was Jack, it was only Jack, and she was running for the door, not thinking of what had happened, the last time that she had let him in, not thinking of her nails raking down his chest.

She opened the door.

'Jack?' she said, fighting to keep her voice steady, wanting to throw herself against him and clutch him. 'It's good to see you. Come in, come in.'

She caught hold of his arm and tugged at him. He pushed his hands in his pockets and stood looking down at her in surprise.

'Are you sure? You weren't as friendly last time I came . . .'

'Last time was a mistake. It all went wrong. Forget it, Jack.' She tugged at him again.

'I'm not used to your London ways, I know that, if that's what it was. But something wasn't right that last time, that wasn't you, Rose . . . I just need to know you're okay.'

She shook her head and closed the door behind him.

'I'm really pleased to see you.' She reached up and

kissed his cold cheek and he gave her a big grin and hugged her. He strolled across to the fire, where he sat and stretched out his long legs.

'By, it's nice to be back here,' he said.

She came and sat at his feet on the hearth. She felt safe with him as close as possible to her. For a moment she wished that she could tell him everything, but how could she begin?

He put his elbows on his knees and looked carefully at her.

'You look peaky, lass. I keep thinking maybe summat's wrong up here for you. You'd tell me, wouldn't you? If you needed help? You're not sick or owt?'

The concern in his voice nearly did for her. She reached out and caught hold of his rough hand. 'I'm okay. I've just got a bad sick headache now, but that's my own fault. I've been doing up some photos in the darkroom and the chemicals have got to me.'

'If that's all it is. Have you fed Lady yet?'

She shook her head.

'I'll do it for you. I've brought another load of wood up for you. I'll bring a sack in here. Then you get yourself off up to bed, lass. Sleep it off.'

It was the last place he should be sending her, she thought sadly.

He pulled her to her feet and kissed her forehead, and she walked to the door with him and stood looking out into the garden. The air didn't seem as cold tonight. There was less of a bite to it and it smelled of earth.

'I'll make you a coffee when you've finished. Thanks, Jack.'

He stayed a long, peaceful hour with her, talking of his sheep, of the farm, and something in her was healed by him being there.

'You love this valley, don't you?' she said, as he stood up to go.

'Aye. But there's other places. Sometimes I'd like to start up again on my own with better land. But there's Mam and Maggie . . .'

And Thomas and Paddy, she finished off in her head. All sitting on your strong back.

'Time you were in bed,' he said, looking at her pale face. 'I'll pop in again to see you, if that's okay?'

He hugged her to him gently as she nodded and went towards the door, stopping to pull an envelope out of his pocket.

'Nearly forgot. I checked your box on my way up. You've not been down for your post today. Night, lass.'

'Goodnight, Jack,' she called after him. She locked the door, relieved that he had gone away so happily.

She went over to the fire, holding the envelope and thinking that Maggie had brought up the post when she came – it had been the postcard from Isabel. So how had Jack brought this up now? Turning over the letter, she saw what Jack had obviously not noticed. The envelope had no stamp on it. The note inside was written on cheap, lined paper, printed in thick capitals. It said:

YOU SHOULD HAVE STAYED IN LONDON
WHORE YOU DON'T BELONG HERE
TAKING WHATS NOT YOURS

Rose's legs began to shake and she sat down quickly.

She had never understood why people got so upset over anonymous letters, why they didn't just throw them away. Now she knew why. It made her feel threatened, sick at the idea that some unknown person was watching her, spying on her. And sitting in judgement. It was like sitting up in the bath and seeing a pair of men's feet sticking out from under the curtains.

But what did it mean, that she was taking what wasn't hers?

She made herself read the note again, dropped it on to the table and went to pour herself a large brandy. There was so much threatening her inside the cottage, it was taking her all her time to cope with that. Threats coming at her from the outside world as well made her feel too vulnerable. She gulped down the brandy.

Why should anyone go to the trouble of sending her rubbish like this? It wasn't so much why that mattered, though – it was who. For of course now that she thought about it, it wasn't an anonymous note at all. It could have been signed Bransdale in large capitals with no surprise at all to her. Only the initial was missing.

Which of the Bransdales? Not Jack, it couldn't be him, not when he was the one who gave it to her so innocently. She didn't want it to be Jack.

Not Maggie, she was too open – what she felt, she would come straight out with, writing it down wasn't her way of doing things.

Not Thomas, for he was still at the 'Here is Janet, here is John' stage – 'whore' wouldn't be in his vocabulary yet.

Which left Mrs Bransdale and Paddy.

One of them making mischief.

Rose strode over to the table, crumpled up the note and threw it into the fire. If she kept the thing, she was going to go on reading it over and over, and it was going to hurt her every time. Hate written down is a very powerful thing.

She felt so sick, and her head was red needles digging into her, and all she wanted to do was to curl up in bed and dream that she was somewhere else. Anywhere else, she didn't care where. Just so long as it was out of this

God-forsaken valley. What did she think she was doing here anyway?

But in the darkest hour of the night, when her lover came again to her, she knew why she was still here. She clung to him as if she would never let him go. He made love to her as slowly as if they had endless time before them, building her up out of her own need for him and tipping her over the narrow edge into pain and back. She flung back her head and howled her triumph as she came, and he bit the white skin at her throat as he entered her.

He lay beside her and nothing existed for her but him.

She reached out and touched the thick seam of scar on his face.

'Who did that to you?' she asked him lazily. 'How did you get such a scar, Nicholas Brett?'

She felt him begin to laugh. Then out of the dark he answered her in a rusty, creaking rasp. 'By a lady,' he said. 'How else, my dear love?'

Then he was gone.

* * *

A week after the death of Tully, her thirteen-year-old sister Emily comes to Throstle Hall to take her place. A week is not long to grieve, but life must go on, and the family need the money. As well for Emily to take Tully's place as a stranger from the village, and Martha has had enough of being on her own in the kitchen, trying to be in two places at once and needing two pairs of hands. So now Emily sleeps in the little room at the top of the house and hangs her good frock behind the door.

Six months after the death of Tully, Emily is standing by Martha's elbow in the kitchen of Throstle Hall, watching her very carefully. It is a grey November day, with a few flakes of snow falling, but the kitchen is warm, for Martha had Emily light a fire in the oven first thing. Martha is making gingerbread. The room is full of the smell of it, and Emily wrinkles her nose and sniffs happily. She has watched all the things which Martha has put in the big bowl, and she lists them again now in her head. Fine flour and treacle, lard and cinnamon, allspice and ground ginger and a pinch of salt. Emily wants to run a big house like Martha does one day, she wants a white apron tied round herself and a bunch of keys hanging from the belt like Martha has.

'How long shall we bake it?' she asks Martha with a frown.

Martha shrugs and looks sideways approvingly at her. She never misses a chance of picking up something, doesn't this one.

'Nigh on three hours. Thereabouts. Less nor that and it's sticky. More and it's black. Make it often enough, thoo'll learn when it's done. It must cook slow and gentle . . .'

There is a scraping sound from the far side of the room, and Martha stops in mid-sentence to stare at the outer door. The latch is slowly lifting, and the door is moving inwards. Emily stares from Martha's face to the door, where a thin fall of snowflakes is drifting through the widening crack.

A man is standing there, staring at them, and all the breath in Martha's body seems to leave her, so that she clings to the edge of the table.

She had hoped never to set eyes on this scarred face again; had hoped that it was finished with. Nowt is ever done with, she thinks bleakly. He is back here and there is Emily now. She stares at him like a risen ghost, sick with horror at what she sees will come again with his return. He did for Tully, she is sure of that, but his white fingers are not going to hurt young Emily.

She straightens up with an effort and, catching Emily by the shoulder, pushes her behind her own wide body. As if that will save her.

Master Brett stiffens at the sight of Emily, then latches the door behind him.

'A cold day for a journey, Martha,' he says cheerfully, rubbing his hands.

Martha can't get a word out. All she can think of is that first time he came, when Tully knelt by t' fire, yelping out at sight of a stranger.

'And who is this, then?' he says gently, and suddenly his voice is sweet as honey, and his eyes are all a-glisten. Emily is as plump and round as a small partridge; she is a riper version of Tully, with skin like cream and breasts swelling like young apples. Emily peers at him from behind Martha's broad back, looking for his horns.

She knows who this is.

This is Master Nicholas Brett that Martha will never talk about. She tightens up her mouth and shakes her head when Emily asks about him. But Emily needs no warning: she was one of t' lasses who walked in front of Tully's coffin in t' summer. Emily misses nowt. Summat that she heard Martha say that day to her father had made her prick up her ears and listen. Summat about Tully's death, about her fall not being what it seemed. Emily has not forgotten Martha's face when she said it.

Martha gropes about blindly in front of her and, picking up her spoon, begins to mix the gingerbread again, stirring it now as if it were something she hated. Her hands are trembling but she takes a deep breath and forces out the words. 'This is Emily Bransdale,' she grates. 'Tully's younger sister. Thoo'll remember Tully, Master Nicholas?' Her voice breaks and she bends and beats the mixture more viciously than ever.

'Indeed I do,' says Master Brett as smooth as silk. 'Where is she now?'

There is a long silence in the kitchen, then from a great distance Martha drags up the words.

'She's in t' churchyard these six months.'

The silence is terrible now, so that Emily wants to scream and crack it open.

'And how did she die, so very young?'

'She died of a fall,' whispers Martha, and can say no more.

Master Brett sighs and nods gravely.

'And this is Emily, then, is it?' He crosses to stand beside the table. 'You have beautiful dark hair, little Emily. Buy yourself a ribbon for it.' He pulls a gold coin from his pocket and drops it on to the table. It spins and rolls towards Emily and she reaches out from behind Martha for it, but Martha is quicker. Her red hand sends it curving through the air off the table into a dark corner of the room, where it is out of sight in the dust and mud.

Emily yelps and retreats again.

Master Brett shrugs and leans towards Martha, whose face is as white as milk now. He reaches out a hand and she flinches, but he slides a long finger into her gingerbread mix, licks it clean with a red tongue and nods at her.

'A little more of your ginger, I fancy,' he says and, smiling at Emily, strides across the kitchen to the inner door, shouting his arrival to the Latimers.

Martha stirs and heaves a sigh and Emily slides cautiously from behind her.

'I only wanted t' money to take home to Mam,' she begins.

'Emily,' says Martha with difficulty. 'Take nowt from that black devil, not gifts, not kisses, not sweet words.'

251

'He frightens me,' says Emily. 'Don't fret, Martha. I want nowt to do with him. I'd sooner have a piece of gingerbread.'

Peering shakily at her, Martha sees that she means it. She sinks down on to a stool before her legs give way under her and wipes her face with her apron.

She failed Tully. She let her die, like that woman in London died. But Emily isn't going to be t' next one, she'll see to that. She knows where she's going for help this time. Feared as she is, nowt is going to harm Emily. Martha knows where to get protection for her.

Chapter Nineteen

THE BINDING

'HE's back, then?' Nan bends and throws a handful of twigs on the fire, and the leaping flame shows the pale face of Martha and the milky green of Emily holding tight to her skirts, as close as she can get.

'And up to his auld tricks.' Martha's legs are shaking with the long walk. Nan nods to her to sit down opposite and she sinks down gratefully on to the battered stool. Emily shuffles to stand as near to her as possible. She looks from the bent figure of Nan to the cat at one side of the hearth and the hare at the other and fear keeps her frozen and still.

'Up to his auld tricks?'

'Aye. In t' house only a day and he . . .' She falters, looks up at Emily and spits it out all in a rush. 'He lifted up t' lass's skirt and fingered her.'

Emily shivers and feels sick, putting out a hand blindly, thinking of how afraid she had been when he had caught her on the dark passage, pushing her against the wall, and of how his fingers between her legs had hurt her. She whimpers and Martha catches hold of her hand and pats it.

'Shush now, Nan will help us.'

'Aye. It's time he was stopped. He's carrying death again with him. Did you bring what I asked?'

Martha lets go of Emily's hand and fumbles in the deep valley of her breasts, bringing out a scrap of old rag which she hands across to Nan.

'It's only his hair combings from his bed-chamber, I couldn't get . . . t' other . . .' She glances at Emily and away again.

'This will do.' Nan unwraps the rag carefully and stares down at the long twist of black hairs. 'His seed or his blood would have been better, but we'll make this do.' She looks up at Martha. 'Once it's done, we can't undo it, you know that? Once it's begun, however it ends, there's no stopping it.'

'Make him pay for Tully,' whispers Martha. 'Make him suffer. His death for hers . . .'

Nan nods slowly and, leaning forward on her stool, from a gap between two stones of the old wall, she pulls something wrapped in a yellowed cloth. She unfolds the cloth and picks up the small, sharp knife it holds. She lifts it high, holding it so that the firelight glints and runs red down it, then lays it down between her feet. The cloth now holds only a round ball of beeswax. She picks this up and holds it between her fingers for a moment, muttering to herself. It is a long time since she made this ceremony. She begins to roll the ball between her gnarled fingers, moulding the softening wax.

Emily drops to her knees beside Martha and leans forward to see better in the smoky light. There is a round head coming, and now a long body. There are two arms and two long legs and between them something long and thick rearing up which makes Emily's eyes widen further than ever.

Nan holds the little poppet up for them to see, then, taking the twist of long, black hair, she begins to wind it round and round the waxy body of the little man, pressing it in firmly with her thumbs.

Then the knife glints again as she presses the sharp point into the chest and turns it. There is a hollow hole now where the poppet's heart should be. Nan turns the knife and slashes it across the ball of her thumb, and blood runs after it in a long, red line. Martha gasps and bites her lip and Emily watches in horror as Nan squeezes the cut thumb until the blood drips, and each drop of blood falls into the gaping chest. Then she rubs her bloodied thumb across and around and over his body until he is all smeared with her blood. The knife drops to the floor again, and Nan holds up the bloody poppet and names him. 'Nicholas Brett,' she says harshly. 'Nicholas Brett!' The cat fluffs his fur and hisses and the hare twitches her long ears at the rising sound.

'These are my orders.
Touch not nor come no more nigh to Emily Bransdale again.
Ride from this valley for t' last time and die out of it.
But after death, thy spirit shall come back.
Then shall Nicholas Brett be held and bound in this place until a woman, long years to come, shall end it all by fire and flame.
I hold and bind thee to Haggabacks. There shall be no rest for thy black spirit for t' evil done to Tully Bransdale.
This is t' binding.'

Nan leans across and takes hold of Martha's shaking hands, pressing the poppet into them.
'Name him. Give him your orders.'
Martha looks at the bloodied little figure between her fingers and remembers Tully, white and still in death.
'Nicholas Brett,' she says unsteadily.

'I give thee my orders.
Touch not nor come nigh Emily Bransdale again.
Ride from t' valley and come here no more.
But I bind thee and hold thee after death here in this

place until a woman in times to come sets thee free
with fire and flame.
And may thoo suffer horribly until that time . . .
These are my orders.'

Nan nods, satisfied, and, taking the waxen man from
Martha's hands, pushes it into Emily's small white ones.

Emily looks at the blood smearing her fingers and
sinks lower to the floor. She looks helplessly from Nan to
Martha, but their faces are cold as stone. Tully was her
sister, and Emily must play her part or ruin all.

'Nicholas Brett,' she breathes on the shadowed air.

'I give thee my orders . . .'

Her voice fades and breaks but she stammers out the
words somehow.

'Touch not nor come nigh me again.
Ride away out of this valley and nivver come back until
after death . . . and I bind thee . . . and I bind thee
here until a woman sets thee free with fire and
flame . . .
And may thoo suffer as my dead sister Tully suffered at
thy hands.'

Tears of distress are running down her face. She thrusts
the figure back at Nan.

Nan takes it from her and nods. Picking up a twig
from the hearth, she pushes it into the red glow until it
crackles into flame. She holds the burning tip above the
poppet's face, then, with a bitter twist of her mouth, she
pushes the red end down into the place his mouth would
be. The beeswax melts and runs with a terrible burning
sizzle, and a strand of black hair crackles with flame and
dies into ash. Nan throws the twig into the heart of the
fire.

Then she wraps the wax man with his bloody chest

and his ruined face inside the yellowed cloth, as tenderly as any baby. She reaches deep into the cleft in the wall again and pulls out a bundle of knotted cords: seven cords with seven knots in each. She binds these round and round the little figure.

She sits and holds it, rocking backwards and forwards, crooning to it.

'Hoof and horn, hoof and horn
He that dies shall be reborn.
Corn and grain, corn and grain
He who falls shall rise again.
Seed and grass, seed and grass
He never from this place shall pass
Flower and tree, flower and tree
Till flame at last will set him free.'

The words die back into silence. The hair on the back of Emily's neck prickles, and there is something here in this place with them, some power she can almost see. Martha is nearly senseless with fright, but it is done. They have trapped him here, the three of them, and he will suffer as Tully did.

Nan pushes the wrapped figure deep inside the wall. It will stay there until it is needed. She is very tired; she has taken a great risk, for using blood in that way is always a risk. You never knew what you might bring in by mistake. Somewhere she thinks that there will be a price to be paid for what they have just done. It may take more blood to bind him than a slit thumb, but they have done their best, even the little lass. Nan sits with her hands upturned on her lap and smiles wearily at Martha and Emily. 'So mote it be,' she whispers softly, and then it is all done.

Chapter Twenty

ONE morning a few days later, Rose came inside from feeding Lady and there was something on the hearthrug, in front of the fire.

Something brown that moved.

Rose thought at first, catching a glimpse of it as she took off her coat by the door, that it was Tibby sitting there. Then she realized it was the wrong colour for the cat. And the wrong shape.

It was a rat sitting there in front of her fire, and she backed up against the door in horror. For she hated rats, she was terrified of them. She had been appalled when Maggie casually informed her that she would get rats up from the beck in bad weather, looking for food.

'Rats?' said Rose in a fading voice, thinking of the night that she had spent with Lady.

Maggie looked surprised at her concern. 'Oh, aye. Right nuisance they are an' all. Tibby will help keep them down, that's why your dad had her. We had a great big rat last year, it got in the . . .'

'Don't tell me!' moaned Rose. 'I don't want to know . . .'

Ever since that little conversation, Rose had been wary of opening the food sacks for Lady; she had peered round the door and made loud 'here-I-am' noises before she would put so much as a foot inside one of the outbuildings.

But one sitting here on the hearth.

What was she going to do with it? How was she supposed to get rid of it? And she had to do it herself, so the longer she stood shivering there the worse it became. She shuffled along the wall until she could see it again, wondering what she could use to hit it. The poker would do, but it was on the hearth at the other side of the thing. It jumped into sight again and she let out a howl of fright before she took in what it was.

It wasn't a rat at all, it was a hare.

She was so relieved that it didn't occur to her that finding a hare sitting in her kitchen was even stranger than finding a rat. It sat up on its haunches now, and looked at her with liquid dark eyes, then it calmly began to wash its long ears, using its licked front paws as a face cloth. She stood and watched it, hardly daring to breathe in case she frightened it.

It was as big as the hare in her dream that night, the one she had seen coming home across the snow. And this one looked completely at home too, as settled there as Tibby ever did.

She'd left the door ajar when she went out to feed Lady, left it open for Tibby, who hadn't come in for her breakfast yet. The bowl was still untouched when Rose glanced across at it. It was just as well that Tibby hadn't been here, though looking at the size of the hare she doubted if one small cat would worry it much.

Rose wanted to photograph it – where had she left the camera? It was on the dresser at the far side of the room. She edged her way slowly and carefully across to it and picked it up, but the hare went on grooming as if Rose wasn't there at all. She stood hesitating with the camera in her hands, watching the hare before she made up her mind to risk the flash on it.

Mad as a March Hare. But it was . . . February, she realized in surprise. Only just, but still into February. And where do hares go in the winter-time? Not into cottage kitchens, surely. Though they had done so once if the tales they told were true, when they had been familiars to the Wise Women. Moon creatures. Magical. Leaping out of the dark death of the year to bring renewal, and a new beginning. Was it *that* the hare had brought her, a sign that it was time that she was moving on? She'd had enough of playing at house, but she couldn't go anywhere, how could she when she was bound and fastened so tightly here?

Rose Thorpe, she told herself crossly. You are quite mad, never mind the hare. Looking for signs and symbols with a great fat hare sitting on the hearth in front of you. Maggie would have had it jugged by this time.

She lifted the camera, and the white flare of the flash filled the kitchen, turning the hare to silver for a moment. It sat on its haunches, nose twitching, and watched her.

This worried Rose, that it wasn't in the least afraid.

She felt she ought to offer it something, as if it had come to her for a reason. What did hares eat, she wondered? There was nothing she could feed it. She looked out of the window and remembered Lady eating the Brussels sprouts in the garden. She thought there were still a few left on the snow-rimmed plants. Reaching behind her again, she picked up a bowl. Keeping her eyes on the motionless hare, she backed slowly across the kitchen and out of the door, closing it carefully behind her. She hurried down the path, crouched and began to pull off the last few sprouts.

Maggie was holding a letter in her hand when she came to the gate.

'Here, whatever are you doing now?' she said, leaning on it to watch Rose. 'You're never going to eat those manky things?'

'They're not for me. They're for the hare.'

Maggie looked blank. 'What are you on about? What hare?'

'There's a hare in the kitchen. I left the door open when I went to feed Lady, so that the cat could get in. It must have come in from the garden . . .'

'Don't be daft!' grinned Maggie. 'Hares don't come into houses.'

'This one did. You come and see.'

Maggie slammed the gate behind her as if convinced Rose was quite mad this time. She followed her up the path to the door of the cottage, still muttering that hares don't go visiting in folks' kitchens.

Carrying the bowl of sprouts, Rose opened the door and pushed Maggie through in front of her. She closed it quickly behind them.

'There,' she whispered. 'See?'

There was a long pause.

'Where?' said Maggie. 'There's nowt here that I can see. Must have been a mouse you saw.'

'I can tell the difference between a mouse and a hare. It was a bit bigger than a mouse,' said Rose coldly. She crouched and peered under the table and the sink. Not a whisker.

'Well, a rat, then. I told you you'd have trouble with rats coming up off the beck.'

'It was a hare,' said Rose through gritted teeth. 'H.A.R.E. Hare. It was not a bloody rat.'

'Well, where is it now, then?'

Rose marched across to the fire and hurled in the frosted Brussels sprouts.

'I don't know where it is now, but there was one, I tell you.'

Maggie looked at her quickly. Rose was wrong but best humour her. 'It must have nipped out again back into the garden when you came out to get its breakfast,' she said hastily.

Rose said nothing.

'Mebbe the hunt disturbed it. They're often up in that wood after foxes. They could have sent it up the valley.'

Rose turned and looked gratefully at her. 'Yes. Yes,' she said. 'It must have been like that.'

But she'd closed the door behind her when she went out into the garden, and there was no other way it could have got out of the kitchen. And even if she had taken its photograph, that proved nothing, for she did not trust her camera now to tell her the truth.

'Here, there's a letter for you. It's a queer one, though, it's got no stamp on it.'

Just what she needed. Another little poison-pen letter.

'Aren't you going to open it, then?' asked Maggie in surprise, as Rose shoved it behind the clock.

'I'll save it until later. I can't stand too much excitement all at once.'

Maggie looked at her vaguely. 'No. We don't want too much excitement all at once. What are we going to do today?'

'Not a lot,' said Rose. 'We've about finished the bathroom. There's just the door to paint, then that's that.'

'Aye, but what about the rest of it – the spare bedroom and the staircase and that?'

'Sod the spare bedroom and the staircase and that.'

'Right,' said Maggie quickly, thinking it was best to agree with everything that Rose said when she was in such a funny mood.

'Weather's picking up a bit, isn't it?' she said brightly. 'Snow's nearly all gone. We've got two snowdrops out at the farm. "February Fair Maids", Mam calls them.'

'Does she? What a lovely old name for them.' Rose was surprised. She would have expected Mrs Bransdale to go out and stomp on them. Stomp, stomp, stomp.

Rose was downstairs at the kitchen sink when she heard Maggie scream. She dropped the brushes she was cleaning in the soapy water and ran up to where Maggie stood transfixed in front of the newly painted bathroom door. White paint was dripping on to the carpet from the brush she was waveringly pointing at the door.

'Maggie, what have you done? Have you hurt yourself?' Rose rescued the brush.

Maggie opened and shut her mouth several times and got nothing out, then pointed shakily at the door.

In the middle of the panel she had been painting was the clear imprint of a spread hand. Rose thought that Maggie had done it herself – what was she making such a fuss for? The paint was still wet, she could just brush it out.

'It doesn't matter, just slap some white paint on it . . .'

'It's not my hand that did it,' croaked Maggie, and held out her shaking hands palm upwards. Clean as a whistle.

'I never did it, Rose. I was painting this bit here, underneath, and it just sort of grew in the wet paint. It's not my hand, that isn't . . .'

'ROSE, ROSE, ROSE,' roared the voice, the sound picking up and gathering from every room in the house, until everywhere echoed and rang with the mocking sound.

'ROSE, ROSE, ROSE,' it came again, swooping and roaring along the narrow passage at them. Maggie's mouth was a round red circle of terror as she began to scream again.

Rose grabbed her arm and pulled her along like a dead weight, her feet dragging and her hands clawing at Rose. They stood in the kitchen as the sound died away, and Maggie clutched at Rose and would not let her go. It died away into silence and there was nothing.

'Maggie?' said Rose tentatively.

Maggie's eyes focused and she stared at Rose, then tried to pull her over to the door with her.

'I'm off,' she whispered, dragging her coat off the hook. 'I'm not stopping here. That's summat bad, is that. Rose, love, you come on down to the farm with me, don't you stop here with that . . .'

'It's all right, it won't hurt you,' began Rose.

'It said your name. It's got your name. You mustn't stop here, come on!'

'It won't hurt you,' said Rose again.

Maggie looked at her. 'How do you know that? You mean it's been here before? You let me come up here with that in the cottage and you never said owt, you never told me. You never said a word, and I thought you were my friend . . .'

She was crying now, desperate to be gone but not wanting to leave Rose.

'Maggie, I couldn't tell you, how could I?'

'The bairn was right all along. That man he saw with a bad face up in your bedroom. I should have listened to him.'

She clawed open the door and burst out on to the path and down to the gate.

'A witch's hare sitting in your kitchen. Handprints that come on their own. And that horrible voice saying your name.' Her voice was rising to a screech. 'I told you. I told you that you should never have opened that cupboard and let the bad out. You should have kept it fastened up like I wanted you to.' She slammed the gate behind her and stood, white-faced. 'You're daft stopping here with it.' She turned to leave and hesitated. 'Please, Rose, please come with me?'

And what if he comes with me, Maggie, what then?

Rose shook her head.

'Then that's the last you'll see of me. I'll not come up here again.'

And she was off, running down the track, stones flying under her feet as if all the hounds in hell were after her.

Rose stood and watched her go. She would not have had that happen if she could have prevented it, but she hadn't even been there with Maggie when he did it. He hadn't needed her to be there to make his mark for Maggie. He was growing stronger.

No more Maggie.

Things were beginning to come together for an ending, and she didn't want to think what that ending must be.

Rose went wearily back into the silent cottage and the unopened envelope accused her from the mantelpiece. She'd forgotten that. She considered burning it without bothering to open it, but then it would only nag at her about what it might have said. Read it, then burn it, she told herself sternly. It was on the same cheap paper, printed in black capitals.

LONDON TART YOU STUCK UP BITCH
SO YOU THINK YOUR DAD HAD JUST ONE
   KID
WELL THINK AGAIN

Rose had difficulty taking this in, it seemed to slide off as if it had nothing to do with her, she was so upset at Maggie leaving like that. She hadn't thought of her father for days. His life here was irrelevant to her – she'd no right to question the way he lived when her own life was in such total confusion. She and her mother had been better out of this place. She saw that now.

She shook her head, crumpled the paper and dropped it into the fire. She stood and listened.

Nothing moved.

Not even the cat was here to keep her company.

The days stretched before her with not even Maggie to talk to now. It was already February and the days were sliding by. She'd made no move to put Haggabacks on the market, for how could she? She'd made no move to leave either. It was not Haggabacks which held her here.

It was her night rider who held her fast.

She couldn't leave him; he was in her blood; he was part of her. She should have known that sooner or later he would make his presence known to Maggie, for he came so easily to her now. And he was growing stronger.

She wondered what sort of a tale poor Maggie would tell them at the farm. Whatever it was, nobody was going to believe her.

But someone did.

Maggie was in tears, incoherent with distress, when she burst into the kitchen. Only her mother was there, looking up from the table, startled.

'Whatever's up with you?'

Maggie wailed and sobbed until her mother caught her by the shoulders and shook her hard.

'Give up,' she said. 'Else I'll make you.'

Maggie gulped and shuddered into silence.

'What's happened, then?' said Mrs Bransdale. 'Summat up at Haggabacks was it scared you?'

Maggie stared at her mother. 'How did you know?' she whispered.

'It's always been there. It's worse when there's a woman in the place, it's women pull it in. Did you see him?'

Maggie yelped and shook her head violently.

'What then?'

'Heard him. I heard him say Rose's name. He put his

266

hand on the door I was painting. Then he called her name.'

'Aye,' said Mrs Bransdale. 'She would be the one to bring him in. I thought she would.'

'How do you know?' breathed Maggie.

'Never you mind. I know. Here, sit down by the fire and I'll make you a cup of tea. You're as white as a . . .'

'As a ghost,' said Maggie hoarsely.

'Aye,' said her mother and grinned.

Maggie sat down by the fire before her legs went altogether. She watched her mother make the tea, and tried to remember the last time she had been so nice to her. And just when she thought she'd be in trouble for making up tales.

'Mam,' she began. 'Will Rose . . .'

'Will Rose what?'

'Will she be all right up there with . . .'

Mrs Bransdale handed her the steaming mug and said nothing.

*　　*　　*

Nicholas Brett stays for four days at Throstle Hall, and by the morning of the fourth day, he is very weary of listening to talk of sheep. Gideon has put a new, young tup in with his ewes, and cares for nothing but to check up on how many ewes the creature has covered. He gets up from the table and goes out into the kitchen now, shouting for Ben. Nicholas wonders why he does not sleep out on the moor with his flock, then he could keep an even closer eye on events.

Nicholas thinks about whether to follow Gideon out into the kitchen and find Emily, but there is something strange about the girl this last couple of days. She is as slippery as an eel, always sliding away round corners when he reaches for her. That's when she leaves Martha, and most of the time it seems that Martha has her tied to her apron strings. They are both looking at him so strangely as well, as if he had a forked tail. He isn't going to get his tail anywhere near Emily, he can see that. It was since that afternoon the pair of them had disappeared up the valley, walking to Ghyll Farm to visit Emily's sick mother, so the tale was. But Nicholas wonders now if they had walked a little further up the valley than that.

He looks at his two companions, lolling at the table, one at each side of him, still half besotted with last night's drinking. They appear to have nothing to say to Nicholas or to each other. The day stretches before them: exactly the same as yesterday, exactly same as tomorrow.

Nicholas pushes back his chair and goes to the window, peering out of the small panes at the valley. There is a cold sun shining, and the early frost has melted. He sighs and stretches. Another day cooped up with these two suddenly seems impossible, and somewhere anger is gathering in him.

He turns to the Latimers and lightly, casually, suggests that they fill in an hour or two by going hunting.

'Hunt? Hunt what? Never known thoo to yearn for a fox's brush afore.'

'Neither do I now, Joshua. It's bigger game than that I'm after.'

'Bigger nor a fox?' Joshua sniggers. 'What, an auld ewe, then, is it? Going after one of Bransdale's flock are we?'

Nicholas thinks sourly that the only one of Bransdale's flock he would like to hunt is clattering dishes in the kitchen.

'Bigger even than that,' he says.

'Venison?' says Nathan in surprise. 'Thoo'll have to climb t' crag for deer. Spoil these boots, will that . . .'

'Not deer. I know where there is a fine hare to give us a run.'

'Hares aren't bigger nor sheep,' says Joshua frowning. 'Not bigger nor deer neither.'

The two look at Nicholas, puzzled, and he looks back and thinks that if this were not such a convenient bolt-hole in which to hide a long way from London when it became too dangerous for him to stay, then he would never see either of these two clodhoppers again.

'A two-legged hare,' he says patiently.

The room is very still now, and Joshua and Nathan look at each other and grin, for now they know which hare they are to go hunting.

'Aye, but we'll need a silver bullet for this one,' gloats Joshua, and their chairs crash to the floor behind them in their haste to be out of the room and saddle up the horses.

Nicholas follows slowly.

Martha is standing in the middle of the kitchen, arms akimbo, roaring after the two boys through the door they have left open. Emily is kneeling by the hearth, laughing at Martha's red, angry face. She turns away her head at the sight of Nicholas. He ignores her, but he has noticed, and his anger hardens a little more. He strolls out after the Latimers, and turns in the doorway to give Martha a courteous bow, then latches the door softly behind him.

Martha subsides like a pig's bladder with the air let out, and fears what devilry he is up to now.

Chapter Twenty-one

Rose bent and picked up the untouched saucer of cat food. The call of the wild must have got to Tibby. That or the tom-cat at the farm. There her food still lay, congealing and smelling fishier than ever. It was not like the little cat to miss her meals. Rose wrinkled her nose at the smell and scraped the dish into her rubbish bag. She washed it clean and put it down, empty, on the floor. She would put fresh food in it when Tibby turned up again.

She stood drying her hands and the day stretched ahead of her, waiting to be filled. The light was too poor to do any outside photos. There was a thin, grey mist drifting down from the moor top. Whatever photos she took she would have to develop. And whatever she was developing, it was neither her present nor her past.

The only thing which didn't seem to change were the portraits she did inside – Maggie and Jack. But she had lost both her models, and that left only herself. On the bedroom wall now there were fastened six self-portraits. Maggie had been cross when she saw them, especially at Rose's name scrawled under them in red lipstick.

'Whatever did you go and do that for, messing up the wall when we've only just finished painting it? And they're not nice pictures either, you've made yourself look right ugly, all chopped up into bits. Writing "Rose" under them like that – didn't you know who you were until you wrote your name?'

Since this was exactly what Rose had not been sure of, she had no answer for Maggie.

She went slowly upstairs, pausing at the door where yesterday the mark of Nicholas Brett's hand had been. Now the white paint lay smooth and perfect. She ran a hand over its glossy surface, where his had lain; then, going into the bedroom, she sat down on the bed and looked at the black and white images of herself. Numbers one to six in her own private gallery.

One: The head and shoulders only. Rose Thorpe, age thirty-two, wearing her usual daily mask. Do not advance beyond this point.

Two: The photograph she had taken of herself the night that the hare came across the snow to her. She glowed luminous and pearly-skinned, ageless compared with the first photo.

Three: The landscape of her body. A breast as huge as a mountain, with the nipple a temple peaking the smooth sides.

Four: The bend of her knee, the soft valley behind it a pale, erogenous zone.

Five: The back of her chrysanthemum head.

Six: Rose in despair, curled like a foetus on the floor, long arms and legs tucked under her.

What Rose wanted to do now was to fit herself into the skin of the cottage, to position herself inside these small rooms. Not nudes this time: she needed something between herself and the air of the rooms. There were some old clothes in a suitcase in the unused bedroom. She opened the door and wrinkled her nose in dismay at the damp, musty smell of the room. Dragging the case from under the old bed, she tipped out the clothes. There was a moth-eaten waistcoat, some yellowing gloves and a bundle wrapped in tissue paper.

She pulled off the brittle shreds of paper, and inside was a wedding veil. It must have been her mother's.

Rose fastened the pearl head-dress to her short hair and the veil fell dustily to the ground around her.

She set up the extension lead and pulled off her clothes. This time when she put on the veil, she turned it round, so that it covered her flesh like a frail shroud. It fell across her breasts and clung to the curve of her stomach, wrapping itself lovingly round her legs.

This neglected, unused room felt right for the photos she wanted – she didn't need the other rooms. There was a terrible discrepancy between the damp-stained walls, the dusty floor and the pink skin glowing through the ivory-coloured veil. She moved in front of the cobwebbed window.

She was Miss Havisham with sex. Forget the Great Expectations.

She began to snatch the images, first facing the camera and then with her back to it, arranging the veil carefully so that it hung in a line at each side of her blind, naked back.

For the last photograph, she turned the veil round again, fastening it pure and bridal about her face, and clasped her hands demurely below her breasts. Her face was beautiful, triumphant. She turned it to the dark space beside her and released the shutter.

Later that night, back in the darkroom in her grubby jeans and sweater, she watched that last image come up towards her out of the developing tray, splintering and forming until she held in her hands a picture of a bride and groom.

Nicholas Brett was there in the photo with her, looking down at her with love. She touched the scar on his face and grieved for the pain of it.

Bride and groom.

Marry me, Rose, marry me.

She stood and held the photo for a long time, wishing

she could interpret the signs which were there if she could read them. The shirt he was wearing, the dark coat – she didn't know enough to recognize when he would have worn these clothes. She would need a book on costume to date them. But to do that would be to acknowledge what he was and how he came to her. She had buried all that somewhere very deep; it was something she dare not consider. He came to her: that was enough. She was full of his presence now, wanting him, knowing that later he would come again to her and she would be ready for him.

He came to her quickly, forming himself out of the dark like a blow. He lay pressing down on her, welcome and familiar. She needed him. At the first touch between her legs she was wet for him, arching up to take the thrust of him, bride come to groom. Then his hands were round her neck, gently holding her still.

'Come with me,' he said. 'I am weary of being alone in the dark.'

And his hands were tightening on her throat so that it hurt her to breathe.

'Let go of me,' she gasped. 'Let go . . .' And her nails were clawing at his hands and she felt the terrible strength in him pinning her down, then very slowly he went from her.

He had hurt her before: this was different. Pain had been part of their loving, an extension of boundaries. She sat up in bed, shaking and rubbing at her throat. And the thing which frightened her most was that somewhere she wanted to be with him, wanted him to take her out into the dark.

She slept for a couple of hours, waking wearily into a cold dawn to sit up abruptly and gaze across the room at her portrait gallery. There was the seventh portrait which she had fastened up last night. It showed a woman in a veil, and beside her nothing but a black, uneven stain. There stood Rose at the altar of her hopes, smiling and smiling at nobody, for nothing remained of the groom.

There was a strange, sickly smell downstairs in the cottage.

Rose thought that it must be the chemicals she had been using, for they left a bitter, sulphurous taint in the air. She went into the little parlour to open the window, and the smell came at her like a green wave. She hurried across the room and flung up the sash window, kneeling on the seat to lean out into the mild, grey air. Winter seemed to have slackened its tight grip on the valley, for there was a soft, green haze creeping into the landscape and some blunt spikes of daffodils were pushing up through the broken earth below her. Rose looked up the path across into the orchard, hoping to see Tibby making her way home, but there was no sign of the little cat.

The sound of sheep bleating grew louder on the morning air and there was a pattering of feet – like small children hurrying – coming up the track. Jack was bringing the ewes up from the farm, the sheep-dog with him chivvying along the last few stragglers. He swung open the field gate and the dog sent the woolly bodies bouncing through. Once they were in the field, their heads dropped and they began to graze eagerly. Jack stood and watched them, with the sheep-dog sitting on the wall beside him. Rose thought how right Jack looked with his flock, how easily and placidly he handled them. He turned and saw her now, coming across the grass to the garden gate.

'Now then, lass,' he called. 'Seen nowt of you for a couple of days. You all right?'

'I'm fine. Isn't it mild today? It feels as if spring's here.'

'Not for a bit yet. There's still snow lying on the moor

there, and when it does that it takes more to shift it. There's more to come yet before we're through . . .'

'Oh, don't, Jack!' she wailed.

He laughed at her expression and came up the path to the window.

The dog followed him slowly, wagging his feathery tail, then stopped and began to snarl softly, staring into the room behind Rose.

'Give over, dog,' said Jack roughly. 'There's nowt in there, only Rose.'

But there was something.

Rose knew what the dog was snarling at. She could feel how cold the room was getting. Nicholas Brett was in the room with her and he was angry.

'Can I come in, then?' said Jack, leaning on the window-sill. He ruffled her hair and she flinched as he touched her, feeling the force in the room behind her strengthen.

Jack frowned and straightened quickly.

'I'll not bite. What's the matter, have you got another headache?'

'No. No, it's not that . . .' Rose could feel the presence at her back like a great weight on her, pushing at her, forcing her against the edge of the window-sill, hurting her knees as it increased.

'What, then? What's up?'

The dog's ears were flat against his head, and he began to whine, high pitched and anxious.

'Will you give over, dog?' said Jack again, giving a half-hearted kick at him. The dog slunk off down the path to the gate and sat there whimpering.

'You mustn't come in, Jack . . .'

'Mustn't?' he repeated, looking worried.

The pressure on her back was getting stronger.

It was pressing down on the top of her head. She

couldn't turn her head to look back into the room – even if she had wanted to. She couldn't breathe properly now. The soft and formless presence of his terrible black anger would crush her where she knelt. Jack moved forward as if he were going to climb in over the sill, and she knew that if he did, then Nicholas Brett would destroy them both.

'No,' she yelped. 'Go away, will you! Just get out of it, Jack!'

Her hands were enormous, impossible to lift, but she heaved them up, scrabbled for the edge of the sash window and brought it down with a crash. Her hands spread wide on the glass to keep him out, white with the pressure on them. Under her fingers she could feel the glass begin to shake, and she knew that if Jack didn't go, the window would burst into his face. She saw how it would be; she saw the razor-sharp slivers of glass arrow into the flesh of his face, stripping it to the bone, and with the last of her breath she screamed again at him to go.

He stepped back from the window, anxious at her distress, and stood hesitating, then shrugged and went slowly away down the path. The dog leaped to his feet and nuzzled Jack's hand, and Jack bent and rubbed the silky ears, then opened the gate for him.

'Come on, lad, we'll not stop where we're not wanted.'

He gave one last look back at the window where Rose still pressed frozen against the glass; man and dog went off down the track.

Rose hurt. Everywhere. She slumped down on the seat and pain wrapped red about her. She rocked backwards and forwards in a daze of suffering, dimly aware that the force in the room was slipping away.

'Poor Jack, poor Jack,' she whimpered softly to herself, and the sound rustled round the empty room.

It was two days before Rose could bring herself to go into the little parlour again. Two days of emptiness, of silence, as if the force which Nicholas Brett had called forth had used him up. Her nights were as empty as her days.

She went in reluctantly and gagged on the smell.

It had taken on a presence of its own, and it wasn't her chemicals. She hadn't used the darkroom for days. There was nothing she used anyway that smelt like this. It smelt of death, of putrefaction. She stood bewildered in the middle of the room, for she couldn't understand what could be making such a smell.

It seemed to be stronger by the fireplace.

Rose walked across and stood in front of the little cupboard, the one where they had found the dried-up cat. How long ago that all seemed to her now. Having two people in the room with her had been a comfort she hadn't appreciated at the time.

She stood looking at the cupboard. The smell couldn't be in there, for she had scrubbed the whole thing out with disinfectant. But the cupboard door didn't seem to be closed as tightly as she had left it. She put her fingers under the bottom edge and pulled, and the door swung slowly open.

The smell poured over her, gagging at the back of her throat. She knew what was in there. She had known at some level since the day that Tibby disappeared, known that she wouldn't see her alive again. The little black cat lay as the mummified corpse had lain, wrapped loosely in a white cloth, with her mouth drawn back in a screaming grin. She must have lain here like that since the day the hare came into the kitchen. Death-bringer.

So who had killed her little cat?

Who killed Cock Robin? she muttered stupidly to herself, tears pouring down her face as she poured herself a glass of brandy. She leant against the sink and gulped it down, wondering if she were going to be sick. She held on to the edge of the sink and waited, and the nausea died away.

Who killed poor Tibby?

She splashed another inch of brandy into the glass and drained it as if it were water, tasting none of it, tasting only the rotting smell of the cat.

The London Rose would not have believed the loss she felt now. She hadn't loved Tibby the way some women do love their cats, but she had been there, and she had needed Rose. In those frozen days of the snow, Tibby had been a comfort to her, sitting on the oven top with her paws curled under her, or warm on Rose's lap.

Now Rose had to bury her. Had to, for there was no one else. She had no choice. There was no Maggie; there was no Jack.

The soil wasn't frozen solid now; she should be able to dig a hole under one of the apple trees. She owed it to the little cat. The thing to do, she told herself firmly, was not to think about what she was doing, just to do it straight away now.

And she managed. She got what was left of Tibby into the shallow hole she had pecked in the soil and covered it carefully. Then she cleaned the spade, put it away in the outbuilding, and went inside and was sick.

After that it seemed impossible to stay in the cottage any longer. She had to get away from it, even if it was only for a couple of hours. She thought of driving the car into Whitby, but her hands were shaking; it wasn't safe to drive anywhere like this. She would go for a walk. She had never been in the wood on the far side of the valley; the one where Maggie said the badgers lived. She pulled on her coat and boots and, snatching up her camera, banged the door behind her. She had left the parlour window open to let out the smell, so there was no point in locking it.

There was a pale sunlight on the hills, and the air smelt fresh. She slammed the garden gate behind her and walked away from the cottage without looking back. She would not think of Tibby and what had happened to her, or of what she had buried in the dark soil.

Paddy stood at his bedroom window and watched the small figure make its way across the valley and into the oak wood which lay like a thick scarf along the far side of the hill. She disappeared among the trees; and, turning, he hurried down the stairs.

'Where are you off, our Paddy?' said Maggie in surprise, seeing him pull on his coat. She was baking, and the kitchen was warm with the smell. A rack of jam tarts stood cooling on the table, and he picked one up and pushed it in his mouth.

'Here,' she said. 'They're for tea, they are.'

'I like a nice tart,' he said, pinching her bottom.

She giggled and said, 'Give over,' in a half-hearted sort of voice. 'Where are you off to, though?' She began to roll out the pastry on the board in front of her, looking up curiously at him.

'Mind your own business. Nowt to do with you.' He picked up another tart on his way to the door.

'I expect you're running after Rose,' she sniffed.

'So what? She's worth it. She knows what to do with what's between her legs. More than you do. She lied to you about what happened that night when I went up. I had her all ends up.'

'That's not what she told me, and she doesn't lie. She's lovely, is Rose,' said Maggie stubbornly.

'So why don't you go up there to play any more, then?

What frightened you off? Had her hand up your knickers, did she?'

'No, she didn't!' bawled Maggie, her face as red as fire, banging at the defenceless pastry.

'Well, what did she do, then? Something sent you home with a face like a ghost and your tail between your legs. You've not been near the place since. It's been days and days and you still haven't told me what's going on. Mam's watching you funny as well. She's said nowt about you going back up there, as if she knows summat that I don't. I don't like that, our Mags. I'll come into your bed tonight and make you tell me.'

She stared at him, horrified. 'You'll never . . .' she began.

'Oh, yes, I will. You just wait and see.'

'You wouldn't dare,' she sniffed, and went back to her pastry.

The wet earth sucked at Paddy's feet as he crossed the fields. He climbed carefully over the fallen stone wall dividing field from wood and stood listening. Nothing. Once or twice he'd seen deer up here in the bracken, small, fragile things. He wished he'd brought his gun with him. He could have waved that at her and given her a fright. He was a good shot – better than Jack.

Not that Jack ever used a gun now, not any more. 'Bloody well think not, stupid sod,' muttered Paddy violently.

He still dreamed of the accident. He saw himself and Jack climb over the wall in the moonlight and felt the red pain when Jack's gun went off. Before that Paddy could run faster than Jack, faster than all the other kids at school. Never again. Dragged one wing like a shot pheasant after that. An old man at fourteen. And all they'd been after was a couple of bloody rabbits.

Where was the woman? Fallen down a hole with any luck. This was her last chance to look at him properly and be nice to him. Stuck-up bitch. Slept with that poncy London git. Slept with Jack. Turned up her nose at poor old Paddy. And what had she done to scare the pants off Maggie?

He stopped to listen again. Not a sound. She must be at the top of the wood by the badgers' sett; Maggie would have told her about them. He scrambled and slid up the steep slope, cursing as the long fingers of spiking brambles clawed at him.

'Looking for someone?'

She was above him, leaning against a flat rock by the mouth of the sett. He squinted up at her, thinking how tough she looked, how cocky. Camera round her bloody neck as usual.

'Aye. You. You could slip up here and hurt yourself. No one would ever know what happened to you.'

He stood uneasily on the sloping ground, peering up at her.

'Well, thank you, Paddy, that's very kind of you to bother so much about me. But I'm not going to slip.'

The faint emphasis on the 'I'm' flared him into rage. 'Think you know it all, don't you!' he shouted at her. 'You come here from London and take one look at us and think you know the lot. You know nowt about what it's like living here. Shut off from everybody, never any money. You come here with your airs and graces, taking what's not yours . . .'

'Now we're getting there,' she said. 'Whose should it be then, Haggabacks? That's what we're talking about, isn't it?'

'It should be mine,' he said bitterly.

'And how do you work that one out?'

'That photo you showed me – this one.'

He pulled it out of his shirt, but she didn't even look worried.

'What about it?'

'Who is it, then?'

She shrugged. 'You tell me.'

'"You tell me,"' he repeated nastily. 'Aye, I will. I'll tell you who it bloody well is. It's my mother.'

She looked at him and waited.

'My mother and your dad,' he said softly. 'And mebbe *my* dad as well. Sister.'

The word fell away into the grey air as he stared at her.

'He took the photos, that's all. It doesn't prove he's your father. And I would be very careful how I used the word "sister" if I were you. I know something of the way that you treat your sister.'

He went white and seemed to crumple as she looked at him, then he swore at her and, turning, began to stumble blindly away from her.

'Paddy!' she called. 'Two things. No more letters. There's no point now we've had this little chat. And what did you do to my cat?'

He glared round at her. 'What d'you mean? I never touched your bloody cat. Okay, I sent the letters, but I never touched your cat.'

'Someone killed her,' she said.

'Not me. What d'you take me for?'

He lurched away from her, banging into the low branches of the trees.

She watched until he reached the bottom of the steep slope, his red hair blazing among the yellow of the dead bracken. He looked back once at her, then was off across the fields. She waited until he was out of sight, then stiffly and reluctantly made her way back to Haggabacks.

*

It was midnight when Paddy came creeping in a cold, white fury to Maggie's bed. She shivered and whimpered up out of sleep to find his icy skin pressed against her.

'You shouldn't,' she moaned, and his hand closed over her mouth.

'*I* shouldn't,' he said with difficulty, breathless with anger. 'What d'you mean, I shouldn't? Don't you mean *you* shouldn't? What the hell have you been blabbing to your girlfriend? How does she know about Thomas?'

Her eyes rolled in terror, and she snatched his hand from her mouth.

'I never told her, I swear I never did. She must have guessed from the colour of his hair being like yours; she kept on talking about how both of you have red hair and none of the rest of us have.'

She lay fearful in the dark to see if he would believe her.

He wanted to. He wanted to believe that she was loyal to him, that he came first with her; if he had lost her, then he had nobody.

'You sure?' he said.

'Paddy, love,' she whispered, sliding down her hand to cradle his small, limp prick. 'Would I be daft enough to tell her about the bairn?'

He lay tense and withdrawn, his anger still burning him up, and she knew that she must give him something to bring him to her again.

'You know what you said to me, that about Rose having her hand up my knickers?'

Maggie sacrificed Rose unhappily, but it was Rose who had made Paddy so angry. She shouldn't have risked that.

There was a pause while Paddy took in what she had said.

'D'you mean that she did?'

283

'Well . . . not really : . . but it was when you cut off all my hair. I thought it looked real ugly, that's why I got so upset.'

Paddy sniggered. 'You looked like a convict.'

Maggie swallowed and accepted it. He sounded a little less angry already.

'Aye, I thought I looked a right freak. But Rose liked it. She said I looked like a model.'

'A model? You? You weren't daft enough to believe her, were you? Model of a dog, mebbe.'

Maggie thought of Rose's face as she had held her, of how soft her skin had been, and fell silent.

'Don't stop now – go on. What happened next?'

'She wanted to take some photos of me,' said Maggie reluctantly.

'What sort of photos – mucky ones?'

Maggie could feel him beginning to harden against her and sighed with relief. It had worked.

'Go on, then, tell me . . .'

'No, not mucky ones. I kept my skirt on, but down to my waist was bare. She took a whole lot of photos of me. She gets right carried away when she gets going, and I was on the window-seat and I was cold. So I told her, and she stopped, and we went over to the fire . . .'

She faltered off into silence, remembering now Rose's mouth warm and soft on her nipple and how good it had felt, how gentle and kind Rose had been to her.

'Tell me, Maggie, tell me!'

And he was on top of her, thrusting between her legs, his mouth against her hair, and she told him what Rose had done to her.

She told him how Rose had kissed her breasts and held her, and Paddy's arms were round her, and he was in her, and she gathered him to her and rocked him against her, and was grateful for what she had.

Nicholas on his red mare leads the way up the lane, the mare's breath smoking white as she prances under him. Joshua holds up his father's long, shining horn, and it blows hard and shrill down the valley.

They hear it at Ghyll Farm and wonder.

Nan hears it at Haggabacks, and she knows.

Nan feels very old and tired today. She gets to her feet at the shrill sound, hobbling across to the door to stand and listen. Perhaps there is still time for her to make her way up to the peat bog where she has hidden before . . . But it is too late for that. They are too near. Her cat and her hare, though, they shall not have those. No harm must come to them.

'Moll,' she calls back urgently towards the hearth. 'You must run, quickly . . .'

The hare slips across the floor and crouches at her feet, looking up at her. Nan bends and strokes the silky head, and urges her away with a thrust of her hand.

Moll flows like a shadow across the patch of garden and over the low wall. For a moment she is outlined black against the sky; then, with a white flash of her tail, she is gone towards the high moor.

'You now, quickly,' says Nan to the cat. He stares green-eyed at her and yowls angrily, his tail fluffed to twice its size, then strops his claws against the doorpost. He is going nowhere. Nan tries to push him out into the garden, but he snarls and scratches at her hand. She shakes her head and moves unsteadily back to the stool. The cat stalks after her and sits in his usual place on the hearth, stiff-backed with his ears flat with rage.

The horn sounds again, almost at the gate.

Nan sits and warms her hands at the fire and forces

her breath to come slow and steady. She will not give them her fear to feed on.

Her stillness, sitting there by the fire and not so much as turning her head as they come crashing through the door, frightens the Latimer boys. Hunting her down in a chase on the moor is one thing; this is something different. They hang back, watching Nicholas Brett.

He folds his arms and stares at her, thinking that now he is so close to her, she is nothing but an old bag of bones. All the same, he is not quite convinced that she has not harmed him somehow, spoiling his game with Emily Bransdale. He can feel some kind of power in the old crone.

'"Thou shalt not suffer a witch to live." Is that what you are, hag?'

'If you say so, Master Scar-face,' she says absently, leaning forward and taking a bundle of something from out of a crack in the wall by the fire. She sits and cradles it in her hands, and Nicholas Brett is not there at all for her.

He swears and kicks out at her stool to send it flying from under her, so that she sprawls painfully on the stone flags of the hearth, ash in her long grey hair, her skirts up round her thighs.

There is a screaming howl as a streak of yellow fur leaps from the hearth and flies at Nicholas Brett's face, clawing and biting in a frenzy at him. He beats at it with his fists, knocking it to the floor, where Joshua kicks hard at the cat, sending him spinning through the air to hit the wall with a dull thud.

The brothers grin at one another and come to stand with Nicholas above the old woman. Cheated of hunting her like a hare, now at least they have a trapped prey. She lies at their booted feet and looks up at them.

'Scar-face,' she says harshly. 'There was a woman

286

with yellow hair who died by your hand in London. You were playing with things you do not understand, trying for power you will never touch. And Tully. Little Tully Bransdale you killed on Fairy Hill . . .'

She yelps with pain as his booted foot crashes into her ribs. The bundle she is holding falls from her hand to lie at Nicholas's feet. He bends and picks it up, looking curiously at the little figure which had dropped out of its white wrapping.

'Nothing but a child's toy,' he sneers and tosses the little wax man into the fire.

And Nan begins to laugh.

She hauls herself up until she can see the wax man, and she screeches with an eerie high-pitched cackle as she sees how it is melting, its small arms squirming horribly as the flames lick at them, its legs bending into nothing. Its round head lolls back and nods, and a tongue of flame licks out from the round hole of its mouth. Then the fire shifts and crumbles, and the figure is gone. Nan points a shaking finger at Nicholas.

'And now you shall have life everlasting, just as you were seeking. You have made sure of that yourself. That was your poppet that you burnt, and as it burnt then so shall you. You may run back to London and hide for all t' good it will do you. You will die there in a brawl, but it will not end there. It will end here, in this place. You'll come again and come again, but only a woman can give you shape.'

She takes a rasping breath and her voice comes more thinly now. 'Nicholas Brett, we have bound you to Haggabacks. We have cursed you to suffer as Tully suffered, and only fire and flame will end it all . . .' She trails off into silence, and Joshua edges closer to his brother.

Nicholas looks from the fire to Nan with a cold, dead

face, then he kneels beside her and pulls out a white-handled knife. He holds it above her; and then, as casually as if he were slicing bread, he rips open her throat.

There is a flash of lightning over the moor, and a drumming roll of thunder. Sleet begins to patter against the window, and Nan's blood crawls wetly across the floor.

The three faces watching turn in a pale circle above her fading eyes. There is only time for her to grieve briefly for her cat, then the faces wheel and spin her out into the waiting dark.

The three horsemen ride away from Haggabacks. Behind them a thick column of smoke is beginning to rise from the rotten thatch where Joshua has lit it.

And in the garden Nan's dead cat spins and turns where Nicholas Brett has hanged it from a branch of the apple tree.

Chapter Twenty-two

ROSE stood by the round table in the little parlour, where the fire of old apple wood smelled sweet on the warm air. There was a ring of candles placed round the edge of the table, unlit, waiting.

As Maggie woke to find the incestuous cold body of her brother clamped to her side, so Rose had woken to silence and emptiness. He had not come to her; again, he had not come to her.

She had forgotten now how frightened she had been that last time, forgotten the pain of his hands at her throat. She had blotted out everything except how much she wanted him. She was burning with a strange, feverish heat, her skin prickling with it. Even her hair crackled as she ran her fingers through it. She rubbed herself roughly between her legs where she was swollen, ready for him. Her nipples hurt as she brushed them with her arm. She was sick with desire for him. It was the evening of St Valentine, and Rose wanted her lover.

She was bathed and sweet-smelling, naked beneath her green velvet gown. She would bring him to her like a moth to her candles. She had lit candles in the windows before, and it had brought Paddy to her. Now she would light this ring of candles on the table, and out of the shadows she would call him to her.

She bent to the fire and lit a taper; then she crossed to the table and began to light the candles one after another, their pale tulip flames flowering in the still air, their ghost images shining in the table.

The ring was done: the circle closed.

She switched off the electric light and gave the room to the fire and candlelight.

It was her own late Candlemas which she was making, her own bridge to the dead world. She began to walk slowly round the table, the velvet folds swishing round her bare ankles.

Round and round the table where the candles burned, round and round in the dark rim outside their light.

'Nicholas Brett,' she said very softly under her breath. 'Come to me, Nicholas, come to me . . .'

Round and round in the darkness, whispering his name like a prayer, the candle flames rising and falling as she passed. What if he did not come? What if she had sent him away for ever when she would not go with him as he asked? She could not go on without him. Not now.

Time fell away to nothing. Rose felt the cottage floating about her like a ship in the dark, and she made herself believe, centring herself down to the circle she was drawing, to the pattern of his name inside her mouth.

Then under the sound of his name there was another sound in the room. Very faint and far away there came the sound of a young boy singing.

'Alas, my love, you do me wrong, to cast me off discourteously . . .' 'Greensleeves'. The notes fell pure and silver round her, and she lifted up her arms and began to dance.

And he was there with her, shaping out of the dark gently, softly, against her. His name died into silence on her lips as he pulled her to him, and round and round the table they danced. The candlelight flickered on his white shirt as they turned and glinted on the buttons of his long, dark coat. He was looking down at her and smiling as he had in the bridal photo.

She was dancing with the Devil in the dark.

The candles burnt and still they danced, until the music dimmed and they came to a standstill in the shadows. Rose wanted to give herself to him, to bind him fast to her. She knelt at his feet with a flowering of green skirts and waited with bent head. He unfastened himself for her and rested a hand on her hair. She lifted her pale face and took him into her mouth. His hand tightened on her head and his teeth grinned down white at her.

But he was so cold in her mouth, and growing colder. He was turning to ice in her mouth, and out of him there came gushing a liquid so bitter, so cold, that it burnt like fire. Her mouth blistered, her tongue was raw pain, and she was held in a black terror, knowing that she must not swallow one drop. She tried to wrench her head free, but his hands held her fast to him. She could not move. The music of 'Greensleeves' swelled and roared round the room, and she struggled to move her frosted mouth; out of her red pain she brought her teeth together hard on the icy thing in her poor mouth.

He cried out in a terrible fury and his fist smashed into the side of her head, knocking her hard against the leg of the table. The world went black and she was aware of nothing for a while. The shadows thickened for an instant where he stood, then paled, and he was gone.

One by one the candles died away with him.

The sound of 'Greensleeves' dwindled to one long note hanging on the waxy air, and Rose lay all unknowing in a crumpled heap of green velvet.

The pain in her mouth brought her round to a faint morning light seeping through the window. She only just made it to the kitchen sink before she was sick, wiping the last of the bitter fluid from her dead mouth, knowing how lucky she was still to be alive. Knowing that it was finished.

It took her a long time to make herself a mug of milky tea, but she managed it, taking it across to the table where she sat down unsteadily. She sipped carefully at the warm sweetness, resting her aching head on her hand. She had to begin tying the threads together to move on from this place, to save herself.

She had come here on the run from Edward, burning with a rage against her father. Looking back now at the woman who had stood here in this kitchen that first night, she wondered at how much she had changed. All those years she had carried that great weight of anger, and none of it mattered. Her father was dead, and whatever he had been she would never know now. He had left her this cottage; he had thought of her at the end.

Did he know of Nicholas Brett? She didn't think so. It was something in herself, some need which had drawn Nicholas into her. And he had fed on her acceptance of him, becoming stronger through her. She had given him shape and form. Her father could not have known what his true bequest to her had been, this twisted thread of love and fear for her night lover.

She owed her father one more thing.

Taking the plate camera, she went out of the cottage like a sleepwalker. She climbed stiffly into her car and drove along the narrow lane which ran across Fairy Hill, which still wore a tattered cap of snow.

She pulled up the car on to the grass verge beside the church and sat looking at it. Bell, book and candle, she thought. Was that what it would take to lay the ghost of Nicholas Brett? She thought of his mouth against her breasts and shivered, climbing out of the car with her camera.

It was a very old church, built of grey stone with a square tower. It stood by itself miles from anywhere.

Perhaps there had once been a village near by, lost now. Rose went through the white gate into the quiet churchyard. She walked slowly through the gravestones, looking at the mossy inscriptions, at the stone-faced angels. She moved across to where she could see a patch of flowers breaking the turf in the newer part of the graveyard. Someone had not survived the year's turning.

Beyond this fresh grave was the one she was looking for. Her father's name and the dates of his birth and death were cut black into the grey marble slab. No more than that. All that was left of a man.

Rose set up the tripod at the foot of the grave and stood for a moment looking round her. How still it was here, how peaceful. Only the sound of sheep far off on the moor top stirred the soft air. She had laid her father to rest since she had come here; she could let go of him and leave him to this place. Whatever he had been, whatever he had done, it was finished here. The reality of his death was hard in her now; this had been a man, had been flesh of her flesh.

She bent her head and looked into the camera, and saw the image clear and inverted, the wild, goose-grey sky, the long grass beyond the grave. The grass stirred, moved as if some wild creature were passing through. Rose thought that for an instant she caught a glimpse of long, dark-tipped ears ruffling the grass, then all was still.

She opened the shutter and distilled light diffused the image.

The shutter closed on its frozen moment, and it was done. There was nothing more for Rose in this wild place.

But there was something more to do before she could go back to the cottage. She pulled the car into a gateway at the bottom of Fairy Hill, and, moving slowly and carefully because of the heavy camera and tripod, she began to climb the steep slope.

It was bitterly cold at the top; the wind blowing the grass flat like thin hair stung at Rose's mouth, flaring the pain up again. She set up the camera and cupped her cold hands round it. Small as a doll's house, there was Haggabacks, crouching in the narrow valley. The pain from her mouth was making Rose feel sick again, but at the back of that pain was the even greater one she knew was waiting for her. She did not know how she was going to bear leaving Nicholas. She took her last photo of the cottage.

She packed up the camera and tripod; she had what she needed from it. Something was caught in the rock where she had balanced the tripod. She bent and picked it up, brushing the crusted snow from it. It was a length of faded scarlet ribbon. She ran it through her fingers, wondering who had climbed up here to lose it; she pushed it into the pocket of her jeans and began to pick her way back down the steep slope to her car.

When she closed her garden gate behind her and went up the path, something moved in the doorway ahead of her. Her heart lurched and banged, thinking that it was Nicholas Brett coming to her. She blinked and the figure spoke.

'Can I come in for a minute?'

Mrs Bransdale. Rose wondered what she could want.

She nodded, pushing open the door of the cottage, and Mrs Bransdale followed her in. She stood by the door watching as Rose put down the camera on the table.

Rose made an effort to be normal, to pretend this was an ordinary day. 'Will you have a coffee?'

Mrs Bransdale shook her head. 'You look rough, lass. Are you okay? Sit yourself down before you fall down.'

Rose sank into the nearest chair and gazed vaguely at the moving mouth of Mrs Bransdale, wishing she would go away and leave her alone.

Mrs Bransdale stood looking at Rose as if she didn't know where to start, then sighed and sat down at the table.

'You've got to get out of here,' she said harshly. 'Maggie told me what happened, about him leaving the mark of his hand on the door. And his voice, saying your name. Looks as if he's had a go at you since then. Your face is a right mess. It's not safe for you, up here all on your own with him . . .'

'Him?' said Rose, as cold as ice.

'Oh, don't play games with me – it's far too late for that! You know very well who I mean. Nicholas Brett.'

The name hung between them like a threat. It horrified Rose, hearing it said by someone else: It made him too real, somehow.

'Nicholas Brett,' said Mrs Bransdale again softly, and there was so much feeling in her voice this time that Rose stared at her in astonishment.

Mrs Bransdale caught the look. 'Did you think you were the only one? You'd never know it to look at me now, but I was a bonny lass once. It's all a long time ago, twenty years or more. I was doing the cooking and cleaning up here for your dad. He was lonely, without your mam. Sometimes I wondered if that was why *she* left – if she'd seen summat, and was afraid for you. Oh, he was a grand big man was your dad. More like you than you'll ever admit. He wanted to take some photos of me. That's all it was, to start with. Just photos of me. But once he started taking them, it was as if I belonged to him somehow. I let him . . . I let him . . .'

Her voice faded out and she stared down at her folded

hands on the table in front of her, twisting her worn wedding ring round her thin finger.

Rose waited, sitting very still, holding the pain in her mouth as if it would spill.

'One time, we were upstairs in the bedroom and your dad was taking some photos of me on the bed. And I saw summat. Only like a shadow of a man at first. Your dad never saw owt. I never told him. But I knew the tales about this place. I knew who he was.'

'Tales?'

'Your dad saw some old letters and records when he was working up at Throstle Hall. Seemingly there was a young girl, a Bransdale, murdered up at the Hall years and years back. They knew Nicholas Brett did it, but they never pinned it on him. And they blamed him for killing old Nan who lived here as well.'

She died a bad death here, old Nan the witch.

'You and Nicholas Brett,' began Rose painfully.

'It's all so long ago,' said Mrs Bransdale. 'But I did love your dad, Rose. I would never have harmed him. And Nicholas Brett got stronger and stronger. I came up to the cottage to work sometimes on my own and he came to me then. It's the only way that he can take shape at all, I reckon, through a woman. He feeds on us. He was my lover as well as your dad. I wanted them both. There was no filling me in those days. I was younger and dafter. But Nicholas came to me once when I was with your dad, when your dad was making love to me. And it all went wrong. Nicholas wanted me to . . .'

'To kill him.'

'Aye. So then I knew that I had to finish it. Finish it with your dad to keep him safe. He never knew why and he hated me for it. I lost both of them, Nicholas Brett being tied to this cottage the way he is.'

'How is he tied?'

'They say Nan cursed him, bound him here to Hagga-backs. Only a woman can set him free by fire. Or so they say. I don't know how. I don't even know what he is, for sure. All I know is, no man between your legs is ever going to fill you the way he does. It doesn't matter to me now, it's all done and dead for me anyway. I did what I did to keep your dad safe – I'll not let any harm come to his daughter if I can help it.'

She scraped back her chair and came to stand in front of Rose, staring down at her.

'You've got to go away. Go back to London, where you belong, while there's still time. Lock the door on this place and leave it like that. You don't belong here and you never will. You buried your father coming back here. Take care that you don't bury yourself along with him.'

Rose shuddered and had nothing to say.

'Jack's not the man for you and you know it when you think about it. You'll never be a farmer's wife, not you. You'll always want to see what's on the other side of the hill. And how could you stay here? If you stay, we'll all suffer. You'll bring Nicholas Brett in stronger and stronger, and how will it end? I'll not have my Maggie harmed. I'm frightened for both of you. For us all. D'you hear me?'

She leant forward and caught hold of Rose's bruised face between her roughened hands.

'Promise me you'll go?' she said, and her voice broke on unshed tears.

'Yes,' said Rose. 'I promise. I'll go.'

Mrs Bransdale sighed and moved back from Rose, tightening her scarf under her chin and fighting to get back her control.

'Now,' she said unsteadily. 'I'll take that goat off your

hands. That's all that's holding you now, isn't it? You lost your cat . . .'

'Hardly *lost*,' spat Rose. 'Your precious Paddy killed her.'

Mrs Bransdale shook her head. 'It wasn't Paddy did that.'

'Then who . . .' began Rose, and swallowed hard.

'You know who killed her. You were getting too fond of her. Paddy wouldn't do that to you.' She hesitated. 'He has some daft idea in his head that your dad was his father. Paddy doesn't remember his own dad, he was killed when he was just a little lad. But my husband Danny had hair like fire. Just like Paddy's. The lad's wrong. Danny was his dad, and I should know.'

She went across to the door and stood with her hand on the latch. 'I'll take the goat now, then, shall I?'

Rose nodded.

'How much d'you want for her?'

'Nothing. Give her to Thomas.'

'Aye, I'll do that.'

Still she hesitated, uneasy with something else she had left unsaid. 'I did love your dad, I really did. Paddy's wrong, he's nothing to you. But Maggie is. *She's* your dad's child. Maggie is your half-sister, Rose. That's why I'll not let any harm come to either of you through Nicholas Brett. You'll not break your promise to me, you will go?'

Rose nodded and said yes, she would go – she wouldn't break her promise. Then she put her head down on her arms and let the tears come, for Mrs Bransdale, for Maggie, for herself, and for the hard knot which tied them. She heard the door of the building slam, then the high-heeled clatter of Lady's hooves on the flagstones of the path. There was one last bleating cry for her, but she would not lift her head. She sat with her face hidden until the sound died away into nothing.

*   *   *

Now Nicholas is all haste to be gone. He packs his bag and rides out of the valley for the last time, halting the mare, as he crests the ridge, to look back. The bitter smoke still drifting from Haggabacks points like a black finger at the winter sky.

He shivers as he thinks of Nan's harsh cursing, but the hag was a witch and so deserved to die. Her death was nothing to him – why should her words be any more?

He turns the mare and urges her forward, for there is a long road ahead of him, and he must be at an inn before the light fails. Death comes to us all, in the end, thinks Nicholas, and feels how strange it is that he has spent so long searching for a way to have eternal life, only to have it promised to him by a dying witch. He does not believe that he will die in a low brawl, he is worth more than that, surely? But wherever he dies, surely he will stay there – the old woman did not have enough cunning in her to draw him back after death and tie him to Haggabacks. And what did she mean, that only a woman would set him free? He had given fire already to Haggabacks. That was an end to it.

But if it wasn't?

Nicholas sees again the waxy little figure twisting and turning in the fire's heart, and the echo of Nan's voice comes faintly back to him. 'We have cursed you to suffer as Tully suffered . . .'

The mare leaps and jumps along the causeway as his heels dig into her sides; then the sound of her hooves is swallowed by the moor wind, and Nicholas is gone.

Chapter Twenty-three

Rose went slowly down the track to the farm. She was carrying a heavy box full of groceries and bits and pieces for Maggie. Maggie. Since Mrs Bransdale had left her, Rose's head had been full of Maggie. Her half-sister. She had at first wondered if it was the truth, but why should Mrs Bransdale lie? Rose wasn't even sure she wanted to see Maggie again, not yet, because it seemed to change so much, knowing that they had the same father.

There were the photos Rose had taken of her, for a start. Not very sisterly. And as to what had happened after the photos . . . Rose didn't want to think too closely about that. It made her feel very little different from Paddy, the way she'd treated Maggie.

And there was Jack. Mrs Bransdale was right: there was no future for Rose with him. No future for her here. But she cared very much about Jack, too much to leave without saying goodbye. She was forcing herself to be very practical, to concentrate only on getting ready to leave. And at the same time she could not accept that she must never see Nicholas Brett again. One thing at a time. That was all she could manage.

Maggie first.

There was no answer when she tapped on the kitchen door of the farm. She pushed it open with her foot, walked in and put down the heavy box on the table.

'Anyone there?' she called. 'Maggie?'

There was no answer.

The slow tick of the long-case clock in the corner filled

the room. It struck twelve heavily, and Rose jumped at the sound. The last of the notes died away, and still there was no answer. Rose looked longingly at the door behind her. It would be so easy just to walk out, to shed all the Bransdales and drive off away from them. Reluctantly, she crossed to the door at the far side of the kitchen and went into the long passageway beyond.

'Maggie!' she shouted.

'Hang on, be with you in a minute,' called Maggie's voice faintly from the top of the house.

There was a curving flight of stairs at the end of the passage, below a beautiful, high-arched window. There were some photos hanging on the wall, and Rose wandered over to them, never able to resist a photo. There was one of an old man holding a horse with a cropped tail, one of Ghyll Farm in a long-gone summer, and a third of a dark-haired woman holding a baby in her arms and laughing at the camera. Was the baby Maggie, Rose wondered? The woman was Mrs Bransdale before the years had blurred her body into fat, before the colour had drained from her black hair. This was the woman in the photos which Rose had found behind the carved angel.

'She was bonny, Mam, wasn't she?' Maggie came down the stairs in a rush and stood looking shyly at Rose.

'It's where you get your looks from,' said Rose. 'Come on, I've got something for you.'

'For me?' Maggie's face lit up. She followed Rose into the kitchen and looked at the box on the table. Rose pulled an envelope from it and gave it to her. Maggie slid out the enlarged photo of herself and stood staring at it without a word.

Rose had chosen one of Maggie's head, turned to look out of the window. She'd wanted to give her one that

301

Maggie could show to the rest of the family. She stood looking at Maggie's bent head now as if she were seeing her for the first time, and suddenly she knew that Mrs Bransdale had told her the truth. Maggie was more to her than just a friend. And maybe Rose had seen something of herself in her the day she took the photos which had opened her up to Maggie. It was done now anyway; Rose had to forgive herself and move on.

Maggie's long silence worried her. 'Do you like it?' Rose asked.

Maggie ran a hand over her head where the hair was growing thickly again in a dark-peach fuzz.

'It's me,' she said. 'I didn't know I looked as nice as that. Paddy said I was as ugly as a convict.'

'Paddy was wrong. I told you that.'

Maggie sighed and looked up, and her face matched the woman in the picture now, tranquil and self-possessed.

'Thank you,' she said.

'Maggie, I've come to say goodbye.'

Maggie looked at the box on the table and back again to Rose.

'Mam said that you were going. I'm right sorry in a way because I'll miss you, I've never had a friend like you before, but I'm glad you're leaving that place. I shouldn't have run away and left you there like I did, I've been that scared that something bad would happen to you. But I just couldn't make myself go up there . . .' Her voice trailed off miserably.

'It's okay. It was best you didn't come up again.' Rose winced as she touched a sore place in her mouth with her tongue.

'He's been back, hasn't he? Has he hurt you, love? You're not talking properly, has he done something to you?' Maggie was pink with anger at the idea.

'Nothing to worry about. I'm going, so it doesn't matter now.'

'Are you off back to London?'

'For a while, anyway. I want to try to get an exhibition of portraits set up. If I do manage to fix it with a gallery, can I use some of the photos I took of you?'

'Me?' Maggie giggled. 'Me, up on a gallery wall in London? If you think that they're good enough.'

'I'll send you a special invitation to the opening. "Ms Maggie Bransdale is invited to the opening of 'Face Value' by Rose Thorpe."'

'Me come to London?'

'Why not? You could come down and work as a model, I keep telling you that.'

Maggie's face closed. 'Oh, aye? And what about the bairn?'

'He won't stay small for ever. Other women manage it. You can make a start by getting yourself there for my exhibition. All you have to do is to get Jack to drive you to the station – then just sit on the train until I meet you at the other end. Look, I still owe you some money for helping me at the cottage. You put it away towards the train fare. I'll send you the rest when it's time. And there's some bits of make-up in the box with the food. Save me carrying it all the way back to London.'

Maggie took the fifty pounds from Rose reluctantly. 'I didn't expect owt else.'

'You earned every penny of it. And that's without a modelling fee.'

Maggie pushed the money into her apron pocket and turned to the box. She pulled out a half-empty bottle of scent and sprayed it lavishly on herself. The smell drifted across to Rose, and she remembered the last time she'd used that scent. She was wearing a green velvet gown, and she was dancing in the dark with Nicholas Brett.

She felt sick and faint at the memory. She would not think of him. She had sealed him off coldly in her head in a tight waxy cell and there he must stay.

The longer she stayed here talking to Maggie the more difficult it was getting. Rose didn't want to leave her here. She wanted to take her away and show her the world outside of this narrow valley. She wanted to tell her that they shared the same father – but that was not her secret to tell. That was up to Mrs Bransdale.

'Maggie,' she said urgently. 'I really must go. I've got one of Jack's photos to give to him. Is he anywhere about?'

Maggie looked upset. 'Did you take some photos of our Jack as well? You never said.'

'Just the one set.'

'But you didn't take any of Paddy, did you? Not him as well?' Maggie didn't like the idea of sharing something so special with her brothers.

'Paddy? No, I didn't take any of him.' She hadn't wanted that foxy face as a memento.

'I'm glad. Jack's down the village. He'll not be long.'

Rose hesitated, looking at the envelope with Jack's photo in it. It would be so much easier if she could just go now, without waiting for Jack.

'Can I leave this with you?'

Maggie stared at her in amazement. 'You'll never go off without even saying goodbye to him? Eh, he'll be that upset if you do.'

Rose felt guilty, for of course she would do that. She didn't want to see Jack's face when she left him any more than Maggie's. But Maggie was right.

'No. No, of course I won't go until I've seen him.'

Maggie nodded. 'I'll send him up to the cottage just as soon as he gets back.'

'Right. Can I leave you and Jack to see to the electricity and the water for me? I'll give the keys to Jack when he comes up . . .'

'Stop fussing. Just go,' said Maggie.

Ah, if it were only that simple . . .

Rose put her arms round Maggie and kissed her, holding her tightly, and Maggie clung to her.

'Maggie,' began Rose, 'don't let Paddy . . . don't let him hurt you. You take care of yourself until I see you again.'

Maggie sniffed and gave a watery smile. 'I wish I was coming with you now,' she began, just as Thomas came bursting into the kitchen.

'Mam, Mam, I've got a goat. Nana's given it to me.' He saw Rose and stopped, scuttling behind his mother.

'A goat? What are you on about? You mean Lady – you've got Rose's Lady?' She looked at Rose.

'I could hardly take her with me.'

'Eh, aren't you a lucky little lad!' said Maggie, ruffling her son's bright red hair. He leaned against her and grinned up at her.

'She's not called Lady any more.'

'What's she called, then?' said Maggie.

'She's called Soddit. That's what Nana called her when she told her to get off her foot.'

Maggie laughed and cuddled him to her, and as she stood and watched Rose realized that not only was Maggie her half-sister, but that Thomas was her . . . what? . . . Half-nephew? She was shaken by the idea. Auntie Rose.

'You smell nice, Mam,' he said admiringly, and Maggie bent and gave him a quick kiss. Rose looked at their two faces, close together, and said goodbye quickly as she left.

Rose walked back to the cottage and coldly, efficiently, finished packing what she was taking back to Islington.

She carried two full suitcases down the track to her car, then came back for a box of stuff from the darkroom. She left the big camera until last, in the middle of the kitchen table. She needed that where she could see it; it was her password out of here and all she was taking of herself. The envelope with the photo of Jack lay next to it. She slid it out and ran a finger down the long curve of his cheek-bone, and wondered what he would do with this image of himself.

Only then did she think of the photos which she'd found behind the carved angel. They were still in the table drawer. She opened it unwillingly, for she had no desire to see the things again. She turned the packet between her fingers and felt the dry paper tear, showing her a glimpse of white flesh. Thinking back now to how violently she had reacted the first time she saw the photos, she wondered at how far she had travelled in understanding and forgiving her father. He had lost so much himself: first his wife and child, then Mrs Bransdale. And he could never even have known that Maggie was his daughter, or else he would have provided for her in his will. These photographs were something best forgotten. They were not important, not now.

She dropped tke packet into the red embers of the dying fire and watched as the images flared to black. Whatever had been between her father and Mrs Bransdale, it was gone now. Dead as the ashes.

Rose stood in the silent kitchen and waited.

She wished that Jack would come. She wanted to go, while she was still holding herself in this frozen stillness, knowing that she had no choice but to leave.

Nothing stirred.

She couldn't sit down and wait for him, there was too much tension in her. The pain in her mouth was less now; she was thankful for that. Perhaps she should wait in the car for him. She hesitated, then shrugged and wandered through into the little parlour, thinking of the day that Jack had swept the chimney for her. The day that they had found the dead cat inside the little cupboard. And then there had been poor Tibby. The door of the cupboard was half open. She walked over to close it, seeing as she did so the corner of something lying at the back of the shelf. She reached in and picked it up.

It was the charm which they had found that day: the charm which Jack had said would be protection from witches. She kept hold of it and, closing the door, looked curiously at the scrap of paper. She had forgotten this. 'He shall keep thee in six troubles, yea, even in seven shall no harm come to thee.' It was a comforting thought. Why seven? Seven for a secret, never to be told. And then Rose realized there was one more thing. One more set of images which she had forgotten. On the wall of her bedroom were her seven self-portraits.

She went to the foot of the stairs and listened. Nothing.

There was nobody in the cottage but herself, yet she felt very uneasy about going up those stairs again. She could leave the photos where they were, but they were good – she needed them and they were a part of herself. She didn't like the idea of leaving them staring blindly at the wall in an empty room, in an empty house.

Jack must come soon. Then she could go. She would get her photos and be ready waiting for him. She began to go slowly up the narrow stairs, step by step to the top and into the empty bedroom. The bed was stripped. She would not sleep there again. She would not let herself think of the nights she had spent there with her dark lover.

All that was left of her now in this room were her

seven self-portraits on the wall. She reached out and gently touched the one of herself as a bride.

The Bride Stripped Bare, even of her groom.

Rose looked at the black, empty space beside her where once Nicholas Brett had stood and felt that inside herself there was a black hole where he had been, which no one else was ever going to fill. She pulled the photos one by one from the wall and, holding the glossy sheaf, crossed to the window, where she let them fall.

For there was his name, cut diamond-sharp into the glass.

She knelt on the window-seat and touched the only proof she had that he had ever come to her. The shape of the letters burned into her, and she knew that she could not bear it, she could not let him go back into the shadows of time without her. The tight hold which Rose had kept on her feelings all this time was loosening, and she was beginning to hurt.

He would go back into the dark, and he would be nothing without her. And what would she be without him: she would be all mind and no body. Nobody. She couldn't make what she had been before be enough for her, not ever again.

Rose dropped her head on to her arms and despair welled up in her, bursting out of her in a long, wailing cry of his name. The sound fell away into a waiting silence, hanging on the cold air.

Then, by the thickening of the shadows, by the faint smell of musty time, she knew what she had done. She had scrambled to her feet and was running for the door before she fully realized what was happening.

'Rose,' he said. 'Rose.' And his voice was full of love and pain, and the smell in the room was changing now to the summer scent of old roses, heavy and nostalgic.

She stood caught in the doorway, looking down the

stairs. She had not meant to call him up to her this one last time. All that she wanted to do was run. She wanted to go down those stairs and out of the door, wanted to get in her car and drive and see the road signs telling her that she was travelling south. She saw herself sitting in her car going back to Isabel, with her father's camera on the seat beside her, free . . . free to be what?

There were other darker images filling her head now.

She was turning away from the swing doors of the hospital where her mother lay dying. She was running away from her father's death and his funeral. Running. Always running.

One more image came to her. It was the look on Maggie's face when she'd understood that Rose would have left the valley without saying goodbye to Jack.

Rose held on to the edge of the door to steady herself and took a shuddering breath. If she ran now, ran away down these stairs, then she would be running for the rest of her life. Nicholas Brett was here because she had called him up, and she had to release him. Finish it.

For how could she go and leave him behind her in the cottage, when Maggie was so close by? For what if he came again, this time through Maggie?

It was not safe. It was not right.

Much as she loved Nicholas Brett, she must see him as something evil, something she must destroy. But she had no power, no protection . . . and then she remembered the charm she had taken from the cupboard, the frail piece of paper which she had pushed into the pocket of her jeans.

Rose turned shakily and walked stiffly back into the room.

Chapter Twenty-four

THERE was nothing now beyond this place, this hour. His fingers touched Rose's throat and she turned to him, put her arms round him and moaned his name.

'My love,' she said. 'My love.'

His fingers stroked her mouth, and all her desire for him came up like a fountain inside her. She wanted him. She wanted him to take her for the very last time.

He lowered her to the floor and lay dark and still on her, stroking his thumbs across her mouth, circling her small ears, and everywhere he touched she burned for him.

For a long time she was aware of nothing but his mouth on hers, of his dark weight. She lay under him in a strange, dreaming state, lulled by the scent of roses, by his delicate touch on her skin. But gradually she began to want more. She wanted him inside her, wanted the release of so much tension dammed up in her. She wriggled and tried to pull off her jeans, but he did not move. Still he lay on her, a dark force pinning her down.

She felt his fingers at the pocket of her jeans: she thought for a moment he had found the charm, but it was not that he was stroking backwards and forwards across her cheek. It was soft and silky. It was the red ribbon she had found on the top of Fairy Hill.

Rose liked the feel of it. She turned her head and kissed his hand, licking greedily at his long fingers, and wondered at how she could ever have thought of leaving him. Now when he was here with her, when she was a part of him again, she knew that she belonged with him, and he was all she needed.

But how heavy he was. She had never noticed before how his weight pressed down on her so. She was hurting. Her breasts were sore, her hard nipples flattened under him. The floor was biting up into her spine, her shoulders. And still he was growing heavier. It hurt her now to breathe.

His scarred face hung above her, and there was a terrible, sad anger coming off him. The scent of roses was gone now: she could smell again the rank smell of wet earth with which he had come to her at first.

'You shall not leave me,' he said harshly. 'You shall not leave me alone in the dark . . .'

He was coffining her into an enforced stillness. She could not move, and he was growing heavier.

Darkness was rising up round her like a fog.

He was holding her so tightly that each finger was marking her frail skin. His mouth came down on hers, moth gentle, sweet and loving, then sucking down until she could not breathe.

And round her neck she felt the first faint pressure of the ribbon. His face and the spinning room grew darker as the ribbon tightened.

'My Rose,' he hissed. 'Come with me . . .'

Something in her wanted to do as he asked. Some part of her wanted to let go and fall away with him through the red dark and be with him for ever. It was easier this way – she could not bear his loss. He was the end of all her choices and all her running.

She was dancing with the Devil for the very last time.

Then, sharp and high through the dark swimming about her, she heard a sound. There was a dog barking, and someone calling to it.

Jack.

Jack was coming up towards the cottage.

He was there in her head as solid as a rock, true and straight. She had been spellbound, choosing death instead of life, choosing fantasy instead of reality. Jack's strong life-force came surging through her as he came nearer to her cottage, and she began to fight.

She was fighting for her life in an agony of hope, clawing at Nicholas Brett's arms as his grasp slackened for a moment at the sound of the dog barking. She had her hands free from under him, but the ribbon was tightening again in a thread of pain round her throat. She twisted and kicked under him, desperate to get at her pocket, sobbing out her terror of dying.

Her fingertips touched the piece of paper and she curled them round it, inching it into the palm of her hand. She scrawled down his scar with the nails of her other hand and his mouth opened in a snarl of pain.

She thrust the charm into the round black hole in his face in a terrible denial of everything that he had been to her. He hung above her for an instant, then his face contorted and black foam coated his lips. He began to scream as the charm burnt like acid into his flesh, charring and blackening. Jerking back from her, he clawed at his oozing, shredding mouth and his terrible screaming was unbearable to her.

Rose was weeping now for what she was doing to him, and great sobs shook her, but she would finish it, she would see that this time there would be no return from beyond the grave for him. Her fingers ripped the ribbon away from her neck, and she rubbed at the pain it left.

She crouched on the floor and watched him, whispering the words of the charm into his suffering: "'Ye are everlasting power of God. Theos Hoc in Vince.:''

His scream sank to a choking gasp as he lifted his head to look at her. His face was falling in on itself: only his dark, tormented eyes stared at her from the crumbling flesh. She put out her hands to keep him away from her and cried out in terror at the heat coming off him. He pulled himself to his feet and reached for her, dragging himself towards her, and she was backing up against the wall, screaming at him to keep away, screaming that she would not come with him. She wanted life, not death.

He was almost touching her with his clawing fingers, and the smell of him rotting and disintegrating gagged the back of her throat.

He cried out her name once, in a long hiss of pain, and fell face-down among the scattered photos. The photo of herself as a bride lay on the top, and his ravaged mouth left a last black kiss smeared across her smiling face. A last rattling, choking shudder ran through him, then he was still.

Then the thick silence in the room was as terrifying as his screams had been.

She had destroyed him.

It was finished.

She could not take her eyes off the thing which had once been Nicholas Brett. She began to edge her way along the wall towards the door. The heat coming off it was even stronger now. She could smell it smouldering on the rotten air.

Something moved. She froze flat against the wall, not believing what she was seeing now. The thing was moving: its fingers twitched, its arms jerked in a frenzy and its legs bent and twisted. The hollow head lolled and nodded and a flame leaped like a red tongue from the ragged hole where its mouth had been.

The photo under its face began to crinkle. Rose's face in it took on a different texture, a different shade. With a soft pop it burst into flame. One by one the seven pictures of Rose licked into fire. A thick, oily smoke rose sluggishly from the thing sprawled across them.

Smoke filled the room and coiled its way down the stairs, drifting into the empty rooms as the first bright flame licked at the floor-boards and the wooden frame of the old window. The frame blistered and crackled into orange fire. The piece of glass with Nicholas Brett's name on it stood out clearly for a moment, then the small pane of glass cracked sharply across the middle and fell to the floor in a shower of splinters.

The bitter smoke fumes curled round Rose where she stood pinned with fear against the wall. She knew that she should go, should get out of the room, but she couldn't move. She would die here after all, he would take her with him in this fire . . . and then she heard her name. 'Rose! Rose! Where are you? The place is on fire!'

She could hear Jack pounding up the stairs towards her, and her legs could move again and she was across the room, wrenching open the door. The flames sucked at the gust of air, silhouetting her in scarlet as she fell through against Jack. He caught hold of her with a shout of relief, hugging her tightly, and she let the spinning sickness inside her ride her out away from all the horror.

Kissing. Something was kissing wetly at her face.

She put out a hand and touched fur, and opened her eyes to find herself lying on the grass outside her garden gate. Jack's sheep-dog was sitting beside her, licking anxiously at her face, but there was no sign of Jack. Rose sat up unsteadily and stared at her cottage, where flames now blazed at every window. A thick plume of smoke was billowing up from it, and she could hear the crash of falling wood.

'Jack?' she moaned, and again more desperately, 'Jack?'

Not him as well. Ah, she couldn't have lost Jack as well. Nicholas Brett was gone but nothing must harm Jack. She staggered to her feet and over to the gate, clinging to it as she screamed Jack's name into the crackling flames.

Then he was there: running down the path towards her.

He was holding her camera. He had gone back into the burning cottage to get her camera.

'We'll be needing this,' he said, and, bending his head, kissed her white face. He was wearing the sweater she had given him with the sheep on, and he was safe. He turned her away from the fire and put his arm round her, holding her tightly into himself. Slowly he began to walk her away from Haggabacks and down towards the farm, with the sheep-dog leaping joyfully round them.

In the red blaze which had once been Rose's bedroom a section of ceiling came crashing down on top of the thing which was now all but consumed, covering every trace of it.

It ended as the binding foretold. Nan's dying words came true, and Nicholas Brett ended by a woman in fire and flame.

Nine months later Rose stood in the Mulberry Gallery, surrounded by blown-up prints of Maggie, Jack and herself. It was a small gallery, long and narrow, looking out on to a garden with the tree which gave the place its name. Two shallow steps led down from it to a small front room with a bay window looking out on to the street. It was the week before Christmas, and the window was shining with silver and blue decorations.

'Face Value' would open to the press and public in

half an hour. Isabel would be on her way here now from Islington with Maggie, who had been staying overnight with them. It was nine months since Rose had seen her: nine months since this exhibition had been conceived. The invitations had gone out some days ago, printed on the back of a photo of Maggie. Rose knew by the response to them that it was that face which was going to bring in the crowds.

She had met the train from the North still wondering if Maggie would actually be on it, because to Maggie getting to Northallerton and catching the London train on her own was the equivalent of going on the Orient Express. A Very Big Adventure. Isabel had taken the day off and first they'd taken Maggie to have her hair cut very short again, then shopping. Maggie had lost some weight over the months; it suited her. She let them try clothes on her like a small girl, anxious only to please and worrying about what was, to her, the appalling cost of everything.

'*That* much?' she kept whispering to Rose. 'That much just for this? Oh, Rose!'

Rose had hidden the price tags on the straight black skirt and shimmering silky top they'd finally found for Maggie. Rose looked down at herself now and straightened the short skirt of the severe grey suit she was wearing. It felt strange wearing stockings and suspenders and such high heels – she grinned at the thought of how much stranger Maggie must feel in hers. Rose walked slowly past her series of self-portraits, grown now to fill an entire wall, and thought that she had become her own final photo: 'Woman Making an Exhibition of Herself'.

Maggie had talked non-stop since she arrived, much to Isabel's delight. Isabel had loved Maggie as much as Rose had expected her to. But Rose had needed to be on her own with her photos, which was why she was here early. She needed to check that they were just as she wanted them, but the lighting was perfect; the photos hung there making their own statements. There was nothing more that Rose could do.

She could hear glasses clinking in the other room. Anna Trent, the gallery owner, was busy getting things ready for the crowds she was confident would come to the opening. Anna was a strong, powerful woman who had taken one look at Rose's portfolio and swept her along as far as this. She'd had the gallery a year; it had been a run-down fruit and veg shop when she'd found it, in an area off Lisson Grove which was not the usual one for a gallery. But Anna was making it work. Rose hoped that this exhibition was a success for Anna's sake as much as for hers.

It seemed so long ago that she had taken the photos of Maggie and Jack. There had been changes in the valley since she had left it. The old couple at Throstle Hall had sold up and moved out to a bungalow in the village. A family called Thompson from York had bought Throstle Hall. They were full of ideas, enthusiasm and money. They were turning the Hall into a rare breeds centre, and had taken Jack on as Farm Manager at a good salary. It was to be opened to the public at Easter. The Thompsons had two daughters: Maggie had told Rose gleefully that Jack was courting the elder of them.

There were changes at Ghyll Farm too. Paddy had come off Income Support and was running the farm now, happier with Jack out of the way and money in his pocket for the first time. The sucklers had been sold; Paddy was going into breeding rare poultry and water-fowl, with Mr Thompson's help, to display at the centre. He had a second-hand car and was taking his test. Then

Maggie had paused for breath, looked at Rose and said, 'He behaves himself now with me. I see to that.' And Rose had hugged her, knowing exactly what she meant.

Haggabacks was still in ruins after the fire. Rose could not bring herself to go back and see it. Not yet. She didn't trust herself to go back: she was too much afraid that somehow, even now, she might call him up to her again.

Paddy had plans for doing up the cottage, rebuilding it as a children's farm that would be a separate part of the centre, where children could handle young stock. Mr Thompson was helping him to find out about the necessary planning permission before they went any further, but Rose liked the idea of a new beginning for the cottage.

'Rose?'

She swung round, startled, to find Anna standing behind her. She was holding a full glass out to Rose.

'Come on, let's drink to us before the crowd arrives.'

'What if nobody comes?' said Rose.

'They will. Believe me.' The two women clinked glasses together.

'To us. To "Face Value",' said Anna.

'To us,' echoed Rose.

Anna put down her glass and went across to the gallery door. She propped it open and the sound of traffic on Lisson Grove spilled in. A taxi stopped at the door and Isabel and Maggie, elegant and poised, crossed the pavement. Rose stood at the top of the steps and caught her breath at how beautiful Maggie looked. Isabel had made her up so that she was all eyes, glowing with excitement. Anna hugged them both, and now behind them there were other taxis pulling up, people were hurrying along the pavement and into the gallery. Isabel was helping Anna hand out glasses of wine, offering something to eat. Voices rose and bubbled, people came up to greet Rose, and the gallery filled up.

Rose watched the door.

The sky was a deepening blue now, the soft blue of a city night. In one of the houses opposite a Christmas tree flickered its message of red and gold lights. A last group of people came hurrying in, laughing and chattering, and Anna closed the door behind them, glancing up to where Rose stood so straight and still at the top of the steps.

Still Rose watched the door.

She knew who she was waiting for: she knew he would not come.

All this in the room behind her, all this which she had worked for, would matter nothing to her if she could only feel his scarred face under her greedy fingers again. She wanted him more now than she had ever done. She knew what Mrs Bransdale had meant when she said that no man was ever going to fill her after Nicholas. It was true: she had tried with several men in the past few months and only ended up more frustrated and lonely than before.

Her hands were shaking with her need for him; she pushed them angrily into the pockets of her jacket. All she had done was to put some photos up on a wall – why had she thought that it mattered so much?

'Rose, love?' said an anxious voice and she turned to find Maggie standing next to her. 'Do I look all right for you?'

'Maggie, you look beautiful!'

Maggie beamed and then caught sight of herself repeated over and over on the wall in front of her. Her full mouth was a round, red circle of surprise. The noise in the gallery rose higher, and more and more heads were turning to where Maggie and Rose stood together. Maggie said something Rose didn't catch.

'What?' she said, leaning in to her.

'I said Mam told me. She wanted me to know before I came down here. I know I'm your half-sister, and I'm that pleased. But I'll say nowt if you don't want me to . . .'

Rose looked at Maggie's worried face and thought that out of everything that had happened to her up in Yorkshire, finding that she had this half-sister was the best thing that could have been given to her.

'Come on, sister,' she said, taking hold of Maggie's hand. Tall and confident, they began to move down the long room. Someone at the far end of the gallery began to clap. More and more joined in. The noise swelled until it filled the room, and as the flashlights of the press flared like white fireworks, Rose and Maggie walked hand in hand into the acclaiming crowd.